STORMS OF PAINE

A Pirate Romance Duology
Book Two

OPAL REYNE

Cover art by: Irene Zeleskou
www.imaginedcovers.com

Trigger Warning
Major spoiler below

Please only read further if you have triggers, otherwise you will seriously spoil the duology for yourself.

Firstly, I will list what triggers **AREN'T** in the duology so you can stop reading in order not to spoil it: No rape, non-con, harm done to the FMC by the MMC, torture, suicide/self-harm, mental/emotion abuse, incest, abortion, drug/alcohol abuse, cheating, breeding, child endangerment, or animal abuse.

Triggers that **ARE** in the duology: brief mention of child bride history, discussions of past domestic violence and child loss/miscarriage. Discrimination towards women. Blood, gore, battle scenes with lots of detail. Wound, and wound care. Ow/om drama – no cheating, though.

Please stop here if you have found your trigger as here on out is a major plot detail and you will truly spoil the ENTIRE duology for yourself. Like truly. Trust me.

Although it is not until the very, very end of the duology (so in book 2), there is baby. It's set in an era where there was no birth control and whoopsies happened all the time. We skip the pregnancy completely, so there is none of that detailed. It's not the celebration/aftermath of the HEA, and actually comes just before it.

Author's note on language

I'm from AUSTRALIA.

My English is not the same as American English.
I love my American English spoken readers to bits.
You're cute, you all make me giggle, and I just wanna give you a big 'ol hug. However, there are many of you who don't seem to realise that your English was born from British English, which is what I use(although a bastardised version since Australians like to take all language and strangle it until it's a ruined carcass of slang, missing letters, and randomly added o's).

We don't seem to like the letter z.

We write colour instead of color. Recognise instead of recognize. Travelling instead of traveling. Skilful instead of skillfull. Mum instead of mom. Smelt is a past participle of smelled. We omit the full-stop in Mr. Name, so it's Mr Name. Aussies cradle the word cunt like it's a sweet little puppy, rather than an insult to be launched at your face.

Anyway, happy reading!

This series is still inspired by TikTok

It was also powered by Redbull and junk food.

There are so many external factors that go into writing a story. So many things that help to drive you, inspire you, and keep you going.

Thank you to all those things that get me through the day and make it easier to sit at my computer for hours without going insane.

CHAPTER ONE

Captain Alister Paine of the Howling Death steered his ship toward the closest port, Vinil City, knowing they needed to resupply.

The violent storm, the one that battered his ship and forced him to lay low for a few days until it passed, showed no sign of returning. It was clear blue skies and calm ocean waves as far as the eye could see. There was barely even a cloud in the sky, a backdrop of clarity past his faded and worn sails.

They hadn't long left the rocky crescent cape of Grutten Valley they'd used to protect themselves from the storm, and the strong winds were now pushing them steadily towards their destination

The port isn't too far.

Maybe a two-day trip if they were lucky.

Their dwindling supplies weren't even the worst of their problems, however. Even if they made it before they ran out of food, they were knowingly heading towards a port unsafe for pirates like themselves to dock at.

No one better try to arrest us. He was already in a foul mood. Getting into a fight with guards was surely going to send him into a fit of blood-thirsty rage.

He had no other option but to take them there, as they wouldn't make it to any other port in time before they starved. Getting supplies without being noticed was their main goal;

otherwise, there would be bloodshed as they stole in their haste to flee.

Currently, they were sailing past a relatively small island covered in tall coconut trees. It was mostly sandy, except for the very centre that had managed to sprout a bit of grass. Life always found a way, despite being hundreds of miles from any mainland.

He'd set sail not long before sun-up, and in a few hours, the sun would be setting over the horizon.

Considering he'd only come to the realisation this morning that Rosetta Silver, captain of the Laughing Siren – who had been sailing next to his ship for the past three months – wasn't going to meet them, he was still rightfully furious. She'd stolen their supplies that were supposed to be shared. *Bitch.*

They had little food, little water, and barely any booze with which he could drink his anger away.

If I ever see her again, I might wring her pretty neck for this.

Then again, he probably should have seen this coming.

She was a liar. A cheat. A no-good, rotten little trickster who had deceived him time and time again.

The idea of having to go to land when he'd much rather not, and the thought he wouldn't have had to for at least another month if they didn't raid another ship, was enough to make him feel spiteful. He hated making port, refused to unless absolutely necessary.

He also didn't like the way it felt, like he'd been emotionally punched in the gut. No woman was allowed to make him feel this way.

I was supposed to be the one to toss her to the side, not the other way around!

Alister was intending to find himself a nice whore to help ease his frustration when he got to land. That should make him feel better and help him forget about her.

Still, it was because of Rosetta he'd gotten the map that led to his most recent spoils. He glowered, his upper lip twisting. Spoils he'd had to share with her.

If only she'd pissed off before we found it.

"You alright?" Pierre asked as he came up the quarterdeck stairs and walked to the helm. The distressed timber slats creaked under his weight. Alister didn't like the expression cast in his direction from Pierre's green eyes behind his tanned face.

It was the first time someone had really come to talk with him since he'd set sail. With the waves of agitation rolling off him like they were something tangible, it was probably a wise move that everyone had left him alone until now. The likelihood that he might have shot someone had been rather high.

He'd at least calmed down a little, after a few *hours.*

"Oh aye," Alister answered, his nose crinkling tight. "Pissed off we have to port, but that's my fault."

Pierre shook his head, his long blond hair tied back in a haphazard ponytail flicking from side-to-side behind him.

"That's not what I meant." He placed his hand on Alister's shoulder like he needed some sort of comfort, giving it a small squeeze. "She disappeared without a word."

He shirked the hand away with a grunt. "Couldn't give damn about that. Woman can do what she wants. She just could have left our supplies."

"You're being rather gracious about this," he commented, making Alister's eyes narrow. "Thought you might have liked her."

The snort of laughter that came from him was instant. "Nay lad. Liked what she could give me but nothing more."

The spark of passion between them had been addictive. Alister had been blissfully drowning in it. So, as much as he wanted to tell Pierre he could get sex like that elsewhere, not even he thought that was true, or believable. He'd asked her to sail with him; it was hard to hide how much he'd obviously enjoyed nailing her.

Pierre wore a strange look before giving a laugh. "Maybe she ran off because she worried she was in too deep."

Hmm. Alister hadn't thought about that. He cringed with disgust. *Could Rosetta have been falling for me?* She *had* tried to stop him when he went to walk away after their argument because she refused to come to his ship.

It was obvious she had been as addicted to it as he was, considering the way she'd been the last time they'd been intimate, right before that destructive storm.

Just thinking about it got his body hot and his blood pumping, despite also making him grip the handles of the helm tighter in spite.

"Nay, I don't think so," he eventually said.

She's too smart for that.

She wouldn't let her feelings get caught up for someone like him after what she'd been through, and Alister knew that.

"Sail ho!" someone yelled from above.

Their heads turned towards the open water to see nothing on the horizon. To his right was the beach; there was no point in looking that way.

"Where, lad?"

Which direction did Alister need to point his ship? Currently, he didn't know what the hell they were talking about. *Is it a ship we can raid?* That would be ideal.

Maybe I won't have to port!

Now that almost brought a smile to his sour face.

"Cap'in," Derek yelled from below, pointing towards the shore. His wooden peg leg made quick tapping sounds as he ran to the railing, his long, brown, shabby beard swaying over his shoulder as he ran.

When all Alister could see was trees, it took him a moment

to see the tips of sails on the other side. *A beached ship?*

Nay, not a beached ship. He could see it as he started rounding the island; it was just so close to the shore it appeared that way, hidden amongst the trees.

It was definitely banked, though.

"Well, I'll be damned," Alister chuckled, his eyes crinkling with humour.

Perhaps I'll get to ring her neck after all.

As he continued to pass the island, he could see the back end of the Laughing Siren coming into view. He'd know that swirling trim and bow patterns anywhere.

"Ha!" Pierre laughed. "Looks like we'll have our supplies after all. Raid and bail like usual?"

"Oh, aye," Alister agreed, steering the Howling Death in that direction, his muscles bulging from the slight strain. The helm wheel made clunking noises as it quickly turned. "I'm not sticking around."

He wondered how Rosetta would feel when he climbed aboard her ship before she could pull anchor and run. He wondered what stricken face she'd give him when she realised her plan had failed, how pale she'd turn when she saw his cruel grin and lack of mercy.

That was until...

"Wait," Pierre nearly gasped. "Look at it."

Alister's lips thinned, causing his short, stubble to poke his lips. The Laughing Siren was damaged and missing half its main sail.

There were rowboats on the shore behind it, laying across the pale-yellow sand. Men were already running towards them. He figured they were intending to come back to the Laughing Siren to stop them.

"Why'd she bank?" Pierre asked, as though Alister would have any idea what went through her thick head. "She could have continued to use the front and back sails to reach us after the storm died if it was due to damage."

"Who knows? She could have come to us for aid but didn't." Alister shrugged and shook his head, causing his long black hair to wave around his shoulders. "She should have known she wouldn't be able to sail away from a shore once she hit sand."

She chose not to meet us. They were half a day's trip from where they'd organised to meet, maybe more with her damaged ship.

Perhaps, if they'd needed to go weeks to reach each other, it would have made more sense to stop, but they could have made it if they'd wanted to. She just simply chose not to.

Still, he found it peculiar.

Steering closer, Alister was able to drop anchor beside the Laughing Siren to keep them in position. His frigate warship was shallower than her deep galleon, allowing him close without becoming banked next to her. A quick escape was guaranteed.

He didn't know what he was expecting.

Cannons to fire at him? The faces of her crew when he tried to swing across to it while his men threw grapple hooks to climb up the taller hull? Yells and shouts?

He got none of those responses.

It looks abandoned.

The ship was dead quiet, not a man to be seen on the surface. The only sounds were the creaking of rigging, the sails that remained flapping in the wind, and the clomping of their heavy footfalls as they made their way onto it. Even the light jingle of their weapon belts sounded deafening in the silence that greeted them.

"Are they all on shore?" Pierre asked, seeming just as dumbfounded as him. He turned his frown on Alister, his brows and lips twisting. "That's idiotic."

Just as he was walking to the railing to see how far those

rowboats were to meeting them, men started climbing over it.

"Alister," Naeem, her first in command, huffed when his feet found the deck. His dark brown skin glistened with sweat, and he wiped the hairline of his short, curly hair with the back of his hand. "Now aren't you a sight for sore eyes. How'd you find us?"

"Saw your ship, lad, as I was making my way to port."

"So, you stumbled upon us?" The man gave a laugh, shaking his head from side-to-side with a grin filled with white teeth. He set his hands on his hips, his thin, yet strong, chest heaving slightly, as if he'd been one of them men helping row. "Isn't that a miracle."

Well, this wasn't the kind of greeting Alister expected.

A fight maybe, but not this.

There was far too much lightness and humour in Naeem's brown eyes, and it didn't reflect the anger in Alister's chest.

"Where's Rosetta?" He made a show of clenching his fist in front of his torso. "Got a bone to pick with her about stealing my fucking supplies."

Naeem's eyes drifted over the men behind him, who had their swords drawn with looks of deadly intent on their faces. He also noticed the multiple pistols trained on him.

"Oh shit." He raised his hands in surrender, understanding they weren't here for a friendly visit.

Those who climbed over behind him raised their hands as well when they realised what was happening.

"Oh aye!" He turned his head towards Pierre, nodding in the direction of the hatch that would take them below. "Get the supplies. I'll get the safe key off her."

"Wait!" Naeem yelled, stepping forward with his hand outreached when they started to move. They all halted. "It's not what it looks like!"

"To hell it's not!"

Alister held his cutlass up to stop Naeem from taking

another step. He pointed the tip so close to his torso, he could cut him in the chest with it if he moved even an inch closer.

"I don't like betrayers and I don't forgive people who steal from me!"

He'd already foolishly done it twice when she'd stolen his ship and locket. A third time was just a mockery. *I should have known she was up to no good.* That mistrust in her was always present, and he'd chosen to ignore it like a damn fool.

Naeem lifted his hands in surrender once more. "You don't understand."

"What's there to understand? She could have met us and instead chose to bank here with our supplies." He nodded his head towards the shore. "I'm guessing you're all working to make a new mast."

It was a difficult task, but not impossible.

With the supplies they had, they could afford to waste the time it would take to cut and shape a tree trunk, then fix it to the ship. It would make do until they were able to reach port – unless they had someone on board who could instruct them on how to do it properly.

"We were on our way to Glutten Valley after we figured out where we were. We'd been pushed around by the storm without our mast and were lost."

"Like I care."

Alister turned away from him to personally lead his men below deck. If Naeem wouldn't tell him where she was, Rosetta would come for him when she boarded her ship. She would come screaming and stomping like an imp.

I can 'chat' with her then.

"We were mutinied!"

That made him pause.

He turned back around, his eyes squinting despite his blind one hidden behind his eyepatch. His lips thinned with suspicion. "A mutiny?"

That was an audacious lie.

"We lost nearly a fifth of our crew, Alister. We took so much damage during the storm." He gestured towards the mast before bringing his hand back into the surrendered position. "Just when we were secure enough to head towards your location, she was turned on."

She's not with Naeem. She also wasn't the first one to climb onto the Laughing Siren to stop him.

Realisation hit just as a cold chill ran down his spine. *Wait...*

"Is she dead?" Alister asked in a choke, putting his cutlass away to show his men to stand down.

Had she been intending to come to him all along but truly hadn't been able? Were they here because they were lost, because she was gone?

Why did a lance puncture his heart at the idea of her death? He was used to people around him dying. Hell, sometimes, he was the wielder of the blade.

"No," Naeem answered with a shake of his head.

Alister didn't think he'd ever felt such a heavy wave of relief wash over him before. *She's alive.*

"But she isn't well," he continued. "She's gotten sick and hasn't left her cabin."

She's ill? Many things could catch them on the seas; scurvy, pneumonia, a simple infection from a wound. He turned his head back to look at his men with a grim face.

"You lot," he barked. "Go back to the Howling Death."

A string of 'ayes' confirmed they understood as much as he did why he was standing down, why he was telling them to leave.

"She still could've sailed towards us afterwards, even with so little of you." At least a mutiny was enough of a reason for her to hastily anchor. "I don't care if she's unwell. She could have put you in charge to command the crew."

Despite not having much contact with Naeem, her first mate, Alister still had a deep respect for the man. He was just as formidable and loyal as Pierre and Derek, and with how much he'd aided Rosetta in the past, it was hard not to be inspired – even with how little he still knew.

Her puffy and naturally defiant lips were constantly sealed with secrets, and he expected half the words that came out of her mouth were lies to avoid spilling them.

He started heading towards the navigation room.

No one had been on board, or at least on the surface, to give any warning. It meant she was inside and hadn't realised he'd come onto her ship.

"Alister, stop." Naeem reached forward and grabbed him by the shoulder. "You can't go in there."

Turning so quickly it made the man stumble back, Alister pointed his finger into his chest. Stabbing him with quick pokes, he forced Naeem to back up as he glared. He was only an inch or two shorter, nearly the same height as Pierre.

"You don't get to tell me what to do, lad. Know your damn place."

His brows furrowed so deeply, they created wrinkles across his forehead. "I'm following my captain's orders. She's told me to keep everyone out."

"Oh aye, I bet." He shook his head with a dark laugh, turning from him once more. "But I'm not her crew and I want to know what the hell happened."

He needed to know the real reason why she'd banked.

Naeem grabbed Alister's shoulder once more to stop him.

Spinning back around, he punched the man so hard across the face, he tripped back, having to stop himself from hitting the ground, spraying spittle.

The teeth-gnashing look Alister gave him should have been enough of a warning not to touch him again.

"Fucking shit, man," Naeem said while palming his mouth,

wiping the blood welling in it. He stumbled like he was discombobulated. "We lost John!"

"Mr Smith?"

"Yes. She's unwell and she's dealing with that. I can tell you're angry because you don't know what's happened, but she can't handle you right now."

Alister's gaze fell to the side, his lips thinning once more. He slowly clenched both of his fists tightly. *Shit. I leave her alone for five minutes and it's chaos.*

"She wants to be left alone. Leave her be."

Alister snorted. "Good for her, but I'm still going in there. She shouldn't get attached to her crew."

"Have a heart, man!" Naeem yelled, coming forward to grab *him* by the scruff of his shirt. "You don't know her like I do. I haven't seen her this torn up in years, since before we left Luxor."

The way his face screwed up tightly in anger was beseeching, like he was desperately trying to reach into an evil man to finally find something good.

Naeem yanked him closer. "We've been through enough shit over the last few days. Give her a chance to get over this before you go in there with all your arrogant bullshit."

Alister grabbed him around the wrist and twisted his arm back. Naeem caved beneath him, almost dropping to his knees at the pain. Alister considered snapping a bone but decided it wasn't in anyone's best interest, considering he needed to man the helm at some point.

"That's what I'm trying to do," he snapped as he released him and headed up the stairs.

He had the courage to fight me. Alister still couldn't believe he'd been grabbed by the scruff of his shirt. Not many dared to do that to him these days.

When he opened the door to the navigation room, with its white walls and blue trim, he noticed the mess inside. Nothing had been put back after the storm, which was odd considering she treasured this room and kept it immaculate. Seeing it was empty, he moved to her sleeping cabin to the right.

He found her curled up on her bed, a blanket covering her all the way to the top of her head. Her boots were lying at the foot of the bed while her doublet coat was thrown over the end.

He eyed the hammock above, knowing she preferred it when she slept alone.

The smell of her, with just a hint of flowery gardenia perfume, invaded his nostrils, and a small sense of ease fluttered within him. It had been a week since he'd smelt it.

"I told you if you disturb me one more time, Naeem, I'll shoot you in the head." The blanket moved back, a pistol waved in the air above her. Then she gave a disgruntled sigh and let her arm dangle off the side of the bed, as though she didn't have the strength to hold it up. "But since you're here, tell the chef to make me soup."

"Nay, lass, don't know who your chef is."

"Alister?" The blanket curled down more so she could peek over it while laying on her side. "Was wondering if you'd find us. Took you long enough."

He noted her voice was raspy and her nose sounded stuffy. All he could see of her face were her blue eyes and freckle-covered forehead, and that arm hanging with the pistol, as though she'd been hugging it like a teddy bear before he'd walked in.

It took *him* long enough? His fists clenched so tightly, he knew his knuckles were turning white. He'd waited three days past their meetup date for her!

Alister had never waited for anyone in his life, and yet she had the audacity to make it sound like his lateness finding her was *his* fault.

"You've got my supplies, Rosetta." He finally slammed

the door behind him and folded his arms across his chest, a scowl forming across his features. "You left us high and dry in Glutten Valley."

A long pause came from her.

"I forgot about that." Her eyes drifted over him before she rolled them. "I can see you're *pissy* about it."

"Oh, aye! You fucking bet I am. You should have sailed to us!"

She let out a long, sullen sigh.

"Take them, I don't care. Raid my whole ship." She started digging through her clothing beneath the blanket before a set of keys looped on a ring, throwing them at his chest. "Take my loot and go away. I'm not in the mood to deal with your shit."

His arms fell away while a frown crinkled his brow. How quickly she'd surrendered wasn't comforting, nor was it what he wanted. It made his hackles rise.

"Get out of bed. You've got a ship to fix."

"No, I'm sick. Can't you tell?" A deliberate sniffle followed her words. "So, unless you want this death cold, leave."

Alister came forward to stand at the foot of the bed to see her better. The hammock strung almost at his chest height above her bed shielded her partially. She'd most likely need to stand on the mattress to get inside.

His frown deepened when he looked down at her. Her face was red, and not even he could tell if it was because of a flu or tears of grief.

"I don't get sick, never have," he said when her blue eyes found him. "And that's not why you're laying here."

"Why else would I be trying to rest?" She pointed her gun at him, but she never cocked the hammer. She twirled it in the air. "I told you, I hate the cold, and now I'm sick because I spent four days covered in rainwater because of a stupid storm."

"You shouldn't get this attached to your crew."

Her eyes squinted into a deep glare while her lips pursed. "You spoke to Naeem."

"Oh, aye. He told me what happened."

"I'm fine. Got over that already." She turned, rolling over to give him her back. Brave, considering most wouldn't dare turn their back to him. "Now, take your supplies and leave so I can sleep. You're making my headache worse."

Alister tsked, his tongue clicking against the roof of his mouth. This wasn't the Rosetta he'd come to know.

"You're usually much better at lying than this."

Alister lifted a leg and grabbed the base of his boot to take it off. He did the same to the other, dropping it to the ground.

She doesn't need me screaming at her right now. He'd rather do it when she was fighting, feisty, and might scream back at him. It always made him want to throw her over something and take her hard as punishment for being bitchy.

"Really, Alister? That's your great plan?" she asked when he started pushing her over to create room in the single bed. "You would try to sleep with a sick woman?"

"Nay," he said as he knelt before falling to his side next to her. His crash to the mattress made her bounce. "I'm going to lie with you until you're feeling better."

He turned to his back and pulled her until she was forced to have her head against his chest. She struggled for a bit, pushing against his side, but he kept his arm secure around her.

She's pretty weak right now. He could tell her pushing had no power to it.

With a sigh, she eventually gave up when she understood he was an unmovable force.

She lay on her side, her face forcibly squished against his chest. Her breaths were huffed, wheezing, as if just that small amount of struggling, like fighting off a newborn kitten to him, had been too much exertion.

"Why are you doing this?" she asked quietly with squished cheeks.

"My mother told me there's nothing better for a sick woman than lying on a man's chest." Alister stared up at the ceiling, remembering the number of times he'd done this for his mother when she'd been unwell. "My da was never around to do it for her."

Shivers rolled over her body as though she was cold, and yet, she felt remarkably hot against his side. He placed the back of his hand against her forehead to check her temperature. *She's definitely running a fever.*

"Your mother was a liar, then."

He pressed his lips together into an angry pout. The short hairs of his stubble poked against his lips as he grimaced. "I think not. She often said she felt better."

"She just wanted to cuddle her child without you realising, you big idiot."

He raised his hand to his chin to stroke the stubble on it. *Could it be true?* His mother was sweet, but she could be tricky when she wanted to be.

After a while, he felt the tension in Rosetta's shoulders lessen and she started to relax into him. She didn't put her arm around him, though. Eventually, she gave a small sneeze, breaking the silence between them.

"Why'd you bank, Rosetta?" Alister was still angry, but he knew she must have had a reason.

"I needed a mast," she answered dully.

Alister gripped her by the jaw to force her face towards him as he moved his head to look down to her. She averted her eyes at the look he gave her, one that told her he knew it was an outright lie.

Her voice was small and filled with so much sadness, he

could hear it. "I wanted to bury him."

He knew she'd cared for Mr Smith, but to go out of her way to not only abandon Alister without his supplies, but also to bank a damaged ship to bury him told Alister he'd meant a lot more to her than anyone realised.

He released her face so she could be comfortable, his brows tight with thoughtful tension as he turned his head back up. His good eye glided over the ceiling.

I wonder if she'd be this sad if I died. He doubted it. Naeem and Mr Smith had been special to her and with her for many years.

There was a pause of silence, and he felt her finally sling her arm across his stomach. Not all the way, but enough to show him she finally accepted the embrace.

Foolish. "You shouldn't get this attached to your men." The words were cruel, but it was the truth.

"I know," she whispered. "But how would you feel if Derek or Pierre died?"

"Upset, but I wouldn't let it get to me. I would just toss their bodies into the sea and immediately hold a vote for their replacement."

"You really have a heart of stone, don't you?"

Alister chuckled, the corner of his eyes crinkling with humour. It made his eyepatch on the left side dig in.

"Aye, kind of have to. I've been on these seas for most of my life and I have seen hundreds die. It pays to never get attached to anyone. They all wash away eventually anyway."

"That sounds... lonely."

"Got to have a heart for it to feel lonely, lass."

Just give him strong booze and let his hand be filled with a woman or the helm of his ship, and he was happy.

"Why are you being so nice to me?" she asked suddenly, followed by a sniffle so it could stop her from being so nasally.

"I'm always nice to you."

She snorted a laugh, as if she believed the opposite of what he'd said. "You think I stole your supplies, don't you? Why are you here doing this instead of shouting at me and taking them?"

Yes, that's what he originally thought, and what he was going to do, but...

"Because now, I know the truth." *She hadn't tried to do it purposefully.*

She hadn't tried to be malicious.

The reason he'd stumbled upon her was because she'd been making her way to Glutten Valley the entire time.

"Pfft. You don't seem like the forgiving type."

He frowned once more. *I'm not.* He was usually the 'kill first and ask questions never' type of person.

For reasons he preferred not to think about, he checked her forehead again gently with the backs of his fingers. He also gingerly moved a few stray hairs that had fallen over her forehead and cheek, allowing her to see clearly. However, it brought a slight smile to his face when they fell back into place – her hair was unruly and untameable, always a nest of knots.

When there was another long pause, he turned his head down to see her eyes had grown heavy, like she might fall asleep. She blinked slowly, but he could see her eyes were moving, like she was thinking.

"I may have done something I shouldn't have."

Rosetta, admitting to a mistake? Well, blow him down; he never thought he'd witness the day.

Still, he asked calmly, "What did you do?"

"I made my men kill those who tried to mutiny against me."

Ruthless. Alister almost wanted to laugh. It's exactly what he would have done.

"I killed almost a fifth of my crew, and now I don't have enough men to sail comfortably. I have about eighty left, I think."

He knew why she was uncertain. Without Mr Smith around to help her count, she could only guess. *I told her she needed to learn.* As always, Alister had been right.

"You can sail with eighty. Your ship may not be as clean, and you might tire your men out, but we often sail with less than favourable odds."

If it was said a ship *should* have a certain number of crewmen, that didn't necessarily mean it *had* to. He just hadn't wanted to argue with her about numbers and logistics when they divvyed up the prisoners. The stubborn woman would've argued with him until they'd both gone grey and died of old age.

"So, what happened here? Where's your mast? Your ship is stronger than mine; you should have made it to Glutten Valley before us."

With a sigh, she started her story. "I almost drowned."

CHAPTER TWO

"We've got to stop meeting like this," Rosetta said while laying her back against the bed, pushing up with both her feet and shoulders so she could make room to wriggle her tights up her legs. She tugged until the wide waist band sat above her navel, then she started doing up the corset ties.

Alister was working on doing up the buttons of his breeches, before he grabbed his worn tunic from the end of the bed. He threaded his bulky and scar covered arms through the sleeves before shoving it down his muscled chest covered in dark hair and more scars, letting it rest loosely around his torso.

They were currently on a small fleet ship they'd spotted in the distance. One they killed every man on board and told their crews to raid while they went to find the safe.

When they walked into this office together and noticed there was a bed, which didn't happen often, one thing led to another...

Rosetta was working on putting all her clothes back on right after letting out moan after moan beneath him. She knew he wasn't going to help her do it.

"I told you this would happen if you didn't stay on your ship where it's safe." His deep baritone voice was nonchalant, hiding the blatant threat in his words.

Tucking in her white, frilly cuffed tunic, she lowered her eyelids into a bland look as she rebuffed, "And I've told you I can handle myself."

"Aye, I know you can," he grinned in return.

Her eyelids flickered. Her wearisome expression fell away so she could blink at him in surprise. Usually, he'd argue with her, not agree with her.

Since he was still kneeling on the bed, he crawled towards her, placing his large hand around the back of her head, lifting until they were almost nose-to-nose.

"But you just look so tempting with a sword in your hand on a sinking ship."

Ngnh! Rosetta's breath was stolen as he crashed his lips over hers to bring her into a deep and searing kiss. He pulled back so he could turn on the mattress and step off the bed. The sound of water sloshing beneath his boots filled her ears.

She squinted her eyes at him with suspicion.

What's going on? Ever since the storm, Alister had been less commanding over her.

He'd spent two days in and out of her sleeping quarters while she'd been sick, coming in to let her rest against him, like he actually thought that would help. It did nothing to help with her terrible cold, but it at least had been comforting.

Her heart had been heavy over the death of her dear friend John, who had been like a father figure to her, and holding someone warm had soothed some of the ache.

She'd spent much of that time in and out of dazed sleep, but the rest of it, she had her head against his chest, listening to his strong heart beating, letting his powerful lungs expand his ribs against her.

She'd told him of the events prior to him finding her; everything about the storm, manning the helm with John next to her, about almost falling into the ocean to be lost forever. The freak accident of her mast being struck by lightning.

Then, the mutiny and how they'd been waiting for her to be alone to do it. She'd hated to admit he'd been the one keeping them at bay, but it had been the truth.

After that, she thought he'd be more overbearing and annoying.

Instead, when she'd woken up alone in her bed and felt well enough to leave it, she'd discovered he was on his ship.

She half-expected him to be on the Laughing Siren, watching the men secure the new mast with a watchful eye. She thought he'd be telling them what to do and threatening the remaining crew. When she hadn't seen him, she approached Naeem to ask him where he was.

"On his ship. He said you know what you're doing and that you don't need him," Naeem had told her.

To hear those words had come out of Captain Alister Paine's mouth, the most arrogant man on Old Gaia and the biggest pain in the ass on the sea, had been laughable. And Rosetta had laughed, waiting for Naeem to stop joking and tell her the truth.

When her laughter had been met with awkward silence, she'd realised he was being truthful.

What had changed? Why wasn't Alister trying to be a manly man constantly trying to make her feel like a helpless, feeble woman?

Since the new mast was more than acceptable for her to sail, that's what she'd been doing. They hadn't touched port because she thought it was suitable.

Her men had done a wonderful job. One of the prisoners had been a ship maker with the experience and knowledge to make them a secure and working main mast. Under his direction and assistance, after six days of being banked, they'd eventually been able to push off.

In the past two weeks that they'd been sailing again, rarely did Alister try to tell her what to do or argue with her about what she wanted.

Actually, after going to where they'd originally been heading before everything had happened and found it empty of treasure, he'd come to her to see what map she'd like to follow next, since there were two close by but in opposing directions.

He was starting to make decisions with her thoughts in mind rather than just pointing in a certain direction she'd be forced to follow. It made her feel... respected as a captain.

She didn't know why the change happened, nor did she understand it. She wasn't about to question him about it either, in case he realised and went back the way he had been before.

"I think a fish swam off with my boots," she finally sighed, letting go of the confusing thoughts.

She tried to look for her boots while kneeling on the bed – that was slowly gaining more and more water around it.

We must have been going for a while.

The water near the closed door was thigh deep and she could see the ship was now pointing towards the bottom of the ocean. The room was on an incline, with the bed at the back of the room and threatening any minute to submerge underwater as well.

Alister looked around before reaching down and grabbing one. He shook the water out of it and then threw it on the bed so she could put it on. He started searching for the other.

"Shit, you're right." She could see his light brown eye trailing all over the floor as his head rotated on his thick neck. "I can't find – wait, there it is."

He sloshed through the water that went from ankle height next to the bed to knee-high in the middle of the room. He grabbed the other boot and threw it at her as well.

She watched him walk over to the safe they'd manage to get open by shooting the lock but hadn't yet opened because they'd gotten distracted. He'd come up behind her and started kissing her neck while shoving his hand inside the front of her shirt to grasp her breast.

She didn't know how watching her shoot the lock off a safe was a turn on for him, but she wasn't upset with it.

Shoving her boot on, in the most convincingly nonchalant tone she could manage, she said, "There's something I've been meaning to ask you."

"I truly fear what you could possibly want to ask me," he answered thoughtfully. He was going through the safe, but not how she would.

She often checked the paperwork inside. He just dumped it onto the floor so he could find the pouch of coins. Different priorities, she guessed.

"This isn't even worth the effort it took to get this thing open," he muttered to himself.

"I want to make port."

He turned his head to the side to look at her over his shoulder. A deep frown crinkled his features.

"We have more than enough supplies to last until we find another trading boat."

Considering everything, Rosetta was surprised he still kept some of his on her ship.

He *had* told her that if she ever planned to sail the other way, he might chase after her with a vengeance if she didn't give him his share before leaving. She told him she'd always intended to give him his supplies when that happened.

The last thing she needed to do was piss off this man who she had seen with her own eyes wasn't good to those he didn't care for. She could only imagine how callous he would be towards those who betrayed him.

"I know, but I still want to," she answered, continuing to kneel on the bed since it was dry. She'd much rather not stand in cold water. "The men need proper food, and we should get fresh water. We don't know how stale the water we have is and it's so sweet now because of all the rum we've needed to add to make it bearable to drink. The original plan was to hold livestock, but we've eaten all the animals we've raided, or they died from the stress of the storm."

He turned to her and folded his arms across his broad chest. He opened his mouth like he was about to argue with her but closed it. Then, with a thoughtful, yet grim expression, he ran his hand over his chin.

She'd never seen him shave, but his short beard was always the same length, only a few millimetres. His hair seemed longer, coming to nearly the bottom of his ribs rather than the middle of his chest like when she'd first met him. As always, only the top half was tied back into a messy, half-folded bun.

"I don't like porting."

"It's been nearly four months since we started sailing together, Alister. I was at sea for three before that and my men are tired. We need to rest."

"Then we'll drop anchor near an island and the men can rest there."

Rosetta rolled her eyes. "They want to rest in beds! They want to eat good food and sleep without the constant swaying of the ocean."

When she could see he didn't plan to budge, she let out a small sigh before turning her face away. She nibbled on her bottom lip in thought.

"Tortaya isn't too far from here," she said after a few moments, her eyes gliding over the wall to keep her gaze averted. "I'll take my ship there and resupply, let my men rest. If you want, we can organise a place to meet so you can continue to the map location."

They were far west, and Tortaya was the last good port pirates could go to before the only option was Austaine, which was the mainland behind Tortaya. The western king paid little mind to what happened in Tortaya, as its business usually benefitted him.

It was a safe haven for pirates and criminals. Trade was popular because everything stolen was sold there. Rosetta would be able to buy everything she could possibly want and need.

"Go to Tortaya on your own while I go to Little Cape?" His tone seemed disgruntled before his brows drew together further, pinching his forehead.

Rosetta gave a small laugh. "I've been there so many times, I've lost count."

Going after the Laughing Siren had been her longest journey from Tortaya, and the only other long journey she'd taken that matched it was right after she'd escaped Theodore, her now dead husband. At the time, she and Naeem had hopelessly wandered the seas, jumping from port to port in disguise. Knowing she'd been the one to kill Theodore still made her heart soar with glee, even after so many months.

Alister grimaced and rubbed his stubble once more, like he was agitated.

"You could go to another port, instead of Tortaya." Rosetta frowned at his tone. *Is he upset with the location?* That made little sense to her. Seeming to sense her disquiet, he said, "It's pretty dangerous there."

"I know it like the back of my hand, and I'll have my men with me." She turned her face back to him with a sombre expression, to see his was crinkled into one she didn't understand. His brows were furrowed in deep lines, and his jaw gritted so tightly the muscle knots had popped on the sides. Even the bridge of his nose was bunched. "I trust my crew. Those against me are dead, and I know the ones I have now won't leave my employ even if I dock."

"I know the face you've got on you." He pointed his index finger at her. "You're going to do this regardless of what I say."

Once more, she turned her head to the side, this time with a huff of annoyance. She sharply folded her arms across her chest.

"Yes," she answered curtly.

"Fine, lass," he sighed, before walking to stand next to the bed. "To Tortaya we go."

"Wait..." Her folded arms loosened, and she turned her head back. "We? You're going to come?"

"Aye, I'll come." A squeak ripped from her when he suddenly picked her up to cradle her smaller form in his big arms. "I should sell the loot we've collected, and I have a feeling that I need to keep an eye on you, so you don't cause more chaos."

"What are you doing?" He started walking with her. He was perfectly balancing her under the crook of her knees with an arm around her back, but he'd never picked her up like this before!

"Can't have you catching another cold again," he chuckled at her in the hip-high water near the door. "You're useless when you're sick. Now, do you mind? Your hands are free, mine aren't."

Considering he was keeping her dry, she did what he wanted without argument and twisted the doorhandle. Once she opened the door, he carefully walked her through the doorway.

Rosetta realised just how sunken the ship was.

Alister had to walk them to the poop deck behind the upper level, since it was the only place that wasn't completely submerged, including most of the railing.

The water looked remarkably light blue above the ship, while around it was that deep yawning colour showing the depths beneath it.

"Swing us a rope, lads," he yelled to the men of her ship while placing her feet on the railing above the water.

He held her up with one hand against her back so she didn't fall, and caught the rope flung to him with the other. He handed it to her.

He spanked her arse with a such a heavy hit, she winced. "Off you go."

The bottom of her boots hit the hull of the Laughing Siren before she started climbing up the side as her men pulled her up by the rope to help.

After she climbed over the railing, she turned back to watch Alister wading through the water to get to his ship on the other side. He may have had to push a dead soldier floating in the water out of his way as he went.

Rosetta turned to her crew, most of whom were on the main deck waiting for her.

She gave them the biggest grin she possibly had. "To Tortaya boys, my shout!"

A ring of cheers sounded.

Alister had collected all his men to the surface so he could speak with them. He towered above on the quarterdeck of his ship and placed his elbows on the railing, leaning against it.

"We've got a new heading, lads," he said, eyeing them over. "We'll be detouring to Tortaya before we go to Little Cape."

"Does that mean we'll be selling our loot and getting more of our wages?" Kent asked below.

"Aye, that's the idea." He crossed his wrists while he spoke. "We'll be spending a few days there, so prepare yourselves because I won't be touching a port for a long time afterwards."

"What about the Laughing Siren?" another person asked.

Their heads turned to the ship sailing beside them but slightly behind.

The Howling Death was always in the lead. There was often a battle in trying to maintain the right speed, since his ship was faster than hers. He eyed the few sails furled away to slow them down. He didn't mind having to slow down, enjoying every moment he was on the seas.

"They'll be joining. We'll be resupplying while we're there. Everyone will be required to help bring the cargo to the surface when we arrive, but after that, you will be free to do what you want for the few days we're there. Those of you who choose to stay near the ship and help sell the loot we've collected will earn additional wages. I need ten, so sort that out amongst yourselves. That also goes for those who stay behind to guard the ship."

Excited chatter began to bustle throughout the crew. Those who were new and didn't understand what it meant to dock at Tortaya were informed about it.

"Do I have any naysayers?" Not that he cared.

"To Tortaya!" was the answer he received before roaring cheers echoed behind it.

Excellent. "Back to your stations."

Alister pushed off from the railing and turned to Derek manning the helm. "Turn her to land; that's our new heading."

"Aye, Cap'in," he answered with a nod, immediately turning the wheel.

He knew these waters and their location just as much as Alister did. Derek would lead the beginning of the two-day trip.

As the crowd of men dispersed, Alister started making his way down the stairs so he could head below deck, intending to check the stocks. He wanted to get a rough calculation of what everything was worth. Eventually, Alister would make his way to the Laughing Siren to know what kind of supplies they would need to buy.

He had a few days, so he wasn't in any real haste to complete his task. He'd probably do it a few times just to make sure all his calculations were correct.

As expected, Pierre came up beside him.

"I'm surprised you're intending to dock, considering we don't need to," Pierre commented as they walked through the halls.

"Rosetta's idea," he answered, peeking at the man who knew to walk on the side of him that wasn't blind.He hated when anyone walked on his blind side. He wished the world on that side would just disappear completely.

Only being able to see from one eye had been disorientating to adjust to when it happened. It also made him vulnerable.

"And you're doing what she wants?"

"Aye. We need more supplies, and she was going to make port with or without us. I'd rather be there to make sure we get the things we need."

It wasn't that Alister didn't trust her to make the right decisions; it's just that what they viewed as important could be completely different.

She'd probably forget to get enough booze. That'd upset his men.

"But Tortaya, Alister?" The tone in his voice gave away his concern as they rounded into the cargo holding area.

The space was filled with carpets, household items, and anything relatively low in price, unless it was large. Anything small and valuable was kept in the safe Pierre guarded. That was his job as Alister's first mate and only they had the keys.

As much as he valued Derek, Alister only held real trust in Pierre. Pierre rarely argued with him or told him he was making the wrong decision. Being older, Derek thought he knew best and that often grated on his nerves. *Annoying old sea dog.*

"Aye, Tortaya. Got a problem with that?" He raised his brow, surprised Pierre, of all people, would have an issue.

"Nay." The man gave a wide grin filled with dark intentions. "We haven't ported since we were left at Dunecaster. I'm excited to have a woman beneath me again."

"Then what's with your tone?"

Alister crouched down and started counting how many bars of soap they'd stolen, then the perfume. The count was correct, but their worth was an estimate, especially since they were of different quality.

I need to make sure I separate what's cheap and what's high-quality before we dock. The men could get it all wrong and mix it together. That would cost him pretty coin, and losing coin uselessly was a sure-fire way to enrage Alister.

"You're bringing Rosetta with us." His cheerful face fell into a thoughtful one as he placed his hands on his hips and bent closer to Alister's crouched position. "Are you sure that's a good idea? We could head to a different port to get everything we need."

Alister brought his gaze away from the candlesticks he'd been going through to look up at Pierre, who was standing there, being unhelpful. He noted that concern once more filled his features.

"Aye, should be fine." He turned back to his task. *I already tried to convince her to go to a different port, and I know she's too stubborn to change her mind once she's set on something.* "Lass already told me she understands."

"And you believed her?" The dark chuckle Pierre gave had a mocking hint to it. "Women always say they understand, until it's happening, and then they suddenly don't like it."

"Then that's her problem," Alister answered dryly, shrugging his large shoulders.

Tortaya was a pirate stronghold. It was an island not too

far from the mainland, a safe haven from Queen Mary Anne and her fleet, the sword in the alliance between herself and the king of the western shores. It was rumoured she controlled him due to her wealth, power, and reach. However, not even her fleet ships could dock – Tortaya would fire its cannons until they sunk.

Bounty hunters still roamed those streets, but they weren't the ones they needed to be afraid of. It was other pirates and criminals looking to make a quick buck by completing bounties.

The city was large and overpopulated, and every minute was a party, regardless of the location of the sun. Drunks stumbled in the streets, and almost every woman was a prostitute, or at least a criminal herself. Those who weren't were just simple maids.

"And what about *her*?" Pierre asked, making Alister's head turn to give him a warning stare filled with so much menace, it'd frighten a rabid beast. The 'her' Pierre was talking about was a prostitute on Tortaya Alister often visited. "If they discover each other..."

"That won't happen," Alister answered with unwavering confidence.

He wouldn't let it happen. He couldn't.

Pierre threw his hands up with defeat. "Alright, if you're sure."

"Aye, I am." He grabbed the man by the scruff of his shirt and yanked him to his knees. They both thudded against the ground, and he gave a grunt. "Now, help check the stocks before I gut you, you lazy sod."

CHAPTER THREE

Alister watched as the Laughing Siren came to a halt next to one of the empty docks of Tortaya.

He was currently waiting in the bay before he steered the Howling Death onto the other side of the same boardwalk.

A grim expression had been permanently fixed to his face the moment he saw land in the horizon. It had nothing to do with the location, and everything to do with the fact he had reached land at all.

Land was filled with people, with strangers he'd have to constantly keep his only working eye on.

Horrible dangers would be lurking in the shadows, hidden behind the laughter and music of happy people. Just how large was the bounty on his head now? Would Rosetta's desire to port be the reason Alister lost his life?

He'd never told her that was one of the reasons he was apprehensive. He wasn't afraid, nor did he fear the possibility of his own death.

No, Alister just hated land and didn't want to be on it for many reasons. He owned the sea. It was an untameable element not many could tame, and yet, he had. For years, he had; he was a king of the ocean. On land, he was nothing but a man. A dangerous, vicious man, but a nobody, nonetheless.

There would be just as many heartless and callous pirates on these shores, those they should all be wary of. The only thing that didn't concern him was that, if they knew who he was, even they would be afraid of him. Afraid of him and his men, known for doing vile things to those who tried to hurt them.

He removed one hand from the helm to look down at his calloused palm. His hands hadn't been clean of blood the last time he'd pushed off from these shores. He clenched his fist until his knuckles went white. Then, he turned his sight to the city of Tortaya with a malicious smirk.

He hoped someone would try to kill him today.

All he needed was one man to try while he was sitting down to relax, and he would shank him with a dagger in the gut.

The bartenders and owners of their taverns would know him; he'd been here often enough. They would know not to get in the way, or he would turn his knife on them. After that, most who didn't know who he was would be too afraid to even look at him.

Only those brave enough to murder in front of others, rather than in the shadows, were the ones criminals and bandits feared. Even though this was an island of loose laws, they still had them. To kill so openly showed he had no fear for repercussions. It proved he had the strength and protection to do whatever he wanted, and no one could stop him.

The permanent citizens would remember him, perhaps not by name, but at least by face. They would stay clear of him.

It's the pesky water rats I need to watch. Other sailors who were new here.

He'd told Rosetta to keep her mouth shut about the depth of their current partnership on the sea, that she was sailing next to him. Some idiotic bounty hunter could try to use her to cut his head off, and he'd had to explain to the poor woman that he cared for his life more than hers.

If anyone saw them, he hoped they thought they were

merely people who knew each other, spending part of their time on shore together. They'd sailed from different angles towards the port for a reason.

Her reaction hadn't been pleasant.

"Why would I want to tell anyone I'm connected to you?" she'd sneered before rolling her eyes. *Hurtful lass.*

Perhaps he should have kept his mouth shut. *Should have known she was smart enough to know the bounty on our heads could affect her.*

Still, her words made him feel like *he* was the shameful problem, rather than the bounty.

Seeing the Laughing Siren was secure through his spyglass, Alister called out his commands, telling his men they were going to sail into the harbour rather than waiting in the bay.

It took an experienced sailor to man the helm while docking. Even a small margin of error could have him crashing into the boardwalk, rather than next to it.

Alister never allowed anyone else to do it.

Once his men threw the rope lines to halt their progression forward, they heaved them to the dock by nothing more than hand and grit, belaying the ship to the pier. A wide gangplank slid from his ship onto the boardwalk so they could walk freely to and from.

Stepping from his ship, he paid the dock hand for the space. No record of their docking was taken down. Last thing Alister wanted was a paper trail of his whereabouts, unless it was in his own captain's log he kept.

They were at the end of the boardwalk where there were no people, but he could see them in the distance, emptying their own ships or stocking them.

From the side of the gangplank, he started calling out commands to move the raided cargo to a certain location so they could sell the smaller, less valuable items at a stall. The bigger ones remained on the ship; they would bring buyers to it when there was interest. All the jewellery he had would be kept in the safe until he located a good buyer.

Behind him, Naeem was calling out similar commands; they had been ferrying cargo Alister hadn't wanted to waste space carrying but was still worth some coin.

But the thought Alister had was, *why is Naeem the one instructing the men?*

With a frown, he grabbed the man's shoulder to turn him slightly. "Where's Rosetta?"

As the captain, she should be the one calling out demands. His eye drifted over her large ship to find her, but she wasn't there.

"She's gone for a walk."

His head shot to the side to look over the busy crowd of people near the port, as though they wanted to clutter it and be in the way. The area was bustling, chatter a loud roar as seagulls squawked like they wanted to join in.

"By herself?"

"She had some business to attend to while we were busy." Naeem gave a shrug, as though he didn't care she was alone in a place like this. "Said she should be back in the next hour or two."

His lips thinned into agitated lines as he gritted the front of his teeth. *Damn that woman.* He should have known there was a reason she wanted to dock before him.

"How long ago?"

"As soon as we threw our lines." Naeem chuckled, patting Alister on the shoulder. "We hadn't even set down our gangplank and anchors before she was gone."

He was imagining she'd jumped from her ship as it was still moving.

"And you didn't think to stop her?"

His smile grew brighter with humour, his brown eyes

twinkling. "Thought you would have learnt by now; no one can tell her what to do."

What is she up to? What was so important she hadn't told Alister, or couldn't wait to take any of her men with her? *Is this the reason she really wanted to port?*

Sometimes, he couldn't make head or tail of her. *She's lucky she's got such a pretty face.* Otherwise, he doubted he'd be able to tolerate her shit like he did.

Then again, he'd seen prettier women and he'd never tolerated them even marginally compared to how he did with her.

Rosetta stepped to the side, narrowly missing being tumbled over by two drunk men, arm in arm, staggering in the busy street. It seemed they were trying to help each other walk, as if they couldn't do it by themselves.

Two halves make a whole idiot, she laughed quietly to herself as she watched them.

She passed tavern after tavern, hotel after hotel, of the most popular street. This island was so large it couldn't be walked from one side to the other in a day. It would take at least two on foot, not that she had ever thought about walking it.

Despite the size, only the town right next to port was used. The rest of it was housing for those who lived here, hidden by trees and hills.

The road was made of broken cobblestone, brick, and dirt. There were potholes and barely any carriages and horses in sight. Those who used them were generally people who lived furthest away and had the most money on this relatively poor island.

The fronts of brick buildings had wooden porches that

enclosed some of the taverns. The wooden railings were patchy in colour, needing to be replaced regularly due to drunk tomfoolery breaking them. A fat man trying to right himself. A man trying to take a woman over it. A brawl launching someone through it.

Already drunk women and men loitered around, a normal occurrence for a sunny Monday morning in Tortaya.

Loud singing of different songs filled the area. Chatter, laughter, yelling, and screaming made hearing anything clearly nearly impossible. The sound of a gun being fired made heads turn, but no one seemed to care.

Rosetta watched a man fall, and then the struggle of a woman trying to help him back to his feet by tugging on his elbow.

Turning her head towards a noise, she saw a man taking a woman against the wall down the side of two buildings cluttered close together, his pants threatening to fall further to his knees than they already were. She seemed to be enjoying herself, as she was bucking back into him as she gave loud cries. Rosetta thought the man sounded like a grunting bear. Neither were bothered they were outside in the middle of the day.

"Get back here, you no-good, rotten cheater!" a man yelled at another as they ran past her. One was holding a cleaver and giving chase, while the other looked rather afraid, a handful of coins in his hand.

She had to quickly duck out of the way when an intoxicated man was thrown out of tavern face first into the dirt. "And stay out!"

Rosetta was sure the man would find himself back inside at some point, regardless of the threat.

Her tricone hat was keeping the bright sun from her eyes while her doublet coat kept her warm and hid most of her womanly curves. A bright smile plastered her face as she took in the buffoonery and chaotic shenanigans that never stopped in this town. The day walkers were just as wild as the night crawlers.

It didn't matter the day, the hour, the season, this place was alive with activity. Those who lived in the town would party until they passed out somewhere, too drunk or tired to care about the constant noise. She thought she even saw one passed out on top of a pile of hay, soaked in questionable liquid, with a bottle in his hand.

Rosetta knew she would eventually join them for the next few days, but currently, she was making her way somewhere important. She needed her focus, to concentrate.

The more she walked, getting further and further away from the heart of the town, the quieter it became. She was walking up such a sharp incline, she doubted any drunk person could walk it without struggling. In the past, she'd seen her fair share of men who had given up halfway, shaking their heads in disappointment as they sat in the dirt facing the decline.

They always looked so sad that they couldn't make it to the top in their state.

The prize would have been worth it if they could.

At the very top of this large and very sharp hill was a grand mansion. It was one of the few buildings on this island that was maintained regularly, and it was one of the biggest highlights. Men would sail here just for this place, as if it was a fabled tale of riches and wonder.

To some, it was.

The road was clean and crisp. Shops got tidier the further she went, and she knew only the most valuable wares were sold near the top before that great mansion.

Anyone was welcome, and it was her current destination.

Two men were stationed at the front. They had swords on their belts, daggers, pistols, while their shoulders had rifles slung across them. They were armed to the teeth like soldiers, yet they wore simple clothing: brown pants, simple vests, and white tunics.

They eyed her over as she approached the three-story building of white limestone. It shone in the sunlight like a beacon in the day. It could be seen from almost anywhere if one wasn't next to a tall building obstructing the view.

Inside the iron fencing were shrubs, trees, and a beautiful garden of flowers. Lush green hedges looked like clouds as they blocked the outside world from looking inside the gardens. A pond with lily pads sat in the centre, with two marble carved ladies pouring water out of vases as the central statue.

The red painted doors were closed. She didn't need to knock with either of the black iron door knocker rings.

Rosetta merely opened the door handles and walked inside.

The massive front room was furnished with multiple lounges of varying colours, sizes, and styles. A large chandelier sparkled with dangling tear drop crystals in a dome pattern, reflecting colours in an array of prisms. Colourful carpets of red, greens, and blue covered the white and black marble flooring, all of them in floral designs.

At the back of the room was a large staircase that split off into two sections to lead higher into the mansion, doors to hallways beside them on the bottom floor.

There was no music, but faint chatter and giggling could be heard.

A string of eyes found their way to her.

A least six beautiful women sat on those lounges, talking to each other. Three more were either seated next to a man or on his lap, happily conversing quietly.

One of the women recognised her.

Her face lit up and she immediately got to her feet. "Rosetta!"

Ah shit, what's her name again? A black-haired woman with pale skin came to put her arms around her for a tight hug.

"Charlotte," Rosetta smiled, hugging the woman back.

"It's been months since I've seen you!" Eventually, Charlotte pushed her arms back to grasp her shoulders tightly with a happy but thoughtful expression. "Are you here to see Madame Lillian?"

"I am," she answered with a nod. "Is she busy? I must be quick."

Alister no doubt had lost his temper that she'd gone off on her own. She could just imagine his dumbfounded face when he discovered she'd left.

"No, she's free. She's in her room having tea." She waved her hand in the direction Rosetta would need to go, despite already knowing the way. "I'm sure she'll be happy to see you."

"Excellent."

Rosetta swiftly turned to the right and walked through a set of large doors that would take her down a long hallway.

There were many single doors leading to bedrooms on one side, while grided windows brightened her path on the other. The walls were painted cream, pale green leaves forking across them in intricate patterns. An occasional pink flower dotted the walls as well.

Mounted iron arbours holding unlit candles would eventually be lit when night fell. They were clean, any residue from old wax candles removed and replaced daily.

At the very end of the red carpeted hallway was another set of double doors that would lead to a large bedroom – one that was different to the rest of the rooms, and far grander.

She knocked on the door.

"Come in," answered an aged, yet feminine voice.

Rosetta opened the door and entered, a strong sweet-smelling incense billowing out to greet her.

Purple silks lay over a neatly made bed pressing up against the back corner of the room. An oak side table sat next to it. A brown lounge was up against the left wall, facing the large windows that spanned nearly the entire wall. Thick, heavy blue drapes blocked out the worst of the sunlight.

Madame Lillian Gunter was seated at a round dining table, sipping at a cup of tea. There was a strip of purple dining cloth through its centre with a fancy three-pronged candle holder in the middle. A pile of papers sat in front of her, as though she had been busy reading letters and ledgers.

She turned her warm green eyes to Rosetta, and they immediately crinkled in a welcoming smile as the corners of her lips turned upwards.

Her blonde hair had streaks of grey through it, but it was still elegantly tied back into a stylish bun. Her lightly tanned face was only gently weathered by age, and even though she was soon to reach fifty, the woman was still one of the most beautiful people Rosetta had ever seen.

"Well, if it isn't Rosetta Silver, as I live and breathe," she said, elegantly climbing from her seat to stand.

Her body was thin, but with her large breasts cupped high on her chest, she knew this woman had been sought after in her youth.

"Hello, Lillian," she answered respectfully with a bow of her head.

The woman scoffed, waving her hand to the side, as if to say she disliked her greeting. "Come here, you silly girl. I demand a hug."

She stood next to the table and waited for Rosetta to approach, her arms opened wide. Like a daughter running to her mother for comfort, Rosetta stomped forward and allowed herself to be collected into those arms.

Her warmth radiated into Rosetta, melting her muscles as if she was melting away all her worries, fears, and concerns.

She couldn't help drawing in closer. The way she smelled made Rosetta feel even more at ease, and she couldn't stop herself from drawing in further.

After a tight squeeze, Lillian pulled back just enough to place her soft hands on either side of Rosetta's face.

"You grow more beautiful every time I see you." She lovingly brushed her long, messy, untamed fringe from her face to see her features better. "You have so many freckles now, my dear. You need to take better care of your skin."

"That happens when you're in the sun as much as I am."

Her smile deepened, causing Rosetta's lips to answer her look with her own.

"Sweet child, how have you been?" She drew away and gestured her hand forward so Rosetta would take a seat at the table. "Where are your men?"

Lilian headed towards her rolling tea table and collected a fresh teacup with a rose floral pattern, placing it down in front of her before grabbing the matching white ceramic teapot. She poured her a cup of tea and Rosetta took in the smell of honey, mint, and ginger.

I've been so long at sea that I've forgotten the smell of something so sweet. She eagerly wrapped both hands around the cup to huddle its warmth and took a sip.

She almost wanted to moan with satisfaction. Lillian possibly made the best tea in the world. *She could have gone into the tea selling business.*

"I've been very good these past months," she answered around another sip, before placing it down to rest on the saucer. "My crew are at the dock. We've only just gotten to Tortaya."

"You walked here by yourself?" The motherly look of concern made fear cut through her faster than any look Alister could possibly give. She filled up her own cup that was almost empty, looking up through her eyebrows with narrowed eyes.

"That's rather stupid of you."

Rosetta couldn't help giving a giggle. "I had to be quick."

Madame Lillian was slow and elegant now due to her age, but Rosetta knew she was a loud-mouthed, hot-tempered, irresponsible woman when she had the energy.

Staring at the blonde-haired, green-eyed, honey skinned woman with aweing respect, she couldn't help noticing she looked similar to Pierre.

Lillian gave a gruntled noise of disappointment before sighing as she sat.

"Considering you're here, you've either gotten the Laughing Siren, or you never got the chance to." At the face Rosetta gave, she answered with an insipid expression down her pointed nose while reaching for the sugar tongs. She purposefully plopped a sugar cube into her tea. "Don't give me that look. If you failed, you'd either be dead or arrested."

"The big girl's all mine."

She gave the woman the brightest grin she could manage, leaning back in her chair with pride. She curled her arm around the back rest while reaching her legs up to place the heels of her boots on the dining table. Lillian said nothing about the disrespectful placement of her boots, but Rosetta was sure if it had been anyone else, they would have received an earful.

"Been sailing her for three months now."

Lillian didn't share in her happiness. "And that Theodore Briggs of yours?"

She gave a curt nod. "Good and dead."

The woman finally gave a smile of celebration. She even clapped her hands together. "Wonderful! Good to see you finally got what you wanted."

"Oh yes, definitely." Rosetta reached forward to grab the teacup and its plate, resting both on her stretched-out stomach.

Lillian's eyes seemed to daze away as she reminisced. "I

still remember the night we had to hide you because it had been discovered you were in this port."

Rosetta remembered that night vividly, often with concern. How close she'd come to Theodore finding her had been too close for comfort.

Someone who knew her had come to Tortaya and seen her walking around. When Theodore heard, he'd hired a boat that wasn't one of Queen Mary Anne's, sailed to these waters, and started a manhunt for her.

Since he didn't have the Laughing Siren with him at the time, Rosetta had put off killing him until he did.

For nearly a week, she and Naeem that sought shelter in this mansion, hidden behind closed doors.

"I'm guessing you've come to Tortaya to supply that boat of yours." Lillian took a sip of her tea, nodding at the sweetness of it. "But why did you, apparently, rush to my estate?"

"I have a favour to ask of you."

She raised a blonde brow at her. "A favour? I can only imagine what you need from me."

"Girls," she answered. "Lots of them."

Her brow raised further. "Well, you've come to the right place, but how many do you need?"

She went to take another sip of her tea with proper, lady-like charm. Rosetta slurped her own, despite knowing full well how to be an elegant, noble lady.

"About eighty-two."

Lillian almost choked on her tea, giving a few coughs. "I don't have that many girls! Dear lord, child, that's a big ask."

Rosetta gave a laugh, shaking her head. "Hire a few from the town for a night."

"You want me to grab random whores from the street?" The disbelief in her tone was unmistakable. "I've never taken in cheap prostitutes, Rosetta, you know that."

"I know." The sigh she gave as her eyes drifted to the walls showed just how much she knew she was asking. "But the men need to be satisfied. They also need to be housed for the night and your establishment is the best in the city." Then she brought her gaze back to eye her up and down. "You also have the only brothel that can house over a hundred. You have room for all of them, and I'd rather they stay close together so they're safe."

Madame Lillian was the owner and mistress of the biggest brothel in the entire northern hemisphere, maybe even the world.

It was famous, expensive, but known for having the highest quality woman. It was also new. The mansion had only been built and established eight years ago. Prior to that, Madame Lillian had a much smaller business in the centre of town. It had still been glorious, but not at its current state.

"You want to bring all of them here?"

"Yes, tonight."

She let out a thoughtful noise before clicking her tongue.

"Hmm. For you, I'll see what I can do." Then, it was her turn to eye Rosetta up and down with a note of apprehension. "Are you sure you don't want to work for me again instead of crew a bunch of useless, brainless men? You could make more coin than most of the girls and save yourself all this trouble."

"No," Rosetta laughed. "I'm quite happy being a sailor, thank you very much."

"A pirate," the woman sneered back.

Rosetta rolled her eyes, taking another sip of tea. "You'll want to have the men bathe. We've been at sea for nearly seven months."

"A room, a woman, and a bath?" Lillian gave a mocking snort of laughter. "Your boys will be paying a pretty penny for all that."

Once more, Rosetta's eyes fell to the side. A deep and

solemn sigh fell from her. "That's where the favour I'm asking really becomes heavy. I need you to be kind to my coin purse, Lillian. I'm paying for it."

When her admission was met with uncomfortable silence, Rosetta looked back to see the woman had a wide-eyed, open-mouthed expression.

"What in god's name do you mean you're paying for it? Get the men to pay for their own whores!" She pointed her nimble finger at her to wag it in anger. "Did they somehow convince you, a woman, to pay for their pleasure? Bloody men, rotten to the core, the lot of them!"

Rosetta reached forward and grabbed Lillian's free hand, clenched into a tight fist on the table. She patted it.

"I worry the men will grow jealous. I need to alleviate some of their stress and show my gratitude for their patience and understanding before I lose some of them."

"Jealous?" Lillian squinted her eyes. The way she stared showed Rosetta she was having her soul examined. "You've met a man, haven't you?"

She tucked a strand of her hair over her ear self-consciously, turning her gaze to the green carpeted floor.

"A no-good pirate, I'm guessing." She threw her hands forward to show her irritation before she folded her arms over her large bosom.

"We've been sailing together for three months. He helped me get the Laughing Siren."

"I told you to stay away from pirates and sailors, Rosie! Nothing ever good comes from getting entangled with them."

It once irked Rosetta that Lillian would call her Rosie, but she had long ago accepted it. Honestly, she found it sweet and heart-warming from this woman she secretly cared for.

She didn't have the heart to tell her to stop calling her the endearment after having done so many times already. It pained her less now that Theodore was dead.

"I know, but–"

"All sailors do is leave you in port with the promise you're the only one, like you're too stupid to know the truth." She folded her arms tighter. "They put a babe in you and then piss off to sea. Then they come back to claim their son when they're nothing but a sweet boy but refuse to claim their daughter."

With another sigh, Rosetta sat back in her chair to let the woman rant. Lillian hated any man who sailed the sea. She held resentment because of things that happened in her life, and she feared any woman being forced to follow the same path.

"I'm not a port girl, Lilian. I sail the sea as much as he does." Even more now that she had her beloved ship. "He's also careful. He never comes inside."

It was the thing she appreciated about Alister the most. Not once had he failed to pull out when they were intimate.

She didn't know if it was out of respect for her or fear of getting her pregnant, but he did it without failure. If he didn't, Rosetta wouldn't take the constant risk with someone so careless. Maybe...

"You know that isn't fool proof!" She squinted her eyes once more to give a disappointed angry glare, because Rosetta was sleeping with a man of whom she would never approve. "And they're always careful until they suddenly aren't."

Rosetta tried to give her a reassuring smile, knowing full well it wouldn't matter. "I've had plenty of men come inside me. You know I don't think I can get pregnant because of what Theodore did."

The way she had lost her child had been horrible. She'd been nearly five months pregnant and had woken up after being unconscious for a few seconds, laying on the stairs with blood running between her legs while servants and maids tried to help her to her feet. It had been a part of her nightmares since the day it happened.

Rosetta would much rather the beating she'd received a few days later than to relive the memory as often as she did.

As much as she'd wanted that child, she hoped she was a broken woman now. She doubted her injured womb could grow a baby, and she'd rather not deal with the possibility of losing one again. She doubted she could survive the heartbreak.

She was also very irregular now, whereas before, she'd had her period every month without fail, like a nice, healthy, fertile woman. *I wish it would just fuck off completely.*

Lillian knew about Rosetta's history; she was one of the only people alive who did. The only people to whom she'd ever revealed the extent of her suffering had been Mr Smith and Naeem. Now, there was only Lillian and Naeem who knew the full truth.

She hadn't, and refused, to tell Alister anything else about those events, other than what he'd discovered the day they'd killed Theodore. She didn't want him to know what she had felt, her heartache and pain, all the things she suffered then, and what she did afterwards.

She doubted he'd care anyway.

"But what if you're wrong?" Lillian looked at her beseechingly.

Looking at the woman in front of her who held nothing but tenderness for Rosetta, it was hard not to feel embarrassed about the man she'd been sleeping with. It was the first time she'd ever felt shame about being underneath Alister.

It was like being scorned by a loving mother.

"How's your daughter?"

"Agnes is wonderful," she answered while turning her head away dismissively, allowing the direction of the conversation to change. "She married the most distinguished blacksmith in town. He's a good man, faithful and kind."

"Your son?"

Lillian was adamant that the same man had impregnated her, despite her being a prostitute herself at the time and her children being born seven years apart.

"Don't know, haven't seen him in two years. He doesn't want to see his mother." Her sullen expression almost seemed resentful. "I miss that child like an ache, but his father turned him from the sweet boy he was into a monster. He refuses to see me, like he doesn't care about the woman who gave him life."

Then, her eyes turned teary, her bottom lip quivering ever so slightly.

Rosetta often kept her eyes peeled when she was in Tortaya for a man who looked like Lillian. She'd love to threaten him for hurting the poor woman in front of her who deserved every ounce of love. She was like a mother to her, after all.

"Every day, I fear he'll be arrested or wind up dead. A mother shouldn't have to worry her son will die before her. It's not fair." She stemmed her tears quickly, her green eyes glistening with them. "Anyway, back to business."

She cleared her throat to rid herself of the lump of emotion obviously present, attempting to push pieces of her hair back into her bun. It was as if she was attempting to tidy her outside appearance to fix her inside emotional state.

"A room, a bed, and a bath." She tapped her knuckle on the table in thought. "Ten pounds."

"Each? I don't even think I have that much!" Rosetta pointed her finger at Lillian. "You would never make this much profit for the rooms in a week, let alone a single night."

She pursed her slightly wrinkled lips. "Seven pounds. I must pay the girls their wages. Maybe their cheapest, but they should understand for a night."

Rosetta knew that price was three pounds, six if the man seemed as though he had fat pockets. The water came from elsewhere and would be costly to get it up the hill, heated, and into that many baths.

"Six. You don't have to pay the street whores that much," Rosetta demanded, folding her arms. "Do remember who it was who stopped those men from ransacking this place three years ago. You did tell me you owe me." She pointed to the large scar that ran from her hip, across her stomach, over her breast, and then all the way to her nipple. Alister always reminded her of it because he seemed strangely fond of licking it over the mound of her breast "I didn't get this scar by doing nothing here."

"I knew when I told you I owed you it would come back to haunt me. Fine! Six pounds."

Rosetta hoped she had that much in her share of the loot she'd gotten with Alister, as well as everything else they'd collected over the months raiding ships.

If not, I may have to pick some pockets.

"I'll bring the men and the money tonight. Make sure the girls are clean so my crew can enjoy fresh women." She looked down to her nails with triumph, stemming the urge to grin. It would only irritate Lillian if she did. "If they want booze, food, or anything extra, make them pay for it."

She'd already told them of her plan to give them a night of pleasure and relaxation. She had also told them to keep their mouths shut about letting Alister's men know.

The last thing she needed was for him to tell her she was making a stupid decision, one she would never tell him the reason behind. Nor did she somehow want to be roped into paying for his men to have the same thing! If they wanted something like this, they needed to pay for it themselves.

It's the bloody price I have to pay.

CHAPTER FOUR

Alister never noticed the short person who walked past him under a tricone hat shielding their face. He was too busy watching over his men work.

Since he knew everything in their stocks, he was making sure they brought what he wanted off his ship and left what needed to stay on it on the surface.

Pierre, the wonderful swindler, was already off trying to find buyers for the expensive cargo. Alister was hoping that by the end of the day, everything valuable would be sold so that he wouldn't need many guards.

He only needed one or two to make sure no one tried to steal the Howling Death. The hatch would be locked, his men forced to find somewhere else to sleep, so it couldn't be raided without being noticed.

As though he knew it would happen, he halted one of his men to check the crate they were carrying. He opened the top to look inside, finding green glass bottles safely nestled inside bits of straw.

"That's sweet wine, you daft twit!" He smacked the man on the side of the head before pointing to the special red wax symbol stamped into the side of it. "That's twice as precious as normal wine. Put it back on the ship."

There must be someone on this god forsaken island who has excellent taste. He wouldn't have it sitting in a stall to be sold for half the price with the cheap wine they'd stolen.

Rosetta's men were putting their cargo with his so it could be sold together. Then, they would split the profits down the middle. What couldn't be sold for the highest price would eventually be sold to a merchant shop for whatever coin they could get for it.

Alister had been surprised Rosetta asked him to help her sell her wares. That was, until her face turned depressed, and she'd mumbled about John being the one who usually helped her sell it.

She was a woman. Merchants and buyers would try to slyly buy it for the lowest price because they would think she was naïve, which she was. Alister knew she wouldn't understand what most of it was worth. She'd admitted that she hadn't traded much, and when she did, John had done all the work while she stood in the background.

She'd put too much faith into someone who was capable of dying.

Thinking of that woman. She still hadn't turned up and the sun had risen higher.

Or so he thought.

He turned his head to check on Naeem, who had gone quiet, to see she had her arm around his shoulders.

He was looking down at her, an obvious chuckle coming from him. They were talking about something that obviously had the man jolly before he peeked his eyes up over her shoulder, as if he was just casually looking around.

His smile died when he saw Alister approaching. He tried to step away from her, but she refused to let go of his neck.

"Unfortunately, since I'm getting you to guard the ship tonight, you'll have to wait until tomorrow."

"Ahhh, Rosetta..." Naeem answered, looking at Alister with his arms crossed over his chest while his eyes squinted.

Her spine stiffened. "I feel the creep of death at my back.

He's behind me, isn't he?"

"Just where in the name of the seven seas have you been?" he bit through clenched teeth. "You had a ship to unload."

Without moving her arm from Naeem, she tilted her head back and to the side to look at him. "Was having tea."

His lips parted in disbelief.

"*Tea*? You left your men on their own and walked these streets by yourself to have tea?"

She finally turned to him, wearing a grand smile that held not a single shred of fear.

"Sure did." She looked around him like she was inspecting the boardwalk. "You did a bang-up job here, Alister. I'm impressed. You really are amazing at what you do."

"You..." *Devious little woman.* He pointed his index and middle fingers of one hand at her. She was trying to get on his good side with a compliment and they both knew it.

He poked her in the forehead twice.

"You're lucky I'm in a good mood when I'm about to make coin." He threw his arm to the side to point towards the end of the boardwalk, towards the town. "Now, move it. You and I are going to get to work selling our wares."

She furrowed her brows into a thoughtful expression.

Since no one else was around to overhear, she leaned in and said, "But you know I can't be of help."

"Nay." Like he did when he was feeling any emotion, anger, pride, or arrogance, he folded his arms. "I don't trust you won't say I cheapened you out of your share if you aren't here to witness it."

Her pouty lips turned more pouted. "How am I supposed to trick you into giving me extra coin when you make it so fair like that?"

He leaned forward to be eye level with her, practically having to lean over. "Because you're a deceptive woman who already revealed all her cards."

Her pout turned mischievous as she reached up and patted the side of his cheek lightly. "That's what you think, big boy."

Bloody hell. He better hope so, because she's already got his sail ropes in knots.

She gave a defeated sigh.

"Alright, let's go." She gestured her hand forward. "Lead the way, *captain.*"

His nose crinkled in agitation. She only called him captain to mock him. Still, he turned and led the way.

Not far from the pier was a street where ships came to sell their wares. The kilometre long street was bustling with stalls and people perusing the wares. His men had already started working, with Derek watching over them until he arrived with Rosetta.

He took the ledger from the one-legged man and gave it to her. He still couldn't believe she'd left to go have tea while he was busy working, forcing him to have to wait for her.

"You sit here and write the numbers and the items sold with it." He pointed to a crate hidden from the sun by the roof of the stall. She couldn't help sell, but he would still have her be useful, since he knew she could write and read perfectly – possibly even better than him. "We will count it all later."

Without argument, she plopped herself onto her makeshift seat with unlady-like grace and folded one leg on top of the other, kicking it like she was bored already, resting her chin in her palm.

Alister leaned his shoulder against the inner wall of the wooden block stall, keeping in the shade to stay away from the muggy heat. It was in the middle of three others they'd taken to occupy since they had a lot of loot to sell.

He eyed her as she brushed the feathered tip of the quill under her jaw absentmindedly, staring at the people walking past.

We have a lot more to sell because of her.

He knew having all that space on her ship would be useful. This might be one of the best trading days he'd ever witness.

When they sold something, she wrote it down, waiting first for Alister to haggle his way to a higher price.

Most things were sold by the crate load. One box of soap? Sold in one go. Candlesticks? All five boxes were bought by one man and the wife who wanted them. A box of bath oils? Sold to another merchant who specialised in personal hygiene wares; he also bought face cloths to go with them.

"They're worth more than that," he heard Rosetta say from behind him.

He was currently in the middle of a trade for a teapot and teacup set, about to accept the offered price for them.

It was the first time she had spoken for nearly an hour, and he turned his head back to look at her with a raised brow. She rolled her eyes, no doubt understanding his question of 'how the hell would you know?'

"They're from the Southern Trading Company." She lifted her head higher to look at them. "Turn one of the teacups upside down; it'll have the insignia on it."

Out of curiosity, he did. When he saw it, he thrust it into the man's face.

"They're rare in the northern hemisphere. I doubt you'll ever find anyone with a set like this." Then, she looked the buyer in the eyes as she said, "Only those of the highest nobility have anything with that insignia."

"And how would you know?" the fat man asked her with his long nose lifted in snobbery.

She gestured to her body. "Am I not a woman? All women know about the quality of tea."

Those words seemed to spark a light in the man, who offered double the price just to have them. Alister got triple.

"The tea we have is also from the Southern Trading Company." She waved her hand towards the metal tins filled with loose herbs and spices. "It's obvious you know your teas, and any guests you serve them to will be delighted at the taste."

For someone who wasn't good at selling wares, she made the man puff his chest with pride at her compliment – even though Alister thought he looked like a brainless moron.

He bought multiple metal tins and gestured to his servant to gather his haul. Alister turned his attention to Rosetta when they were gone.

"Good job, lass." She'd saved him from losing good coin. "No doubt you learnt that from being a duchess."

"Yes," she grinned. "I learned that those teacups are ones of thousands, and he'll be very disappointed when he walks into any tea shop on the mainland to discover them there."

"Wait." Alister stared at the man as he walked further into the crowd. "You lied to him?"

She gave a snort of laughter.

"Of course, I did. The Southern Trading Company usually have the rarest and most prized items. Everyone knows that, but those were fakes." She scribbled down how much they'd gotten for them. "The insignia is usually stamped in blue, not black. That's how I knew."

Regardless, Alister grinned at her. He was always up for stealing from fools.

Eventually, they were pulled away from the stall by Pierre so they could sell the valuable items from the ship.

A singular man, who intended to ferry everything he bought to the mainland to sell to vain and rich nobles, bought most of it: carpets, rugs, drapes, all the fabrics they'd stolen. He'd also taken the wine and perfume.

Since that task was completed rather quickly, they were able to return to the stall in no time. It was getting late, and they were currently down to one stall out of their three, consolidating everything together. Most of what they had left was slow to move, less desirable or worth very little.

With her feet up on another crate, her arms folded, her head tilted back like she was moments away from falling asleep with boredom, Rosetta nearly jumped out of her skin when her name was called.

"Rosetta?"

"Who wants to know?" she answered almost immediately, as if that was her go to when her name was called in port, said with a hint of wary suspicion.

She eyed the crowd of people until her gaze finally fell onto the tall, thin man approaching their last stall. His hair was short and looked flaky. His nose was large, his lips so thin they could barely be seen. His eyes were a beady, pitch black.

Alister was still leaning against the wall as he watched the man carefully. *She's known in these parts.* Even just one person recognising her could be troublesome.

"Well, if it isn't Alexander Olofam."

She gave a pouted smile Alister had only ever seen when she was getting heated with him. It deepened as she walked over to the counter to lean across it, twirling a strand of her brown hair.

It was the kind of flirtatious smile he didn't like her wearing for another man when he was standing right next to her. Even more so when she started brushing the fingertips of her other hand over the skin high on her chest to tickle herself.

"I haven't seen you in these parts for quite some time." His eyes fell to her chest where she was playing, then lower and remained fixed there. The way she stood showed most of her cleavage, to the point where her breasts were almost spilling out of her tunic. "You cut my brother's ear off the last time I saw you."

"Then he shouldn't have hit his wife in front of me."

His eyes shot back up, and he gave her a laugh. "That's true. You taught him a real good lesson with that."

"It's my favourite thing," she giggled. She reached forward to start playing with one of the buttons of his tunic, twisting it playfully. "How have you been?"

When some of Alister's crew shuffled behind her, his gaze fell on the men, before freezing at his dark and menacing face. Alister was being patient because he wanted to know what the hell she was doing and why, but he wasn't pleased.

"I've been good," he gulped, shying his gaze away from Alister to place it back on her. "You've got a new crew, I see."

She waved her hand back towards the men behind her, including him. "Do you like them? They're dumb but they get the job done."

Alister's eye twitched in irritation. He was a moment away from losing it. He wasn't part of anyone's crew, and he wouldn't allow her to pretend he was beneath her!

"They're a lot scarier than the last." The man's shoulders caved inwards in nervousness. "Where's Mr Smith? He's a friendly fellow."

Her smile never fell as she said, "He's around, off selling some of my better wares."

Why'd she lie? Alister couldn't help but frown. Then again, talking about death could dampen any conversation. His confusion was lost the moment she started walking her fingers down the man's chest.

"So, you going to buy my wares or are you going to leave me *unsatisfied*, Alexander?"

The man gave a shudder of obvious want, and Alister thought he may have seen something small growing in his breeches.

"For you, Rosetta, anything." He started digging into his pockets to pull out his coin purse. "You promised me you would come see me before you left last time."

"Sorry about that," she pouted, drawing her finger back up in a teasing manner.

She was making a sale, and as much Alister didn't like this, he wasn't about to say no to coin. His greed hooked him like a curled fishing hook.

She bit her bottom lip, tugging on it lightly before she spoke. "I did try to find you, but your brother refused to tell me where you'd run off to. Might be because of the whole ear thing."

"What are you buying?" Alister finally bit, wanting this interaction over with as quickly as possible.

Rosetta turned her head over her shoulder to look at him. "All of it."

Alister's head reared back. "All of it?"

He looked over what they had left. There was much here, and not all of it was valuable or useful. *He wouldn't buy lace doilies.* What use would a man like him have for lace doilies?

"Yes." The man nodded when her fingertips started trailing back down, then dangerously lower. She started twisting the top button of his breeches. "Everything. Whatever you have left."

"A hundred and seventy pounds."

Rosetta stared up at the man while giving a subtle, yet suggestive, lick of her lips. She gently reached over for the man's coin purse with her other hand and took it from him.

He didn't seem to notice as he relinquished it.

"How much is in here, Alexander?"

"T-two hundred and four," he panted when her finger strolled over the buttons of his pants to touch the third, then the lowest one.

"Thank you. You won't regret our little trade, will you?" The man shook his head like he'd lost the ability to speak, his oil-covered cheeks turning pink. "Make sure you stay near your home. I'm busy at the moment, but I'll be in Tortaya for three days. I promise to come. I'll make up for not being able to see you last time."

Her smile grew as she stared to lean away, reaching up to pinch his cheek while giving him a wink.

"I'll stay home," he finally answered, his trance broken now that she'd removed her playful touch.

"Good boy." Then she turned to everyone behind her, looking around at the wares before she clapped her hands. "Well, this all belongs to my sweet, dear Alexander now. We should leave so he and his servants can collect it."

Before Alister could say or do anything, Rosetta walked away from the stall. She started heading back towards the dock without sparing him a glance.

His crew looked at him the same way he looked at them; with confusion. He fell away so he could chase after her. Just as he was about ask her what the fuck that just was, she nearly punched him in the stomach with the coin purse.

"I hate that little prick of a man," she sneered with a tight expression. "He's a coward, but he always buys the shit no one else will when he sees me."

He noticed her lips were not only pursed tightly, but also slightly twisted with disgust. The angry squint to her eyes showed him just how much she despised him.

She drew her gaze to the side to look at his frowning face.

"He's got a thing for me, absolutely incessant about it. It makes it easier to steal his coin." She turned her eyes forward once more. "And I've just made sure he stays home and out of my way while I'm here."

Alister turned his head to look back at the stall they were walking away from, realising she'd just finished the last of their work in the span of ten minutes. He'd been thinking this would take them the rest of the day, considering what they'd had left.

She even got more than it was worth. The man had just handed her his entire purse without care! *So, it's not just me she has this power over.* The thought made him grumble with disdain.

"Naeem!" she yelled when she saw him on the boardwalk. "Help me, my hands are unclean!"

She threw them forward like they were on fire.

Naeem came running over with a look of humour. "Alexander again?"

She nodded, looking down at her trembling, shaking hands. "I-I think I have to remove them."

"I'll fetch the axe," Naeem sighed, walking away to head towards the ship. He shook his head along the way.

Alister knew he wasn't actually going to, but he did turn to Rosetta with his brow raised. "You're a nasty piece of work, you know that lass?"

It was said both with pride and a disgruntled infliction.

"Don't be too upset that I play the same game with all men to get what I want." She stepped forward to play with the seam of his doublet coat near the centre of his chest. It seemed she was trying to distract him in the exact same way she just distracted Alexander. "Just know you're the first who's ever gotten to play with me."

How Rosetta made her words suggestive and body awakening, he didn't know. He even had to stifle a groan when she ran her palm over his pectoral muscle and grazed his nipple at the same time.

Then, she turned away to head towards her ship.

"Now, let's go split our hard-earned coin so we can pay our men and relax."

CHAPTER FIVE

"Oh, my sweet, bewitching Rosetta," Pierre called as she walked down the boardwalk by herself. "You're a vision as always, my dear." He bowed to her like a gentleman, taking her hand to kiss the back of it. "You are so beautiful, even the moon seems to shine less brightly against your decadent radiance."

She ripped her hand from him and held it in the air like she was about to back-hand him. "It's as if you just want me to hit you."

He wiggled his blond brows at her, his green eyes shining with a mischievous glint. "I might enjoy that." When she lifted her hand higher, he flinched. "Wait, no. Please don't."

She let out a silent giggle while letting her hand fall. Then, she turned to Alister with a bright smile, her heart swelling.

He gave her a nodding grunt. "Let's go."

Her smile fell and a sigh fluttered from her when he turned to walk off.

"Don't worry, I think you look beautiful," Pierre commented once more, eyeing her and the yellow dress she wore with appreciative eyes.

She turned her chin up at him as she picked up the skirt of her dress so she could walk. "I don't particularly care if anyone finds me beautiful."

But she'd kind of been hoping for more than that from

Alister. The last time she'd worn a dress in front of him had been the day she'd first met him.

Perhaps it was a silly notion, but she'd been hoping he'd appreciate it, especially since she'd worked on untangling her hair and pinning it back into an elegant bun. She'd even worn her red lipstick and a touch of blush.

I guess it doesn't matter.

Some of his men, those she knew were closer to him than others, were walking with them. Her men were at the mansion waiting for Rosetta. She'd organised for Madame Lillian to keep the gate closed until she arrived so she could speak to them. She also needed to pay first.

After splitting up the profits of the day and getting Alister to help her count it out, she knew she had enough.

Unfortunately, it was going to leave her with very little for herself after expenses. *But I don't need much.* Just enough to get her through their stay in Tortaya and have as much fun as she wanted. She could get more later when they sailed again.

She eventually let the skirt of her dress go and walked with her fingers caressing her lips, deep in thought.

Booze and food. Maybe even something small for myself. Rosetta hadn't bought herself much since she'd left her home three years ago. *I was hoping to buy a new dress.*

She'd been gifted this pale yellow one the last time she'd come to Tortaya by one of Lilian's girls. When she was in port, any port, Rosetta liked to feel like a woman. As much as she enjoyed being captain of a ship, she missed being feminine.

Wearing a dress also had its uses.

It hid a pistol and a sword underneath. She'd cut openings into the sides of it so she could reach in at a moment's notice. It also hid the hefty coin purse she strapped to her for Madame Lillian, and the smaller one with her spending money.

Alister stopped after choosing the tavern he apparently

wanted to be in for the night. When Rosetta kept walking, he grabbed her wrist.

"And just where are you going?"

"For a walk." She looked up at the sign of the tavern called '*The Drunken Sailor*' before turning her gaze back to him. "I won't be long."

"By yourself?" His eye seemed to move over the fact she was no longer surrounded by anyone, since his men had gone inside. "Where is your crew?"

"You're so protective, it's almost sickening." She gripped his jaw and shook his head gently. "I'll be fine. Got a loaded gun and my sword under this frock."

"You do?" He came closer to pat her sides, feeling them for himself. "The fact I never felt these on you that first day still amazes me." He gripped her weapons, jiggling them with a grin. "Aye, I feel better knowing you've got these on you."

"Exactly. I won't be gone long, and I won't be far."

His grin faded and his eye examined her, and her outfit, carefully. "The degenerates come out at night in these parts, lass."

"I'm meeting up with my crew. They're off at another location and I want to check on them." She gestured to the front door and the lack of porch this place had. This building had two small alleys down the side, leading to another street, an entrance on both sides. "Go, drink; I'll be back shortly."

Seeing she wasn't going to listen, he rolled his eyes and turned to walk inside. She was still surprised at how easy their arguments seemed to be lately. Even in port, he was calmer.

Is he losing interest? She pondered the question as she made her way down the street, and once more climbed the sharp incline. The brothel was built on the top of this hill for that very reason: they didn't want stumbling drunks making their way inside. They wanted determined men with heavy pockets of coin.

If he is losing interest, then why would he port with me? Or get more supplies if he is planning on cutting ties soon? It didn't seem to fit.

Seeing her men loitering outside the front of the gates stole her attention. She put her thoughts to the side. Looking at the collection of them, she was rather thankful she hadn't walked with them through the street. They'd all made their way here on their own.

I'm sure a crowd this big would have been odd.

The gates opened when she arrived, and they followed in behind her. Madame Lillian came to the front porch, standing at the top steps with her hands placed firmly behind her back. Rosetta stood next to her so she could speak to her men.

Leaning closer to quieten her voice, Rosetta asked, "Is everything organised?"

"Yes. I somehow managed to wrangle up the number of women you needed."

Rosetta doubted it was Lillian herself who rounded up the street whores. She probably sent one of her own girls to collect them, so she didn't have to leave the mansion.

She nodded her head in understanding.

"Alright boys, this is how it's going to be." She eyed them as she boomed. "The girls are going to come out and pick their man for the night. She will lead you to a room and you filthy, disgusting lot will bathe. She will then attend to you anyway you see fit."

A bustle of chatter began. She noticed some of the men elbowing each other, like they were giving each other teasing, offensive comments.

"There are some rules." She stepped forward to point her finger at them. "These are high class whores and I've paid a pretty penny for them. If you even so much as dare lay a harmful hand on them, you will lose said hands. Speak nasty words, you will lose your tongue. If one of you so much as dares to make a mistake that could lead to an increase in population, you will be boarding my ship as a eunuch. Do I make myself clear?"

"Aye," was the answer she received from them all.

"There will be no brawling, but you are allowed to wander the halls and be randy. Have fun with your women, swap them if they allow it. If you want to drink or eat, you will be paying for it yourselves and they only sell the best here, so expect your pockets to leave lighter."

When they confirmed that they understood, the women came out to grab their men. Each was taken inside with a giggling whore on his arm, a pretty woman who would make sure these men felt loved and desired for a night.

"Thank you for this, Lillian," Rosetta sighed when they were all gone, taking the hefty purse of coin from her dress.

Lillian took it, knowing Rosetta would've made sure every single coin was accounted for.

"I think you owe me now," the woman said with squinted eyes, before giving her a smile. "Where are Naeem and John? I didn't see either of them in the crowd. I expected Naeem at the very front, whistling like the naughty boy he is. He's always the loudest."

Rosetta laughed, knowing she was right.

"Naeem is guarding the ship. He'll be here tomorrow night. I plan for him to pick his woman, or three if he so chooses." He'd told her he was happy to pay for it himself when he learned of how much this was costing her. Rosetta's smile fell away and her gaze lowered as she said, "But Lillian... I have terrible news on Mr Smith."

The wrinkled corners of her eyes bowed as she bit the inside of her lips. "He's gone, isn't he?"

Taking a deep breath to steady her own heartache, Rosetta nodded slowly. "He took a bullet for me when I was mutinied against. It's one of the reasons I've chosen to do this."

Lillian raised her fingertips to her lips to stifle any noise. She couldn't stop the welling of small tears as she quickly tried to blink them away. Like they were contagious, the tickling of tears tried to rise in Rosetta's own eyes, but she was much better at being able to shove them down.

"He was such a nice man. A true gentleman." She cleared her throat. "He was one of the few I would lay with when he came here."

Rosetta already knew this. Lillian rarely sold her body to men anymore, only to those she *wanted* to, not because she had to. There was usually mutual desire between them.

Apparently, even some younger men came to her, desired her for the beautiful woman she still was at her age and the sexual prowess she had in the bedroom. Rosetta was sure they compared every woman they met against her.

"Anyway, he was a sailor, and he knew the risks," Lillian said, dismissing the heavy conversation. She pulled on the skirt of Rosetta's dress. "Well, don't you look splendid tonight. I've always hated you in that little pirate outfit of yours. You said you sailed here with a man. How did your Jolly Sailor Bold take your outfit change?"

She gave a grand smile. "He said I looked dashing."

"You're a no-good, two-timing liar, Rosie." Her lips thinned into a disappointed motherly pout. "He didn't even notice, did he? Argh! Men! They're so stupid."

She gave a laugh, a genuine one despite being caught in her lie.

"I don't care what he thinks." She ripped the skirt from Lillian's hands. "I didn't wear it for him, I wore it for me. Naeem told me I looked like the fairest maiden in the world and that's all that matters."

"He's a good boy, that one. He's always looked out for you."

Rosetta gave her a warm smile.

"He has, hasn't he?" She didn't know why Naeem had chosen to follow her, but she knew it wasn't for love. He had no interest in her like that, but he had been with her every step of the way. "He's the one person I don't want to lose."

"You won't." Lillian reached up to pat her cheek gently, comfortingly. "He cares for you. Just feed him well and watch his back as he watches yours, and you'll both live forever." Then, she clapped her hands before intertwining them near the side of her head. "Now, are you going to come in for a finger of whisky?"

Rosetta shook her head. "No, thank you. I'm going into town."

"By yourself?" Her eyes filled with worry.

"You're the second person to ask me that question tonight," she said with a snort and a shake of her head. "But no. I will have company."

"Don't do anything stupid." She folded her arms across her large chest, shadowing her cleavage from the light spilling out from the open door next to which they stood. "You're a rare woman, Rosetta. Don't you dare let any man hurt you because of their own foolishness."

"Yes, *mother,*" she sneered jokingly.

"I am thankful every day I am not your mother!" Oh, she definitely cared for her. Rosetta knew it was because of everything she had done when she first came to this island.

Lillian had taken her under wing when she'd discovered why she fled Theodore, and she'd housed both Naeem and herself until they were able to get firmly on their feet. They'd formed a close bond and never seemed to have lost it.

"Now, off you go." She shooed her hands forward. "Quickly, before I put you to work."

Rosetta did just that, heading back to town.

That woman always raises my heckles. Rosetta didn't need her pushing doubt into her mind like that.

Even though she'd been beneath many men, Lillian wasn't very fond of them. She often pushed her opinions and distrust onto those who worked for her. It was her own way of caring and trying to help shelter their hearts, but it could often be upsetting.

I wouldn't let Alister hurt me, right? She liked the man, that much was obvious, but she wasn't *in love* with him.

Her forehead crinkled into worried lines as she nibbled on her bottom lip. *How could he possibly hurt me anyway?*

What they had was a mutually beneficial agreement but nothing more. He shared her bed, she shared her body, they shared their loot, but there was nothing between them but desire.

Am I being silly? Was Lillian right? Was Rosetta making a terrible decision getting caught up in a man like him, a pirate? One more vicious than any she had met.

But he's not like Theodore... He'd never struck her or spoken terribly to her. She would've gutted him the moment he tried. He'd put her down for being a woman, but she often thought that came from a deep place of caring for her wellbeing. *He's stopped doing that, though. Why?*

She let out a groan, her head falling back in annoyance as she walked. *Damn you, Lillian!* She hadn't been confused until now.

She was pondering these harsh questions all the way to The Drunken Sailor, but they faded the moment she saw him sitting with his crew.

He was pointing his finger at one of his men with a grin, making the entire table chuckle. The firelight from the candle on the table in front of him made his scarred, yet handsome face glow, despite the shadow of his short beard.

A smile crept onto her face before a laugh hit her. She even shook her head. *Why was I even worried?* She walked further into the tavern, feeling rather light-hearted.

CHAPTER SIX

Alister sat at the head of a long, distressed wooden table in the very middle of the large, two-level tavern. There was no second level roof above him, since the second level was a small walkway around the edge people could sit at with a railing.

It meant Alister could see all those above them.

There were four walls cut out from the middle up to the ceiling, like glassless windows holding the top level up. He couldn't see those sitting on the other side unless he got up and walked to peek over the half-wall. It separated them like a square ring.

There were many people inside the tavern, sitting at small, round tables fitted around where he and his men sat. The sound of chatter was deafening, and the terrible music made it even harder to hear.

There were at least a dozen of his men with him, those who had been with him the longest. They sat on the long benches of a grand table, he in a single chair at the end with no arm rests, leaning back casually with his knees apart.

He slammed his bottle of scotch down and clicked his fingers at a barmaid for more him and his men. He paid for the round.

They cheered when they were handed their bottles, and Alister took his own with a grin. He looked down at the label.

"Can't remember the last time I had good scotch."

"I like my rum, but we should stock up on other booze now that we've got the space," Pierre commented, taking a swig of his own bottle.

Pierre and Derek sat the closest to him right at the end of the table.

"Aye, but it's expensive. Rum is cheap." He let out a thoughtful noise, inspecting the label again. "Perhaps we can get a barrel or two."

Alister would covet it, since good alcohol was the only thing that seemed to get him truly legless anymore.

"He'll just drink it all," Derek nearly growled, pointing at Pierre. "Yer a carouser, ye pisshead."

"There's nothing else to do but drink and work on our ship!" Pierre threw back at him. "Even blind drunk, I can still man the helm better than you."

Someone came to sit on Alister's lap, and he paid her little mind as he leaned forward and pointed two fingers at Pierre.

"You've got a bottomless pit of stomach, lad." He motioned towards Derek. "He's right. Any food or drink we buy goes straight into your wide gob. If you want extra booze, buy it yourself!"

Chortles of agreeance flittered around the table as his men joined the conversation.

"Don't be like that, Captain," Pierre chuckled, knowing full well Alister was right.

They often called him Captain on land, keeping his name and who they were to a minimum. The bounty posters had their faces; the last thing they needed was to share his name so openly in a crowded place like this.

"The kraken has a smaller gut than ye!" Derek yelled. "Yer nothing but a lazy, eating pig!"

"And you're nothing but an old, one-legged seadog."

"Come here and say that." He leaned across the table to

grab Pierre by the scruff of his shirt. "I'll gut ye so quick–"

Alister kicked the underside of the table with his free leg to stop them.

"Nay. I'm not drunk enough to deal with you two starting a bar fight. Do it later, when I may want to join."

"Aye, Cap'in." Derek gave Pierre a glare but released him.

"Woof," Pierre barked at the older man, earning a kick in the knee. "Ah shit! I think you broke my leg, Captain."

Alister let out a bellowing laugh, fixing the person on his lap so she was seated higher. He hadn't even looked at her yet. Actually, he'd barely noticed someone had come to sit on him – especially since she'd sat on his blind side.

When he did turn to her, he expected to see Rosetta. Instead, Alister found he had a blonde-haired woman on his thigh.

He shrugged, leaving her where she was. and grabbed the bottle of scotch from the table. He took a deep swig of it.

"What would you prefer?" Alister asked them. "Whiskey or scotch?"

He felt a finger tickling over his jaw and down the side of his neck, before a hand rubbed over his chest. It dipped inside his tunic.

Considering this woman had only come to him after he'd bought a round, he figured she was after his coin. The wenches who usually came to sit on a man's lap in these places were generally cheap street prostitutes. Some come to sit on the laps of his men and not one of them was dismissed.

"Whiskey," Pierre said.

"Scotch," Derek argued.

"You're only saying the opposite of me!"

"Aye, yer darn right I am. Don't want ye getting nothin' ye want."

"Whiskey it is," Alister sighed, shaking his head with a laugh. It was cheaper and would get the job done.

"I also kept a few bottles of the sweet wine we plundered," Pierre said, taking a swig of his scotch.

Alister frowned.

"Why did you do that?" He leaned forward, disturbing his lap partner. "I didn't say you could do that. We could have sold that today!"

How dare Pierre do anything like this without his say so!

"Yer did it to sweet talk, Rosetta." Derek slammed his fist on the table. "Yer a rotten traitor."

Pierre placed his other hand over his heart like it was wounded. "I need her to like me! The woman keeps hurting me when I'm just trying to be nice to her. You and I both know she likes wine."

"And how the hell do you know that?" More importantly, why didn't Alister know it?

"She was drinking it the day she stole our ship and invited me and this old bag of skin for dinner. She made a comment on missing it to be teasing." Pierre leaned back, looking around at the table. "Speaking of her, didn't you say she'd be joining us?"

Now that he mentioned it, Alister didn't see her. He looked down at his unoccupied thigh, wondering why she wasn't seated on it. Then he looked at the nearly empty bottle of scotch he had. It was his second.

I expected her to be here by now.

His gaze fell on the pretty woman who'd been sitting on his lap for quite some time, who he still hadn't spoken to.

Why should he care? If Rosetta would rather spend the night with her crew, then why should he care? He tried to tell himself he'd turned to the blonde not because of irritation and dismay, but rather with interest.

"Need a drink, lass?" he asked her with a cocky grin.

She reached forward to hook her finger around the neck of the bottle he was holding, tilting it towards herself to peek inside, as if she was trying to figure out what it was.

"What are you drinking?" Her voice was undeniably gentle, the kind that would be sweet to hear in bed.

He figured she couldn't read the clearly written label.

"Scotch."

"I like whiskey," she answered. "We can share it if you like."

Well, wasn't that just kind of her, offering to share his own spent money with him. "Aye, whiskey it is."

He hailed for the barmaid again, just as Pierre got up and started making his way outside the door. He went to the front of the tavern from whence they'd entered, no doubt to rid himself of the liquid he'd just drank.

Alister downed the last of his scotch. He grabbed the bottle of whiskey when it was given to him, took a swig, then handed it to her.

"I haven't seen you in these parts before," she said after a deep draw from the bottle. It was as though she wanted to drink as much as she could, like she thought she may not be able to get more.

"Nay, don't come here often. I'm a sea loving pirate."

She gave him a pout. "All the pretty ones go to sea."

He gave a deep chuckle. *I like this one.* She obviously knew all the right things to say.

Just as he opened his mouth once more to sweet talk her, placing a palm over her breast from behind, a hand grabbed his shoulder on his good side.

Pierre was leaning closer to whisper to him.

"You should go for a piss mate," he said quietly, before talking his seat.

He had a grim look on his face, grabbing his bottle but not taking a drink of it. The usually joyful man was glaring at the table.

"I'll go when I'm good and ready to."

Christ! Someone was trying to tell him what to do with his own body. He was quite in tune with it, since he'd been using it for twenty-nine years.

Pierre peeked at him, his sour look darkening.

"Then it's your own fault. I'm not getting involved. Last thing I want is you biting my head off."

Seeing the man was quite serious when he usually wasn't, and it had been a while since Alister used his legs, he rolled his eyes.

"Fine, take her for me." He turned to the woman on his lap. "Sorry, lass. I'll be back."

He threw her into Pierre's lap, who grabbed her but didn't start trying to steal her from Alister like he normally would. That alone was enough to make his hackles rise.

He made his way to the front of the tavern, went outside, and then down the side of it while unbuttoning his breeches. Not even a few moments later, he was walking back inside, admitting he did feel better.

He picked up random strings of chatter, since he always listened out carefully while on land. Mostly, it was useless things he had very little interest in.

Eventually, though, a conversation caught his ears. He was about to pass the wall that separated him from the people sitting on the other side – those sitting on the outer rim of the interior of this tavern.

"You got your chance when she was here last. I want tails of her this time!"

"Didn't we flip a coin back then? We'll just do that again. Whoever gets heads, gets head," a woman giggled. "Just hurry up. I'm ready to leave this god-forsaken bar."

When he realised the feminine voice sounded awfully familiar, he halted and stepped back to look down the walled area his men weren't seated in.

That's where he saw Rosetta sitting in a booth. She was

seated not on the lap of one man, but two.

She sat with her legs spread over each of their thighs, touching between her knees. She was in the middle of them, her arms over their shoulders, and the table was not enough to hide that one of them had a hand deep up her skirt. The other turned her head to bring her in for a kiss. She welcomingly accepted it.

What in the absolute fuck am I seeing? He couldn't believe she was doing this, that he was witnessing this!

"Enough of that," she demanded, pulling away. "I'm getting impatient and if you boys can't deliver, I'll find someone else. I know you have coin. Now, flip one to decide who goes where."

Red frayed the very edges of his darkening vision. His knuckles turned white as he clenched his hands into tight fists. He stormed forward and slammed both his hands flat against the table, loud enough to give both the men a fright.

Rosetta was used to loud noises and merely turned her head to him slowly. Realising who it was, he expected her to go white with fear at being caught. The bitch had the audacity to give him a bright smile!

"Well, hello," she laughed. "Fancy seeing you here."

"What do you think you're doing, Rosetta?" he barked loudly.

"Whoever you are, you're going to have to wait your turn with her," one of the men said, waving his hand dismissingly. He had brown hair, was short and thin.

"Yeah. We haven't seen her in months." This one had short black hair, was thicker in body and looked tall. He was also the with his hand up her skirt. "Get lost before we make you."

Something dark began brewing in his gut, his upper lip curling up on one side in anger. It strengthened when that hand went even deeper, to the point he knew he must be cupping her at the apex of those toned legs Alister liked to nip, lick, and touch.

"Boys, be nice." She smacked them on the back of their heads but didn't lose her smile. "This is the pirate I was telling you about. The one who helped me get the Laughing Siren. Show him some respect."

Then she patted one of the men on the head before doing the same to the other, saying, "This is Chip and Jimmy. Old buddies of mine."

They suddenly turned to him with laughter, their sourness fading while Alister felt something nastier grow at their jolly attitudes.

"She wouldn't shut up about getting that silly boat last time she was here. Thanks for helping her out," Jimmy said, a genuine smile brightening his face. "Apparently, you made it easier for her."

"What's your name? I'd like to know of this great captain who helped Rosetta Silver get her ship. She wouldn't tell us a peep about you."

"Captain Alister Paine of the Howling Death," he sneered, leaning forward to tower over them. "And she's been sailing with me for four months since then."

Silence boomed between them all as they registered who he was.

"Really?" Chip said, his brows crinkling in concern. He turned that look to her, his hand slowly coming out from underneath her skirt. It didn't stop him from kneading her thigh right in front of him over her dress. "Don't you know he's got a bounty on his head?"

"Yeah. He's one of the biggest murderers Queen Mary Anne is after."

Rosetta looked at him, suddenly giving him a frown with a confused shake of her head. Probably because he'd revealed their relationship when he'd explicitly told her not to.

Then she shrugged, twirling her index fingers near the

sides of their heads like she had a tune in her head. She looked unconcerned about the situation.

"Yep. We've been high tailing it all over the seas. Collecting loot and sinking ships. Oooo!" She bounced with excitement, turning to one and then the other. "He's got a big one. I might actually be able to fit both of you at the same time now. No need to toss a coin!"

Alister's jaw dropped, his eyes going wide. It didn't take a genius to realise that she meant taking both their dicks inside her pussy at the same time.

He pulled his pistol from its holder and slammed it against the table. "Both of you leave, before one of you finds a bullet between the eyes."

Chip and Jimmy stared at his gun, their eyes going stark with fear. They turned to each other with a cowardly expression he had seen many times over in his life.

"Not worth it?"

"No way."

They both scattered.

Alister kept his eye on Rosetta, who watched both men bolt from underneath her within the breath of a second, shock plastered on her face.

"What the hell do you think you're doing?" Rosetta yelled at him, her face finally turning into something angry.

Good, he thought. *Finally.*

"I should be asking you the same thing!"

She leaned back and folded her arms across her chest. Then she placed one leg on top of the other, bouncing them while giving him a glare.

Looking at this woman, red lipstick smudged across her face from passionately kissing other men, he felt that bubble of rage boiling faster.

"I was having fun," she answered with a tone that said it was supposed to be obvious. "What are you even doing here?"

"What are you doing with *two* other men?"

"I'm not your wife, Alister. You don't get to make me feel like I'm being unfaithful when I'm not. I have no tie to you."

He blinked at her words. It was true, she wasn't his wife.

"Currently, you are *my* woman," he sneered back as a rebuff.

"No, I'm not," she laughed between each word with a mocking tone. "Lacey is currently your woman."

"Who?" He scrunched his nose up as he reared his head back.

"You didn't even know the name of the prostitute sitting on your lap? She's a lovely girl, but as dumb as they come."

"I won't change the way I do things in port because of you!"

Alister was used to having strange women sitting on him. Half the time, he barely paid them any notice and didn't even know they were there. It was harder when they snuck up on him on his blind side. He only gave them attention when he was bored and thinking of finding something to bed at the end of the night.

Rosetta's brows turned into a deep frown. She unfurled her arms, like her anger was lessening while his grew by the second.

"I'm not asking you to."

"I don't like jealous women, Rosetta." Rather, he hated it.

She gave him a bellowing laugh, one of those horrible ones he often found cute, which meant it was genuine.

"The only one who seems jealous here is you."

"Nay, I'm not," he bit with spite. "You didn't think it skipped my attention you decided to do this in the same bar as me? If you wanted to be discreet, you would have gone somewhere else!"

She gave him a sigh, as if she thought this conversation was a waste of her time and energy. It made him grit his teeth harder, the knotted muscle of his jaw popping.

"Do you see any of my crew here?" She gestured to their surroundings.

Alister looked around, wondering why that was so damn important.

"They're busy and I can't stay with them. It's not a place for me." She leaned her elbows against the table, placing her cheek against her enclosed fist in boredom. "I'm a woman in a town full of, as you put it earlier, degenerates. If I found myself in a situation where I needed help, I knew I had people I could run to close by."

She looked away from him, nibbling at her bottom lip.

"I'm not an idiot, Alister. I wouldn't leave myself alone in a place like this, and it's common for me to stir up trouble."

She'd placed herself nearby for protection? Shit, even he thought that was the best thing she could have done for herself.

"I didn't wish to disturb you from having your fun, so I came here and hung out with Chip and Jimmy because I know them." She turned her face to him to give him a grin. "They think I'm a sailing prostitute or something. It's rather funny, and it's so easy to make money that way."

He clenched both his hands into fists and punched the table. "Rosetta, you better stop talking before I fucking lose it."

She looked him over, at the snarled-up face he wore and the way he towered over her.

"I'm not asking you to change the way you do things," she said, before waving her hand towards the direction of his crew. "Go back to your men and Lacey. Enjoy yourself. I can see in port, things change between us. You obviously want variety, like most men."

"I was expecting to have you with me tonight as well!" Not her in someone else's bed!

She gave a mocking snort. "I'm not the kind of woman to

fight over a man. I'd rather not have to wait my turn for a dick." She shook her head with a scoff. "You've only got one, whereas I've got three holes that can be filled. I'd rather have all the attention on me than fight for it."

Once more, she looked off to the side, but this time with a small smile. She even twirled a strand of hair while giving a dreamy sigh.

"There's something about taking a man at each end that just throws a woman's brain off. It's like a button that just turns our brains to goo."

A chilling coldness rushed over him. Alister realised she was serious. She didn't see anything wrong with this; she didn't care. She thought *he* was the one being ridiculous.

She doesn't care if I sleep with other women. He should take this for the free pass it was, do whatever he wanted without a shred of dignity. He wouldn't have to worry about how she felt, not that he had seen anything wrong in the first place.

She told me she understood I would have port girls and prostitutes. So why didn't he like her acting the same way as him?

He eyed her, realisation hitting him heavily. *She really would have done it.* And she probably wouldn't have known Alister would have tossed her aside for it, either.

I don't share my women. He expected his rare port girls, those who weren't cheap whores, to keep their legs closed except to him, just like he expected from Rosetta.

He leaned back, creating space between them.

She really would have slept with them. It would have been his own damn fault and he would have been furious about it.

Furious because he liked having this woman beneath him. It was like a constant ache he was very content to have, and she would have stolen that from him.

It hadn't been because of jealousy; she was just mirroring him. She thought him having another woman on his lap meant she had a free pass too.

But he didn't feel jealous. Jealousy meant he wanted something that belonged to someone else, and how he saw it, Rosetta currently belonged to him.

She's my woman.

She gave him a reassuring smile, not seeing how it twisted him up inside. The bridge of her nose was the slight pink colour she got when she was either drunk or aroused, and she seemed too quick-witted right now to be intoxicated. Her breaths came out in pants, like she felt hot, and he looked down to see her nipples hard beneath that yellow dress she wore.

Rosetta looked ready to be taken, like she *wanted* to be taken.

"Go have fun, Alister. I'm not trying to stop you." She looked around him like he was in the way, muttering to herself quietly. "Now, where did those boys go?"

Nay. A confusing mix of emotions strangled his throat. Confusion, spite, anger, disappointment. They all held onto him with gripping claws.

Red still frayed the edges of his vision, and his blood boiled higher until he thought smoke might billow off his skin.

He reached forward and grabbed her wrist, dragging her behind him as he took her the few steps outside.

She stumbled behind him at his quick pace. "Hey!"

Turning them, Alister tossed her back against the wall next to the door.

If she wants a cock, she can fucking have one. His.

He hooked his arm around her back to keep her where she was as he lifted the skirt of her dress.

His teeth were gritted so tightly, he feared he'd shattered them in his mouth while his lips were pressed into thin lines. His eyepatch cut into the inner part of his cheek because of how tightly the bridge of his nose was crinkled.

"What are you doing?" she asked, a frown furrowing her features. She looked down at their chests pressed together, like she was trying to see what he was doing.

"I'm horny, lass."

Rosetta was aroused, and like it often did, seeing her like this got him hard and wanting, but there was something else driving him. Something dark, and heavy, and evil.

Once he had the front of her skirt bundled around her waist, he slipped the hand from her back to under her thigh, keeping her skirt up as he worked on undoing the top button of his breeches. With his other hand, he moved to free his cock, already hard and ready for her.

She didn't remove her lifted leg from around his waist, nor did she try to push him away. She tightened it around him instead, like she usually did.

"I'm going to fuck someone right now. It can either be you, or another woman," he said with his teeth still clenched in resentment. He was unused to the way he was feeling, the way this terrible emotion had crawled inside him like the kraken bringing its tentacles up to destroy his ship and drown him. "And I'd much rather it be you."

"I don't understa-oh!" She threw her head back and gave a sharp moan when he slammed his cock inside her.

Her nails dug into his shoulders, and they buried deeper when he hefted her off the ground and forced both her legs around his waist.

Despite the terrible emotions inside him, the feel of this woman gloving his cock felt splendid.

Bloody hell. He leaned his forehead against her shoulder as a breathless groan fell from him at the feel of her. His brows crinkled. *She's so wet.*

Dripping. He could feel it around him, and it made those kraken tentacles slither tighter. Rosetta was prepared and wet... because of other men.

He pulled back, then shoved in with such force, she bounced, the back of her head hitting the wall. He dug his fingertips into her thighs as he held her up, gripping her tightly as he did it again, again, and again, slamming as hard as his body would allow.

Take it, take my cock. He wanted her to feel it, to know he was deep inside her, that it was Alister currently pounding between her legs instead of someone else.

Rosetta slipped her hands from his shoulders to trail them down his back. He could feel one hand had snuck its way under his tunic. She dug her nails in as she buried her face against the side of his neck.

She tried to spread her legs wider for him, welcoming him like she always did. "Oh!"

She let out a little moans while Alister glared at the wall, grunting deeply whenever he hit the end of her, and it resonated down the length of him.

She didn't care that he was taking her against the wall of the tavern outside in the open. They were even right next to the front door. There were dozens of people walking behind them in the street, watching them, hearing him take her.

A part of him knew they shouldn't be doing this here. He was leaving himself vulnerable to someone coming up behind him to slit his throat. He was putting their relationship on show for all to witness.

Hell, someone even walked out of the tavern door right next to them.

He hadn't cared. He'd needed to take this woman to remind her she belonged to him. To remind himself she still did.

He was so impatient that he'd refused to wait a few seconds more to deliver this message to her hot, quivering insides. With harder than normal thrusts, he knew he was delivering it.

I almost didn't stop her. His glare deepened, his eyes narrowing further as his lip curled upwards into a snarl.

The air was cooler than it had been during the day, but it was still muggy. It was nothing compared to the blazing inferno between them, though, as hot as ever as they shared in each other's heat.

Alister pulled her from the wall so he could slam her against it, but in such a way that her hips were tilted differently. He started pumping his cock faster, wanting to drown out this sharp emotion he didn't like with the blissful feeling of her. He didn't want to feel like this when he could blissfully ache in her like usual.

I almost lost this feeling. The way the smell of her tangled in his senses like it wanted to sweetly suffocate him, and he was desperate to breathe her in.

Her body was soft in his strong arms, squishing against his body, under his palms, around his shaft.

The way she was always tight around him like her body was stretched as far as it could take around his girth, how it got wonderfully tighter when she started to come.

In the exact way she was now as her core clenched and spasmed. How she gave a burst of wetness that made thrusting through that mind-numbing squeeze easy.

For a moment, those clutching emotions faded out as his eyes rolled back in his head at the feel of her orgasm.

For a moment, Alister was suspended in that aching bliss. *She feels so good.*

She let out a loud cry, not one shred of concern about quieting so those behind them didn't know she was currently trying to milk his cock.

They were fucking in the street like the rest of the depraved and shameless fools of this town. This was something he'd never done before. Hell, he'd mocked others for this exact thing, but *damn,* he didn't care when it was Rosetta moaning for him while he did it.

When she started to relax, she curled her arms around his shoulders to hug him to her, sweetly, softly, almost tenderly. She even started lazily kissing at the side of his sweat-covered neck as his hard, grinding movements caused more to seep to the surface of his skin.

Alister picked up his speed when the ache faded back to those hateful tentacles that she'd softened a little. *She almost slept with other men.*

She almost shared this with someone else. Would they have appreciated it like Alister did? Would they have drowned in her the way he was? Would they have been as addicted to her like he was?

But she hadn't.

It was Alister she currently held between her legs. It was *his* cock she just melted around. She was in *his* arms, under *his* breath, under *his* warmth, under *his* gaze.

It was *his* name she softly moaned directly in his ear.

A rolling shudder passed over him, from his head all the way down to quake in his legs.

She was moaning his name while pressing her lips and face against him, like she wanted to nuzzle beneath his skin. Her little pants brushed over him like torture, haunting and lovely. The warmth of them tingled his flesh and made prickles of goosebumps raise the hair around his ear.

He had her legs spread wide so he could force her to take his wild thrusts, but he could feel she was trying to wrap them around him now.

"Don't stop," she moaned, her nails biting harder. "Please don't stop. Right there, Alister. Oh!"

His sight dazed out and his head tilted back. *Fuck, I want it.*

Alister started pistoning as fast as he could, hearing her thighs slapping against his hips. He no longer cared how hard or deep he was. *I want to claim it.*

He wanted to own the feeling of her around him, to claim this hot, wet channel so no one else could take it, to ensure she remained around him and him alone – until he was done claiming her.

Rosetta threw her head back against the wall, tugging on his hair as her back arched. She came once more, clutching him everywhere; her thighs, her hands, her pussy. Everything gripped him like her body didn't want to let go of him.

I'll kill them. If anyone threatened to take this away from him, Alister would make them regret it.

He turned his head and sunk his teeth into the side of her neck, wanting to bruise her, to plainly show that he'd been at her. She gave a sharp gasp in reaction, even though she was orgasming around him.

I'll kill them all! His hips slowed completely when he felt his balls drawing up, the heavy throb in his cock worsening, the agony in his groin tightening. *Because it's fucking mine!*

Alister froze, his teeth losing their grip as his mouth opened wide. Instead, he pressed them against her as he started to lose his senses. His eyes snapped open, his hands gripped tighter, his body arched into her.

"Haa." His breath quivered out. "Haaa." Everything started to seize. "Ha!"

The dam burst and the first rope of semen unleashed from him. A long deep groan strangled its way from his chest and throat. Like he couldn't help himself, his hips twitched as he rode out his orgasm. *Oh god,* he thought, his eyes closing so he could tightly clench them shut at the sensation.

Surrounded by her heat, her wetness, her grip. Alister delivered deep yet shallow pumps as he filled Rosetta with his seed.

Nothing felt better. To release inside this horny, devious bitch who drove him crazy, made him so feral it sometimes brought out the worst in him.

The number of times he'd wanted to, pushed so close to the edge to give caution to the wind and do it, had never been as overwhelming as it had been this night. Spite, and need, and possessiveness clung to him.

And to do it...

Fuuuck... He nestled the side of his face against her jaw as he trembled.

Every drop he'd given had felt amazing. No orgasm had felt so warm, so wet, and so damn deep that it nearly felled him and his ability to stand.

He pushed her harder against the wall like that was the solution to him staying upright. His knees threatened to buckle.

Shit... I want to do that again, was the first thought that came to him when his cock finally ceased twitching and filling her.

He shouldn't and he knew it.

Alister hadn't come inside a woman since he was a foolish young lad losing his virginity. He didn't make mistakes like this. So why, when he pulled his head back so he could look at her, did he not feel an ounce of regret?

"Wait," she said around huffed breathes, her brows furrowing. "Did you just come inside me?"

He didn't care for her question, not when there was nothing either one of them could do about it.

"If you want to sit on my lap, then come sit on it," he snapped at her, pushing his hips against her to go impossibly deeper.

Her eyes squinted into a vicious glare. "If my seat is taken, I will sit elsewhere."

The gall on this woman, to tell him she'd sit on other men when she still had him inside her, filled with his seed!

Alister clenched his jaw tight once more. He thought this

would make him feel better, but she'd ruined it by opening her fucking mouth.

He ripped his shaft from her and placed her down so he could do up the buttons of his breeches.

He shook his head, muttering angrily to himself with hope she couldn't hear him cursing her. *Sometimes, I just want to wring her pretty neck.*

He grabbed her wrist in a hold she couldn't escape, stomped his way back inside The Drunken Sailor, and made his way back to his men.

Alister plopped himself in his chair. He flung her backward so hard she would have almost fallen over his thigh if it wasn't for him catching her. He forced her to sit on his leg.

Whether she was being compliant because she actually wanted to sit with him, or she knew angering him further wasn't wise, it didn't matter to him. She was doing as his actions dictated, and that's what truly mattered to him.

Alister reached into his boot and pulled a dagger from it, slapping it into her open palm.

"If someone tries to take the other one." He gestured to his other thigh with his head. "Stab them."

He didn't care if a woman hurt another woman in front of him. As long as it wasn't his own hands doing the crime, he saw no issue.

One side of Rosetta's upper lip curled up in disbelief, the bottom one falling a little. Then, she turned to him with a mocking laugh.

"I'm not going to fight over your lap." She tried to hand the dagger back. "I'm not some petty woman."

He curled his arm around her waist tighter, so she couldn't even think of moving from him. *I'm going to keep a close eye on her tonight.*

He leaned closer so they were almost nose-to-nose. "Then don't be upset when someone sits there."

He turned his gaze away from her to the table, remembering he'd given his last drink away. He saw a fresh bottle in front of him.

He looked up at Pierre, who was already staring at him with that grim expression, but not as tight. He gave him a nod.

Good lad. He'd ordered another for Alister, knowing he was going to want a good, stiff drink and would have been furious when he realised he didn't have one.

He'd been gone for a long while, after all. It must have been obvious he'd discovered her.

He pointed two fingers at him. "You and I will talk later."

If it wasn't for Pierre, Alister wouldn't have caught Rosetta before she'd left with two men.

At that thought, he snatched the whisky, turned the bottle up, and chugged the entire thing in one go. Once he was done, he threw it against the table, watching it shatter across the worn timber.

Everyone flinched.

"Get me another two." He carelessly threw coins onto the table, rattling as they settled.

CHAPTER SEVEN

Rosetta looked down at the dagger in her hand with such a deep sense of confusion, it felt as though her heart was sinking.

What just happened?

How did she go from giving Alister his space and freedom, to having him take her up against the wall *outside* until her mind forgot everything around them like a mindless, screaming, begging whore, to this?

To sitting on his thigh with her closed legs between his open ones, a dagger in her hand, and a demand that she guard his lap for herself.

All his men were chatting and laughing amongst each other, like they didn't know what just happened, except for Pierre, who was sipping on a bottle, staring at the wall.

Where's Lacey? Rosetta couldn't see her as she glanced around, her brows frowning deeper. Why was Rosetta here instead of her? *Isn't that what he wanted?*

Rosetta knew her. The girl was sweet but dumb, simply because she'd grown up in these parts. She was a nice girl who liked good looking men who would pay her a pretty penny for her to rock their world. She was good at being a prostitute, knew how to make men feel good, not just with her body but also with her words.

She made men feel special.

If Alister was looking for an excellent street girl, Lacey

was one of the best. So why pass her up for Rosetta, someone he could have anytime?

She peeked at him from the side to see his cheerless expression. His lips were pressed behind that stubble, his eyes narrowed as he glowered at his men. The energy radiating off him was thick and charged, like a bout of violence could sprout from him any moment.

He looked murderous.

When a barmaid brought two bottles, he grabbed the necks of both with the hand not currently gripping her side in a tight, inescapable squeeze.

He shoved them both against her stomach.

"Drink," he demanded, releasing one so she'd take it before it fell.

"I can pay for my own." She held it with both hands despite the dagger, her face twisting further.

"Nay." He lifted his own bottle and took a swig. She watched how his Adam's apple drew up, then down as he swallowed deeply. "I pay for the first night."

She noticed all his men were given a bottle as well, regardless of whether they were finished with the first or not.

He didn't look at her, and eventually, he joined in the conversations with his men. Rosetta just sat there quietly.

She'd never sat on his lap before in front of his men. Her eyes observed the warmly lit tavern as she fiddled and tapped on the blade's sharp point. She didn't feel like drinking with her stomach knotted the way it was.

I thought he didn't want anyone to know the depth of our partnership.

She realised it didn't matter, not when he was flaunting his coin the way he was, so much so that another woman noticed how much he had.

Patrons would think she was another prostitute sitting with him, since a black-haired girl came to take his other thigh.

He didn't seem to notice as he lifted his arm up behind her back to take a sip of his drink, answering back at one of his men.

I don't want to do this. She didn't want to sit here with him and another woman. She also didn't like the idea of battling for her position with a dagger like... like some jealous, crazy girl.

Rosetta went to stand. The hand around her side gripped tighter, forcing her back down.

"You are staying," he demanded, looking at her out of the corner of his eye. His glare was sharp and menacing. Then he turned forward to point down the table, giving his attention to someone else. "You wouldn't know how to catch a fish even if it jumped out of the water and slapped you in the face. Only Glen is good with a net."

A small lump of emotion settled in her chest, extinguishing her usual flame for defiance.

Why is he doing this?

"Rosetta?" a feminine voice said quietly, and she looked up at the woman in front of her.

Her brows drew together in concentration. *Wait, I know her.*

"Claire?"

Claire smiled brightly and leaned forward to take Rosetta's hands, currently holding a bottle and the dagger.

"I haven't seen you in ages."

Since they were in the way, Alister shot his body through them so he could hear the table. They both had to lean behind him to speak.

"I heard you'd left and was upset I never got the chance to thank you properly for what you did."

That lump of emotion faded so she could give Claire her full attention. She waved her hand forward dismissingly, giving an awkward laugh. "It's fine. I did leave on short notice."

"But that money was everything I had saved. The fact you got it back for me meant I was able to buy my way out of that place so I could hire my own room."

Claire had been living in a brothel that allowed women to pay for their boarding by whoring themselves out to any man. She was poor, had been saving so she could buy a small room in one of the housings so she could work the streets for herself. She wanted to pick her partner, rather than be desperate enough to take anyone.

A man had gone through her room after sleeping with her and stolen everything.

Rosetta and her crew, the last time she was in Tortaya, had hunted the man down after she'd discovered the girl crying on the steps. They not only got it back but stole all his coin for her. Rosetta hadn't even taken a cut of it as compensation.

"Like I said, it's fine." Rosetta wasn't used to receiving gratitude and her cheeks heated in embarrassment. "I'm just glad things are working out for you."

"Did you get that little boat you wanted?"

Who hadn't Rosetta told about it? She'd never shared which ship she was after, only that she was after a specific one.

"Yeah, I did," she smiled.

Claire returned her smile. Then, she pointed to the back of Alister. "Is this one yours for the night?"

Rosetta eyed him over. *Apparently so.*

"Yes."

She reached behind his back and patted Rosetta's shoulder. "I remember you're selfish when it comes to coin. I'll leave him to you."

Claire got up and left, giving her a wave before she went down the table and fell into Pierre's lap.

"Well, aren't you a pretty boy," she said to get his

attention, lying across both his legs.

The playboy, whose mood seemed to mirror Alister's, jumped like he hadn't expected a woman to fling herself into his lap. She hung onto his neck with a bright giggle, making his lips quirk in reaction.

He let her go. She blinked at Alister, who was still leaning forward like he didn't know Claire was even gone.

With a sigh, she reached her arm forward to push at his chest, making him recline in his chair so it was more comfortable for herself.

He lifted his arm to take a drink, but he halted when he must have realised how easy it was, then turned to her.

"Stab that one, did you?"

"I knew her," she answered with a shake of her head.

His eyes squinted into a look of mistrust as he took a sip of his drink. "You know a lot of people in this port."

"I told you before we came here that I've been here a lot."

Rosetta had made an impression with quite a few of the permanent residents.

She had made herself a vigilante, fighting for the women of this town since no one else was going to do it. The soldiers and guards were always paid to look the other way and Rosetta refused to not help just because of their greed.

"That's not always a good thing," he muttered.

Despite their conversation, the tension between them was thick enough that Rosetta thought she actually might choke on it. *Why does he want me here if he's displeased?*

It was obvious he wasn't in a good mood. He'd been grinning when Lacey had been here, so why be sour with Rosetta?

He turned back to his men and Rosetta drank quietly, listening in. It's not like she could go anywhere else with her crew currently preoccupied. It was mostly the playful banter and light conversations frequently heard on the ship.

Rosetta hadn't even finished her drink before another round was placed on the table in front of her. Since he'd given a large collection of coins to a barmaid to pay for it, another woman came to sit on his other thigh.

Rosetta let out a sigh.

The idea of doing this all night was already grating on her nerves. *At least Claire left easily enough.*

Rosetta looked over the woman.

She was busty, thicker than most, but stunning. She had dark brown hair waving around her face, large breasts pushed high with a deep cleavage line to show them off. She was beautiful with prominent features that made her look feisty with naturally seductive quirks.

She immediately started twirling his long hair around one of her index fingers.

He reached forward to grab his new bottle and Rosetta realised he barely noticed the woman. Actually, he was talking to Kent about how he wouldn't have the brain capacity to navigate the ship like himself, Pierre, and Derek did.

Kent often liked to get under everyone's skin by being an arrogant man with both his brawn and brain – not that he had much going on in that thick skull of his. He refused anyone betting him to wear Rosetta's lipstick again, though, as if he was truly afraid of that outcome.

Can he not see her? The woman was on his blind side, and he was too distracted by drinking and conversation to even know he had someone there.

Knowing she wasn't going to be able to escape Alister, considering their earlier actions and his current mood, she stared at the woman while nibbling at her bottom lip.

Maybe if I just ask her to leave, she might. She didn't know this one like she did Claire.

"This one is taken," Rosetta said to her quietly.

The woman looked away from Alister's face to her and

gave her a sultry smile.

"I know this one; he has a fat purse. He'll share us."

She narrowed her eyes at the woman.

"I don't share." She moved the bottle hiding it and flashed the dagger. "Leave."

The woman giggled. "Jealousy isn't a colour they like. You're not the first to fight for *his* coin and lose it all to me."

The woman spoke as if this wasn't the first time she'd stumbled onto Alister's lap. *Looks like I'm not the only one who's known.*

A spike of anger prickled the back of her neck. Rosetta wasn't used to people not doing what she said.

She brought the dagger more forward and pointed the tip at her. It glinted from the candlestick melting on the table. "You've got five seconds to leave."

"No," she giggled again, before leaning forward to press her lips to the side of his neck. She eyed her while she did it, her eyes crinkled in humour.

Just like that, something tore through Rosetta. *Screw this, I don't take anyone's shit.*

Not his, not this stranger's, not anyone's.

With such a quick motion that not even Alister could hold onto her, Rosetta launched forward and tackled the woman.

They both went flying over his leg and landed on the ground, Rosetta above her. She straddled her waist, and with the fist holding the dagger, she punched the woman across the face.

She gave a squeal of pain before Rosetta drew her fist back and punched her across the cheek again.

"S-stop!" No one came to assist her as Rosetta unleashed one last strike.

"You may not know me, but I am not a prostitute, sweetheart."

Rosetta then slammed the blade of the dagger into the

timber floor so close to the woman's head, she almost took her ear off. Their noses touched as she leaned down.

"Aren't you going to help me?" The woman turned her face towards Alister.

Rosetta glared down at her. If he tried to get in the middle of this... Well, she'd wreak havoc.

"Nay," she heard him say with a dull tone of nonchalance. "The lass will turn that dagger on me if I do."

"If I *ever* see you again, I will cut up that pretty face of yours so badly, not even a squealing pig will want to fuck you." She twisted her head at the woman with an evil sneer. "Got it?"

Blood had welled in the corner of her lip, and she gave a nod with stark eyes. She must have realised Alister didn't care, and that Rosetta was much more dangerous than she first appeared.

She grabbed a fistful of the woman's beautiful long hair and used the dagger to cut a chunk from it, throwing it at her trembling form.

"Get the hell out of my face."

The woman crawled to her feet and bolted from the tavern without glancing back, her short heels tapping loudly against the floor.

Once she was on her feet, Rosetta eyed the patrons now watching her. Most turned their gaze away, especially the women trying to earn their money for the evening. *That should get everyone to leave me alone.* At least for a little while.

Rosetta had made a big statement. If Alister growled at her for it, she'd sink this knife into his thigh so he wouldn't want *anyone* sitting on it.

A hand grabbed her by the back of her dress and yanked her so hard, she'd have fallen over his thigh if he hadn't caught her like before. She turned to him with a shout ready in her throat, only for it to catch.

Alister was grinning, a light, breezy chuckle falling from his lips. "I think I like you fighting over me, lass."

With a huff, Rosetta slammed the dagger into the chair between his thighs, right near his groin. He flinched back to avoid it, then turned his head up with a raised brow.

She folded her arms and turned her face away from him, disliking that she enjoyed his reaction to her fighting over him. *Arrogant bastard.*

Deciding she wasn't happy with her arms folded, she grabbed a nearly empty bottle and drank the last of it.

"You don't notice them there, do you?"

"Not at all," he answered, leaning back in his chair. He pointed to his eyepatch. "It's worse when I can't see them. Unless they somehow grab my attention, they get ignored." He sighed, taking a swig of his drink before swirling the contents of the bottle as he watched it with a thoughtful expression. "I may buy them a drink, but they eventually leave when they realise it'll be a long time before they make any coin from me."

He hefted her higher on his thigh, bringing her closer. "Which is why I need your help with this. I'm so used to women sitting on me in port, Rosetta, I barely register it."

If I want it, I have to protect it. Ugh, that didn't sound enticing, but at least she understood.

I can't change him. Not that she was trying to.

She had to work around him, but considering she had nothing better to do, and it might lead to her having fun later, she was at least tempted.

She grabbed the handle of the dagger and yanked it from the chair. Pointing the tip of it in his face, she gave him a scowl.

He seemed to read her expression for what it was, because he answered it with a grin. "Atta girl."

She just hoped she wouldn't have to do it again.

It seemed her violent display had scared everyone else off because no one came to take his thigh and she was finally able to relax.

His mood also lifted. He reclined back in his chair, as if he wanted to sprawl out, no intention of leaving it again.

Eventually, most of the men had a woman on their lap and a great discussion started about one of the raids they had done. She wondered if it was done to impress women, or because they just liked to reminisce about loot they'd stolen.

She'd never tell them that the women didn't care about great heroics. They just wanted their coin and were only listening to gratify them.

"And Greyson here." One of the men pointed to who she assumed was Greyson. "Almost fell off the side of the enemy's ship when one of the sails turned and knocked him over."

"I ducked!" the man roared, slamming his bottle down with a loud thud, causing some of the liquid to slosh out. "It missed me. I just stumbled because of how low I had to crouch!"

Wait, Rosetta thought to herself, blinking in surprise. *This is a raid with the Laughing Siren.*

"I thought I was going to die that day!" Pierre exclaimed. "One minute, I'm killing a man, the next Rosetta is flying at me like some monkey, screaming 'catch!'"

She let out a giggle. "I underestimated how much rope I needed and swung too high."

She'd been too high on the rope, flying through the air with her legs kicking when she realised she was going to swing back towards her own ship. Hers had been taller, and she hadn't estimated how much rope she'd needed.

"But did you have to land on top of me? I thought you were going to kill me with that arse of yours!"

They'd both gone crashing to the deck, her sitting on his chest with her thighs around his head.

"What else was I supposed to do?" She leaned forward and pointed at him. "It was either land on someone or go into the water. Everyone else was busy!"

"You almost got my head cut off."

"Liar! I stopped that sword."

A large smile filled her features at the conversation. This was the first time she'd heard them talk about one of the raids they'd done with her. It was one she'd instigated because it had been a fleet ship she'd wanted to destroy.

She'd always wanted to join in their banter.

"We overtook that ship and sunk it within an hour," Alister added in. "Worst raid we've ever had. There was nothing on that boat worth taking."

"Still one of the funniest," a man said further down the table. "Philip broke his finger because he tripped over his own feet and landed into the hatch grate. With the way he wailed, you'd think he'd broken his entire arm."

He cradled his arm under his elbow, flopping his hand around with a false, exaggerated, blubbering *boohoo*.

"The most successful raid we had lately was that trading boat with all the carpet," Pierre said, starting a new conversation about a different raid.

Rosetta turned her attention to Alister, ignoring the new conversation to talk to him about the old one. She fingered the seam of his black doublet coat.

"You smeared so much blood on me that day. I barely had a drop on me before that."

He gave a small chuckle, turning his eye to her. "I told you, lass. If you step off your ship to help, I'll take you, no matter what I'm covered in."

She brought her hand up to touch the stubble on the side of his jaw. "It doesn't count as punishment if I like it."

His chuckle deepened, his mood seeming to lift by the second.

"Haven't figured out anything you don't like yet." He turned his head back and took a swig of his drink before he muttered around the rim. "Guess I'll have to keep trying."

Halfway into her third bottle of whatever drink was ordered, she'd tried to pay a barmaid to bring her food. Alister noticed and swiftly handed the woman coin before Rosetta could finish reaching into the tear of her dress.

"I'll be paying for all your drinks and food tonight."

She looked down the table and realised others were buying food since she'd started a trend. They paid for it themselves.

"I have my own money, Alister."

"Don't give two shits what you've got." He finally turned his head to give her a disgruntled look. "Don't say my name. My face is one thing, but people remember a name on a bounty page a lot better than the drawing."

Someone walked behind him, and she eyed them cautiously. Thankfully, the person didn't pay them any notice.

"You've said it enough tonight." His words were curt, but she could see the corners of his lips turning up, as though he was trying to stifle a smile.

She tried to think of the other times she'd said his name since she didn't think she had, until she realised what he was talking about. Her eyes widened and she thought she felt a flush of heat spread over her cheeks.

Oops. She'd moaned it a bunch.

It was a nasty habit of hers she'd only ever had with him. She'd never chanted another man's name so enthusiastically as she did with him during sex.

It may also be because she didn't always know it.

Food was placed in front of her, and all earlier thoughts faded. Her stomach grumbled at the sight of fresh meat and vegetables, one of the best-looking meals she'd eaten in weeks, if not months. She speared a piece of meat and began to nibble on it. It melted in her mouth, sparking her abused tastebuds to joyous life.

The first thing to go on her plate was the vegetables: potato, carrot, and broccoli. Being on a ship with men, they preferred to satisfy their hunger with as much meat as they could. They even choose dried smoked meat over any vegetable from a ship they'd raided. She knew much good food had been lost to the ocean simply because of that.

When she'd eaten as much as her stomach would allow, she noticed Alister's gaze fall back to her half-eaten meat.

"Have you eaten since you entered this tavern?" she asked with curiosity.

"Don't eat much when I drink."

She gave him a pout, eyeing the three bottles in front of him and wondered how many others he'd drunk.

"Do you want some?" She gestured to her plate.

He shook his head. "My hands are full."

Of her arse and booze. His hand had eventually slipped from her side to knead her cheek firmly.

"Here." She leaned forward and speared a good cut of meat. Cupping underneath it in case it fell, she brought it closer to him. "Have some."

"Nay." He ducked his head back to evade it. "I bought it for you."

"I can't eat any more and it'll go to waste."

She brought it closer, and he eyed her carefully before slowly leaning forward to take the bite. He washed it down like he didn't care how it tasted.

She speared another piece and brought it to his mouth. She smiled when he took it, which seemed to make him frown in bewilderment.

Her eyes took in his face; the light brown of his eyes, the black convex shape of his eyepatch, the scar running underneath it. It was the partial shadows cast by the bright candles hanging from a chandelier above that caught her attention.

"This reminds me of the last time I fed you myself," she said, a devilish smile pouting her lips.

Just as she had thought then, she found him handsome. He was strong and mean looking, rough around the edges with black hair around his jaw.

"You don't know how close you were to losing your fingers."

Rosetta let out a loud laugh, shaking her head as humour filled her face.

"You were so angry!" She kicked her legs in excitement at the memory. "You looked like you wanted to kill me, but you couldn't."

"Oh aye," he laughed, throwing his head back a little. "Would have put my hands around your throat and wrung the life out of you if you'd unshackled me. You were smart to drop me off in Dunecaster."

"Do you still think about killing me?" Her tone was light, already knowing the answer.

"Almost every day."

"Then why haven't you?" She lowered her voice until she knew only he would be able to hear as she added, "Mr Paine."

He gave a snort of laughter, bringing his bottle to his lips. "Because I can always kill you dead, but I can't bring you back to life."

Her smile grew as she leaned forward once more and speared another piece of meat. She brought it to his mouth, knowing he'd take it.

While he was chewing, she said, "I thought you looked rather handsome all tied up and defenceless."

His humour died instantly. He gave her a dark look, his eye squinting to the point it almost shut. "I still haven't gotten you back for that."

"Sure you did. You marooned poor helpless me on an

island..." She tried to stifle her giggle as she added, "For half a day. How long was it supposed to be again?"

"Bringing up a man's failures isn't wise, Rosetta." She noted the hint of anger in his tone.

She leaned forward and pressed her mouth to the side of his throat, her lips curling into a smile. "You could always tie me to my bed in revenge. We have yet to do that."

His head turned sharply to her, forcing her to lean back. His anger faded into surprise, his mouth slightly ajar.

"You're giving me ideas you shouldn't." A light chuckle fell from his lips, his sourness lifting swiftly. "Don't be upset with me if I use them against you."

"Have I ever been?"

He placed his bottle between his legs, allowing him the freedom to grab her jaw with his entire hand. Her cheeks squished in a little as he shook her from side-to-side gently.

"You're a cheeky woman," he said with a grin. "You better not be up to one of your tricks.

"I'm always up to one of my tricks."

He grabbed her bottle from the table and handed it to her. "For that, I'm going to make you swallow the rest of this in one go."

"It's almost full!" And she just ate!

CHAPTER EIGHT

Rosetta felt a buzz creeping over the front of her skull as she watched the men at her table playing a game of dice.

She knew at some point, they would gamble their wages away.

It was giving her much entertainment hearing them squabble, whine, and cheer.

Six of them were rolling five dice in a cup before placing them upside down. They sneakily looked under the cup to see what they rolled without showing anyone else.

After they rolled, they had to successfully guess the number combination of the dice on the table for a single number. The first person generally picked the number that was going to be bet on. If it was four, they had to guess how many other fours or under were on the table. If they picked three, they had to be correct with the total amount on the table or under.

The next person would then raise their bid on that number. If someone thought there were seven fives, that was because they had more than one under their own cup.

Someone would call back to the person who gave the most recent bid by exclaiming they were a 'liar', saying that they had guessed too high a number on the table. Then a bet was placed between the challenger and the accused liar.

If the challenger was right that they'd over estimated, they got a coin. If the accused was under the amount of the collective dice on the table, they got a coin.

It was a game of counting, guessing, and luck.

Her nose was fuzzy, her cheeks warm, and she knew she was swaying slightly with how unsteady she felt.

Rosetta was getting drunk, thanks to Alister constantly making sure she had a bottle in her hand.

She was having too much fun to care.

She'd always enjoyed spending time with her own crew when they were in port, and watching others was interesting.

There was a difference in this dynamic; these boys were rougher and rowdier than her own, and she was able to freely share her thoughts about them with Alister in the same way she did with Naeem.

However, she was able to be a lot naughtier with him.

She teased him a lot, making him scowl, grin, point at her in anger or laughter. Rosetta was sure she was sending him on wave after wave of emotion.

She gave a tipsy hiccup after she took another sip of her bottle, no longer sure how many she'd drunk. Her eyes never left the table.

"You look like you want to play," Alister commented, tucking a strand of hair from the side of her neck that must have fallen from her bun.

As always, whenever he touched her lightly, which just so happened to be rarely, a tiny trace of goosebumps would rise where he'd stroked his fingertip.

"I've never played it before," she answered quietly. "You know I can't."

She didn't understand the game completely, nor was she confident enough in counting quickly to play. Still, she watched with enthusiasm.

A tiny squeak left her when she was pushed from his thigh to be seated between them, her arse precariously pressed against his groin. He reached a hand forward since the round had ended and grabbed one of the dice rolling cups.

"She's in," he told the table, sliding the cup in front of her.

She turned her head back, giving him an uncertain face. Her brows were twisted in worry.

"I told you I can't play."

He leaned forward to the point his chest was resting against her back, arms on either side of her against the table. His head was over her shoulder, almost pressing his cheek against hers. His thick stubble scraped against her skin, and she almost considered rubbing against it in appreciation.

"It'll be fine," he whispered. "I'll help you."

He explained the game so she could better understand it, which did little to help with her apprehension. Then, he shook the dice in the cup, turned it upside down, and allowed them both to peek under it.

She struggled to quickly count the dots on the dice, and then the number same number of dice pairings.

"Four fours," he told her.

But we only have two. Despite this, she voiced his estimate.

Bets began around the table. She felt lost the moment it changed from bets of four, to fives.

"Eleven fives," he said, and she echoed his guess.

"Liar," the person next to them threatened, ending the bets.

They all revealed their dice from under the cups, showing that she and Alister had overestimated by a single die. He threw one of his own coins on the table.

We lost. She shied her hands away from the table to withdraw from the game.

Alister grabbed the cup, shook it for the new round, and then turned it upside down. He waited for her to peek under the cup for them.

The person who got Alister's lost coin started the new round. While bets were being played, one of his hands slipped from the table to hold her around the waist. It didn't escape her notice that his fingertips grazed over her breast.

It was their turn to bet, and he tilted the cup with his other hand to check it. He turned his head towards her, pressing his lips against the side of her neck as he said, "Seven threes."

She echoed him.

They weren't challenged and the round continued.

His hand started roaming down her side and Rosetta felt her dress slowly creeping up her legs as he used his fingers to bunch it in his fist. Once it was at her knees, and she felt his palm pressing directly against her skin, she turned her head slightly.

"What are you doing?" she whispered, just as his tongue dipped out to lick her.

"Nine sixes." She quickly echoed him.

As men called more bets, eventually someone called a 'liar', his hand started lightly moving along her inner thigh. The muscles in her leg twitched all the way up until her abdomen gave a small spasm.

"Wait," she said, just as she felt him sneaking further under her dress until he was almost touching the sensitive apex between her thighs.

"Roll the cup, Rosetta."

Her eyes fell over his crew, realising none of them knew he'd sneaked his hand up her skirt. They were too preoccupied with their own women or the game.

She grabbed the cup, shook it, and then turned it upside down. Just as she was peeking under it, she felt one of his calloused fingers slip through the lips of her pussy and she tensed in his arms. She felt slicker than usual, sticky even, having forgotten about his release still inside her. She was gripping the cup with both hands and her fingers dug into it when he started to lazily move his finger over the nub of her clit. He pulled on it, making it and her inner walls throb.

"Five ones."

Once she echoed him, she grabbed her drink and chugged it for courage.

As much as she felt awkward about it being discovered while they were playing, in the middle of a tavern, surrounded by his crew and other patrons, she also found it oddly titillating.

It wasn't the first time she'd felt a hand under her skirt in a bar, but she'd never had it done to her while there was a crew she knew in front of her, one she sailed with!

More so, it was Alister's men, and he usually didn't like being intimate in front of them. She didn't think he'd ever kissed her in front of them, so for him to have shoved his hand up her skirt was a whole new experience.

The game continued. Bets were called, coins lost and won. So far, she'd won two games.

All the while, Alister continued to move his finger in mind-scattering circles, and it took every ounce of concentration to keep her focus on the table. It didn't help that her eyes were unfocused already from the alcohol swimming in her system.

Just as they won their third hand, he slipped his exploring touch further and pushed a finger inside. She felt her body clench around it, a flush of heat spreading from her chest to rush over her upper arms.

His lips were playful against the side and nape of her neck, his tongue trailing out in subtle strokes. It made her skin prickle each time. Then, a sharp nip made her jump.

"You're wet," he rasped quietly, a certain kind of grit in his throat. "Are you enjoying me touching you here, in front of my men?"

Her hand shot from the table so she could grab his when he pushed a second finger inside, stretching her, filling her all the way until she felt his rings stopping him from going further.

His fingers were thick and long, covered in coarse callouses that wonderfully abraded her insides.

S-stop, she mentally pleaded, hoping it could somehow reach him. It didn't, and she was both relieved, as she wanted to chase her orgasm, and anxious about someone noticing.

He started moving them back and forth, spearing her channel slowly. His mouth became rougher, and she had long ago felt his shaft hard against her backside.

"A-Alister," she whispered, trying to not let it come out as a moan. It was their turn, and he hadn't given her a bet.

"Hmm?" As if he had only just remembered the game, she felt his head turn as he reached around her to the table.

He grabbed the cup and tilted it back further so he could see while moving his fingers.

"Nine twos."

That wasn't the bet number. They had been betting on sixes. She echoed it with a frown.

"Liar," a person down the table said, and she cringed.

She tensed when she felt his fingertips pressing right against that sensitive spot inside her and rubbing it directly. A warm rush swept through her.

No... Not there. She felt her body dipping into his hand like it was begging him to press deeper, despite her thoughts.

Everyone moved their cups.

"Well, I'll be damned, they were right. Nine twos."

They were given a coin and she gave them a broken grin, trying to hide the fact that her thighs were starting to twitch and spasm. "Lucky guess."

The game continued, but every second, she could feel her breath coming out as heavier pants.

"Aye, you're about to come, aren't you Rosetta?" Alister whispered so quietly, no one else would be able to hear. Humour trickled through his tone while a rumble of deep laughter vibrated in his chest.

She knew she wouldn't be able to control the loudness of her voice to answer him, not when she felt her body clench around his fingers as he moved them faster, in and out.

She looked at her dice and threw out a random guess that was only slightly higher than the last bet.

Oh! Her brows drew together, and she had to fight against her own bottom lip to avoid letting out a moan. He was right; Rosetta was about to come, and it took everything in her not to grind into his hand as she did.

A shiver ran across her skin like a rippling dance.

Her hands squeezed the cup tighter when she felt her body starting to stiffen, her core clenching those sensual moving digits. *I'm... about... to...*

"We're out," Alister said when the rounded ended, pushing the cup away.

He slipped his fingers from her right before she could blissfully come around them. *Wait, no!*

Bringing his hand out from under her skirt, he pulled her until she was seated over his right thigh again.

"But I didn't get the chance to win my coins back off her!" the guy next to them laughed.

Alister grabbed the four coins she'd won with the hand that had been playing with her. He placed them into one of her open palms, spreading her own dampness across her hand, plus something a little whiter and milker than usual.

Her nose crinkled with just how much liquid spread over her fingers from his.

He was staring at her dishevelled state with a sly grin, as if he knew she was aching for the orgasm he'd denied her.

She knew her cheeks must be flushed with drunken arousal, her lips wet since she'd licked him, her breaths short and shallow. Even her breasts felt heavier than normal, her nipples itching for attention.

With her eyelids heavy, she peeked back at him.

"She's got beginner's luck all over her," he said to them as his eye flickered over the features of her face. "She'll steal all your coin if I keep playing with her."

She understood his double entendre.

The game continued without them, someone else joining to take their place.

She gripped his jaw while squeezing her thighs together, trying to put pressure on her throbbing clit. "That wasn't fair."

Now she was horny and well into being intoxicated since she'd been drinking the entire time in an attempt to hide her noises. She'd been using the bottle as a way to stifle them.

"I like you in a skirt, lass." He hefted her higher up his thigh.

He pushed another strand of hair back from her neck that had fallen from her bun, almost like he was trying to show rather than tell her that he liked it the way it was.

"It has it's many uses," she mumbled, surprised he'd complimented her in some small way, and a little nervous by it. He didn't do it often. "As you've discovered tonight."

"I thought you wore it to hide your weapons." He raised a brow at her, grabbing at the sword hidden beneath her skirts.

"I do, but it's also easier to get under it." She gave a mocking snort to herself. "Can't really wear a dress on a ship; it's near impossible to climb the shrouds in one. Tights make it easier to move around, but they aren't easy to play in."

Hell, she and Alister sometimes struggled when they needed to be quick. It wasn't often they came off when they were on a sinking ship they'd just attacked.

"You were expecting to be played with?"

She didn't understand why his expression darkened, his eyes narrowing at the table while his upper lip twitched. Whatever thought had struck him, it soured him completely.

Knowing she was going to need to rescue him from his own mind, Rosetta placed her hand on the other side of his face so she could press his head closer. She slipped her lips over the corner of his jaw to give it a sweet kiss.

"Knew you'd eventually shove your hand up my skirt." She placed her hand on the erection pressing against his breeches, hidden under her dress. She even gave it a stroke. "Didn't think you'd deny me if I let you."

He turned his head to her while pointing his index and middle fingers at her face. It seemed her words eased whatever had been eating at him because he said, "You're a horny bitch, you know that?"

He only asked questions like this when he knew she was teasing him, and he liked it.

"Takes one to know one," she threw at him, stealing a quick kiss on the mouth before anyone could notice.

He seemed surprised that she did.

If Alister had known Rosetta would be playful and seductively taunting like this on his lap, he may have gotten her drunk on it sooner.

They'd had ample opportunity on their ships in the past.

She'd managed to figure out a way to claim his lap for herself completely by throwing one of her legs over his other thigh, leaving no room for anyone to sit.

Currently, she was curled into him, her arm across his stomach, the other around his shoulders. Her face was buried against the side of his neck and occasionally, he'd feel her lips move against him, or her wicked little tongue.

Having a warm woman on him while his hand was constantly filled with a cool bottle made him rather content.

His men were still talking, but the crowd had thinned out a while ago. They'd been dragged away to tup the women on their laps seeking coin, happy to oblige them. He'd lost Pierre a few times, but the man always came back and found a new girl on his lap. Derek had left long ago.

Now that they'd thinned, chatter was less frequent, but Alister enjoyed listening to those who did talk while others rested their sorry, drunken faces against the table, as if they might fall asleep. He would occasionally drop in a few words, especially if there was a disagreement he could settle.

As his eyes scanned the table, he noticed a collection of full bottles in front of Rosetta.

She's slowed down. At some point, he thought she may have been trying to match him, but it was obvious by the two bottles and the half-full one in her hand that she'd long ago fallen behind.

Actually, she hadn't moved for a while.

He wiggled his shoulders. "Aye, lass. You alright?"

"Mmm." She seemed to clutch him closer. "You always smell so good," she softly slurred with her face still buried against his neck.

Well, he shouldn't. He should smell of salt, sea, sweat, and often booze. Occasionally blood.

Oh, nay you don't. He pulled her until her back fell against his arm.

"Don't you dare fall asleep," he demanded as he watched her head fall back limply, her eyes barely open.

She gave him a small smile, like she'd known that was what she was doing.

He reached forward and tapped her cheek with his hand, lightly slapping her a few times. "I've got plans for you later."

"I'm not."

He knew that must be a lie, and yet, she lifted her bottle to drink a quarter of it. She tried to place it on the table, missed it completely, and emptied the last quarter onto the ground.

It looked as though Alister was going to have to leave sooner than he'd originally planned. He started moving her so she could get to her feet.

"Can you walk?"

"Yep!" She stood, stumbled to the side, then steadied herself by putting her arm around a random patron to stop herself from falling. "Well, aren't you a helpful chap."

She bopped the confused man on the nose.

As he was getting to his own feet, he watched her dip like her legs were buckling before she righted herself. He watched her do it again and had to catch her right before she hit the ground.

"Nay, up you go." He put one arm under her legs while the other he curled around her back. She squealed when he cradled her in his arms and he chuckled at her. "You're a funny one when you're drunk."

He turned them both to Pierre.

"Little help here, lad." He nodded towards the two full bottles on the table with their corks still tightly squeezed into their necks.

The man laughed with a shake of his head. He stood to place them on her stomach, and she curled her arms around them so they didn't fall.

"You off to the ship?"

Shit. Despite the fact he was hiding it, Alister had to right his footing by stepping back when he himself felt his legs caving, both from the booze and from the fact he hadn't used them in hours.

"Nay, won't make it that far."

Pierre looked over them with a hint of concern. "She's pretty drunk, Captain."

"Don't give a crap what she is."

Rosetta had been teasing him all night and he was going to make her pay for it. The more intoxicated she got, the worse she seemed to be. She even tried to undo the buttons of his breeches so she could slip her hand inside, right in front of his men, as though she'd forgotten where they were, that they had company.

He walked them from The Drunken Sailor into the street.

Other drunk pedestrians walked past, like obstacles he was sure he was going to struggle getting through. Thankful he knew there was a hotel close by he'd stayed in a few times, he headed in that general direction.

"Do ye not know how to walk in a straight line, lad?" she said, mocking the way he spoke by exaggerating it.

"You wouldn't know a straight line if it spanked you on the arse right now," he laughed back, stumbling to the side to right his footing. "At least I can walk."

Albeit not well, but walk nonetheless.

She gave him one of those laughs that always made him shake his head. *Such a horrible sound.*

Holding the bottles with one arm, she slipped her hand up over his tunic, into the open vee of it, then up the side of his neck to hold onto him. The way she did it had been sensual, caressing his skin slowly. She'd even scraped her nails over him.

He picked up his pace when he noticed her head slump forward. Walking inside the hotel, he went straight to the counter. "Aye, give us a room. Now."

"That'll be four pound," the attendant told him, looking over the rim of his square glasses.

"Don't care what it costs. I'll pay it in the morning."

The man folded his thin arms across his surprisingly well-tailored chest. "You pay first."

Alister leaned across the counter. "If you make me put this woman down, you'll find a knife in your gut. Four pound, in the morning."

"Knife?" Rosetta giggled with a hiccup, pulling out his dagger from goodness knows where and flashed it in the light. "Do you need it back?"

The attendant's face whitened. He quickly reached under

the counter to give them a room key and told them the way.

"You better appreciate this," he grumbled when he was climbing the rounding staircase to make it to the upstairs sleeping quarters.

Alister didn't think he'd ever carried a woman to a bed. Doing it up a set of stairs while drunk himself was a battle he wasn't sure he was going to win. *Shit, my legs feel heavy.*

When he got to the door, he realised he had to put her down anyway so he could open it. She held the bottles while he did.

Just when he was about to pick her up again, she curled her arms around his shoulders. They crossed behind his head, the bottles clanking together.

Rosetta pulled him down to her height and crashed his lips against hers. A small groan fell from him as he returned her messy kiss, lifting her to her toes by squeezing her arse so he could push her inside.

Just as he smacked the door closed, she jumped up and wrapped her legs around his hips, forcing him to catch her.

A sense of need and urgency rushed through him as he searched for the bed while trying to stay with the kiss. Finally locating it, he rushed towards it and fell on top of it with her. He felt the bottles roll over his back and fall to the mattress as she let them go to dig her fingertips into his shoulders, her arms crossed over his back.

It was like a wave of spiralling need, desire, and lust washed over him. Previously held back by an invisible force, it split apart under her hot kisses and touch. It heated his skin and made his muscles tense.

He slipped his tongue into her welcoming mouth to taste alcohol and the sweet scent of her. He deepened the kiss to where he thought he might be crushing her beneath his lips. Another groan fell from his mouth as he thrust his hardening shaft between her open legs.

His fingers dug into her hair, messing up her bun. He

gripped the brown strands while drawing her closer. His hands itched to touch her and they left her hair, roaming down her body. He realised they still had their clothes on; impatience drove him, but he was determined to have this wicked woman naked beneath him.

He lifted her so to undo the ties at the back of the dress he'd been slyly loosening all night for better access to her breasts. He didn't care if he tore the dress as he pulled it from her body before removing his tunic. He kicked his boots off as he reached down to take hers from her feet.

She was the one who placed her hands on his breeches to undo the buttons and it gave him the opportunity to grab one of the bottles.

Popping the cork off, Alister tilted his head back, threw the bottle up, and attempted to down the entire thing. He knew it was going to be a while before he'd get the chance to drink again.

He threw it to the side once he was done and turned his attention back to her.

He paused, seeing she was laying back and waiting for him. His heated gaze glided over her as he felt a moment of pause. What he saw was near damning.

I don't get her naked enough.

Rosetta had a body like a goddess made purely to be fucked, a body that called to ruthless men like him.

Her weapons belt still attached to her waist made her appear dangerous and treacherous behind that sensual swell she always held.

Lightly tanned skin spread over deep, womanly curves, and he ran his palm over her side. Her legs were toned, her arms flexing with small, yet feminine muscles. Her hips flared wide, helping to give that pert arse its shape while her strong thighs helped to support it.

He palmed a handful of her round breast, thumbing the red,

rosy nipple. It flicked under his touch, and she twitched along with it. Leaning down, he brought it into his mouth. She immediately dug her fingers into the strands of his long hair, pulling him in with a small pant.

With a bent arm holding him up, his other hand came down to brush between her thighs, spreading them for him.

He slipped two fingers inside her, finding she was already wet and ready. She gave him a small moan, arching her back, and he released her nipple to turn his head down to look over the flat plane of her stomach.

Fuck... What does she taste like?

He'd never gotten the chance, hadn't thought about it before when he usually just wanted to slam himself inside her so he could feel her grip him. Call it selfish, but he just really enjoyed this woman around his cock.

He started running his tongue and lips over her scar, from the breast he'd been sucking down to her opposite hip. Then, he peppered her abdomen in sucking kisses he hoped would bruise her skin as he pondered what he wanted to do.

Alister didn't usually like going down on a woman.

The idea of putting his tongue somewhere when he didn't know where it had been, or more importantly, who had been there, was off-putting. To taste the seed of another man?

He couldn't think of anything worse.

But he knew who had been inside Rosetta, and it had been himself. He'd made certain of that tonight.

As he moved his fingers in her, he noticed her wetness felt stickier than usual.

A swell of desire clenched his abdomen at the reason why. *I came inside her.* Dammit, he wanted to put his tongue on this woman more than anything.

Alister realised he didn't care right then. It was his seed, and tasting this woman sounded like the most delectable treat.

He started pressing his lips lower. He nipped at the skin

just below her navel, brushing his chin over the small thatch of hair on her mound, until her folds greeted him. Removing his fingers, he slipped his hand down her inner thigh as he lowered his head.

"Where are you goin-oh!"

He ran his tongue in a flat stroke over her clit, and his shaft pulsated at the touch.

Wetness coated his tongue when he slipped it lower. He was unsure if it was himself or her he was tasting, but he couldn't help thinking he didn't mind them together.

Alister knew he'd made the right decision when she spread her knees further apart, gripped his hair tightly, bucked her hips, and let out a sweet little cry when he swirled his tongue around her clit again. He dipped his tongue back to tug on it.

Then he buried his face against her, tonguing her in unshy, confident sweeps. Every time he felt her hard nub move from his attention, her thighs would spasm around his head and she'd let out another soft cry.

He curled his arms around her legs to hold her to him when her hips tilted back and forth. He just wanted her still so he could do this his way, but he also kind of liked the idea that she was trying to greedily fuck his face.

She likes this. A grin formed across his lips, only to die when he finally looked up at her. He hadn't realised he was being watched through a heavy-lidded gaze.

Chin against her chest, her mouth was open as pant after pant fell from her. Dark brown brows were drawn tightly together while her eyelids crinkled.

Rosetta looked like she was loving this, her blue eyes glazed and wetter than normal. *Shit, she likes this a lot.*

"M-more," she demanded because he'd stopped, pulling his head back down to almost force him.

He absentmindedly ground his cock against the bed when a heavy, pulsating throb racked it, and his breath fanned over her pussy lips when he gave a deep pant.

He started moving his mouth like he wanted to devour her. Which he did; he wanted to feast on this woman.

His strokes became rushed, the press of his lips hard, his tongue exploring. He slipped lower and pressed it inside her, and she threw her head back. Apparently, that was enough to send her over the edge.

"Alister..." Her hips twitched as a rush of slick erupted from her.

His nose crinkled, a groan falling from him at the taste of her, knowing she was coming against his tongue.

He lapped her up, never stopping, never removing himself from this new delight he'd discovered. He wanted more, to steal it from her like a thief hunting for a pocket full of coins. He sucked on her clit, harshly tugging on it, and her little moan turned into a scream of ecstasy.

Only when her legs stopped squirming and she was pushing his head away did he finally break from her. Alister knew he'd made her come hard by the end.

Leaning back, he fervently licked at his lips covered in her orgasm, knowing what he was tasting was purely her, as he stared down at this woman.

Rosetta was relaxed, her eyes dazed and off elsewhere. She lay limp against the bed, her arms beside her head as if she'd thrown them back. Her freckled nose, like someone had thrown sugar across her face, was pink. Even her cheeks, ears, and chest were red as she tried to catch her breath.

Her chest was heaving with high-pitched huffs, making those breasts pump up and down. They subtly jiggled with her after tremors.

Alister looked down to see that her thighs were loose around him, her pussy spread and glistening from her orgasm.

It wasn't often he saw this placid side to her, meek and innocent, so vulnerable that he knew a man had to earn the trust it meant.

He was one of the worst criminals around. For someone like Alister to have obtained it... well, that was a miracle in itself. Usually she was reaching, trying to take control.

Rosetta had an aching hint to her heated gaze. It was an invitation that said he had freedom to do as he pleased, so long as it felt good for her.

The way she looked when she was like this always stirred something inside him. It weighed heavy on his chest and cock, gripping them both with undeniable lust.

I'm going to take her senseless tonight.

Rosetta was going to learn why Alister usually took more than one woman to bed when he was in port.

CHAPTER NINE

A disgruntled groan fell from Rosetta before she even opened her eyes. She could see the brightness of the sun behind them and knew if she were to open her eyelids, she'd be terribly blinded.

She curled her body into the side of the person she was lying against, her head burrowing deeper into their chest to hide from it.

"Someone shoot the sun," she grumbled to herself, her head feeling like it was splitting open the more she woke.

I'm so hungover. Deathly hungover. She couldn't even remember how much she'd drunk, or how she'd gotten to this bed to wake up next to someone who felt wonderfully warm and comfortable.

"I don't think that would be wise," he chuckled next to her.

Her brows drew together, and she peeked open her eyes. She tried to use his broad chest to shield her from the sunlight filtering into the room through the window.

"Alister?"

"Who else would it be, Rosetta?" There was a heavy bite to the tone as his head turned down to her. His eyes peeked open, as if he also wasn't ready, but there was a tight glare in them.

"You're usually still asleep when I wake up," she answered plainly.

She had a feeling the entire time she'd been cuddling into Alister. The body next to her had smelt like him, felt like him.

"Nay." He tilted his head back to the pillow, closing his eyes once more. "That's because you wake up as soon as the sky does."

True. It was as though the moment the sun gave just a fraction of light over the horizon, Rosetta was awakened like a beckoning call. It made waking up with it high in the sky strange.

To wake up gently next to him like this, while he was already awake to share it with her, was actually rather enjoyable.

He made their cuddle more intimate by turning towards her to lay on his side. He brought his other arm over the top of her body and dragged her closer. Facing each other, he made her face squish against the centre of his chest as he placed his chin against the top of her head.

His warmth helped soothe her raging headache. She sought it, not wanting to jar herself out of her satisfied state.

Yet, she also felt something else: a strange wetness over the front of her stomach as her skin stuck to his. Her brows came together to knot in concentration, feeling her body with her mind when she thought she felt it lower.

She squirmed a little at the odd sensation she felt. Rosetta dug her hand between them and felt the lips of her folds, finding them slippery and tender.

"Alister..." she asked with a thoughtful tone.

He answered her with a sleepy, "hmm?"

"Did-Did you come inside me?"

"Oh, aye." She felt his jaw moving against the top of her head as he spoke. "In you, on you, around you. I think I even hit the ceiling, lass."

That made her eyes open wider than she wanted. "But you never do!"

"Was a wee bit drunk last night; almost dropped you twice carrying you here."

He tightened his arms around her, holding her closer like nothing was wrong with the world. He even kneaded her ass with one large hand, pushing her hips against his.

She'd never experienced him this lax and satisfied before.

"But you never get drunk."

She'd seen the man drink rum like it was water and never miss a step, even on a rocking and unsteady ship.

"I do when I'm in port. Give me a belly of whiskey and scotch and you'll see me walk like a landlubber on the ocean."

A chuckle followed his words.

She was too shocked to move. "But you never come inside me. Why would you do that?"

And why was he so damn calm about it?

"You were riding me like you wanted it." She felt something growing against her abdomen. He was getting hard at just the memory. "Wasn't really in the soberest state of mind to stop you."

That seemed to make the worst of her anxiously beating heart settle. Rosetta could remember fractions of her night the more she woke. She could remember being beneath Alister for a lot of it, as well as on top of him once.

"So, it was only once."

Still not good, but she'd had men stupidly come inside her before, even though they weren't supposed to.

What also helped calm her was that she truly did think she was a broken woman. Either it didn't matter at all, or it was just extremely difficult to get her pregnant.

Once more couldn't be that bad. *Fuck, I hope so.*

"Oh nay. More than that. We were going until the sun rose."

No wonder she was so tired!

She felt her heart slapping hard in her chest. She started

pushing against his torso.

She could forgive once, maybe twice if they were going all night and he was drunk. She knew she must have been plastered. Trying to get a riding woman off him in the middle of coming and clinging desperately would have been difficult.

It was probably Rosetta's fault. In the throes of her climax, too drunk to care, she could picture herself riding him as he came, so long as she got to come too. He probably even told her and she'd been too focused on reaching bliss.

But she couldn't stay calm for the rest.

"What about at the bar then?" When he wouldn't release her, she started bashing on his chest. It wouldn't do much, considering her arm was twisted between her. She could only deliver small punches. "You have no excuse for that!"

She was suddenly flipped to her back, Alister kneeling over her on a straightened arm. His silver locket dangling from his neck almost brushed over her naked chest.

One of his knees was between her thighs as he gripped the underneath of her jaw in one large hand. He clamped her jaw shut, tilting her head back slightly, and she was forced to stare at his snarl-like face.

The content and relaxed Alister she'd been experiencing for the first time had turned into a murderous looking man who held her down.

"I was angry, Rosetta."

His hand gripped tighter, and if he'd been holding her neck lower, he would have been strangling her.

She tried to pry herself free, not feeling a shred of fear when she felt her own anger rising like a monstrous beast.

"If you touch other men while we're sailing together, you'll regret it."

Then, his grip softened, as did his expression. He was looking over her face like he was mesmerised by it, his thumb rubbing across her bottom lip as though he couldn't stop himself. It moved to the side under his rough touch.

Even though everything became gentler, the way he said his next words made dread pool in her stomach.

"I'll hunt them down and kill every single one of them."

Her lips parted in shock while her eyes widened in realisation. Because his hold on her had lightened, she was able to push her way free.

"You don't get to make such a threat!" she yelled as she crawled to get off the bed and away from him, taking the sheet with her to hide her nudity. "It's not fair when you have your girls and prostitutes. If you're going to–"

Rosetta's words were cut short when her feet found the floor... and her legs immediately gave out. A sharp gasp of pain cut its way from her throat before she even hit the ground. She found herself on her knees right next to the bed, gripping the sheet as agony shot through her.

Because she hadn't been moving, and had been too distracted, she hadn't realised just how much her body ached.

Her thighs were so sore she couldn't stand, as if they'd been stretched apart further than they'd ever been before. Her belly ached, like she'd been punched in the gut repeatedly. Her core was so tender, even the singular step she'd taken had made it throb so deeply, it'd sapped all her energy in one go.

What did he do to me? She was sure if she really tried, she could stand, but that felt like a battle she knew to be too difficult.

She hadn't even noticed he'd come closer until she felt his hand wrap around the nape of her neck and pull her forward. He pointed at the headboard.

"Do you see another woman in this bed with you?" he yelled so loudly it made her flinch.

Her eyes turned away from his furious face to scan over the bed. No, she didn't. She knew from her hazy memories slowly returning that it had only ever held the both of them.

"I never bring a woman alone to my bed when I'm in port, Rosetta, and now you know why. I'm not the same man when I'm on the sea. When I'm in port, I get drunk, and when I get drunk, I get horny." He let her go so he could start backing off the bed. "I drink all evening and then fuck all night since I usually don't get to."

"But you currently do!"

Why did she have to take him like he was a rutting beast when she'd been satisfying him for months?

He stood, stomping around the room with loud, echoing footsteps. His round, muscled arse flexed as he reached down to grab his breeches, stealing her attention for a split second, like she couldn't stop herself from ogling his scarred body.

"Oh aye, I know," he answered as he stabbed his leg into it. "Tell that to my dick that wouldn't go down even though I knew you couldn't take much more."

Talking about it, even now it was semi-hard!

"You can't change a habit I've had for over ten years." He shook his head as he made his way to the door once he finished putting his breeches on and nothing else, that wide and glorious chest covered in hair in full view. "Be thankful I stopped when you *begged* me to, because I didn't fucking want to."

Then he opened the door and slammed it behind him as he left. Rosetta stared at the doorway, dumbstruck.

She couldn't believe what this morning had turned into.

She tried to stand so she could collect her dress, but her legs wobbled and refused. Giving a groan of pain, she stayed on her knees and pressed her face and upper body on top of the mattress in dismay.

Why do I have to pay the price for his habits? she thought with a scrunched-up face, feeling the twinges, aches, and pains radiating throughout her body.

Rosetta knew she had enjoyed every minute of it when it

was happening. One of the reasons her channel probably ached was because she'd come until she couldn't anymore. She didn't think she'd ever reached that stage before in her life.

His threat had been a powerful message. If Rosetta took another man, she'd see Alister at his worst... and his worst was not kind.

She'd already seen it. When they took over ships, she'd seen him beat others who wouldn't surrender, strangle them, cut them slowly with a knife. He could be undeniably cruel when he wanted to be, and that never bothered her before because it usually had nothing to do with her.

Honestly, she'd usually laugh or ask if she could join in.

She would be upset about it if his message wasn't as clear as it was. *He's not going to bed other women.* That's what it meant, and he was expecting her to take the brunt of it.

Her eyes crinkled into heavy bows of sadness and confusion.

As much as she'd hidden it from him, Rosetta hadn't liked seeing Lacey on his lap. She'd hated the way it cut through her like some petty, jealous, pathetic woman.

She'd laughed out loud at herself – she'd been worried about any other reaction she could have had.

She refused to show it and told herself she shouldn't care. He'd already made it obvious he'd been planning to sleep with others while in port the day they'd killed Theodore. She told him the whole reason she'd been hit so hard she fell down the stairs was because she'd been upset he had port girls and gotten one pregnant.

She'd seen by Alister's reaction he would do the same.

At the time, she'd resigned herself to that fact and would allow herself the same freedom when the time came. But Rosetta had forgotten, and when she'd first stepped foot on land, she'd been intending to share her time with Alister.

So, when she'd seen Lacey with him, she'd tried to snuff out her jealousy and gone to men she'd trusted in the past. It would have grown her coin pouch, and she was hoping two could make her forget why she was even upset in the first place.

Her eyes bowed further, her eyebrows crinkling tightly together as she turned her head to stare at the empty room.

The spark of hope she felt having him all to herself was trapped in the despondent emotions strangling it. What was the point in having a spark of hope when it had nowhere to grow?

Other than desire, there would never be anything else between them. They had a mutually beneficial agreement and nothing more. It gave them pleasure, it got them gold, and it gave them both security on the sea.

Eventually they'd sail in different directions. What's the point in getting caught up in any other emotions?

Why is he even doing this? That cruel possessiveness he'd displayed should have worried her; instead, she couldn't help finding it delicious. A body thrumming, core quivering, delicious display.

Rosetta let out another disgruntled groan. *Shut the hell up, body.* She couldn't handle its shit right now, getting turned on for him when she was too sore and bewildered to do anything about it.

She figured Alister knew she wouldn't listen to the threats he made if he still took other women.

Does he want me so much that he's determined to keep me to himself like this? She had to purse her lips by force to stop them from trying to curl into a small smile.

It didn't matter. Her smile faded anyway when she remembered the current state of her body. That's when she finally felt fear.

Dear lord, I can't even stand! And they were in port for

another night. *I'm going to die!* Rosetta didn't think she could handle another night of port Alister.

Just as she was pondering what she was going to do, she heard the handle to the door wiggle and turned her head sharply to it.

She brought the sheet back to her chest when he entered, his eyes narrowing when he saw she was still in the position he'd left her. She was thankful she covered herself when people came in behind him.

All this room held was a large bed and a chest of drawers. They carried in a medium-sized, wooden bathtub and started filling it with buckets of steaming water.

"Place the food on the bed for her," Alister told a woman holding a plate.

He stood there with his arms folded, watching them carefully, waiting as they went back and forth with more buckets until the tub was halfway full.

The maid placed the food at the foot of the bed next to Rosetta, a concerned crinkle to her forehead. She also placed a glass of pure, unsweetened by rum, water on the ground.

"Are you alright?" she whispered quietly, her gaze wandering over Rosetta's position while she looked seemingly helpless and naked. She knew she must look worrisome considering her state; her once neatly pinned back hair was loose and everywhere. "Do you need help?"

Not all women wanted to work the streets and many sought employment in the many bars and hotels this large island had.

She was sure this maid had seen the aftermath of many tragic regrets some street workers would feel from taking a man for coin and finding out he was brutal. Some even tried to keep unwilling women permanently after getting a taste.

Rosetta knew there was also the possibility they may have been unwilling the entire time, may not have been a street worker at all. A helpless woman dragged to a man's bed when she never wanted to be there to begin with.

The way she looked at her was to beseech Rosetta for any indication that she might need rescuing, that there was a possibility she might be able to assist.

Maybe the owner of the bar would help protect those who needed saving by throwing the man to guards while sheltering the poor woman until he was gone. It wouldn't be the first time she heard of something like that happening in this often repugnant town.

"Oh, piss off," Rosetta said with a roll of her eyes, making the woman flinch. "He may be a brute, but he isn't a monster."

Couldn't the maid tell the difference between an abused woman and one who had spent her entire night screaming with lust and just simply couldn't walk afterwards?

It probably didn't help that Alister looked like an evil man with the scarred state of his body and the dark, mean expression he currently wore.

"M-my apologies." She bowed and quickly ran from the room with her head down. She refused to make eye contact when she passed Alister.

When Rosetta brought her gaze to him once more, the grim, tight press of his lips had softened at her defence.

He must have noticed something had changed with her temper, because he finally came over to her and nudged the plate closer. "Eat; it'll make you feel better."

He walked away when the workers told him they were done with filling the tub and closed the door behind them, locking it.

Her stomach grumbled at the food, but her mouth salivated for the glass in front of her. She grabbed it and chugged half the water down in one go, nearly moaning.

When was the last time I had water like this? It was as though her mind had forgotten its existence after being at sea for so long. She finally turned to her plate. Two pieces of toasted bread were buttered and glazed with honey.

As she took large bites, she watched him dip his hand into the tub to check the temperature of the water.

The silence between them was strained while she ate, even though he kept looking over at her. When he did it again, and saw she'd stopped eating, his brows creased.

"Eat more. You barely eat at all." She knew he meant in general and not just now.

She gave him a shrug, turning her head to the side to rudely dismiss him. "I can't help when my body tells me I'm full."

She turned again when she heard his heavy footfall approaching. He grabbed the piece she hadn't eaten and brought the whole thing to his mouth so he could hold it with his teeth.

A squeal of surprise squeaked from her when he used both hands to slip around her, picking her up to cradle her in his arms.

Before she could even ask what he was doing, he was lowering her into the tub as if he knew she didn't have the energy to walk to it herself.

The tub was longer than it was wide, and she had plenty of room to sprawl out. She sat with her feet in front of her, forced to bend her knees when he removed his breeches and hopped into the other side. It was perfectly big enough to fit them both and, because it was only filled halfway, it didn't overflow.

He started eating the piece of toast while staring at her with an observational, dull gaze. Rosetta turned her eyes away.

I've never had a bath with another person before. Or a man, for that matter.

It felt rather private. She couldn't help covering herself like some silly, shy virgin, as if they hadn't spent the night intertwined.

"The hot water should help," he said once he was finished chewing the last bite.

He removed the tie holding the top half of his hair away from his face, so it was all loose before putting his arms around the rim of the tub.

Surprisingly, it is. Her body felt less stiff the moment she'd been encased in the delectable heat.

She eyed the empty plate, her glass of water, and then the filled tub.

"Did you do all this to make me feel better?" She couldn't hide the tone of disbelief in her voice even if she wanted to.

"Aye," he said, letting his eye trail over the wall in thought. "It's not your fault I'm the way I am."

He isn't usually this considerate.

She scoffed out a laugh. "I'm going to tell everyone you have a sweet side."

Eyes narrowing quickly into a scowl, he turned his head and pointed two fingers at her. "You better not."

His scowl faded into a face of light confusion when she started laughing more. Not loudly, but enough to show she found this humorous.

He just looked perplexed. She figured it was because they had been shouting at each other only a short while ago. He wouldn't know of the whirlwind of emotions and thoughts she'd had before he'd come back into the room.

"I see you've calmed the fuck down."

Then he reached forward and grabbed her arm, dragging her across the tub until she was seated between his legs, her back against his chest.

She wasn't sure if he'd done it because he wanted her closer, or because he wanted to stretch one leg out while he kept the other bent so he was comfortable.

Just as she was considering whether she wanted to stay where she was, she tried to leap forward when she felt his hand cup her between her legs.

"I can't!" Rosetta couldn't take anymore. She was too

tired, too tender, too... everything.

He wrapped his arms around her waist to hold her still while two of his fingers moved to find her entrance.

"Aye, I know."

"Then why are you–?"

"I'm cleaning you of my come." He pushed them into her channel, and she let out a gasp, gripping the edges of the tub. "Didn't really mean to do it inside."

"It's a bit late for this." Yet, she couldn't help finding the gesture oddly reassuring. "And I can do it myself!"

"Nay, it should help. I also don't mind doing it."

He may want to do it to make certain it was truly done.

Her legs twitched when he pressed them deeper, split his fingers apart, and she felt the heat of the water gushing in.

"You shouldn't lock your ankles around a man. That's how you make your own regrets."

While she was gripping the edge of the tub in tension, she nibbled at one of the corners of her lips. She vaguely remembered doing that.

Rosetta knew she sometimes did it when he was hitting just the right spot and didn't want him to move right before she reached orgasm.

Usually, Alister would pry one of her legs free of him and hold it to the side so he could withdraw when she was too thoughtless and gone.

Last night, she could remember at least one time when she may have been doing that while she was coming, had felt him trying to move her unbudging legs, until he eventually started shuddering with a low groan. He released her legs to grab her hips and pull her hard on him, grinding himself in while she felt him pulsate.

She felt herself clench in memory.

She was thankful he didn't seem to notice her do it around his fingers before he removed them. He placed his arms over the rim of the bathtub and reclined back to be comfortable.

"Why are you so calm about this?" Rosetta asked with a sigh, turning her head to look at him.

"Nothing else I can do about it, now is there? I don't dwell on my mistakes. I've done too many bad things in my life to do that." He rolled his head to the side to punctuate his nonchalance in his words. "Things also tend to work out for me anyway. A lot of the reason I'm still alive is because I've been extremely lucky. One night isn't going to hurt."

She considered telling him it may not matter anyway, but she decided against it. She didn't want to give him the freedom to think he could do it in the future.

She lifted her arm and pointed her index finger in his face, dangerously close to poking him in the eye. "Never again, you hear? I don't care if we're both too drunk, never again."

He gave a small chuckle, leaning his head back against the tub and turning his face to ceiling. He closed his eyes like he was tired.

"Oh aye, don't need you to tell me twice. I court death enough; don't really need to court life as well."

Feeling comforted, she turned forward to let her body simply rest. She laid her back against his chest, deciding he deserved to be used as a pillow.

"Have you ever had a bath with a woman, Alister?"

"Nay. Must say, I don't mind it."

A small smile curled her lips.

After a short while of just relaxing, she felt him move. His hands started rubbing down her aching thighs in deep, yet careful strokes.

"You're giving me a massage?" *This morning is full of surprises.*

"Don't think too deeply into it. We've got work to do today, and I can't have you walking around like some feeble sick person."

Oh, right. They had to get the supplies for the ship.

Once the water was too cool for Rosetta to enjoy, she finally got the courage to use her legs. She let out a sigh of relief when she felt minimal twinges.

While she was putting on her weapons belt so she could finally get some clothes on, she noticed he hadn't hopped out directly after her.

He had removed his eyepatch and was dunking his head in the water. Hoping to get a peek at that side of his face for the first time, she kept her sight on him.

Unfortunately, he covered it with his hand as he felt around for one of the towels next to the tub. He dried his face and then placed his eyepatch on before she had the chance to see him.

Disappointed, she grumbled to herself as she put her dress on, noticing the tear in the neckline she didn't have the day before.

Once she had it tied at the back, she reached into the slits she'd cut so she could reach into her weapons belt. There was a small, rectangular pocket with a button in the centre.

It held her bullets, but she'd also stashed her comb into it just in case she'd gone to a hotel instead of her ship to sleep.

Rosetta sat on the edge of the bed and started combing her hair of the tangled web of knots. While he was getting dressed, his gaze fell to her before quickly looking away when he realised he'd been caught.

I wonder... She'd seen him look at his own long locks the day she'd been torturing Pierre with a hairbrush.

"Do you want me to brush your hair?" she asked, trying to hide the humour in her question.

He paused as he was placing his second boot on, nearly dressed besides his tunic. "Nay. I don't trust you after this morning."

"Come now. You're painting me as a spiteful bitch. You've been nice to me since; least I can do is be nice back."

His eyes squinted, as though he found her suspicious.

It seems she won though, because he came over to her. She spread her legs so he would fit his wide body between them as he slowly turned and sat with his back resting against the bed. He rested one of his arms over her leg while the other draped over his hips.

Rosetta started by gently combing the tips first, rather than raking her comb from the top of his head to the ends like she had done to Pierre. This was far less painful and showed care.

"It's pretty long now," she commented. It came halfway down his back.

He nodded in agreeance, reaching into one of his boots. "Too long. Cut it."

Blinking at the dagger he'd slapped into her palm, surprised he was trusting her with this, she eventually turned her head up.

"Well... how long do you want it?"

"Don't care, as long as I can tie it back when its windy."

Rosetta brought it all together in a fist and measured to just past the tops of his shoulders. She held the dagger above her fist and in one quick slice, she cut away a little over one third of the length.

He pulled a couple of strands forward to inspect how long she'd left it. He pushed it back with a shrug and waited for her to continue combing his hair.

He made a thoughtful sound when it was untangled enough that she could run the comb over his scalp, letting out little expires.

"You're enjoying this," she stated, trying her best to keep humour from her tone so he didn't think she was mocking him.

"I haven't had my hair brushed by another since I was a young lad. Forgot how nice it felt."

"My mother used to do it for me too, even when I was a teenager." She welcomed the sad pang that swirled in her heart. She missed her parents. "The maids at the mansion weren't as gentle. Can I plait it for you? It means you won't have to brush and retie it every day."

"I don't." She figured as much by how messy his hair often looked. "But aye, do what you want, as long as I don't look like a girl."

She dipped her body over the top of his head so she could meet his eye.

"Alister, I could put you in a dress, put make-up on your face, and give you a frilly umbrella to walk around with, and you still wouldn't look like a woman."

He finally gave a large grin as he chuckled. "That's true."

Instead of just plaiting the half of his hair he usually tied into a folded bun, she braided the top before plaiting it. She smiled when she was done, finding he looked neater.

"I need to go back to my ship before we start looking for supplies."

Her ship funds were locked behind the safe. She also wanted her hat so she could shield her face from the sun.

He didn't seem to mind.

CHAPTER TEN

Alister occasionally looked at the woman walking beside him with her hands clasped casually behind her back. The sun was showering them with its brightness and warmth, making her clean hair look glossy and her skin shine.

He swore that her freckles seemed darker the longer they walked through the biggest market in Tortaya, not that he was usually so attentive.

It was the same market in which they'd sold their own wares, almost a kilometre long of stall after stall of trade merchants and pirates selling their stock.

Although it ventured further into the town, it neared the pier for easy access for stocking and suppling ships for travel.

They had barely made a dent in walking down it, since most of the fresh food was at the very edge. Rosetta also slowed him down by checking every single stall when usually, he just rushed past and picked what grabbed his attention. There were generally several stores selling most items anyway.

"Our men aren't monkeys, Rosetta. They won't eat an entire barrel of bananas before they become overripe."

Completely disregarding what he said – as she had done the entire time – she reached inside her large coin bag reserved for supplying her ship to pay the seller for a barrel.

Two of her crew were following them, since most of it would go onto her ship because of the cargo space it had, and they moved to hoist it onto their shoulders.

They left to carry it back to the Laughing Siren. They would be back in a little while to help grab more supplies they bought. The same men rotated through to find them in the crowd of other buyers to assist.

"Then we can make sweet bread with them. If Mr Darkley doesn't know how, my chef can teach him. I taught him."

Glen definitely doesn't know how to do that. Alister's brows pressed together. *You can make bread with overripe bananas?*

He was learning there was much he hadn't eaten before today. *Turning overripe berries into sauce instead of gravy?* Pickling vegetables he'd never heard of in jars because they lasted longer. Drying herbs when they went old to season their smoked meat so it didn't taste so terrible. Turning grapes into raisins that could be eaten as they are or added to other foods.

Perhaps we should have docked in a port earlier. To learn that he and his crew could almost eat in luxury like kings on the seas... well, that might just be a good enough reason to port more often.

They led their men very differently; they also organised their ships differently. The more Alister watched Rosetta as a captain, though, the more he understood she was excellent at it.

With everything she was buying, and making him pay half for, she was guaranteeing them a higher chance of staving off sickness.

She also regularly threatened him that if she bought something he didn't chip in for, she would remember and wouldn't let he or his men eat it.

Once they were done with the food, they started buying tools. This often got them separated, since their ships required different, yet similar, maintenance.

Other than making sure his ship could be repaired to perfect sailing conditions, he didn't care how clean it was, how warm it was, or how comfortable it was.

That's why, when he turned around to find Rosetta in the crowd and saw a small line of her men holding thick blankets, he stomped toward her.

"What are you doing?" he asked, staring in disbelief when he saw another one of her men grabbing an armful of blankets.

He seemed to be the last one; Alister realised he was too late in stopping her. Tilting her head back so she could see under her tricone hat, she gave him a puzzled frown.

"What do you mean?" She turned her gaze towards the back of the last man. "We're coming into the colder months."

"So? Your ship should already have blankets."

"They're barely acceptable!" she exclaimed, raising both her hands in an annoyed gesture because of his tone. "They may be just fine for spring and autumn, but my men will freeze if I don't get them something thicker."

"That's not an opulence you should be affording. They know they're about to go back to sea for a long time. They can buy their own warmth if they don't want to go cold." Alister palmed his own face in frustration. "Just because you don't like the cold, lass, doesn't mean we men can't handle it."

"Just because you can, doesn't mean you have to." She folded her arms across her chest. "It's my ship and my crew. I can buy whatever I want for them."

He hated it when she was right.

Although Alister was going to keep a closer eye on her now, he worried he was too late to stop her from stupidly buying everything her heart wanted.

Of course, she wants to spend all her money on that ship. She just recently got it. She probably wanted to do what women did when they got a shiny new thing to play with: doll it up.

He watched her carefully as she bought cleaning supplies, disgruntled by it. He at least approved of the ropes, timber planks, and tools she'd need to fix her ship.

Since she'd lost the top half of her mast, she needed to buy new sails to give him back the spares he'd lent her. She also bought extras in case it, somehow, ever happened again. There was also a small team adding a new crow's nest and checking that the mast was fully stable.

Lightning striking a mast through a storm was rare. It had never happened to his own ship, or any ship he'd sailed on.

He doubted she'd have to deal with the issue again, but she seemed set on making sure she was prepared. Trying to talk her out of it was useless. She refused to listen to him. Him! The more experienced one who had been sailing for years.

He almost lost his mind when he turned around for two seconds and turned back to see she was two stalls down buying paint! Paint, of all things!

It worsened when he reached her and saw she'd dug her hand into her dress as if she was reaching into her own personal coin sack.

He grabbed her wrist before she could pay the vendor. His other palm felt the bag in her hand that she had been using to pay for everything with today, and felt it was completely empty.

Don't tell me... "Was this all the money you'd put aside for your ship?"

He'd calculated this with her, had budgeted what he thought she would need and then an additional sum for the occasional whim he couldn't foresee.

"Yes," she answered while ripping her hand from him.

"You shouldn't be digging into your own funds. If you've spent your quota on your ship, then you've failed to hold back from what you want to buy to what you *should* buy."

Despite what he said, she gave him a bright smile.

"This is the last thing I want to get. I may not find another blue that matches the colour of my ship the next time I port." She reached forward and paid the vendor. He gave three ceramic pots of paint to her men, and Alister thought his eye might twitch when they were also given high-quality brushes rather than the cheaper ones. "Since you paid for my booze and food, I have coin I can spare."

"We may not be so successful the next time we set sail." They'd found a medium chest of mostly silver coins. It was unlikely they'd find anything that grand again if they didn't find Dustin's trove. "You should have kept some in case you need to port for an emergency."

He slapped the bag upwards to show her it was empty.

"Now you have nothing to lean on except your own funds. That's how you make yourself poor."

She reached up and patted the side of his face in a teasing gesture. "I have faith you will help me earn more coin, big guy."

What if he didn't? They could part ways in a month if he chose. Just as he was about to tell her this, ask her what she would do then, he realised he may not like the response he got.

Rosetta turned to her crew currently following her.

"You can all get lost and leave me alone now." She shooed them with her hands, including him, by waving them forward. "Anything else I buy is for myself and I can carry that."

He watched her walk further into the markets alone, a small hum floating up from her.

"Wait." He trod after her. "Are you planning to spend the day by yourself?"

"Aye, laddie," she chuckled. "Not afraid of no one in the daytime in a busily crowded area. The worst of the degenerates have passed out in a filthy hole somewhere." She tilted her head and narrowed her eyes. "Before you say anything about it, Naeem is back at the ship directing everyone bringing back the supplies. He's too busy to join me and I'm free to do whatever I want."

His gaze wandered over the fact she was still wearing the dress from the day before, as though it was the only one she owned.

He didn't like that his thoughts weren't only for her safety. *She would also be free to do* whoever *she wanted.*

He may have told her what he would do if he discovered she'd been with another man, but he didn't know what she had been truly upset about: the fact she thought he may touch others, or because he'd stopped her from having the freedom she'd wanted. Would she try to hide it from him?

After knowing the man the day before was attracted to her, Alexander whatever his name was, he wondered just how many other men were interested in Rosetta. Would they approach her if she were alone?

She was very pretty. He bet even strangers would approach her with the intention of bedding her.

Shit. Alister ran a hand over the top his hair, feeling the bumps of the braid she'd put there and jerked his hand away in surprise. He wasn't used to the sensation. on his hair being tied into a braid.

I'm not used to feeling like this.

How was he supposed to handle these unexperienced jealous and possessive urges? Ones he didn't particularly want her to know the full extent of.

He'd eventually realised that's what he'd been feeling, but he hadn't been bothered to learn that, so long as she remained his for as long as he wanted her.

"I'll come with you."

She stopped to turn with a frown.

"You want to come with me?" She gave him a laugh that brightened her eyes with disbelief. "I'll be fine on my own."

She patted her sides and rattled her weapons. "I get you think I'm in danger because I'm on my own, but I'm sure you don't want to follow me around while I look at dresses."

He folded his arms across his chest and tried to make his tone light to hide his true intentions. "Are you saying I don't like going shopping because I'm a man? That's rather presumptuous."

"Nooo," she giggled, stepping forward to poke him in the chest. "I'm saying you probably don't like going shopping because you're a cheapskate who doesn't like spending his coin."

Bloody hell, she has me dead to rights there.

Instead of responding to her hurtful, but truthful, comment, Alister turned her and slapped her arse so hard, she jumped.

"Move it. Let's go find you something better to frolic around in."

She gave a loud squeak at the heaviness of his spank before walking forward to lead the way.

Because they were on their own without men guarding them, he kept his hand firmly on the hilt of his cutlass. Without a care, as if the world was filled with innocent bunnies and pretty rainbows and not the criminals around them, Rosetta skipped along.

To his annoyance, she stopped at every stall that held something of interest to her – which happened to be almost every single one. She even stopped to lean over and smell some of flowers at a florist. He noticed she paid special attention to the roses and the white gardenias.

"Actually, it might be good that you're here with me," she said under her hat, walking once more with her hands behind her back. "You can pay for a new dress."

"Nay," he chuckled with deep humour. "You can pay for your own clothes."

She tilted her head back to look at him while pointing to

the neckline of the yellow one she was wearing. "I only have to get a new one because you ripped this one last night."

"You're a cheeky one, but you can't pull the wool over my eyes this time." He raised his brow when he thought he may have seen the corner of her lips twitch, as though she was going to smile at being caught. "I still remember the day you took my ship from me and screamed 'get me out of this god forsaken ugly dress'. You wanted a new one regardless."

"And here I was, hoping you were forgetful!"

She threw her hands up in frustration, but the smile that broke from her showed him she wasn't really bothered in the least. He shook his head at her, cracking his own small smile as they continued to shop.

She darted around, moving back and forth to look at everything, but was always drawn to return to his side. Alister thought he might have been enjoying himself a small amount, watching her flit around the market like a fairy.

That was, until she started trying to feed him different, strange foods.

From their supply hunting, she'd already figured he hadn't tasted much. Now, she seemed to be on the prowl to make sure he tried everything possible and made him pay for it!

If he refused because he wasn't sure if he would like what she offered, it forced them to move on. Occasionally, he'd try something just to make her shut up. Unfortunately, they got to a stall selling something specific and she refused to budge.

"You have got to try this. I only ever got to eat it when I was in the mansion. My family couldn't afford it. The fact they even have it here means you *have* to."

"Nay, I don't want to."

He eyed it over with a grimace. He didn't like the brown colour of it. He also didn't fully trust that, after everything nice she'd gotten him to eat, she wouldn't trick him into eating something foul.

He could picture Rosetta playing a prank on him too easily.

She would very much learn that Alister didn't like messing with his tastebuds. He was enjoying himself. The last thing he wanted was to be put into a sour mood because he'd eaten something that made him shudder with disgust.

Rolling her eyes, she was so adamant he try it that she paid for it herself.

"A whole silver for just that piece?" he howled when he saw she was holding a tiny sliver of this brown food that looked like it came from the backend of an animal.

It was no bigger than his thumb nail.

"Only nobles can afford to eat something like this," she said, inching closer. "Just try it."

"Why should I care what nobles eat?"

He'd tried things like caviar and snail once because he'd been curious to know why the rich wanted to eat them. Alister didn't often purge what was in his stomach, no matter what he ate or how much he drank, but even he'd almost emptied his stomach when he tasted them. Their gross consistency also hadn't helped. Since then, he'd refused to eat something just because they did.

"Please?" she asked with a giggle, bringing the piece closer to his face. "I used to love eating this."

His hand shot forward and he grabbed her wrist to stop her.

"I. Said. Nay," he bit with so much malice in his tone that he noticed some of the people around them stepping away.

His teeth were tightly gritted, and he knew his face would be twisted into something nasty. *Why does she never listen?* It was as if she was getting under his skin like this on purpose.

Her lips parted. He watched her eyes bow at the corners, her cheeks lifting as she cringed at him. It took him a moment to see past his own anger to understand why she gave him such a pained expression.

Alister's eyes widened. He immediately released her small

wrist when he realised he'd been crushing it within his meaty fist. He brought his hand back so quickly, like it was on fire, that he knocked it into a pedestrian behind him.

The small man acted as though Alister had punched him in the face when he stumbled back, holding his cheek.

"Ah, shit." He felt a hit of shame prickle on the back of his neck. "Rosetta... I didn't mean to."

Alister may be forceful, but he didn't think he'd ever actually hurt her by grabbing her before. Not because he was afraid she'd shoot him for it, but because she'd run and fought from a life filled with abuse from a man. Alister didn't want to be cast into that same category.

Her eyes narrowed on him, her lips thinning into a scowl.

"If you eat it, I'll forgive you."

He winced when he looked at it near his face, then back at her. *Fine then!* He hesitantly opened his mouth and let her place it on his tongue.

His face was crinkled in worry as he started to chew, but eventually, it faded into a widened state of mystification. Seeing his expression change and keeping to her promise to forgive him, she gave him a bright, happy expression.

"It's good right? Apparently, it's hard to make."

Alister thought it may have been the most delicious thing he'd eaten, besides maybe a perfectly cooked piece of meat – which he never got at sea.

His sight moved to look at the remainder in the stall. "What is it?"

"It's chocolate," she answered with a smile. However, he noticed she started rubbing her injured wrist with her other hand in an attempt to soothe it. "It's made from cocoa and milk, which is why it goes to waste so easily. I haven't seen it since I left Luxor."

After watching her when she stepped away from the stall, Alister's feet felt stuck to where he stood. With a solemn sigh, he reached his hand into his coin pouch and flicked a gold coin at the vendor.

Catching back up to her, since she hadn't noticed he hadn't followed straight away, he grabbed her good wrist. She gasped when he slapped a small bag into her upturned hand.

"What's this?" She looked inside before frowning at the small pieces of chocolate.

"A smart man knows when he's right *and* when he's wrong."

"Al–" She paused before she finished saying his name out loud in the overcrowded marketplace. "I told you it was okay as long as you ate it."

"Aye, but that didn't sit right with me."

Her expression remained thoughtful, before a look of sweet contentment curled her lips. She pulled a piece from the pouch and popped it into her mouth. Her cheeks grew flushed like they often did with arousal at the taste. He blinked at her reaction.

They continued their shopping, but Alister noticed Rosetta hadn't bought anything but the piece of chocolate she'd forced him to eat.

He'd never had any intention to buy anything in the first place, but he wasn't too beaten up at losing an entire gold coin since he'd gotten her to smile so warmly.

She stopped them at a jewellery store, and he rolled his eyes so hard, he thought he may go blind in the other.. He knew she would at some point start making them peruse some.

In rare times in the past when Alister may have spent time with a woman and walked market streets, there was always tension within him. Women always wanted him to buy things for them, commenting on how something was pretty, or saying 'I've always wanted something like that'.

He despised it.

He hated it all the way down to his bones, his soul.

The number of times he'd stormed away from a woman in a huff because of her insistent, annoying begging, he couldn't count on one hand. He expected the same from her and already, the swirl of fire began to swell in his belly.

He tried to supress his growing anger.

His brows drew together while she looked over a golden necklace and placed it over his collar bones like she was trying to pick something for him. She must not have thought it suited him because she placed it back down and moved them along. She didn't seem interested in anything for herself.

She's not going to ask me for anything?

"You wear a lot of jewellery," she commented with humour. "Have you ever bought a piece of it?"

He looked over his fingers that almost held a ring each. He could feel his golden ring dangling from his ear and his mother's gift still knocking against his sternum.

"Nay. Almost all of it is booty."

For the first time, Alister noticed Rosetta didn't wear a single piece of it. She had no rings, didn't wear a bracelet or necklace, and her ears weren't pierced to hold anything.

"For a woman, you wear none. I find that strange."

She took them to a clothing stall and placed her fingers over her lips in thought as she looked through the white tunics available. "I've been gifted enough, but I sold all of it. I'd rather wear something I've bought myself or stolen."

Her face brightened. She pulled a bright white, crisp tunic and pressed it against his chest.

"Hmm. You, shop vendor." The man came forward and respectfully nodded to his potential customers. "Do you have anything like this, but bigger?"

Alister looked down at the shirt, and then back up when the man said yes. He started rummaging through the crates on the ground.

"I don't need more clothes."

"You do," she laughed. "A man should feel good in what he wears."

"I'm comfortable in what I've got." He gestured to the breeches he wore, the dull tunic covering him, and the doublet coat around his shoulders. He had a couple of spare pants and shirts. "Don't need much more than this."

She pinched the front of his shirt, tugging it away from his skin. "This thing looks a hundred years old. For someone wanting to show off wealth with fancy jewellery, you dress like you're poor."

She pressed a bigger tunic to his chest and nodded in approval. She gave it to him, despite what he'd said.

"I'm far from poor, Rosetta."

"Yes, but you dress it," she answered blankly while she went through more shirts and eventually pressed one against herself.

The wrist cuff was slightly frilly and would droop, but other than that, it was similar to the button up she usually wore.

"I'll take this one." She handed the man the cost of it.

Damnit, Alister didn't want to look poor. Relinquishing the price of the tunic she'd picked for him to the vendor, he chased after her when she walked away. She was surprisingly spritely.

She tilted her head to the side to peek up at him from under her hat, giving a small look of triumph. *How does she always get what she wants?* She always managed to say or do the right thing that had him on the backfoot when it came to her.

Why am I buying this? He asked himself as he emptied more of his pouch to buy new black breeches at a different stall. She'd bought a new pair of tights, a dark brown pair this time.

"I don't need new boots," he complained when she made a comment on the ridiculousness of his foot size after going inside a boot maker's store. The shop was dimly lit and smelt of leather and shoe polish, shoes lining multiple racks.

He was a big man, not just in muscle but also in height. He needed strong feet to keep him steady!

"How long have you had those things?" She gestured to them with a cringe marring her features. "I'll bet years."

She shook her head at him, sitting down on a stool to try on a boot herself. She measured the bottom of it against her old ones first to make sure it was the correct size.

"A man wears a good boot until it's got holes."

"Ew! That's how you lose your toes to foot rot!"

"Not if you take care of them," he huffed, folding his arms across his chest. He couldn't believe he was having this argument with her.

"And do you?"

Well, no. Still, didn't mean his toes were going to fall off.

She started stomping around in the boots she'd tried on, her face heavy with concentration. Then she placed her hands on her hips and nodded at no one, almost as though she was having a secret conversation in her mind.

When he didn't answer, she raised a brow at him.

"I bet in the storm we faced, your feet were slipping about." His lips thinned at her words, not liking that she was right. "That wouldn't have happened if you'd had boots with grip."

Now that was an argument he found hard to disagree with. Being steady at the helm at all times mattered to Alister.

She's too bloody smart for her own good! He bought the black pair she'd picked out for him by slapping coins onto the vendor's table so hard, it thudded and spooked him.

Since they had both bought multiple items, they were wearing satchels over their shoulders to carry everything. She'd made him throw out his old boots and wear his new ones while she tucked her new ones into her satchel.

"Enough, lass!" he eventually shouted when she was trying to put a hat on his head. The yellow dyed feather sticking out of it was disgusting and the idea of wearing it made his skin crawl. He felt ridiculously foolish with it on his head. "I don't need help dressing. Been doing it myself my whole life."

Tilting her head back with glee, the loud boisterous laugh she let out made multiple people jump with fright. "I was wondering how far I could go before you stopped me."

You! "You!" He pointed two fingers at her with squinted eyes. "You're an annoying little pain, you know that?"

She placed her hand over her heart. "I do try my darn hardest to be."

The tension in his shoulders swiftly dissipated, her playfulness deflating his irritation quickly.

She took them from the stall and led their stroll once more, her feet stepping over the cobblestone pathway and dirt that covered it.

Concern started to creep into his features when she began to lead them away from the markets and into town. There were less people, and although that made him more relaxed, he was unsure as to where she was leading them.

Since most people were shopping in the market or busy on the street that held most of the taverns, there weren't many where they were walking. He eyed those they occasionally passed.

"I thought we would be going back to our ships when you were done," he commented, tilting his head towards her.

"Dixy's house of garments is the only place I can guarantee will have quality made dresses," she answered, tilting her head back to him. "I've always wanted to buy one from there."

"Wouldn't any do? You don't even wear dresses often."

A mocking snort came from her.

"Just because I don't doesn't mean I shouldn't own one I like." Her head turned forward and a thoughtful expression fell over her. "Even though I consider myself a commoner now, I was once a duchess. Sometimes, I like to pretend I still am."

It often slipped Alister's mind she hadn't always been a lowly commoner like him. To him, she was a cutthroat pirate. A tricksy thief. A daring sailor captain. A murderer.

What was she like before? Before her hands had been tainted with blood like his. Before she had set out to change her own fate.

He couldn't picture Rosetta any other way than what she was now. A brutal woman who shot and cleaved at men, who wore weapons underneath her skirt. Who moaned and bucked her hips like a whore, rather than stay still like a pure maiden.

But as he examined her while they strolled, he noticed the upturned point of her chin and the way she looked forward through her long bottom lashes. How her shoulders were rolled back with her chest pushed forward. Her hands behind her back showed composure and calmness. Her footsteps were so short, she almost seemed to gracefully glide over the ground.

It was a walk that held superiority and confidence.

Rosetta was usually a stomping imp, walking with one shoulder forward as if she was ready to barge people out of her way.

How had he not seen the difference in the way she had walked on a ship in tights to walking on land in a dress?

She couldn't hide the true her, not with the way she teased him, mocked him, did her horrible laugh, but in between that, she had been playing pretend.

Not once had he noticed.

"Don't most noblewomen walk holding the arm of their male companion?" Alister asked to ridicule her for her act.

"Sometimes." She gave him a raised brow. "I didn't think you wanted me to be that openly affectionate with you."

"Nay, I don't think that is wise in these parts."

"Then why bother asking?" Her words were like a stab, almost as if she had read between the lines of his question.

"Well, I don't know," he grumbled, palming the hilt of his cutlass tighter.

Why did I ask? He wondered if it was because when he walked with a woman, she tended to reach for him. They smothered him in unwanted touches to appease him – mostly for coin.

Not once had Rosetta done that. He was unused to the lack of intimacy he was usually trying to escape.

It made him frown in thought. *Do I want her to do that to me?* The idea of Rosetta holding his arm didn't seem abhorrent to him.

"Also," she said quietly as she leaned closer. "It's rude for a woman to just grab a man's arm. It should be offered."

Hmm. Alister ran his palm over his chin. *I never considered this.*

So, his reaction to shirking a clinging woman from him was not unfounded. He couldn't help crinkling his eyes in humour. Well, that made him feel better about the reactions he'd received for it.

Although Rosetta had purposefully tried to pester him, he'd been surprisingly comfortable beside her while they walked. He thought of her as a part of his crew, and Alister was content being around his crew.

"Unless you want her dead, I wouldn't draw your sword," he heard someone say behind them.

A surprised breath left his chest before Alister turned his head to find Rosetta was no longer beside him. He spun around and found her caught in the arms of a man who had a small knife pressed to her throat.

"Or your gun," another man said next to them with a smirk. This one held a long, thin sword in his hand, semi-crouched as though he expected Alister to suddenly attack, was prepared for it.

Shit. He'd been so preoccupied by their conversation that he hadn't been paying attention to their surroundings. He was used to having his crew with him to protect his back.

"You're barking up the wrong tree, lads," he answered, folding his arms across his chest to appear unphased. Yet, observing Rosetta in danger got his pulse unsteady. Strange; usually, he didn't care.

Her head was tilted back like she was trying to shy away from the edge of the knife at her neck. It exposed the pale column of her throat, making her look undeniably helpless.

His brows twitched to a frown when he expected her eyes to look beseechingly at him, and they didn't. She appeared relaxed, her expression almost... bored.

"We know exactly who you are. There's a pretty bounty on your head."

When his eyes narrowed into a glare, the one holding her pressed the knife closer. Alister didn't take in the details of the men, unable to tear his eyes away from Rosetta and the blade glinting menacingly in the sun.

They're not bounty hunters. They would have gone straight for the head if they were. Bounty hunters were generally smarter than this.

"It's double if I'm alive so that wretched queen can hang me herself."

Alister scoffed out a laugh at the ridiculous notion. The only way he would ever face the Queen was when he was nothing more than a head without its corpse.

Bounty hunters knew this. Too many had died by his hands to risk being this foolish.

"You're awfully attached to this one, aren't you?" the one holding the knife laughed.

Aye, I am. How attached was the question.

Would he risk his own life to save Rosetta?

When they'd been sailing in this direction, he'd told her he would protect his own skin before hers. Now that he was faced with this dilemma, he couldn't say he felt the same.

"She's rather pretty." The one holding her brushed his crooked nose over the side of her face, as though smelling her. Her lips twitched into a grimace; seeing her uncomfortable at the touch made his gut twist. "Wouldn't mind having her for myself for a night."

The second man revealed a set of iron shackles he had hidden behind his back. "Give us your wrists or we'll dice her."

His eye once more found Rosetta, who was still staring at him. Her expression had fallen back to the previously dull one, but she must think he had no intention of helping her.

He was unsure how to do that without complying with what they said or risking her life.

Then a grin formed across his features.

He realised he didn't need to do anything.

"Nay," he chuckled, unfolding his arms. "I'm not the one you should be worried about."

They turned their heads to each other in confusion, right before Rosetta snuck her hand out from inside her dress.

She pulled her pistol from its holder, threw her hand up, and placed it under the man's chin. He had no chance to react before she pulled the trigger and shot him.

Blood sprayed over the side of her face, shoulder, and neck. Alister swiftly grabbed his own gun and shot the one beside her before he could do anything.

One fell to the dirt right after the other.

Pedestrians scattered quickly, avoiding them after witnessing them murder two people. It didn't matter they had been attacked first; they were the ones who had killed.

"Thanks for giving me the chance to reach for my pistol,"

Rosetta stated as she bent down and started going through their attackers' clothing, flipping their coats and tugging at their pants.

"Smart thinking on your part."

"They always think I'm helpless because I'm in a dress. It's why I love wearing one in port." She shook her head, but he could see her shoulders shaking with silent laughter. "Nothing is more priceless than watching a man realise he's made a grave mistake. Instant regret is such a wonderful expression."

She straightened to her feet while keeping her hands hidden behind her back. "That's why I was never worried if this ever happened. Now, pick a hand."

His forehead crinkled deeply, but he picked her left hand.

"Ha! Unlucky choice." She threw a very light coin purse at him. "I get the heavier one."

Just as he caught it in his fist, she brought her other one forward and poured a few silver coins into her palm. She placed them inside her dress and threw the empty pouch onto the ground on top of the bodies.

Alister did the same, eyeing her over. *She's not upset?* She just had her life threatened because of him.

Although he was thankful she wasn't shouting at him – he wouldn't have reacted well if she had – he thought the hot-tempered Rosetta would have been berating him for this. Instead, she placed her palms on either side of his face to gently hold it.

"What's that expression for?" His brows drew together between her hands. Her expression seemed soft and sincere as she looked up at him, her blue eyes catching the sunlight and shining behind her freckles. Those spots seemed even darker than before, and he thought perhaps even a few new speckles had joined them. "Thank you for coming with me today. I'm actually having fun."

Has she always been so... bubbly?

Had Alister just never noticed Rosetta could be warm like this or was this a new development? The way she'd been with him this day felt strange, but it didn't completely feel out of character.

A sweet woman surrounded by filthy pirates. It was like she was a giant sunflower surrounded by nothing but dirt. She'd stood out the moment he'd met her, and even from a distance, she drew attention.

Why was he only just now realising this? He'd been witnessing this for months.

When he didn't respond, too busy losing himself in her glowing pretty face, she moved her hands and flicked him on the forehead.

"Despite the fact that you would have let me die."

She turned away from the crime scene they just created, heading towards the shop as if nothing had happened.

Alister was sure he'd have to pay off the guards at some point. That's if he wasn't with his crew when they tried to arrest them for this. If he was... well, good luck to them.

"Considered helping you for a moment."

"Pfft!" She waved her hand dismissingly. "Liar. Even if that were true, there was very little you could have done."

"Too bad for them you're a tricky bitch," he chuckled, earning himself a smirk. She even threw him a wink.

Then she started wiping the blood from her skin with the skirt of her dress, revealing the layer of white frills beneath the top layer.

"And I just had a bath. Was hoping to stay clean before we set sail again." She pulled a few strands of her hair forward and groaned. "Maybe I can dunk my head somewhere."

He reached his hand forward to wipe splatter from her jaw that she'd missed with his thumb. "Blood's a good colour on you."

While she was laughing at him for what he'd said, he turned his head to look over his shoulder, to make sure they weren't being followed. He was still rather angry they'd been snuck up on.

"We're a pretty good team," she mumbled.

He'd been thinking the same thing. "You argue with me too much."

"That's because you're arrogant!"

"You also never listen to me!"

She elbowed him in the kidney, so he pushed her to the side by palming her head. Their banter was cut short when she took them to a shop door and opened it. A bell rang above.

Alister stood in front of it, unsure if he was meant to follow inside or not. He'd rather not stand in a shop meant for women, so he leaned up against the wall next to the door with his arms folded.

People gave him odd looks, since he was standing in front of dress shop, but they didn't stare long when his glaring good eye captured both of theirs.

Impatiently, he waited.

CHAPTER ELEVEN

Rosetta yanked the crossing ties at the back of her dress. She had her back to a mirror in her navigation room so she could see what she was doing.

The new dress she'd bought was made of much better quality than the pale yellow one she'd had. This one actually had boning in it to make it stiffer around the torso and chest. It pushed her breasts up and together, creating a much more obvious line of cleavage.

It also had an additional layer underneath, making it fluff out to the sides more. It was a three-layer dress and should keep her much warmer, especially since it had long sleeves.

She brushed the front of it with her hands once she was done tying it, a smile forming as she looked it over in the mirror.

I love this colour. It was a dark forest green with light green leaves stitched across it.

It looked rich, and she couldn't help noticing it made her dark hair stand out even more. It made her look strong, like a tree that could never be knocked over, no matter how much it was pushed or how hard the elements bashed it.

She felt like it represented her perfectly.

As usual, she'd altered the sides so she could easily reach in to grab her weapons. Sewing it neatly had been one of her tasks this afternoon once she was done shopping.

When she was dressed, she worked on getting her hair into a large braid that eventually ended behind one ear before plaiting over her shoulder.

She gave a sigh. It wasn't neat – it was a messy, uneven braid. She didn't think she could be bothered re-doing it. Sometimes, Naeem helped her to do her hair, but he wasn't here to do so.

Her new boots were hidden beneath her skirt, and they made heavy clomping noises against the timber of her ship as she made her way off it.

Those of her crew she had been with for the longest were waiting for her on the other side of the gangplank on the boardwalk.

"Hey, Captain!" one of them greeted with a grand smile.

She was thankful they looked refreshed after their stay at Madame Lillian's brothel.

"Where are we off to?" asked another, his smile just as bright.

It appeared they all wanted to impress; they looked clean, had their best clothes on, and even brushed their hair.

"Well, don't you all look dashing!" she giggled, gesturing her hands at them. "What's the occasion?"

"We still haven't had a proper celebration for getting the Laughing Siren."

She noticed a blush heating the cheeks of Keat, the man often in her crow's nest, as he said, "We thought we should look as lovely as you normally do when we're in port."

There were eight of them, and Rosetta would trust every single one of them with her life. The fact they were dishing out fine words and wanting to celebrate with her meant much.

She started walking down the pier with them in tow.

"Well, I was thinking we could go from bar to bar until we find one we like." Then she clapped her hands together with a squeal of joy. "Ethan knows how to play the piano! We should find a tavern with one."

"Rosetta!" a loud, boisterous voice called, making her stare further down the boardwalk to see who called her. "My sweet Rose," Pierre called again, waving his arm in the air like an idiot. "Don't you just look– UCK!"

He was pushed so hard to the side, he almost fell over. She watched Alister chasing him with a finger pointed at his face. He was the one who'd pushed him.

"Not again," he snapped when Rosetta came upon them.

He quickly turned to her. Just as she opened her mouth to say something, he rubbed the back of his neck and said, "You look nicer than you did last night."

Her brows drew together. *Was that supposed to be a compliment?*

She realised it was when his lips drew together into an irritated pout. He pointed at Pierre again. "This is your fault."

The blond-haired man threw his hands forward in a confused shrug, not sure what he'd done wrong when he was just being himself. Maybe that was the problem.

Needing to save them both, Rosetta grabbed the skirt of the dress and pulled it to the side.

"As much as I like the sea, I miss the colour of forests. I thought I should bring some of it with me."

"It looks good on you," Alister grumbled, turning his sight away from her.

She smiled. *That's better.*

"I thought I said I'd meet you at The Lazy Mermaid," she commented, eyeing the different crowd of his men he had with him, besides Glen Darkley and his son, Derek, and Pierre. They must spend most of their time with Alister when he was in port.

His gaze almost seemed to caress over her plaited hair, her face, the way her dress fitted over her torso, all the way down to her skirt hovering just slightly above the ground. There was something more to the appreciative look he gave her, something *darker*.

"Aye, but I thought this would be easier for you." He brought his eye up and turned his head to his men. "We didn't mind waiting, did we lads?"

A ring of 'nays' followed his question.

"But I was going to hang with my crew for a little while." She gestured to them behind her. "I haven't spent much time with them."

Alister surprised her by coming over and putting his arm around her shoulders, turning her so she was facing her men. Her body stiffened under his arm, unused to open attention in front of others.

"She's hanging with us again tonight, lads. Got it?" Her lips parted in shock at his words. "If you want her, you'll join us."

They looked between each other but nodded while shrugging. They didn't seem to mind who they were with or where they were, so long as they were with her.

With a defeated sigh, she nodded. "Looks like that's the plan now."

He turned them and took a step forward to start their walk before he removed his arm. Pierre came to take over, putting his arm around her shoulders and forcing her to walk under his heavy weight as he rudely pushed most of it onto her.

"Did you dress him?" He hiked his thumb at Alister. "Never seen him look so nice."

Alister's lips thinned tightly, and she tried to stop the snort making its way through her nose.

"He doesn't need help dressing. He's been doing it for years, apparently," she answered with a sly grin of humour.

She had to admit, Alister did look rather splendid tonight. He was wearing the crisp white tunic she'd picked out. It wasn't a button up but instead had a deep vee tied with strings.

His black breeches weren't as baggy and shone with newness. Even his boots sticking out from under the cuffs of his pant legs drew her attention.

With his hair still the way she'd styled it earlier, he looked wealthier. It suited him better with all the jewellery he liked to wear. *He looks rather handsome tonight.*

Seeing Alister was growing sourer by the minute, when Pierre opened his mouth to comment on it further, she stepped on his toes.

"Ow!" He shied away from her. "Why is it whenever I'm close to you, you hurt me?"

"It's not my fault you're so clumsy!"

Both their crews chuckled as they made their way further into town. People made way for them, considering they were a fairly large crowd of rugged and ruthless looking pirates.

Eventually, they made it to The Lazy Mermaid tavern.

"Get lost, ye lot," Derek demanded as he barged his way to a group of men sitting at the end of a long table, pushing them by the shoulders to leave.

The table was more towards the back of the bar than the one they'd occupied the previous night. To accommodate all of them sitting together, they dragged another one to the end.

Pierre and Derek took the end again just as Alister took a single chair and placed it at the head. The person who was about to sit in it fell to the ground.

Just as Rosetta went to sit with her men, he pulled her arm and made her sit on his lap. Her men spread themselves out amongst those of his crew who joined them. He eyed the table, seemingly pleased with the collection, before his brows drew tight.

"Where is Naeem?" He turned his head to her. "Since he isn't guarding your ship tonight, I expected him with us."

Rosetta turned her gaze away to look at the table. "He's busy relaxing. He'll be back in the morning to help me make sure the ship is ready."

"Hmm." It looked as though he wanted to ask about it, but eventually, he just shook his head. "First round's on me, lads. The rest you can pay for yourselves."

He told one of them to get their drinks since there didn't seem to be any barmaids working in this tavern.

Rosetta squinted her eyes. "You are so stingy with everything else but paying for booze. Why?"

He gave a laugh when a bottle was placed in his hand, before one was given to her. "Because, if they are having a good time, I'm having a good time."

"So really, it's for a selfish reason."

"Oh aye, got me dead to rights there, lass. If you haven't noticed, I don't move from my seat. If I pay, they stay with me."

"Lazy," she poked.

He wrapped his arm around her waist tighter and placed his elbow on the short armrest of his chair, leaning his cheek against his fist.

"I spend most of my time at the helm or checking the stocks of my ship." He gave a small, disgruntled scowl. "Let me be lazy; I think I've earned it."

She swiftly moved her hand forward to point at him. "I do that too."

"Aye, but you're younger than me. You've got energy I don't."

After last night, she couldn't help thinking that was the biggest lie that had ever come out of his mouth. *I'm still sore.*

The night was similar to the previous one. They gambled, but with different games of dice. They spoke of different events they'd shared together. The chatter seemed livelier with her crew present, all of them speaking about achievements before they'd met.

They all get along really well. Since they'd sailed together for so long, they'd all gotten to know each other enough that there wasn't any tension. His men were speaking about a time quite a few years ago when they had their old sailing vessel.

"Actually," Rosetta murmured, playing with the ring dangling from Alister's earlobe. "I've never heard how you acquired your ship."

A beaming grin spread across his features, revealing his wide, sharp canines. She only ever saw them when he smiled this brightly.

"She wants to hear how we got the Howling Death, lads," he said to the table, hefting her higher up his thigh, as though he wanted her to be closer like he was pleased.

"Now wasn't that a day!" Pierre exclaimed.

Alister raised the hand holding his bottle and held the neck with his thumb and index finger, splaying his other fingers out. He waved it through the air like he was showing her a painting.

"Picture this. We'd been high tailing it over the seas after a heavy storm damaged our old ship because we hit some rocky shallows. What was this, four years ago?"

"Maybe a few months more," Derek confirmed.

"We were taking on water, rushing to fix that old thing as best we could. She was a good ship, but smaller." He placed the bottle on his knee, swirling it. "We were all tired, working day and night to make sure she stayed afloat. Just when we got it in working order, there it was, sailing over the horizon and heading straight for us."

It wasn't often Alister was the lead storyteller.

She couldn't help smiling as she watched him speak with a sense of glee. He was obviously very fond of this tale.

"They were pirate hunters. They knew our ship, wanted the bounty on our heads. They didn't know the old captain had died a year before and were still after him."

"So, your ship came sailing towards you?"

"Oh, aye!" he laughed. "Came sailing right into my hands. I knew when I watched it coming towards us with the bony finger of the grim reaper pointing from the bow, like death was coming for me that I had to have it."

"It helped that our old ship had seen better days," Pierre added. "We needed a new one anyway."

"When I saw that grim reaper pointing at me, I knew it would send fear into the hearts of our enemies. I sacrificed our old boat so we could jump ship and take over theirs. We lost many men that day."

"It was a sea of blood on the deck," Kent threw in. "It took days to clean it all. I should know, I was one of those who had to!"

"It was also the day Cap'in lost his eye," Derek said, his gaze fixed on Alister's face.

"I haven't lost it!" he yelled, smashing the end of his nearly empty bottle against the edge of the table so hard, it shattered. He threatened Derek with the jagged spikes of glass. "It just doesn't bloody work."

The murderous, foul glare he wore showed just how angry he was.

"You hurt your eye that day?" she asked to draw his attention away from the old man who had narrowed his eyes in return.

"Aye. Was fighting the captain. He was an ogre of a thing, nearly as big as me. Managed to cut me down the face right before I sliced his throat. They fought until their last breaths, refusing to surrender."

Pierre nodded with a ponderous expression. "If we were destined to die, it would have been that day."

"Sounds like a battle," she said, pretending to appear wowed, just to make them feel good.

"It was like a war in the middle of the ocean," Kent laughed. "Guns firing, swords clanging. Men swinging on ropes while others jumped from the quarterdeck railing to try and sneak up on us from above."

Pierre smacked his shoulder to shut him up so he could speak. "If it wasn't for Derek, I'd probably be a hobbling peg walker like him!"

"I regret saving yer life every day, ye piece of shit!"

Rosetta bounced when Alister kicked his leg forward to boot the underside of the table, stopping them from arguing before they'd even started.

The conversation continued, men sharing little details, how they had saved another man or were saved themselves. It was obviously a day that brought them tightly together and deepened their bonds.

The conversation fizzled out into another tale.

The only time Rosetta was able to get up was when Alister was challenged into an arm wrestle by Kent. Of course, he accepted, refusing to back down. When she went to step away to give them room, Alister pulled her by the skirt of her dress.

"Nay. You'll be staying here."

"I'm just going to the bar."

With his elbow on the table and his hand in position for Kent to grab it, he looked her over. Then he nodded – not that she was looking for his approval. He reached into his purse sack and pulled out a few coins, asking her to get him another as well.

Leaving the men to be men, Rosetta made her way to the bar. She bought herself a bottle of rum, since it was one of the cheapest liquors she could stand drinking, getting him something stronger.

On the way back, however, she overheard a conversation that caught her attention. She slowed to listen in, her gaze falling over three men seated in a booth. There was a map rolled out on the table between them, their gazes fixed to it. The candlestick in front of them seemed to make their awed faces glow with heat.

"How'd you get it?" one of the men said, excitement and shock widening his grin. He was half-bald with a receding hair line, his face shaven but dirty.

The one who spoke next obviously owned the map. "Stole it from some drunk passed out last night. He'd been showing it to everyone. It was like he wanted someone to steal it."

His hair was short and dark, his eyes near onyx. He was thin, but had a piercing hint to his features, a meanness to him present in the way he sat. It was obvious he was either a pirate or had been at one point.

The third man never spoke, his hair hidden under a plain red bandana.

"With all the coin we got, we could pitch in to buy a small boat."

"Those fools gambled us straight into a boat! Could you imagine what we could do with this much treasure?" He tapped the map with his index finger.

"Finally get our own ship and crew. We've been waiting for this day!"

Unable to help herself, she stepped a little closer to see the map better.

I haven't seen that one before. It wasn't one she'd given to Alister, nor was it one he had crossed out in his desk.

My funds are low. Alister was right; there was a chance they may not be so successful when they sailed again.

Her eyes fell to where she saw their crews sitting, watching Alister take back his own seat. The wrestle must have ended, and she'd missed seeing who the victor was.

She glanced back to the three people with the map.

With a sultry smile, Rosetta walked with both the bottle of rum she had for herself and the scotch Alister asked for.

She fell into their laps.

"Hello boys," she giggled with slurring words – even

though she wasn't drunk at all. "Fancy a drink and a woman?"

They quickly rolled up the scroll and eyed each other.

"What do you want?" the map owner asked with squinted eyes. His tone was quick and sharp, telling her he didn't appreciate her little interruption.

She was laying across the one who never spoke so she could have her shoulder against the map holder's chest.

"Well," she pouted. "I just discovered my man was sleeping with another woman. Decided I would pay him back by trying to find multiple others to take me. You lot looked rather fun, so brought booze and the space between my thighs... for free."

Once more, they eyed each other. Slowly, she watched their faces turn into grins.

She had to hide the devilish smirk trying to make its way onto her own. *Tricking morons like this is like taking booze from a drunk man.*

"Well, little lady," the map holder chuckled. Grabbing her, he pulled until she was seated over his lap so he could cup between her legs with a rough grab. She had to stifle the wince when he squashed her delicate pussy as if he was an ill-mannered barbarian. "Aren't you lucky we are more than happy to help you get revenge."

"We also don't mind sharing you," the balding man added, reaching forward to take the scotch from her hand. He bit the cork off and was about to take a deep swig as he said, "Looks like the gods are in our favour tonight!"

Alister gripped Kent's fist in a tight grip and started pushing sideways as the gorilla of a man did the same.

Their clasped hands shook violently with strain.

Kent had always been strong and, on the rare occasion Alister was exhausted from manning the helm, he'd beaten him.

But not this time. Even though Alister's hand started moving towards the table like he was about to lose, a smirk formed across his features. They'd already had the battling waves of almost touching the table, fighting for dominance while waiting to see who had more endurance.

Alister gave a sudden burst of strength behind his push. His hand came over to slam Kent's down against the table with a loud thud. Cheers rang out while others gave disgruntled noises. Coins were thrown on the table as bets were paid up.

Alister moved to return to his seat.

"You should have asked me when I was drunk," he chuckled to the man. "You may have won then."

Others began challenging Kent and he took up every one, needing to prove himself after losing. Alister watched with humour, knowing he'd most likely win against the rest.

Even Pierre wasn't as strong as Kent.

Derek may be, though. Unfortunately, the old sea dog didn't like playing. He said it hurt his withered bones.

It took Alister a while to realise something was missing. He wiggled the fingers of both arms. His hands were empty of a cold bottle and a warm Rosetta.

It's been a while. His head lifted from the table so he could look around the tavern.

He knew he'd spotted her at the bar right after he'd won, but he could no longer see her. *Where the hell did she run off to?*

A terrible feeling grabbed at his stomach. He started to get up just as he thought, *she better not be on top of another man.*

His question didn't linger long – not even a few seconds later, he saw her coming towards them. His brows drew together as he sat back down.

Actually, she was running.

Alister watched someone grab her by the wrist, holding onto it as they spun her. They backhanded her so hard across the face, she stumbled to the side and into the table of their crews right near the middle.

The man who hit her had two others following him.

Alister immediately got to his feet, his chair sliding back so swiftly, it overbalanced.

"You fucking bitch! Give it back!"

The man stepped forward, as though he intended to grab her, but tensed when he saw the entire table stand. They rose behind her like an ocean wave of eyes and brawn.

"Say hello to my friends," she laughed, pushing off the table to get back to her feet. She placed the back of her wrist against her cheek as a small crowd of men surrounded her.

Alister was already stomping his way towards the man. He looked at Alister steadily approaching him, right before he grabbed his wrist and twisted his arm behind him in a hold he couldn't escape. It arched his back and forced him into submission.

"I'm going to break every bone in your body for that," he nearly growled, twisting the man's arm harder until he gave a yelp of pain. "How dare you fucking hit her."

The other two had already gone wide-eyed in fear, taking a step back. They were outnumbered and they knew it.

"But she stole from us!"

His teeth clenched, the bridge of his nose crinkled tightly. "I don't give a shit what she did."

"He's right," Rosetta said in his defence with a mischievous smile. "Have mercy on him; I did steal something."

Alister leaned closer to his ear, looking at him through his good eye. "I don't give mercy."

He proceeded to bend the man's arm until he felt it give

way, the long bone of his forearm snapping. A loud crunch filled their ears right before he let out a high-pitched scream.

He pushed him into their crews while the two other men fled from the tavern before they could be targeted. Their men started beating him he fell, taking over from Alister while he turned his rage to Rosetta.

"You leave my sight for two seconds." He pointed his index and middle fingers at her as he stomped closer. "And you put yourself in danger."

She got herself hit!

She should have backed away from him in fear with how he approached her with his face twisted. She'd stirred up trouble when all he wanted to do was relax with his men! Instead of retreating, she lifted her hands and unfurled a piece of parchment in front of him.

When he tried to swipe it away, she literally pushed it into his face. "It's another map to Dustin's trove."

That made him pause.

He eyed over the piece of parchment when she drew it back. She moved it to the side so she could see him, that smile still present on her features.

"I knew you didn't have this one." She turned so they could both face it, her back almost pressed against his chest. "I've never seen this island before, so I'm wondering if it's not charted by Queen Mary Anne. That must mean something, right?"

The treasure hunter in him outweighed the fury he felt, and he reached forward to hold the side of it to examine it better.

I don't remember seeing the name of this island either. Its shape was familiar, though. *Dead Man's Island?* The shape was odd, almost triangular.

His eye fell over her in front of him, sweeping over the braid of her hair before he ran it over her cheerful expression. He even looked at the curve of her small nose, her pouty lips, her rounded chin.

She risked herself... to get this for me? He knew she did when she let him take it so he could look over it further.

She knows how much finding Dustin's trove means to me. She'd gone out of her way to help him procure another map so he could be a step closer to his goal. Maybe it was selfish of him, but even he thought it was worth the risk.

"You said you weren't ready to go south," she said. "Hopefully, this one is in the northern oceans."

He pointed at her with the hand holding the map. "Don't put yourself in danger next time. Let me know and we'll help you."

She gave a shrug, tilting her nose up at him. "Didn't want to risk them leaving before I could grab you. I knew you would help if I got to you."

His lips pressed into thin lines of irritation. He couldn't fault her logic.

He went back to his seat, and she followed behind. He threw the map in front of Derek and Pierre, the rest of their men throwing the man who'd hit her outside. Whether he was alive or not, Alister didn't know. He dearly hoped not.

"Looks like she got us another map," he said while Rosetta sat over his thigh. He was pleased she'd returned to it willingly since he was rather fond of her perched there.

Pierre swiped it from the table before Derek could, making him grunt. He placed his hand on his chin in thought as he looked it over. He eventually gave it to him so he could examine it as well.

A small conversation started over it, the men posing similar questions about its unknown location as he and Rosetta had. The fact it was unknown meant it very much could be the real deal rather than the fakes he kept finding.

"I hope you don't mind, but I had to sacrifice your drink to get it," she said, turning her face towards him.

He shook his head. "Nay, don't mind losing a few coins for a map." He frowned when he realised he could see a welt forming on her face. "How's your cheek?"

He lifted his hand to softly brush the tips of his fingers against it, a bruise already blooming.

"Fine," she shrugged. "It's how stupid men assert their dominance over women they can't control." Her voice quieted, almost as though she was talking to herself rather than him. "I'm used to it."

Alister didn't like hearing that admission.

"Are we going to head to this when we leave Tortaya?" Pierre asked Alister when their conversation finally turned.

"Nay. We're right in the middle of two locations that could hold booty. We'll check them first before we head back out to open seas. I also have to figure out where this is."

"Where do *you* think it is?" Pierre asked Derek, who had been sailing for much longer than both of them.

Alister slid his chair closer so they could speak in hushed whispers. He didn't mind that Rosetta was with them; Alister just rarely let his crew know where they were heading. Only the three of them knew where they were sailing or what direction they were going.

Once he discovered Dustin's trove, he didn't want those on his ship to jump off at port and lead others to it.

It's mine. He wanted to own it, possess it for himself and his men only.

"Maybe it'll be on the painted map in my navigation room," Rosetta offered. "It's much more updated than anything you have on your ship. Some of the places don't have names because they have only sailed past them."

She's absolutely right.

Every second he sat looking over this parchment she had procured for him, the more he felt it might actually be real. It made him very appreciative of this cunning, beautiful woman he had on his lap. He knew exactly how he wanted to reward her.

He started bunching up the skirt of her dress to lift it, excitement brightening his features. She was going to have a very happy Alister between her thighs tonight. He was so pleased with her, he might focus on her pleasure rather than his own.

Her thighs pressed together when she felt his palm caress between her knees, but that didn't stop him from brushing his hand up between her thighs.

With how close they were to the table, no one would notice he'd snaked his hand under her skirt and was making an unmistakable path to his favourite place on her body.

"I think I've seen this island before," Alister told them to make sure they weren't aware of what he was doing. "Even if it's not on the wall, I'll eventually remember where."

He felt her tense when he pushed his hand between her closed thighs to cup her with his entire hand.

"H-hey," she whispered, her hands coming forward to grab his forearm, as if she was trying to stop him.

She gasped when he slipped his middle finger inside her core to find she was wet, surprisingly snug around it.

"You owe me a drink," she mumbled unhappily, yet he could feel her channel spasming around his finger, like it wanted to suck it in further. "I lost mine getting this for you."

She wants a drink? More than what he was currently doing as he started to move his finger back and forth?

That didn't sound like the Rosetta he knew.

Even last night, when he'd been touching her while they were playing dice, she hadn't truly tried to stop him.

She leaned closer to whisper, "I'm not drunk enough to do this in public yet."

A grumble fell from him, and he slipped his hand away, palming one of her thighs to knead it in appreciation. He liked the way her thighs felt under his palm. He often gripped them just feel the squish.

"Fine, lass. I'll get one of the lads to get us a drink."

She shook her head. "I want to get it. I don't trust they won't get it wrong again." They did like to get one type of drink, since they were lazy and forgetful.

Alister gave a sigh, releasing her so she could stand. He knew she'd be more receptive to him if she was pleased. When she was on her feet, he grabbed her arm and pulled her to lean over him.

He pointed up at her. "Keep out of trouble this time."

She gave him a warm smile, kissing him on the cheek sweetly and making it tingle in reaction. A frown formed on his face; she rarely did this to him.

"I promise."

He watched her carefully as she walked away.

Before she made it to the bar to order, Pierre and Derek grabbed his attention once more. They were thrilled about the map and wanted to keep talking about it. They were trying to guess where it was, one thinking they knew better than the other.

Even Alister was joining in on their banter; this was a mystery he was excited to unfold.

"I bet ye one silver it's in the east," Derek said to Pierre, the hairs around his lips curling inwards as he grinned confidently.

"I'll take that bet since it's got to be north. That way has more oddly shaped islands."

"It'll be good if it's in the western waters," Alister commented. "We're already this way."

As they were betting, he felt Rosetta sit on his thigh and hand him a bottle. He took a swig of the bottle, tasting scotch on his tongue like he'd asked.

Although he was hoping it was near their current location,

he couldn't help saying, "But I think Derek's right. I think I've seen a land like this near the Sthrill Islands."

That was close to where Rosetta had stolen his ship all those months ago.

"Maybe I won't take that bet. The Sthrill Islands are pretty far east," Pierre commented, once more rubbing at his clean-shaven chin in thought. He even thumbed the small scar over his lips.

"Ha!" Derek exclaimed. "Ye can't back out now. One silver if I'm right."

Ignoring him, Pierre's brows drew in tight. "If you're right, Captain, it'll take us months to sail there if we're going to look at the other places first."

They weren't maps to Dustin's trove, but Alister wouldn't give up the potential for free booty.

"Cap'in knows what he's doing," Derek bit, leaning across the table to smack Pierre upside the head. "We're going there first."

Alister gave a deep chuckle.

"Thanks for the faith, old salt." Then he smacked Pierre up the other side of his head as well. "Listen to your elders, mate."

Rosetta giggled in humour while placing her lips against the side of his neck to kiss it. His skin prickled at the feather light touch.

She must be content now that she has her drink. Since she'd started teasing him, he started to bring her skirt up so he could be happily beneath it.

She freely let him, and his grin grew.

"Hey! You're only a few years older than me." Pierre shot his head towards Alister to defend himself. His words were cut short. He shook his head in what seemed like bewilderment. "Ummm..."

He looked between him and Rosetta, which made Alister

turn his head to the side so he could see it wasn't her who had come to sit on him. He instantly removed his hand from under the strange woman's skirt.

He'd thought it was odd she'd come sit on the side of him he couldn't see with.

"Where's Rosetta?" he asked the men in front of him, looking around the tavern and not finding her.

Shit. Where'd she go? How long had this woman been sitting on his lap?

They gave a shrug in response, looking around as well.

The woman sitting on his lap was a pretty redhead, her face sweet and fragile looking.

He removed his other arm from around her waist. He realised that she'd taken Rosetta's seat and she may have stormed off on him for it! She might be angry, considering she'd just taken a hit to procure this map for him and he hadn't pushed this woman away.

"Are you looking for that woman in the green dress?" She gave a cute pout, as if she was offended.

"What of her?" Alister asked with a deep growl-like tone, anger bubbling beneath his skin.

What if Rosetta had seen his hand up her skirt and decided to let someone else up hers, not knowing he'd thought it was her the entire time? He felt a rush of dread creep over the top of his skull and down his spine. *I'll kill him.*

"She told me to give you this." She lightly smacked the bottom of her bottle into the side of his.

Alister looked at his drink in his hand.

Was that before or after she came to sit with me?

"And that you had lots of coin."

Alister turned his head to Pierre. "What the hell is that supposed to fucking mean?"

"I don't know, man." The emotion he wore was the same one that crawled down Alister's spine. He'd told him to help keep an eye on her, explaining what had happened last night and that he wasn't intending to share her... or himself. "But you might want to find her before it's too late."

Alister pushed the woman, making her gasp in surprise. She stumbled into Derek's lap, and he put his arm around her.

"I'll take care of ye. I like 'em red."

He didn't know how she responded, not when Alister begun making his way through the tavern to see if Rosetta was still inside. He pushed the heads of people sitting down to make way for his large frame.

She's gone. She'd already left, and he found himself running outside into the fresh air. Well, as fresh as this foul-smelling town could give.

He turned around in the street, having no idea which way to go.

Of course, she's already gone! She wouldn't be so stupid to stick around like last time.

She didn't even tell her men she was leaving.

He didn't tell his own as he started making his way down the street, having no idea where she could have gone. For some reason, he found his feet heading towards the hotel he'd taken her to the previous night.

"You, keeper," Alister demanded as he walked up to the counter. "Have you seen the woman I brought here last night?"

He shook his head and righted his square glasses. "No, but you're both welcome to come back here tonight when you do."

Of course, they were. Alister had paid a pretty penny for her bath since it was a luxury most didn't want to afford. He'd done it for her since he'd known it would help her recover.

I took care of her, and she still ran off!

He ran back onto the street and stood there with his fists clenched tightly, feeling his arms shake. He slowly turned his head from side-to-side as he looked each way down the paved road.

I should go back and take that redheaded woman. If Rosetta abandoned him because a woman he didn't want sat on his lap, why should he care? She didn't get rid of her when it was obvious she was on his blind side, and he'd been expecting her on him the entire time.

He should take that prostitute and still kill the man she was planning to be under. *I'll still keep her.*

Alister had decided he wasn't done with her, regardless of if she took a man from port. He'd be angry for a long time, but he wouldn't be able to stop himself from desiring her and he bloody knew it. He'd just take his anger out on her.

He wanted his feet to turn back towards the bar but found himself unable to go that way because, deep down, he didn't want her beneath someone else. He wanted her selfishly to himself. He wanted to stop her.

His eyes scanned over the busy street, trying to figure out which direction to take. Two people caught his attention.

"Oi!" he yelled, stomping his way over to them. "You two are meant to be guarding the ship!"

He couldn't believe they'd abandoned their post. *She told me she trusted them!*

"Oh, Alister," one of them said as he turned around to greet him, dragging the other with him since his arm was around his shoulders. "We were."

"What do you mean you were? Who said you could leave it?"

"Rosetta did," the other said, giving him a wide grin. "Told us we could have a few hours off. We're trying to find some of the crew. Do you know where they are?"

His brows drew together in a deep frown. "When did she say this?"

"How long have we been walking?" one asked the other.

"I don't know, maybe less than ten minutes?" He gave a laugh. "Said she'll take over for a while."

Alister didn't stay to speak with them any longer. He headed straight for the pier.

Why would she go to her ship? Had she taken someone there with her? If she did, he couldn't help finding that foolish.

His pace was brisk, pushing people who got in his way. His bootsteps sounded loud and heavy on the timber of the boardwalk compared to the softness of them on the dirt. As soon as his feet found the gangplank to the Laughing Siren, he heard a soft voice, one that made him slow with a frown.

"And as he sails for his heavenly lagoon,
He finds himself washed in never ending horizons.
Lost and craven, for sweet glittering pearl eyes."

It was a woman singing, and quite beautifully at that. It was almost like a whisper so very few could hear.

"He dost not care if her kiss is filled with dread,
If she drags him down to the swallowing depths.
Not when she has lips of silk that taste like longing."

When he finally finished the incline of the gangplank, keeping his step quiet, he found Rosetta laying against the shrouds in the air. She was by herself, staring off at the black sea crashing small waves.

"Oh, dear sailor, he'll never return to shore.
After finding the young maiden surround by water,
He'll leave with her promise of glittering silver.
Oh, foolish sailor, you'll never return to shore."

She began to hum to herself, a small break in the song.

I thought she couldn't sing. That's what he'd been led to believe. Yet, the voice fluttering over the light wind to him was lovely, tantalising, like a lullaby.

He opened his mouth to speak while taking a few steps closer, but her arm shot to the side. She held her pistol up in the air, unable to point it at him since he was behind her.

"If you're trying to rob my ship, you've got another thing coming," she threatened, wiggling her arm to make sure he could see her gun. "You've got five seconds to get off it before I–"

"What are you doing, Rosetta?" He folded his arms across his chest.

"Alister?" He heard the frown in her voice before she turned on the shrouds to show him there was one crinkling her features. Even with the darkness, the light from the town barely brightening her, he could see it. "What are you doing here?"

"Why do you always ask me that when I ask first?"

She gave a shrug, turning back over to lay against the netted rope holding her up in the air. She wriggled her shoulders as though she was trying to make herself comfortable.

"You surprised me. I just didn't expect to see you." She tilted her head back to take a deep draw from her wine.

His arms folded tighter, his lips thinning harder. "Why did you leave the tavern? I told you you'd be spending the night with me."

Her bottle fell away from her mouth, her shoulders seeming to slump.

"I'm tired, Alister," she sighed, but he noted a hint of creeping sadness in her tone. It strengthened once more. "Decided to let the prostitutes have you for the night. I told that girl to tell you."

She told that woman to come to my lap?

His arms loosened as his forehead crinkled deeply. "And you came here to be by yourself?"

"Yes," she answered quietly.

He couldn't believe this. *She left me with another woman on purpose.* She obviously had no intention of being with another herself. Alister rubbed the back of his neck, unsure how he felt. *Does-Does she actually not care?*

He realised he wanted her to. Alister wanted her to feel as possessive of him as he did her, wanted her to desire him all to herself. *I thought she did.*

"I told you I understand," she continued just as quietly. "I'm too tender to help you tonight. If I can't take you, then I must be understanding that someone else has to." She gave a mocking snort, like she had a thought that made her laugh humourlessly. "Even if I'm alone."

Then she tilted her head back and downed more of her sweet wine.

Alister gave his own snort of quiet laughter. It didn't take a genius to figure out she had done this and very much didn't like it. That quelled the worst of his anger, instead making a swell of warmth spread through his gut.

Oh aye, she wants me to herself.

Alister came forward and put his foot on the railing so he could climb the shrouds.

"What are you doing?" her voice sounded with a hint of confusion.

He threw his back against the netted rope with a harrumph, making himself comfortable next to her.

"I told you, I–"

"I know," he said to cut her off. He put his arm around her shoulders and brought her closer so they were laying against the shrouds together. "It's fine."

It had to be fine, because Alister didn't want Rosetta feeling alone or possibly sad and upset because of him. He didn't want to taint whatever was driving them to be desperately intertwined. He wanted it too much, ached for it too deeply.

Alister also knew women were fickle things. She said she was alright with it now, but he knew well enough that it'd fester inside her. She'd hate him out of resentment for her own decision.

If that means I have to go without for a night in port, so be it. She wasn't trying to change him; he'd come to this decision on his own. It just meant he shouldn't drink much more. *Can't get drunk.* He'd make himself horny if he did.

It took her a while, but eventually, he felt the tension in her body go lax. Her head fell against the nook between his chest and arm.

Alister looked up at the stars twinkling past a clear sky, a subtle wind blowing against them. The air smelt heavily of briny saltwater and the gentle waves crashing against the side of the hull beneath their feet was constant.

The moment was peaceful.

"I thought you couldn't sing."

CHAPTER TWELVE

Rosetta stared up at the sky with a thoughtful pout.

Why is he staying with me? She didn't understand.

The stinging emotion she'd felt in her chest, with no one else to blame but herself, faded. She felt the tension and pooling disappointment in her stomach leave as her body went lax beside him.

"I thought you couldn't sing," he commented.

Rosetta pursed her lips in annoyance.

"If you tell anyone, I'll cut your tongue out," she threatened. "If the men discover I can sing, it'll be relentless. They'll make me sing sea shanties until my throat hurts."

Rosetta sung and danced like a baboon on purpose.

"Your secret is safe with me," he chuckled. "'The Siren's Sailor' is a sweet song. I haven't heard it in years."

She doubted he would have, since it was a song mostly sung by women. It was a song about how a man gave up his search for riches by falling in love with a mermaid with fangs, a beautiful monster who would drag him to depths to be eaten.

She tilted her bottle of wine towards him. "Want some?"

"Did you get that from Pierre?"

It took him a moment, but he eventually grabbed it and drank a small amount.

"No. Half that sweet wine was mine to do with what I wanted and I may have taken a few for myself. You guys kept any booze you found for yourselves, so I had every right to do the same."

She expected him to have more than a large sip, but she shrugged her shoulders when he gave it back.

Her head was resting against his chest, and she found the warmth comforting while they shared a small silence. She was surprised he was letting her lay on the blind side of him. He'd once told her he didn't like people on that side. She figured it was just because he hadn't thought about it when he climbed the shrouds.

She had been feeling despondent earlier, so Rosetta had been thinking about her life, mulling over everything. "Did you think this is where you'd be in life?"

"Aye, always knew I'd be a pirate."

She couldn't help furrowing her brows. "Even when you were a boy?"

"Ever since I was four."

She knew she was stating the obvious when she said, "I didn't." She let her eyes fall over the stars that made her feel small and insignificant in such a large, cruel world. "I never thought about sailing until I was suddenly doing it."

At the time, she was just so miserable that she wanted to escape her life, but it had been daunting. Running away had been frightening and she'd been terrified the first time she stepped foot on a ship.

"I grew up with flowers, tea parties, with the belief that I would go to fancy balls. I was a girl showered with affection and told I had society at my fingertips." A pang lanced her heart as she thought of herself as a child, of the parents she missed dearly. "I never thought I would go through the things I have, that I would do the things I have, that I would one day captain a ship and crew." Rosetta's voice grew small as she whispered, "I never wanted to be a pirate."

The arm around her shoulders drew up, his hand landing

on top of her head in a comforting gesture, but he didn't say anything for a long while.

Rosetta realised she may have said too much and turned her head up. "Sorry, I was just thinking out loud."

She saw he had a thoughtful expression, his gaze remaining on the sky. "My father was 'Mad Dog'."

"You mean Captain Cole 'Mad Dog' McCarthy?"

"Aye, my real name's Alister McCarthy. Didn't like it much, so I changed it."

"Didn't you say he was the last captain of your crew?" Her eyes opened wide, and she patted him on the chest. "Wait... You shot your own father in the head?"

He gave a curt nod, tapping his forehead with a finger. "Right between the eyes. Asked me to, was so sick he could barely stand."

"Why didn't you tell me earlier?"

"Because people thought he was insane. I changed my name because I didn't want people to think I was insane too. Paine suits me better, anyway."

She guessed that was true.

I didn't tell him my name was Briggs. She probably never would have if he hadn't figured it out on his own.

"How did you end up on his ship, then?"

He stayed quiet for a long while. She could see he was unsure about sharing his past with her. *I'm surprised he even told me of his father.*

"It's okay, you don't have to tell me."

"My ma was a prostitute, and he didn't trust that I was his at first. Refused to claim me. He knew it when he saw me a second time when I was four." He reached up and grabbed a couple of strands of his own hair to look at. "Apparently, I looked so similar to him even as a child that it was hard to deny it."

He dropped his hair and stared up, seeming to think on his

next words.

"Mad Dog was a nobleman before his sailing ship was taken over by a band of pirates and he was forced to join them. He got a taste for killing and raiding ships, realising he could earn more money than he had ever earned doing good, honest work. He eventually worked his way up to captain."

He started wriggling a ring around his finger with his thumb until it was almost off. He handed it to her to examine.

The ring itself was made of gold, an etching of a simple family crest on it, some sort of dog, mostly likely a sniffing hound.

"That was his family's ring, and he told me when I was old enough to wear it, he would take me from my ma and make me a pirate. He visited her almost every year, checking in, paying her for raising me, making sure I was growing well." He gave a dark laugh, a small shake of his head making his hair sway. "She hated it, fought him on it, but he eventually took me when I was eleven, despite her protests."

He gestured for her to return the ring and he slipped it back on his finger. "It didn't fit, but he knew he wouldn't be coming back for a while."

"You were eleven when you started sailing?" That meant he'd been sailing for eighteen years.

She frowned. *Unless he's had his birthday since we met.* She'd had hers but never told anyone.

"Aye, and I have barely been on land since." He tapped her in the forehead a few times. "Which is why when I tell you how to do something, you should do it."

She grabbed his hand to stop him. "No, I don't think I will."

"Of course not," he sighed roughly. "Why would you listen to me?"

She turned her body so she was tilted towards him, subtly bringing her outer knee up to rest next to his. That gave him room to bring his arm further down to hold her better, resting his hand against her lower back.

Rosetta carefully brought her hand up and ran her fingers through the long, black stubble on his jaw. She gave him a small smile when he turned his head so he could see her, since she was laying on his blind side.

She took a large sip of her sweet wine and offered him some. He lifted his hand and shook it. "Nay."

Alister saying no to booze? She gave a snort of laughter. *Well, isn't that strange?* Honestly, this whole night was strange.

She continued to stroke his jaw. *He told me of his family.* Rosetta didn't think he ever would, considering he shut down any conversation about his mother. He told her it was none of her business.

"Do you know how to navigate using the stars?" he asked, making it obvious he wanted to deviate from their current conversation.

"I may not be able to count well, but I know how to follow the sky, Alister."

He pointed to a group of stars. "So, you know that's the Ursa minor?"

"The little bear? Of course." She pointed to another, larger group . "That's the great bear."

"Ursa major," he nodded before pointing to another. "Cepheus, the king." His arm moved to point somewhere else. "And that one far over there is Triangulum, the triangle. You can't really see it right now, though."

She threw her hand forward and pointed to another constellation before he could. "That's Draco, the dragon."

"Aye!" he chuckled, drawing the curved line of the Draco constellation. "That one is my favourite."

Rosetta turned her head to see his bright smile. She realised he was sharing an activity he enjoyed, and it made her heart jump precariously.

Who would have guessed Alister likes stargazing?

Rosetta knew he couldn't see she'd stopped looking at the stars while he pointed to more constellations. She was too busy admiring his face. It was filled with abundant joy, so different from the serious, stern faces he often wore.

She wanted to see all of him.

She wondered if he would let her.

With slow and hesitant movements, she brushed her fingers up until the tips were running over that scar cutting across his face. His hand snapped forward to grab hers just as she touched the bottom of his eyepatch.

"What I've got under there isn't pretty, lass," he warned with an ominous tone, his face turning grim.

"I don't mind." She pushed her hand forward through his.

His grip loosened, letting her reach higher so she could grab the bottom of it with her thumb and middle finger. Making sure she wouldn't hurt him as she did, she started lifting it up until she revealed his eye and pulled the patch away completely.

In the light of the nearly full moon, Rosetta was able to see him entirely.

The scar ran down his hairline, thickened over his brow, made a shallow divot over his eyelid, as though he'd closed it when he'd been sliced, before it came down his cheek.

His eye, however, was not its usual brown. Instead, it was blue, milky and discoloured. The whites of his eye seemed normal, and when he blinked or moved his good eye to look at her, it followed like it was undamaged. Rosetta could tell he was completely blind, though, as it had no pupil.

"You're right, it's hideous," she sighed playfully, seeing he look tense at how she was staring.

"That's it, give that back." He turned so he could grab his eyepatch from her hand.

She stretched her arm out and held it above her head so he couldn't grab it.

"Give it to me Rosetta," he snapped, rolling until he was above her on his hands and knees to reach it better. The shrouds shook around her, making her bounce.

The bottle of wine wedged between them fell and smashed against the deck, glass exploding everywhere below them.

She brought her arm forward so she could shove her hand through the webbing of the shrouds where it would be more difficult to reach. She giggled quietly the entire time.

They were almost chest to chest as he struggled to grab his eyepatch from her. She grinned when she looked over his face; he was so close to her, she kissed his cheek right over his scar.

He never saw her coming.

He paused with his own arm through the netting of the rope and slowly reared his head back as she placed her hand on the injured side of his face, lightly stroking his cheek.

"You look like you have the moon in your eye," she told him, letting him know she didn't actually find it hideous.

It did look like the moon, with the way the orb reflected into his eye as it loomed over them with its bright white light.

She often thought he held the sun in the other when the sunlight hit it just right, almost seeming to glow.

She brushed her thumb over his eyelashes, giving him a warm smile. His eyelid flicked under her touch. She thought it might have been uncomfortable, so she brushed over his eyebrow instead.

"You don't need the eyepatch, Alister. You look just fine without it."

With his brows furrowed in uncertainty, she watch both his eyes move over her face, seeming to dart over it as he took in her soft expression.

She leaned forward and pressed her lips to his cheek, right over the bottom of his scar again. Perhaps she shouldn't have been so teasing about something she knew he was insecure about. She just hadn't expected him to react so suddenly.

When she pulled her head back, she saw that the hard press of his mouth had lightened, his brows unwrinkling.

Alister leaned forward this time and took her lips with his own, bringing his arm back through the shrouds to cup the side of her head. It was light, almost shy, and Rosetta kissed him back just as tenderly.

They had never kissed like this before, a gentle coax. Not even his tongue snaked forward, as if it was bashful and hiding. Instead, she felt his lips brushing over hers lightly, growing quicker and quicker, as if he wanted to get in as many as he could rather than bury her under them.

It didn't take long for him to tilt her head himself while he tilted his own to the side, that soft press becoming harder.

His tongue came in to lick against her own for a moment and she heard him take in a deep draw of air. His shuddering groan forced her to answer with her own. The kiss was passionate, heated, filled with emotion rather than unbridled lust – at least, she felt it was for her.

His hand seemed unsteady as it shook slightly, and he slipped it down the side of her neck just underneath her jaw, brushing his thumb over the column of her throat..

She brought her hand back through the shrouds so she could hold onto it tightly with both hands. She felt her head swim as their lips started to move in rougher sweeps, hungry to taste each other.

Then his head tilted the other way, forcing her to move hers the opposite direction. She felt his tongue lick across hers again and this time, she let out a little moan first.

His hand moved away, and she felt him press his body against her so they could be closer. His other arm pushed through the netting of the shrouds so he could hold onto it while also wrapping his arm around her back. He grabbed the cheek of her arse, hefting her hips closer to his.

His mouth broke away when he let out a deep expire, just as she felt something hard, thick, and long slip over the mound at the apex of her thighs.

He buried his face against the side of her neck as he drew his lips across the tender spot over her pulse. She let out a quiet gasp when goosebumps washed over her skin in a wave. His breath was hot and sweet with whiskey and wine.

"I don't think I've ever wanted to be inside you as much as I do right now, Rosetta," he whispered against her.

Heat warmed her skin, flushing as her core grew slick at the mere idea. His tongue lashed against hers in a deep, flat stroke, tasting her skin like he was desperate to.

"I–I can't." But gods, did she want him.

Rosetta couldn't handle Alister pounding between her thighs right now. She wouldn't be able to take the usual strength and unyielding passion he seemed to dole out to her like a savage.

"I'll be gentle," he rebuffed while nipping at her skin, making her abdomen tense.

His heated breath wrapped around her throat, seeming to make her own temperature rise and spur her body on further.

"You don't know how to be gentle!"

A breathy moan broke from her when he suckled on the tender spot, bringing more goosebumps to the surface. It almost distracted her from the fact that he'd started lifting the side of her skirt to place his palm on the outside of her thigh.

"Sure, I do." He broke away so he could kiss his way up her jaw, up and over the side of it. "Let me show you."

He took her mouth with his own once more, and she realised he'd never been this affectionate before. From the moment he'd started kissing her, he hadn't stopped; little pecks rained over her.

Something was different this time. Alister was almost

being... tender with her. There was affection in each kiss, no matter where he placed his lips.

He lifted her leg until it was bent, her knee pressing against his side. He pushed her arse forward while pressing his hips against her again, this time slipping his shaft hidden away behind those breeches right against her clit.

She felt herself undulating into him when it felt just right.

I want him. She could feel she was wet, that her sore and tender core ached for him to fill her.

He stayed with me. She returned his fiery kiss that seemed to make her mind go numb. *Told me about himself.* She slipped her tongue against his when she felt it twist past her lips. *Showed me his face.* She curled the leg he'd lifted around his side to pull him in.

Their day together in the market had filled her with joy and contentment. She'd felt swell after swell of emotions with him, sweet and pleasant ones. She wanted to share them.

Understanding she was accepting him, he finally moved his hand from her thigh and reached between their bodies. She heard the buttons of his breeches popping one-by-one.

Each time she heard the sound, desire flipped low, making her feel like something was fluttering deep inside her. It made everywhere delicate throb.

"Please..." she begged in between kisses. *Please be gentle with me.*

Under her skirt, the broad head of his cock brushed against her clit. He used her folds to guide his way lower to tuck it against the pooling dip of her entrance.

His heated kisses continued even when a mew came from her as he started pushing in, until she felt the head pop inside just past the rim. Her leg tightened around him when he slowly pushed his cock further inside, and she felt the burn of him stretching her.

"Haa, shit," Alister gasped nearly breathlessly. "You're so

fucking tight."

Rosetta was so swollen and tender, and he felt so much unbelievably bigger than usual. She knew she must be snug around him, and she had to force her body to adjust against the strain and the pressure.

Her mouth drew open when he pulled his hips back to collect her wetness, before pushing the rest of himself inside. She felt the tip kiss against her cervix before his hips pushed in deeply, almost lifting her.

He finally moved his hand from between them so he could hold onto the netted rope supporting them, but he grabbed it right where her hand was, interlinking their fingers.

She didn't know if he did it on purpose, but she had to squeeze his hand back as she felt her core quivering around him.

Rosetta didn't know if the wild, deep throbbing she could feel was coming from him or her, but it made her legs weak. The one around him tried to fall and she had to keep moving it back up.

He placed his lips against the side of her neck as he murmured, "I've got you." He squeezed the cheek of her backside to show her he wouldn't let her fall.

She was able to lift her other leg up around him, tilting her hips forward for an easier perch, making it feel like he was impossibly deep. Rosetta could tell her back was pressed tightly against the shrouds, the rope curving around her body, helping to hold her up.

She almost couldn't believe they were doing this here, a metre off the ground, out in the open, on her ship.

Her head fell back when he started to withdraw before he pushed his cock in. Her vision went hazy, and she thought the stars had split in two.

He's everywhere. She felt him everywhere.

Her channel was so sensitive, it felt like she was being

stroked all along it.

Rosetta knew if he had gone any faster, it may have felt like a scrape rather than the careful glide that made her clench onto him in bliss. If he had hit the end of her hard, it would have felt like a deep, painful slam rather than the light kiss that made her pull her legs in so he could press deeper.

His breaths sounded so loud, laboured, shaken in her ear, she wondered if she felt as good around him as he did inside her. His pace was slow, finding a soft but deep rhythm, and Rosetta could feel it all.

Instead of being lost in the pleasure she was feeling, she was losing herself to him. To the way he felt. The shape of him. The way his hips ground against her folds to massage her needy little clit rather than tapping it. The hard warmth she felt not only deep inside, but also blanketing her body. Muscles squishing into her and forcing her soft form to mould around him.

The smell of his skin wasn't tainted by sweat, or the sea, or the smell of heavy booze. She was breathing in all of his essence as a pure scent, and it made her eyelids flicker in heavy arousal. Woodsy. Musky. *Fuck, he smells so nice.*

The sound of his deep voice as tiny, barely noticeable groans tingled her aching senses. She'd never heard him sound so delicate before.

His beard tickled her skin as his lips pressed messy kisses against her neck, like he couldn't stop tasting her. They slipped over her jaw, over her ear, making her shiver when he touched somewhere sensitive.

She wanted to wrap her arms around him, draw him closer. He was being so sweet with her, so gentle; nothing had ever felt like this. There was the passion always present between them, heat and fire, but she felt like this was something more.

Her eyes crinkled into deep bows when she felt a sensation swirling in her chest, around her heart that almost seemed to stop every time he was as deep as possible. There was this strange feeling of warmth spreading over her, over her breast, leaving an ache she was afraid of.

Her throat felt tight with a clogging emotion she didn't understand – like it'd choke her if she let it. It would break her, destroy her if she continued to let it grow.

They were only having sex. They'd done this many so times. So, why did Rosetta feel like something was changing inside her? Every steady and perfect thrust from him was pushing her further and further towards emotions she'd never felt before.

"W-wait," she gasped, her brows furrowing deeply.

Alister shuddered against her.

She realised he'd stopped kissing her, had been so focused on what was happening between her thighs that he'd been laying his forehead against her like his head was swimming and weak.

"Fuck, Rosetta." His hand squeezed hers tighter. "I'm being as gentle as I can."

But it wasn't her core that she needed to run from. It was how she felt like she was drowning in tenderness. *Why do I feel like this?*

Her emotions pushed her, driving her closer and closer to the edge so swiftly, he grunted as she suddenly clenched around him.

"A-Alister!" she screamed.

Like a wave pushing her underwater backwards, she felt her body arch. The tension that clamped her body forced her quiet, her legs shaking as they wrapped and squeezed around his waist. Rosetta pulled her arms up on the shrouds as wetness trickled from her core as she came.

His hips broke their rhythm when they twitched in response to her milking him. Such a loud guttural groan broke from him, she knew it would have been accompanied by an oath if he had the thought process to speak.

Sparks seemed to flash behind her clenched eyelids, making her brows draw together even closer as she was swept up by pure, aching rapture.

Her body slumped against him when she'd finished wringing his cock, all her energy sapped from her. *I-I feel so strange.* Good, but undeniably strange.

Alister was still moving, his big cock still spreading and penetrating her over and over in such bliss, her mind felt exceptionally dizzy. *Why?*

Penetrating her deep. Penetrating her slowly.

Every time he prodded and glided over the ridge of her G spot, her eyelids flickered, and her eyes rolled lightly. Rosetta felt like she was floating as the sensation of drowning seemed to intensify.

She no longer cared if she was saved.

Why...?

That question was all she could think about, and she no longer understood what she was even asking. All she knew was when he pulled his head back so he could stare at her, and she looked back into both his eyes, she was irreparably doomed.

His mouth came down to kiss her.

Rosetta was so desperate to breathe that she kissed him back hard, slipping her tongue into his mouth to taste him. She needed his breath, needed him to breathe for her.

Light-headedness began to eat at her. Her head fell back before she felt like she'd gotten enough. Dizzy. Hazy.

Her blood was rushing, tightening her body once more around him. It was too much; she felt tears prickling against her eyelashes.

The balls of her feet pushed against his backside, trying to force him harder, faster, forgetting that she needed him to be kind to her body. She ached, she needed, and was desperate as she came.

"I'm about to come." His voice was so croaked and hoarse, under so much strain that it rung in her ears. Those four words made her abdomen flutter so heavily and strangely, she wondered if it felt odd around his cock.

A split second of clarity spiked through her mental freeze. "N-Not inside."

Despite saying this, she clung to him, didn't want him to pull away, didn't want him to end this. Rosetta was afraid of what she was feeling, but it felt so good, she wanted to live in this moment forever.

"I need you to move your legs," he told her, just as she felt his hips break their rhythm to twitch.

A groan fell from him, and he placed his chin against her shoulder, his arm wrapping around her tighter.

He continued to thrust, slowly, gently, but she could feel it was becoming uncontrolled. Suddenly, he'd be too deep. Suddenly, a thrust would slam before softening. He'd give a few quick pumps before shaking his head and slowing down once more.

His hand squeezed her arse so hard, she knew he must be bruising it.

"Uhh." She felt him shaking and knew he needed to take her the way he normally did, to pound her and wreck them both until they were both almost yelling.

But he wasn't, for her, and she could tell he was suffering for it. Instead, she was experiencing Alister losing his own mind, feeling his body spasm out of control rather than being too disorganised by her own.

Rosetta adored it, mewing contently every time something changed from his steady pace.

She could feel him trying to tug back.

"Now!" he choked.

Rosetta unlocked her ankles and let her legs fall so that

they were bent beside his hips to cradle him.

He withdrew immediately and she felt a burst of lukewarm liquid splatter against her clit before he even got the chance to press against her. He almost hadn't pulled away in time. The undershaft of his pulsating, throbbing cock slipped between her folds as more ropes of his seed came from him.

It hit against her belly and dress.

"Aa! Haa!" He pushed their bodies together to help stroke himself as he came, continuing to thrust over her swollen clit so it made her legs twitch every time.

His head was tilted back, as if he didn't have the strength to lift it forward as his body shook and quaked against her. Watching both his eyes crinkle, staring blankly at the sky, was wonderful.

A final moan fell from them both before they both placed their foreheads against each other's shoulder.

The broken sounds of their heavy breaths were all that was shared between them as they held each other. Neither moved, neither spoke as they cuddled.

The more Rosetta laxed, the more she felt her legs slipping away, the strength in them lost. The heels of her boots found the shrouds, and she was able to support herself with his help.

That seemed to be his cue to move, because he pulled his head back to gaze at her, his eyes lingering over her face when she did the same.

He was still holding her, and she could feel his cock still against her, throbbing lightly.

What was I feeling? Why did the worst of it fade but leave little remnants behind to make her ache when she looked at his fully uncovered face?

Her eyes flicked between his. *The sun and the moon.* She didn't think she would be able to not think of them that way again.

"Why do you always get what you want?" she teased with

a false cry. Anything to get her mind to stop fixating on the strange emotions pestering her. She punched the top of his chest with the hand he wasn't still holding.

"I was gentle, wasn't I?" He gave a chuckle, like he already knew the answer. "Told you so."

He leaned in to give her a quick but deep kiss.

His arms started to pull away so he could fall to the side and rest against the shrouds. He tucked his shaft away and buttoned up his breeches while she pulled her skirt down.

"This dress was clean before!"

"Aye, I know." He turned his head towards her, brushing the back of his hand against her stomach. "Now it's got me all over it."

She tried to look angry. She pouted her lips, but she couldn't stop them from curling at the sides.

He didn't seem to mind that he was no longer wearing his eyepatch as he looked over the water. His breaths were still puffing out in short and shallow hits, and she watched his chest rise and fall.

"Do you do this often?" he asked quietly.

"Lay against the shrouds and look at the sky?"

"Aye."

"Sometimes." She tilted her head back to stare up at it. "It's peaceful when there is no one else on the deck."

He rolled over and grabbed her hand, trying to yank her to her front as well.

"Then come, I've got something to show you."

He made his way further up the shrouds and curiosity ate at her. She followed behind him as he climbed to the crow's nest bucket at the very top of her main mast.

It had only been replaced once they were at port; Alister's ship had been acting as watch for both of them.

He hopped inside and reached over, his hand extended to help her into it. Once she was standing, he turned her so she was facing the bay as he stood behind her.

"Where the hell is it?" he grumbled with concentration. "Ah ha!" He lowered his head next to hers from behind and pointed at a spot on the water. The stars were reflecting against it, moving because of the sea.

"It's a constellation my pa made up and it can only be seen on the water from high up." He started moving his hand to draw it. "It's like a boat sailing on the waves."

It took her a long while to see it, but she eventually did. She drew what she thought was the shape of the boat and he laughed.

"You got it."

He backed away so he could come up beside her, placing his forearms against the rim of the bucket to stare with her.

"My pa taught me everything I needed to know on how to be a sailor. He wasn't the greatest father, but he had his moments." He looked up with an odd, lopsided smile. "He was the one who taught me the stars, how to count my coin. I don't know what I would have become if it wasn't for him taking me away as a kid, but I doubt I would have been anything more than one of the petty street urchins behind us."

Rosetta turned away from the water to look at Alister grinning up at the stars next to her.

"I like being a pirate, lass. I'm bloody good at it."

Those remnants of emotions stabbed at her like a knife as she observed him. Her brows pulled together so tightly, it put pressure on the skin of her forehead.

I'm such an idiot.

CHAPTER THIRTEEN

Rosetta woke slowly in very dim light, the sun just touching the horizon, calling to her.

She let her eyes lazily peek open to stare at the tunic-covered chest her cheek was currently squished on top of. They drifted across Alister's sleeping cabin that held his desk on one side, a dining table in another corner, with his bed just a metre below them.

This room wasn't as big as her navigation room and looked worn and untidy. It had always been darker, since the windows were aged and stained with time and grime.

Her eyes fell to him sleeping on his back, an arm crossed behind his head with the other around her. His hand was curled over her hip, and it gave her the opportunity to examine the ring he had showed her.

How did he convince me to do this?

Currently, their legs were entangled, each having a knee between the other's, Rosetta half-lying on top of him. Although she was completely inside the hammock they were lying in, he had a leg hanging outside it.

It had been no easy feat getting inside it together.

He'd needed to get in before her, and she had to jump on top of him. He'd covered his precious groin but told her he didn't care how she kneed and elbowed him, as long as she got in and made herself comfortable.

She didn't think she would be able to with her dress on, but she'd managed to fall asleep rather quickly.

How am I supposed to get out without waking him? Maybe this had been his way of making sure she couldn't escape like she usually did when she woke before him.

Then again, he looked rather content and comfortable. She was as well. It was a cocoon of warmth and strength. Even though he looked as though he was about to fall out, she knew he wouldn't.

Tentatively, she raised her hand to brush her fingertips over the eyelashes of his blind eye.

The hand on her side shot forward like it usually did when she touched his face when he was sleeping. He rarely ever woke, but it meant she'd never been able to pull that eyepatch off before.

Eventually his arm fell away, but she watched his eyelids flicker open, showing her both of them. She thought, because she'd touched it directly, that might be the reason he woke this time.

"Hey, lass," he greeted with a rumbling voice filled with groggy sleep. Her stomach quivered in response to its husky sound. "It's too early for me to deal with your shit."

Then, he shoved her head against his chest. He also kicked the leg hanging from the hammock so it started to swing, as if to rock them. He laid his head back once more and closed his eyes.

"Go back to sleep."

"If you keep me here against my will," she whispered. "You'll regret it."

"Will I now?" he asked with humour, his lips quirking upward.

He brought his leg into the hammock and turned over, curling his arms around her head and upper back to hold onto her. His embrace was warm, cushioned by relaxed and squishy muscles surrounding her.

She let him sleep just a little longer, waiting for his breaths to turn light and even. *He looks so soft when he's asleep.* Boyish, even. It was a shame she was about to ruin that.

She bit his chest hard, making him flinch back awake.

"Shit, Rosetta!" He grabbed her hair and yanked her head back. "What the hell is your problem?"

"Told you you'd regret it."

He rolled back over, putting them into the position they'd been in when she'd first woken up.

"You're bloody right about that."

"Does that mean you're awake now?"

"Oh aye! Not really how I wanted to wake up but sure, I'm awake."

She let out a loud giggle. "Good, because I wasn't going to lay here bored."

"Well, you could have touched my dick instead of biting me. Both would have woken me just the same."

She'd known he was hard, since it had been pressing against her all morning. She thought biting him might make him go soft and she'd been hoping for that. Rosetta had been recovering and their moment of intimacy had made that harder. She still felt twinges, which should be gone by midday.

"Maybe next time," she teased, letting a playful smile fill her face.

His grumpy face turned grumpier. "Nay, because this is the first time I've gotten you into my hammock. When we're back out at sea, you're not going to come to my ship."

Rosetta shook her head, knowing she needed to save the morning she'd basically destroyed.

"I trust my crew now. If the few who don't want to sail with me don't return today, I'll know those who do want me as their captain. I'll be more comfortable moving between our ships from now on."

His brows knotted together, his eyes moving over her face to inspect it, as though trying to see if she was lying.

"Is that one of the reasons you wanted to port?"

"Mhm," she nodded. "If the men return, I shouldn't have to worry about them anymore."

"Does that mean you'll sleep in my ship with me sometimes?"

She pointed to the bed beneath them.

"Never in that. It feels like a block of bricks." She reached up to play with the ties of his tunic with a little pout. "But I guess I didn't mind being in the hammock with you. It's very warm."

"Aye, lass," he chuckled with a grin. "That'll do."

Rosetta didn't like the way she felt when she stared at his face for too long, how strange emotions bubbled up into her throat. Instead of letting herself melt in them, she tried to direct herself away by either averting her gaze or starting a conversation. So, when it happened while laying with him, she reached up and brushed her fingertips over his eyebrow.

"How did you lose your sight? It doesn't look like the blade really cut your eye."

"Nay. It only just nicked it but it, uh, got infected. With no doctor on board, there was no way to save my sight as it slowly got blurrier and blurrier. I woke up one morning and all I saw was black. We just focused on trying to make sure it stayed intact." He placed his hand over the side of his face. "The pain was excruciating. I thought it was going to pop right out of my skull."

She lifted his tunic to look at the scars crossing over his abdomen. "Healed all your scars the same way, huh? How's that working out for you, Alister 'One-Eye' Paine?"

"I believe there should be a captain in there somewhere."

"Nay, lad. Only good captains get to be called one."

"That's it!" He started to push her. "Time for you to get the hell out of my bed, you foul wench."

She held onto it with a death grip, but he was moving himself on purpose so he would eventually fall onto the bed below.

"That's one way to do it," she said, curling her chin over the edge to look down at him.

"You're lucky I'm in a good mood this morning. Otherwise, you'd be regretting this."

"Oh yeah," she scoffed, her tone mocking. "You're a real ray of sunshine."

"Aye, and you're a fucking sunflower."

She gave a laugh, until she realised she didn't really understand what he meant. She decided not to dwell on it.

As he crawled to get to his feet and find his boots, Rosetta rolled out of the hammock to put her own on. Then, Alister approached her with his hand out flat. "Need my eyepatch."

"Oh." Rosetta averted her gaze. "I, um, lost it?"

"What do you mean, you *lost* it?"

She turned her gaze back to him and nearly cringed.

"Oops?" She watched his eyes widen in horror. "Don't you have another?"

"Not one as good! It's the only comfortable one I had."

"You don't need it." She tried to smile reassuringly for him, using the same words from last night. "You look fine without it."

"That's because you're pretty, Rosetta! You don't know what it's like." He shoved his hand through her hair, gliding over her cheek and then back to cup her head. He brought her closer. "It's never been about what I look like; I don't give a shit what people think. I just hate the way they stare at it, the pity I receive!"

She didn't know what made her gasp.

The fact he was angry? The way he grabbed her, aggressive

but tender? The compliment he'd given? Or was it the real reason why he'd never shown her before?

"What more do you want me to say? I'm sorry."

His lips pursed together in annoyance.

"I know when you lost it." He bit out a curse she couldn't distinguish. "It was when we were on the shrouds. So, it's really my fault."

"Sure is!" she grinned, making him snap his head to her with a scowl. "Anyway, we've got ships to get ready."

He grumbled and went to the drawer of his desk. He pulled out a different black eyepatch, one that laid against his eye rather than giving it room by being convex.

They parted so she could go back to her own ship.

After calling out for Naeem a handful of times and finding he still hadn't returned, she let out a long groan of frustration.

He's supposed to be helping me with the ship!

She stomped her way back across the deck and down the gangplank, ready to kick his ass when she saw him.

When she found one of Alister's men on the boardwalk, she grabbed him by the scruff and pulled him closer. "Tell that captain of yours if he goes looking for me, I had to go to find Naeem."

"Ah." He held his hands up in surrender. "He's not here at the moment."

That made her frown. She let go of his tunic.

"Well, where did he go?"

The man gave a shrug. "Not sure. Said he'll be a few hours."

Well, good. It gave her a few hours as well; hopefully, she'd beat him back. She didn't want to hear him berate her because she wasn't getting her ship together.

She stopped by the leatherworker first, needing to buy a few things she hadn't the previous day. *I forgot I need gloves.* Winter was coming; she hated holding the wheel of her ship and having her hands freeze. She'd been planning to quickly run off to do it while Naeem got her ship and crew started anyway. Plus, she had an extra errand she was hoping to slip in as well.

"How long until it's ready?"

"For you, Rosetta? Give me an hour."

She looked over the leatherworker, letting a small genuine smile fill her face. He was one of the few men who didn't bother her, had never been up her skirt, and was just generally a nice person – which was rare to find in places like this.

"You're a good man, Garth." She tapped the table. "Fastest in the business, no one better."

She placed a few silver coins on the table as she walked out. Once more, she started her brisk walk, eventually climbing up the long hill to the mansion.

Rosetta opened the double doors to the brothel and was greeted by women relaxing in the front room. Not wanting to take out her anger on them, she gave a small sigh.

"Where is Naeem? He's supposed to be with my ship."

"He's in Victoria's room," a beautiful, dark-skinned woman with her curly hair tied back in two braids answered. When it was clear she didn't know where that was, the girl awkwardly laughed. "Come, I'll show you the way."

She followed behind to the second level, walking up the staircase to the left. When they got to the room, the girl gestured to the door.

Without caring to knock, Rosetta opened the door so hard it slammed against the wall. "Wake up, you lazy whale!"

Naeem's head shot up to look at her, bashing himself in the sternum with his chin. The man was sprawled butt naked on the bed like a starfish, nothing but the two women under his arms covering him. He didn't care to cover his groin, despite Rosetta being able to see everything.

It's nothing I haven't seen before. She'd seen this man's

bare backside more times than she really cared to.

"Ah shit! Is it morning already?" He threw his arm across his face with a deep groan. "Sorry, Rosetta, was up all night."

The women in the room looked at her with pouted faces because she'd woken them. Then one of them said, "Does he have to go?"

For a prostitute to say something like that meant she'd actually enjoyed herself.

Rosetta shook her head with a laugh. *I guess we do have a little time now that Alister's busy.* Plus, there was something she *should* do since she was here now, not that she really cared to.

"I guess I better get up." Not that Naeem was making an effort to do so.

"You have thirty minutes," she told him. "Make them count. I'll be with Madame Lillian."

"Thanks, Captain!" he yelled as she turned away from the room. "So, ladies, which one of you wants to ride my face and who wants to ride my—"

She closed the door before she could hear him finish.

"Is Madame Lillian available?" she asked the girl who brought her here.

"I'll go check."

She ran off while Rosetta calmly made her way through the mansion, finding herself back downstairs.

Just as she hit the bottom step, someone entered through the double doors. The early sunlight filtering through shadowed the large, tall, and obviously muscled man before her eyes adjusted.

Is that...?

She gave a shrug when she didn't know him and walked down to the side of the mansion that held Lillian's living quarters.

The girl came running back. "Yes, it appears she's

available. I've told her you wanted to see her."

Gesturing her hand forward to let Rosetta know she could continue, Rosetta did just that. Knocking first, she entered before she even got a reply.

"Good morning!" Rosetta exclaimed, throwing her hands open in front of the doors that slammed against the walls.

Lillian immediately frowned at her. "You know its rude to be so loud this early in the morning. I've barely just gotten out of bed."

"And yet, you're already dressed and covered in make-up."

Her slightly wrinkled lips thinned into agitated lines.

She raised her hands holding the teapot she'd been using to pour herself a cup and gestured at Rosetta. She nodded, accepting the tea offered. She'd been in the middle of pouring herself a cup already.

"What's wrong? You're only ever this cheerful when you're actually not."

She hated how well the woman could read her. "I'm here because Naeem wasn't at the ship when he was supposed to be."

"Doesn't he always do that?" the woman asked with sincerity. "You've never been this upset before."

"Things aren't the same anymore." She turned her head to the side as Lillian placed a teacup in front of her and poured honey tea inside. "We've got another ship sailing with us. Can't have them waiting around because he's forgotten to get up at first light."

"The other captain will be upset? Men, always so impatient."

Rosetta folded her arms across her chest while placing her boots on the table. "Exactly. I'd rather not be yelled at when it's not my fault."

"Aren't you sleeping with this man, though?" She waved her hands to get Rosetta to move her feet from the table. "He shouldn't yell at you when you're regularly shining his cock."

While Rosetta did move her feet, Lillian also got her to stand by holding her hand out and gesturing her up.

"Yes, but we argue a lot. He's a big, arrogant meathead."

"Sounds about right." She pulled the sides of Rosetta's skirt. She hadn't changed yet like she wanted to because she'd needed to come get Naeem. "Well don't you look absolutely beautiful. This colour is *perfect* on you."

Of course Lillian wanted to talk about a feminine aspect with her. It was a rarity between them.

She spun her finger to make Rosetta turn and she let out an irritated, sullen noise, spinning so her dress would wave out. It felt like a show a young daughter would do for her mother.

"I actually got a compliment this time," Rosetta grumbled quietly.

"From your dear Jolly Sailor Bold? I find that hard to believe." She scoffed while waving her hand as they finally fell to their seats. "They hardly notice things like this."

Rosetta went to take a sip of her tea, but it fell back to the plate before it even made it to her lips. The sound of the porcelain cup hitting the saucer rang in her ears. She found it hard not to reflect on the three days she'd had in Tortaya so far.

She knew the dynamic between her and Alister had changed, and she worried what it meant. Were they closer, or was Rosetta being foolish?

"Stop that!" Lillian leaned forward to smack the side of Rosetta's knee with the back of her fingers. "You only nibble at your lips when you've got something on your mind. I've told you not to. That's how you get peeling lips."

"I'm fine," she said, finally taking that sip. "Just tired from getting drunk like a sailor."

Her eyes squinted at her in suspicion.

"It was another woman, wasn't it? I told you sailors are no

good! Probably got drunk and tried to play it off like some accident when they know full well that–"

Once again, Lillian was trying to nestle doubt into her mind like she always did.

"It's not that," she laughed. "I was the only woman he slept with while in port."

"That you know of," she sneered, and Rosetta hated the way her words made her gut twist. "Were you with him the entire time?"

"I don't care either way." Rosetta bit her lie, folding her arms across her chest. "I have other things to worry about and I had a great time regardless."

She just needed to get the woman to stop talking like this.

Her lips thinned once more, her eyes narrowing this time. "What other things? For you to honestly say there's something worrying you, it must not be good."

Crap. Rosetta cursed to herself.

She gave a bright smile to the woman in front of her. "I have a large ship to set sail today. Did you forget that I got the Laughing Siren?"

"You're a terrible liar."

She stabbed her hands through her long, loose hair, since Rosetta had let it down when she'd gone to sleep.

"How do you do it?" The laugh she gave came from a place of pure frustration. "How do you know when I'm lying and when I'm being truthful? You're the only one who can seem to fucking tell!"

Lillian pointed her nimble finger at her.

"Don't you swear at me, Rosetta Silver!" She withdrew her finger from the air to hold her teacup like a proper lady, even though she'd never been raised one. She puckered her lips, making them wrinkle further as her eyelids fluttered lower. "Your eyelids flicker when you're telling a lie. Always have."

"My eyes?" She brushed her cheek right below one of

them. The fact Lillian could pick up something so subtle from her was puzzling.

"Yes. Now, are you going to tell me what's bothering you, or are you not going to talk to me about it?"

With a grumble, Rosetta aggressively folded her arms. "Fine. So, you were right."

"About?" she said blankly, lifting her teacup with a sense of superiority as she wiggled her head side-to-side. "I'm often right."

"He was careful, until he suddenly... wasn't."

The cup nearly fell from her hands and her composed posture turned into one of unmasked shock. "What?"

"Do you have any of that tea you make for the girls? It may or may not have been once."

Rosetta had been intending to bring this up the entire time; it was why she'd come to see her when she'd much rather have not. She'd seen her enough over the past few days to last her months.

Lillian leaned forward to grasp her hand reassuringly. "Rosie, when was this? You know it's not as effective the longer it's been."

"Not last night but the previous one."

"That's too late! You should have come here straight away."

Rosetta shrugged her shoulders like she didn't care. "You know I don't think I can bear children, but I'd rather be safe than sorry. Will it still work after two days?"

Lillian quickly got to her feet and started making the special tea. Her actions were jarring, like she wanted to be swift to make up for lost time.

"I don't know. There's a lot of terrible or terrific luck, depending on your perspective, that goes into making a child. I don't even know if this works. I just hope it does."

Lillian eventually placed a different cup down in front of

Rosetta and she chugged its contents in one go. She scrunched her nose at the pungent, mud-like taste.

"Look, I wasn't even planning on coming here at all," she told her as Lillian sat back down. "I just thought while I was here collecting Naeem, I might as well."

"Silly girl." She shook her head in disappointment.

"Eh," Rosetta said, shrugging her shoulders once more. She placed her boot against the table and started rocking her chair back and forth on its two back legs. "The first time was because he was pissed off I was letting other men play with me."

"Why did you do that? You know how men can be. They think women are theirs until they no longer want them."

"Because I was teaching him a real good lesson, wasn't I?"

It wasn't why Rosetta had done it, but she'd rather play it that way than tell Lillian the hurtful truth.

"Why would you–" Her eyes widened, before she gave a laugh Rosetta often associated with evil coming from the woman. "You saw him with another woman and made sure he understood you'd do the same thing back! I knew you were wonderful! Such a clever girl. I was just like you when I was younger."

"Well, it worked, didn't it?" Rosetta gestured to the cup she'd just fully emptied. "A bit too well."

The humour between them died and Lillian turned to her with her motherly eyes.

"You'll be careful, won't you?" The care and sincerity in her voice made Rosetta's heart swell with a painful ache. Lillian reached forward to cup her cheek and Rosetta found it was rather cold this morning. "Don't go giving your heart to someone who doesn't want it."

"Of course not. I've lost faith in men after Theodore." Rosetta turned her eyes to the window to stare out of it. It was a beautiful, early autumn morning, reflecting nothing about the way Rosetta truly felt. "I really thought I could love him. I wanted to, but then I realised love isn't real. It's just some made up fantasy mothers tell their daughters to keep them smiling."

"It is real," Lillian responded. Her expression looked filled with sadness for Rosetta. "I love both my children dearly, no matter what they've become."

"Yeah, well, I won't ever experience that."

Why did Lillian have to bring something up that could possibly be painful for her?

"I also loved the father of my children," Lillian mumbled, turning her eyes away to stare at the cup in her hands. "It was foolish of me, but I couldn't help it when he kept coming back to me."

"You told me he never claimed your daughter. You don't even know if she's his."

"She is his daughter!" Lillian shouted in a high pitch scream, her face scrunched up in anger Rosetta rarely saw. Her hands even clenched into frail fists. "I know she is. Just because her hair is blonde like mine doesn't mean she came from someone else. I see pieces of his face in hers, in the colour of her eyes. It hurts to look at my children and see his stupid face."

Lillian had a love hate relationship with this unknown man. She often spoke of him, of her children, of her past. It was obvious she longed to go back to the days she had with them, to experience them again.

"I knew when he was coming to port. He always came around the same time of the year. I knew I was pregnant with her not even a few weeks after he left, and I hadn't taken another man after him before I knew." Her shoulders slumped forward, a heavy emotion weighing her down. "He always gave me enough money that I didn't need to. That's how I know. He just didn't like hearing I had to still work months later. He thought I was just being greedy when he didn't understand the money he gave me for our son just wasn't enough."

It was Rosetta's turn to reach across the table to hold her hand. She brushed her thumb over the back of it. "I'm sorry. I shouldn't have said anything. It's none of my business."

"No," Lillian sighed, shaking her head. "It's fine." She turned her face up to give Rosetta a warm smile. "Did I tell you Agnes married the blacksmith last year? You should have seen the wedding, she looked beautiful. Unlike me, she got married, and because she was pure, she was allowed to wear a white dress. I've never been so proud."

"Yeah, you told–"

Rosetta's words were cut short when she heard a commotion coming from the hallway. They shared a look of worry between them when they heard heavy, stomping footsteps approaching.

"Stop! You can't go in there. She's got a client," a woman yelled with panic when the commotion got to the other side of the door.

"I told her if I caught her with another man that I'd fucking kill him."

They flinched when both the doors to Lillian's chamber swung open so fast, they slammed against the walls with an ear-piercing thud.

Her brows drew together instantly. "Alister?"

His eye visibly widened before it darted between her and Lillian. *Did he seriously follow me here?*

"You know each other?" Lillian asked them both.

He stayed frozen, seemingly unsure of what he wanted to do. Actually, it looked as though he wanted to slowly back out of the room but couldn't now that he'd been seen. His hands were frozen in the air from when he'd shoved the doors open.

Her eyes squinted in suspicion, more so when his nose

bunched, as though he knew he couldn't escape.

"As you can see, I'm currently busy." Lillian gestured to Rosetta. "Give me a few and I'll be right with you, Alister."

He isn't here because of me? Rosetta's gaze fell on Lillian. She had a terrible feeling about this.

There was a long silent pause between the three of them, so thick with tension it could have been cut with a piece of paper.

"Nay," he finally said with a shake of his head, brushing his palm against his stubble of his cheek. "It'll be fine."

He turned around and closed the doors on the woman's face with one hand before greeting the room once more.

At first, his steps seemed hesitant as he came closer into Lillian's living quarters. Then he leaned down and kissed the side of Lillian's face. She reached one of her hands up to cup the side of his before giving his cheek a kiss.

Rosetta's lips parted, unsure of what to make of this, especially when he walked to Lilian's bedside table, grabbed the vase full of fresh, vibrant flowers, walked to the window, and carelessly dumped them out of it.

As though he knew it would be filled with water, he grabbed a container and filled the vase once more. When he walked away after placing it back down, she saw the vase now had a bouquet of white flowers.

"You never forget, do you?" Lillian turned her face to the flowers with a warm, gentle smile Rosetta had never seen before. Her expression made her appear years younger. "You've always remembered they're my favourite."

"Aye," he answered, plopping himself down in one of the chairs at the table. He sat between them, since they had been sitting opposite each other.

"I'll get you some whiskey," Lillian said, turning from her chair to play host.

"What are you doing at a brothel?" Alister whispered while

she was gone, his eyes narrowing while his lips pressed hard together.

"I should be asking you the same thing!" she exclaimed back just as quietly. "I came here to get Naeem."

His brows drew together, and he opened his mouth to say something. Their hushed conversation was cut short when Lillian returned, leaning over to place a glass of whiskey in front of him.

"Why does he get booze and I have to sip tea?" Rosetta complained when Lillian sat back down.

"Because he's a man. Women shouldn't drink until it's evening."

Then, as if she couldn't help it, she gave them a loud, sudden burst of laughter. Her green eyes lit up brightly as they flickered between them, her usual downturned, grim expression turning upright with humour. She even shook her blonde hair around.

Alister and Rosetta gave each other a bewildered look.

"What's so funny?" he bit between clenched teeth.

"Just never thought I'd see you two in the same room without trying to cut each other's throats. I just can't believe it." She patted the table in Alister's direction. "Do you remember how I told you how one of the girls who worked here stopped those men from stealing from the safe?"

"Aye," he chuckled, rubbing his jaw like he was trying to think back. "I asked how a prostitute could stop a bunch of men ransacking a place."

Rosetta's eyes widened and she put her hands up to shake them at Lillian, wishing this conversation would suddenly end. *Shut up, shut up, shut up.*

"And how she would most likely turn that knife on you if you ever met because she doesn't like men like you?" Not seeming to understand what Rosetta was trying to say with her hands, Lillian gestured towards her. "This is she."

Rosetta snuffed the urge to place her head in her hands in embarrassment.

His head shot to her. "You worked here?"

"Three years ago," she mumbled, turning her gaze away.

This couldn't be more embarrassing.

"I'm just surprised you've met and don't hate each other," Lillian laughed, lifting her tea and trying to stem her giggles, like she truly found it too hilarious to drink. "It's not what I expected."

We far from hate each other.

His eyes squinted as he placed his arm on top of the backrest of her chair to be closer to Rosetta, hushing his voice. "Why didn't you tell me you worked for her?"

"Because it's none of your business."

He grunted in answer.

"How do you even know each other?" Lillian asked, a frown of confusion crinkling the smile she wore. "From memory, I don't think you have ever been at Tortaya at the same time."

Rosetta's eyes widened. *Oh no.*

She didn't get the chance to stop Alister from saying, "She's been sailing with me for the past few months."

The smile Lillian wore slowly faded, little by little, as realisation seemed to settle in. A cringe started to blanket Rosetta's features.

"*Him*, Rosetta?" Her teacup lowered so she could gently place it on the saucer. "He's the one you've been sailing with?"

"Aye," he chuckled. "Helped her get that little ship of hers."

Even though she wanted to bite at him that her ship was bigger than his, she couldn't stop herself from palming her face because of his response.

That's it, I'm dead. Lillian obviously knew who Alister

Paine was, and she would never approve of a pirate like him.

I'll never hear the end of this until the day I die.

She'd seen the wanted posters of his face while she'd been walking around, posted to bulletin boards and occasionally in a bar. She now knew just how large that bounty was, and it was impressive, to say the least.

Shame, embarrassment, and chagrin sailed through her.

"You! You!" Lillian started to yell before she reached over and grabbed Alister by the ear and yanked.

"Ow!" His face morphed into pain. "Watch the earring!"

Her lips parted in a gasp as she watched them. She was surprised Alister wasn't flipping into a fit of rage at what she was doing to him. His head started to lower as if he was trying to follow her to reduce the damage.

"You're just like your bloody father!" She yanked even harder.

His head turned to Rosetta, his face twisted into a horrible wince. "What the hell did you say to her?"

Never had Rosetta wanted to disappear more than at this very moment as realisation dawned.

Her eyes opened wide. *She's... She's...*

"Oi! Ma, stop it!"

Alister was Lillian's criminal son. *Someone kill me, please.*

CHAPTER FOURTEEN

When Alister came to this mansion, he hadn't expected to see Rosetta sitting down, having tea with his mother.

When they'd told him she was busy with a client, he'd gone into a murderous rampage, wanting to kill the man laying with her. He'd warned her if he came here and found out she was sleeping with a man, despite his father being dead for years, he'd kill him.

He knew she still worked, despite Alister regularly giving her so much money, she didn't need to anymore. He just didn't want to know that the faces his mother had been beneath were still alive.

So, to find Rosetta with her instead... that had come as a surprise.

Not once had he ever come here and found his mother having tea with a woman who wasn't a girl working for her. He figured they must have a close relationship and he'd been curious to unveil exactly what it was.

He knew the secretive Rosetta probably wouldn't have told him if he'd asked. Part of him had wanted to back away, knowing if he entered this room that the truth of his relationship with Lillian would be revealed.

He just hadn't realised he should be worried about his mother finding out about the fact he'd been with Rosetta! Or currently was. Whatever.

However she saw it, it meant his ear was coping a firm yanking!

"Let go!" he finally yelled with a stern, firm tone when she hung on tight.

He was moments away from being truly furious. Alister wouldn't lash out at her, wouldn't dare touch or grab her that was in any way aggressive.

These two women weren't the same.

Rosetta was strong, and he saw her as such. She could take his strength, his brutality, and had proved that repeatedly. She even seemed to like it.

His mother was older and had always been a little frail and fragile. She was often sick. He feared, truly feared, that if he grabbed at her in anger like he did Rosetta, he'd break her.

With one last tug, she finally threw his head back.

Lillian folded her arms across her chest, anger and disappointment clear on her face. Alister hated it when she looked at him with that expression, and he gnashed his teeth tightly.

He turned his head to Rosetta so he could yell at her. "What did you–"

His words were cut short when he saw her head in her hands, as if she was either ashamed or embarrassed. He didn't like how it felt to know that.

Well shit. He didn't know what he'd done wrong, but he couldn't blame either one of them for talking to each other when they didn't know the other's relationship to him.

He grabbed his glass of whiskey and threw his head back to down the whole thing in one go.

I shouldn't have come into the room. He'd just wanted to spend time with his mother before he left port, like he always did.

He always came on the last day. It was generally when he was the calmest after being out at sea for so long. He liked to adjust to the land before he came here to be weighed with the despondent emotions that would sink him when he was with her.

He'd gone to the florist first, the same one Rosetta had stopped at the day before, so he could buy her the healthiest bouquet of white gardenias. He'd been performing this task since his father died, taking over for him in his death.

Finally, Rosetta lowered her hands to look at them, slowly drawing them down her face and hollowing it.

"I'm sorry. I–I should leave you two to be reunited," she said, turning her head to the table and pushing her chair back.

Alister pushed it back in, making her gasp. "Nay, stay."

Whatever he was being punished for had already been dished out.

He watched Lillian's lips purse. "I also want to give you something before you leave."

She got up and walked over to the side table next to her bed to open the drawer. *She wants to give Rosetta a gift?* That was strange. *Just how close are they?*

"Because he's here, I know I can give you the last bottle I have."

She started to hand a medium glass vial to Rosetta, and he took it before she could. He inspected the clear liquid.

"What is it?"

"A perfume," she answered him. "I make it from the gardenias you bring me when they're starting to die."

Alister fell back in his chair with a shocked laugh.

No wonder Rosetta often reminded him of the sweet memories he had of his mother; she'd been wearing the flowers he brought her the entire time!

He gave it to her, his laughter still rolling as he shook his head. *What are the bloody odds?*

"Thank you," Rosetta said quietly, staring at it with a frown, like she'd come to a similar realisation as him.

"Were you the one who dressed him?" His mother gave him a bright warm smile. "You look so handsome. I've never seen you look this clean and nice before."

She started playing with the ties of his tunic and his eye fell on Rosetta, whose cheeks seemed a little redder than usual. He blinked. He didn't think he'd ever seen her blush that wasn't from arousal.

"Aye," he sighed. "She told me I looked poor."

"Of course, she did! When she's honest, she's brutal with it." She let out a giggle and he finally saw the expression on Rosetta's face curl into something lighter. "You did look poor, my dear. You dressed for comfort on the seas, not the niceties of land." Then, she turned her attention to both of them. "Anyway, you have yet to tell me how you met."

Alister leaned back in his chair and put his arm around Rosetta's, patting her on the shoulder.

"I let her borrow my ship so she could get hers."

"Borrow?" Rosetta practically shrieked.

He grinned, knowing his words were exactly what she needed to brighten up. Getting her riled up was Alister's sure fire way of getting her to stop being so upset. He did it often.

"I stole his ship from him and left him in Dunecaster so he could watch the back end of it sail away!"

"But he obviously got it back," Lillian said with a raised brow and an upward curl to her lips.

"So? I still had to convince him to help me get the Laughing Siren, and that was no easy task."

"She tricked you, didn't she?" Her smile turned knowing. "Rosie's always had a way of using that mind of hers."

He was about to agree, since it was so obvious, but his words fell short. His grin faded.

"Wait." His head turned to Rosetta. "Why does she get to call you Rosie?"

Rosetta looked surprised that he'd asked. *I want to call her that.*

"Oh my," Lillian gasped, placing her forehead against her fingertips in disappointment in herself. "I always forget you hate being called that because of–"

She didn't finish her sentence, instead looking at Alister warily.

"It's fine," Rosetta sighed, gesturing towards him. "He knows. He was there when I killed him."

"I hated that man the moment I saw him!" His mother yelled, her thin fingers curled into weak fists on her lap. "He was a horrible, rotten cretin!"

"How the hell did you meet him?" Alister did *not* like the thought of Theodore Briggs being anywhere near his mother.

They both threw a hand at Alister.

"Long story," Rosetta answered. "Could we move onto something else?"

A knock sounded at the door.

"Rosetta?" a man called.

Why is a man calling for her here? A brothel.

"Don't come in!" Rosetta yelled. "Go wait out front, Naeem. I'll be out soon."

The tension in his shoulders relaxed.

Her eyes fell back to Alister. "He wasn't at the ship this morning and I knew I had to come get him, otherwise he wouldn't have woken up until noon."

"That's right, you're sailing away today," Lillian murmured. A deep frown of worry and sadness crept over her, clouding her eyes. "Both of you."

"Aye," he nodded. "Got ships and crews to lead."

She sighed, as though she hated it but understood, until her head snapped to the side, as if she suddenly realised something.

She pointed her index finger at Alister with deeply disappointed eyes. "I should yank on that ear of yours again!"

Alister never surrendered to anyone – except his mother. He put his hands up. "What did I do this time?"

He didn't even know what he did the first bloody time!

"How dare you make this girl pay for her crew to enjoy themselves here by herself because of what you've been stupidly doing with each other!"

He slammed not only his fist, but his entire forearm on the table as his head snapped to Rosetta. "You did what?"

She cringed while his mother flinched.

"O-Oh," she stuttered, covering her mouth with her fingers. "You didn't know?"

"What the fuck did you do that for? That must have cost a bloody fortune!"

"What I do with my–"

He put his hand up to silence her. "Don't need to hear it again, lass. How much do you have left?"

She turned her head to the side, as though she was dismissing him, and yet, she dug into the slit in her dress to get her purse. She threw it on the table so he could hear it only had about three or four coins in it.

"I didn't mean on you. I meant all together."

Without looking at him, she gestured to the purse on the table again.

No, it couldn't be. He picked it up and looked inside to confirm he was correct.

"This is all you have left? You had over six-hundred pounds for your own personal pocket."

She'd spent almost every coin she had on her by coming to port. He realised she didn't have any personal funds to lean on should things go astray when they went back to sea.

What she had left was barely enough for a meal.

"What...? Why...?" He pressed his fingers against his crinkled forehead in disbelief. "How could you be so stupid, Rosetta?"

When she didn't say anything, squeezing her arms across her chest tighter in defiance, he bashed his fist on the table again.

He snapped his head towards his mother when he felt both her hands cup one of his. She shook her head at him as if to tell him 'no', like he shouldn't be angry!

She reached up and brushed her thin hand against his cheek in a comforting gesture to settle him. "She's a woman, Alister."

"What does that have to do with anything?"

"This is none of your business, Lillian," Rosetta bit. "Stay out of it."

His mother ignored her request like she would have with most. "Men are cheered for their endeavours, whereas women are scorned, dear. She was worried her men would be jealous, so she paid for them to have a night of the same, on her behalf."

A cold rush seemed to roll over him. *It's because of me?*

"I'm leaving," Rosetta said, quickly sliding her chair back before he could stop her. She stepped away and then turned to bow at Lillian. "Thank you for your help, Madame Lillian."

"You *will* be coming back here," she demanded with narrowing eyes, eyeing her up and down carefully. "I won't have you disappearing on me after everything."

Rosetta's lips thinned, as if that was exactly what she'd planned, before she gave a curt nod. "I promise."

Then she turned from the room and exited.

"How much was it?" he snapped when she was gone.

She gave a sigh, brushing her hand over his cheek as if she missed doing it. "Four-hundred and ninety-two pounds."

He frowned. That was so expensive. "I expected more."

She gave a short scoff through her nose. "I owed her for what she did for me. She almost died saving this place from ruin. She didn't get that scar from standing by and doing nothing while three men terrorised the place."

Alister had been furious when he'd come into port nearly a year later to discover what had happened.

"You mean the one across her stomach?"

She nodded. "Just the one."

His eyes wandered across this room. It wasn't the one he'd grown up in. No, this place was new, and he was the reason for it. He'd built this place eight years ago so she could take in women she wanted to help, give them a safe place. It gave her meaning. He also wanted to make sure she always had a roof over her head, food in her belly, and people around her so she wasn't alone while he was out at sea.

A way she could be surrounded by guards and be protected.

He knew he had a sister, one he counted as a half-sister since his father had never claimed her. However, Agnes was rebellious and avoided their mother as much as possible, even though they lived on the same island.

Alister cared for one person in his life, and it was the frail woman in front of him. No expense was too great to make sure she was comfortable. Her business now made her so self-sufficient that Alister didn't need to give her coin unless he wanted to.

No one except for Derek and Pierre knew their relationship.

As much as learning Rosetta was taken under his mother's wing came as a shock to him, at least he knew it meant she'd been taken care of, since Lillian wouldn't have let her go without.

"How did she come to be in your employ?" Alister asked, turning his eyes to the window in thought.

"It's not my story to tell, dear."

"Aye, but you're going to anyway." He brought his gaze back to her with a look she knew would mean he wouldn't let this go. "If it was before the last time I came to port, then it wasn't long after she left Luxor."

Lillian leaned back to sit comfortably in her chair while grabbing the pot of tea and refilling her near-empty cup.

"I'd heard about a young girl working the streets, someone who new in port but quickly making a name for herself." His mother raised her cup and gave a humourless snort. "That's not always a good thing."

"She was popular?" Alister wasn't sure if he liked hearing that. *I did ask.*

"Yes and no." She eyed him warily, her gaze flicking to and from him when usually, they were able to remain fixed on his face. "She was violent. If a man treated her wrong, she'd lash out. If she witnessed one hit another street girl, she'd turn a knife on him. Men wanted her because she was pretty; they wanted to be the one to tame her."

Her lips thinned as she paused.

"If it wasn't for Naeem watching her back while helping her steal coin by pickpocketing as well, I don't know what would have happened. The girls on the street loved her because she protected them. They had someone to turn to when they were wronged, someone who would fight for them when no one else could or would. She wanted to mete out justice."

"You brought her in because of this?"

She shook her head. "No. I wasn't sure if I wanted to bring someone like her into my business. I didn't want her to bring trouble."

"So then how–?"

"The girls who worked here begged me to, especially when they brought her and Naeem here, injured and bleeding because someone cruel discovered they'd been sleeping on the street and were easy targets." Her eyes bowed in deep sadness. "She was a broken woman, Alister. She was so determined to get her ship, she wanted to make coin any way she could and refused to pay for somewhere safe to stay so she didn't spend it. She didn't care for her safety. I couldn't bear to know I'd turned this girl away."

She cleared her throat of the clogged emotion in it and recomposed herself.

"I let them stay in two of the rooms for free, knowing they wouldn't stay if I made them pay. There were many unoccupied, so I knew it wouldn't matter. Naeem became a guard while Rosetta worked as a girl and helped to protect this place along with him. If a man mistreated one of the women, she was the first to step in and help her." His mother gave a great laugh. "She also hunted them down and took all their coin to give to the girl as compensation. Once she was safe, she started to flourish in the year she was here. She eventually got enough money together to buy a small ship and a crew, right before you came back two years ago."

"You didn't tell me about this last time I was here. You only told me people tried to ransack the place."

She reached forward and cupped his cheek once more to rub her thumb over it. He felt the hairs of his face bent the other way and the sound of it scraped his ears like sandpaper.

"I didn't want to worry you, since I knew there was a chance she'd return." She gave him a small smile. "And she did, with a newer and bigger boat each time, with more men who wanted to follow her."

He gave a light chuckle. "She's got a way at getting men to do what she wants."

Alister had been the victim of that time and time again.

He wasn't happy to learn this part of Rosetta's past. She had endured much more pain and suffering than she originally let on.

She can be so light and bubbly sometimes, he thought to himself as he rubbed the back of his neck. It made it hard to see she hadn't had an easy life. It often made him forget.

What else has she gone through?

"Leave her alone, Alister," his mother pleaded, her eyes bowed into heavy arches of concern. "She's been through enough. Don't make it worse."

"She's a grown woman," he answered with a dead expression. "She can make her own choices." He rather liked that one of them was sailing with him so he could ride out this lust he seemed to have for her.

"If you hurt that girl..." Her voice turned stern in the way it did when he knew he was deeply angering his mother. "I will be very disappointed in you."

He pointed two fingers at her. "Don't turn me into the bad guy. I don't lay a hand on her that she doesn't want!"

She lightly smacked him upside the head. "I'm not talking about that. I know you wouldn't – I taught you better than that."

Yes, she did. His mother was the reason he didn't like to lay a heavy hand on women or do anything violent or unkind to them. If he didn't like the idea of it happening to Lillian, then why should he do it to others?

He finally understood what she was trying to say, and he gave a deep, bellowing laugh while tilting his head back.

"Nay," he chuckled with deep-seated humour. "She's too smart for that, knows it would be foolish."

"Then don't do what your father did to me!" He opened his mouth to say he would never, but she pointed to a cup on the table. "I had to give her special tea today, so don't try and tell me you wouldn't."

He winced. *Damn lass, you really threw me off the pier here.*

"It was an accident." He couldn't believe he was having this conversation with his own mother!

She squinted her eyes at him. "Men always say it was an accident, but you're not the ones who have to deal with it!"

Before she could get into one of her tantrums about his father, he dragged her in for a tight hug. He patted the back of her hair, taking in her motherly scent that had been a comfort for him since he was a child.

"How have you been, ma?"

"Been missing you, you ungrateful child," she murmured against his broad chest.

Nay, never been ungrateful.

Rosetta was working with Naeem to make sure everything was shipshape before they set sail.

She had long ago changed into her new brown tights and the white, button up tunic. She threw her now worn-in boots onto her feet, and they almost came to her knees.

"I've chosen Mr Andrews as our new helmsman for the night shift," she told Naeem as they walked through the hallways below deck.

They had just gone through the stocks and supplies one last time, making sure they had everything they could possibly need. She also checked on the livestock they'd bought, checking how much feed they had to keep them alive for as long as possible.

They had cows, chickens, a pig, and a goat she was set on calling Reginald. She called every goat Reginald, and she would grow close with it over the course of the next few months.

Men had been tasked with caring for a certain animal, and they would treat them like a beloved pet before they were sadly eaten. It gave them something to enjoy doing on the ship while out at sea.

"Thomas Andrews?" he asked, putting his hand over his

chin in thought as they rounded a dimly lit corner. "He's a good man; strong, too."

"Yes, well, he's been with us for just as long as Mr Smith and I know he can do all the same tasks."

He could read, count, navigate the stars. He had never been a sailor before he'd become a part of Rosetta's crew, but she knew he was up for the task, and she trusted him explicitly.

He was a few years older than them, but she knew Mr Smith had taken him under his wing like a son, showed him how to do everything. *I feel like he did it so he had someone to replace him when he died.*

She snuffed out the ache that started to rise before it overtook her.

"I think you've made a wise decision," Naeem answered. "I'm glad you made it before we set off."

She'd been thinking about it for the past few days, trying to make her choice. He'd already been temporarily performing the requisite tasks, but she thought she should finally give him the official title.

"I'm glad I've got your approval," Rosetta said. "I'll put his name forward and hopefully, the men will vote him in."

Naeem nodded his head. "Good idea, but I don't think there will be any naysayers. Will he be bunking with me in my cabin?"

"Yes. I know you've enjoyed the space to yourself for a while, but he will need to be near the helm as well."

A bright grin showed the humour of his loud laugh.

"True! But I don't mind sharing. I kind of miss John's snoring now that I don't have it."

She gave a soft, sad smile, before walking in front of him to climb the steps to the surface. The repairs for her ship were done, the railing rebuilt.

She saw Alister leaning against said railing next to the gangplank on the main deck. His arms were folded, and his head snapped up when he noticed her emerge.

A deep sigh left her. *I knew he would come.*

"I have to go. I think he wants to discuss exiting the port."

Naeem, never one to question her or see through her lies, nodded in understanding. "Makes sense. I'll keep making sure we're ready."

She threw her hand up and poked him in the chest. "Check everything."

He rubbed the back of his head with another laugh. "Sure thing, Captain. We won't make the same mistake as last time."

Rosetta turned from him and made her way up the stairs to the quarterdeck. It put her in the path of Alister, and she looked at him from the corner of her eye.

"Let's talk in the navigation room."

With a nod, he unfurled his arms and followed behind her.

Rosetta let him close the door as she made her way to the desk, turned, and leaned her backside against it. She crossed her arms over her chest, turning her head to the side.

"I'm sorry," she grumbled. "I didn't know she was your mother. She never told anyone the name of her son and I didn't tell her who I was sailing with because you told me not to."

He walked further into the room, his bootsteps heavy and echoing. "Aye, I know."

He threw a bag of coins onto the desk next to her, making them rattle and clink together when it landed.

She frowned, looking down to grab them. "What's this?"

"It's half of what you paid," he answered, stepping back from her. "Not going to make you pay for something that's half my fault, lass. Not that I approve of what you did."

With a sneer, she tried to hand it back to him. "I didn't ask for your help."

"Nay, but you're getting it." He raised a brow when it was obvious she was going to argue with him. "Take it. I told her I would."

With a sigh, she placed the sack back on the desk. *At least I have funds now.*

"About Lillian..."

"You can't tell anyone she's my mother," he told her. "I'm a criminal, Rosetta. Not just any criminal, but one of the most wanted men on the seas. The moment anyone discovers who she is..."

"They'll capture her to use her against you," Rosetta finished for him. "I know, I figured as much already." She finally turned her eyes away from the sack to look at him with a sigh. "I'm sure you didn't intend for me to find out about her until you saw me sitting with her."

"Aye, figured there was no point in hiding it once you saw me."

Her lips thinned tightly. "I'm guessing you forced her to tell you why I was living in that house."

"Nay. She refused to tell me."

"Liar," she scoffed, making his eyes narrow. "Although I very much wanted to keep that part of my life hidden, I know she would have told you if you coerced her enough. There are things I've done that I'm not proud of, Alister, ways I behaved to get where I am now." She turned her gaze away to look at the cabinets, needing to look away from him. "I wanted this ship and Theodore dead to the point where I didn't care what happened to me, as long as I reached those goals. I didn't even care if I died."

She clasped her hands in front of her, circling her thumbs together as she stared down at the floor.

"Lillian is very dear to me. She made that time bearable, helped me get through the first year I escaped. I would never do anything that would put her in danger." She finally turned her face to him to see he had a deep frown, his lips tight with emotion. "I will never reveal your relationship with her, regardless of what happens."

No matter what happened between Alister and Rosetta, she would never break their trust, would never reveal this dangerous secret.

He gave her a singular nod to say he understood. "Is your ship ready?"

"Yes. Naeem and I have been working on it while waiting for you to return."

Rosetta had peeked over at his ship to see Pierre and Derek doing the same.

"Good, start leaving the bay. We'll go after you."

Then Alister turned from the room to leave. *Things were never meant to get this complicated.*

"Wait," she demanded, making him turn back around.

She grabbed a small leather pouch sitting on top of her desk and threw it at him. He grabbed it from the air and opened the fold of it.

"My eyepatch?" He pulled his usual, black, convex eyepatch from it. "You had it all along?"

Not only did Rosetta roll her eyes, she rolled her head on her shoulders as well. "Look further inside, you big idiot."

When he did, he pulled out a second black eyepatch that looked exactly the same – except for one important feature.

She watched him rub his thumb over the convex shape, thumbing the pattern etched into it. His brows drew into heavy creases.

"My family crest?" He turned his head up to her. "But you didn't know my ring was my father's until I told you last night."

"I know," she answered, lifting her shoulders.

With her heel against the ground, she started to sway one of her feet from side-to-side to appear casual, as if she didn't care how he reacted, even though she very much did.

"I took your eyepatch so I could have its exact dimensions, since I knew you must favour it. I've never seen you wear any other." She turned her gaze to the wall. "I'm good friends with the leatherworker here and I asked him to make it for me while I got Naeem. I studied your ring while you were asleep this morning and drew it for him."

Somehow, she felt a little uncertain and... shy about giving Alister a gift. She didn't even know if he would like it.

Alister's family crest had been pressed into the convex of the patch and painted with a leather-safe paint.

"I picked blue for the crest since you like the sea so much and I figured it was your favourite colour. Sorry if I got it wrong, or if it's supposed to be a specific colour." She pouted. "It should be as comfortable as your other one, since I got him to make it the same. Actually, it should be better, since he would have used the highest quality materials for me."

When Alister stomped towards her with an undecipherable expression, she felt her gut twist. *Perhaps I overstepped.*

It was often hard to tell where the boundaries were between them, especially since the line seemed to be heavily blurred these days.

"If you don't like it, you don't have to wear it," she started, turning her gaze away once more while nibbling at the corner of her lips. "I just knew you wouldn't give me your patch without asking why."

He was also a little sensitive about the whole thing.

Alister grabbed her jaw in a firm grip and forced her to face him. There was a dark hint to the way he stared at her, one that wanted to swallow her whole right there and then.

He ripped the flat eyepatch from his face to stare down at her, both of his two different eyes directed at her.

"You're lucky we have ships to set sail," he said with a deep rumble, before he crashed his lips against hers.

A small moan caught in her throat at the contact, his tongue swiftly coming forward to brush against hers. The kiss was deep, controlling, unyielding, and he ended it too soon, staring down at her with that same hungry look before backing away.

He walked from the room to go back to his own ship without a word.

A soft smile curled her lips when she saw him don the eyepatch with his family's crest instead of his old one.

CHAPTER FIFTEEN

3 months later

Rosetta was seated in a small rowboat along with Naeem and four others rowing the oars. She could see Alister and Pierre in a boat just in front of them.

They had finally arrived at Dead Man's Island, and no one wanted to wait to find out if it was Dustin's Trove or not. They instantly dropped anchor in the shallows and headed out.

They knew this must be the island on the map she'd stolen in Tortaya all those months ago. After circling once, they mapped it as the exact shape as the drawing. Even the cliff that had been vaguely drawn was the same.

It had taken three months to get here after going to the other two locations of maps that could hold booty. Neither did, but one looked as though they had at one point, been dug up by other treasure hunters.

They'd seen a speck on the painted map on her navigation room wall that looked like the parchment. It was close to the Sthrill Islands, where she'd stolen Alister's ship from him.

After a long discussion between herself, Alister, Naeem, Pierre, and Derek, they decided unanimously to come here first. It appeared their gut feeling had been correct.

But is this Dustin's Trove?

It was out of the way, far from any trading sea routes. This island was in the middle of nowhere. The fact it had been on her wall at all was a surprise.

It looked like a giant hill of sharp rocks that eventually ran up to a long, deadly cliff. It was relatively small, no sandy bank for them to row up to in order to hop onto land. They would've needed to take their rowboats to some rocks and try to climb out without falling into the water.

Luckily, they weren't doing that.

The map didn't say they needed to set foot on the land, but rather go through or under it. With the late noon sun shining directly against the cliff, it lit the way as they started rowing.

She expected a wall to stop them, that they would have to turn around and deem this a failure, but the closer they got, the more she could see a shadow. She watched Pierre point to it. Alister patted him on the back and directed his men rowing the oars in that direction.

It was impossible to tell from afar, but the shadow led to a small cave with ocean water running through it.

They lit torches with flint and steel so they could see in the darkness. Eventually, it became so narrow that the men brought their oars into the boat and started pushing against the walls of the cave to steer them.

"We'll need to watch out for the tides," Naeem commented when they turned around a sharp bend. His voice echoed against the walls, as did those from the boat in front of them. She couldn't hear what they said, since they were too far away to be distinguishable.

"I don't think so." She looked up at the high, rocky ceiling. "We'll know when it's starting to rise, and we'll have plenty time and room to escape."

Silence fell, and it gave Rosetta time to quietly reflect on the last three months of their journey.

Not long after they'd left Tortaya, they'd gone through a tough storm. The Laughing Siren and the Howling Death separated during those few days, but had always been in spyglass distance from each other.

It hadn't been as dangerous as the one that damaged her mast and they'd been able to navigate through it relatively close to each other. Still, they had chosen a location to meet if they were truly separated.

After that, they'd raided a trading boat and sunk one fleet ship weeks apart from each other. They'd tried to raid it first. It had added to their supplies but had mostly been unnecessary. Rosetta was adamant about destroying the Queen's fleet ships, blaming her for putting a man like Theodore in a position of power to hurt someone vulnerable.

Now that she trusted her crew completely, Rosetta felt comfortable crossing between their two ships at will and had no fear of spending an extended period away from her own.

Before Tortaya, she could have cut the tension between herself and her envious crew with a knife. There had been obvious unspoken spite and jealousy brewing.

As time crept on, she'd seen the way they acted or looked unhappily at her, and it had always been worse after she spent any time with Alister.

Now, months later, the tension on her ship was almost non-existent. They'd appreciated what she had done for them, understood she knew it was unfair, and had gone out of her way to make amends.

They also knew she would most likely take them to a port to satisfy their needs again. She wouldn't wait so long to do it, and she definitely wasn't paying for it this time. Madame Lillian's girls had made sure their one night had been spectacular and worth every penny, with Alister's help, of course.

Now, she had freedom.

Freedom she used to be entangled with Alister whenever she pleased on either ship.

Some nights, she'd have dinner with her crew, others she'd

eat with Alister so they could spend the night together. She often slept alone, but sometimes, he'd be in her bed. Other mornings, she woke in his hammock.

As though they were inescapably drawn to each other, he'd swing over to her ship to talk to her while she was manning the helm before going back to steer his own. He'd let Pierre take over to talk to her about an island they were passing, about where they were in the world – any excuse to come and interact with her.

She would often do the same.

When he could see she was tired, he convinced her to let him man the helm for a few minutes. It allowed her to take a break and rest her arms, get a drink, eat, until she was ready to take over.

It was common for those who manned the helm to do this regularly throughout the day, but Alister had begun to involve himself in her rotation. He occasionally allowed her to do the same for him, since her shift was shorter than anyone else's on both ships.

He trusted her, as she trusted him.

Rosetta lacked his endurance, so she often did short morning and afternoon shifts, making Naeem do the peak of the day. It had always been that way between them. Mr Thomas had taken over John's position at night.

Alister also forced her to help count the stock and supplies regularly, forcing her to learn despite how much she tried to annoy him when he did.

There were days they didn't see each other at all, except from a distance. It was a silent truce of quiet and peace.

But as the months drew further into the year, the colder the winds became. Since they had entered the cold, bitter months of winter, she sought Alister out at night.

Rather than crawling her way into Naeem's hammock, she found it more comforting to crawl into his. So, even if she didn't see Alister at all throughout the day and well into the evening, she'd find him to soak in his warmth while she slept.

Not once had he seemed to mind.

She thought it might be because he could easily get her under him before they crawled into their chosen sleeping arrangements. Warm, naked, and curling into him with the blanket thrown over them, Rosetta often woke next to him and watched him sleep.

He'd stopped wearing his eyepatch while he was alone with her, and she'd take in the heat and sight of him for a little while. It was often accompanied with having to encourage herself to abandon his hammock to dump herself into winter air so she could man the helm of her ship.

Alister woke every time, would let her free before rolling back over to sleep, calling her some sort of oath for waking him. She'd giggle at him for it.

If she woke in her bed with him, he never knew she'd left it at all. She often tried to convince him to come to her instead.

Although the days were broken up by different, small events, a routine had formed, one she was comfortable and content with.

It also sent dread through her.

When she'd originally set sail alongside Alister, she had expected the passion between them to fizzle out by now.

He hasn't grown bored yet. Neither had she.

She'd never intended to sail with him for this long, and as every day passed, every week, every long month, Rosetta knew she was growing more and more attached, to him and to a life filled with security, safety, comfort, and pleasure.

The oceans were rough. It was a torturous element to have to live on, but she'd found happiness for the first time since she was a teenager.

It frightened her.

She never thought she'd ever experience something like

this. To have a wonderful crew who shared their laughter and entertainment with her. To have a second ship with a crew who would swing over to talk to hers, sharing memories and chatter.

Close friendships were built over games, food, drinking, and general rough housing. To see the two ships integrating closer together was joyful.

Naeem and Pierre were an insufferable pair who seemed near impossible to separate if they weren't on duty. There was a joke they were now married with how much time they spent together.

She didn't want to destroy that, didn't want to rip them or their crews apart, just as much as she knew she didn't want to part from Alister.

Those emotions and feelings were swirling and she grew saddened by them. Rosetta didn't want them.

What do I do?

At first, they only swelled up when he was sweet to her, when they were intimate. It made her heart warm or made her feel crazy, depending on the intensity of their passion.

Unfortunately, they were starting to pang even when they argued.

She refused to recognise them completely, refused to even think it. When she felt them, she turned away from those feelings because there was nowhere for those sparks to grow.

Like sparking flint and steel against sand, no matter how much she tried, it would never light.

It was a hopeless endeavour and she refused to even try.

It was like she was watching them roll against the sand by themselves while she sat with her arms wrapped around her knees in the dark. They sparked on their own, and she refused to give them anything flammable on which to light.

She sought Alister because she was like an addict who couldn't seem to get enough. He made her uncaring of what was happening within her beyond him touching her. She sought his warmth because it was comforting, and she hated being cold.

Rosetta also desperately wanted to draw away.

I will never tell him. She didn't want to tell him the truth she refused to acknowledge it herself. In some way, she was regretting agreeing to sailing with him.

A voice broke her from her depressing thoughts.

She faintly managed to hear Pierre's voice, since they had crept closer as they travelled. "The tunnel is opening up to a cave."

Darkness enveloped a large, open space as their boats floated in. They began to paddle into the middle side-by-side, bringing their lights closer together so they could see.

"It's empty," Derek mumbled.

"Nay, it's not." Alister pointed just to the right. "Go that way; I think I see rocks we can climb."

The closer they got to it, however, the more a distinct shape formed. Their flame torches reflected against parts of it and the further they rowed, the more it came into view, reflective metal glinting back at them.

"It's a chest," Rosetta gasped.

Not just any chest, but a large one.

"Is it...?"

"It's not enough," Alister said with a shake of his head. "This isn't Dustin's trove. It's fabled to have much more than this."

"No, but it's something!" Rosetta exclaimed with a grand smile. "I hope there's something good inside."

A few of them chuckled as they rowed closer to that bit of land. The ledge was made of rocks the height of their boats, eventually growing taller and taller until reaching the chest that sat on a small rise.

"At least we don't have to dig this time!" Pierre joyfully

chuckled as he used his hands to pull them towards the rocks.

"That's because you're lazy!" Naeem shouted at him.

Holding a flame torch, Alister was the first to climb out as Pierre followed, carrying a shovel just in case they needed to break a lock. Derek stayed in the boat, and she figured it was because of the instability of his peg leg.

"Circle off," Alister said while using his hands to shoo them away. "We'll call you when we've seen what's inside."

They moved and allowed Rosetta's boat to take their place so she and Naeem could step off. Hers stayed behind, since it wasn't in the way, and Naeem carried the torch for her as they exited.

They climbed up to the top ledge and approached the chest. The height of it almost came to her hip and must have been at least five feet long.

"There's no lock," Naeem said with a raised brow.

"What's the point?" Pierre gestured to the cave. "It's not like many people would come here."

"It looks like it's been here for a hundred years. It could be empty."

Despite their conversation, Rosetta stood next to Alister as he bent over and pushed the lid open.

They all held their breath as he raised the lid.

A ring of gasps sounded, their jaws falling. Rosetta's eyes widened at the vast amount of gold coins she saw.

"They're pieces of eight," Alister chuckled loudly, reaching inside to brush his fingertips against them before grabbing a small handful.

"Golden Spanish currency," Rosetta added with a tone of disbelief.

Each coin was about the size of her palm and had the same Spanish symbol pressed into it. She'd seen one of these coins before but never this many.

"One of the rarest, but the most valuable," Alister told

them with a large grin. "We're rich, lads. Very rich."

Even though his words were joyous, she knew him well enough to note the hint of disappointment in his tone. It wasn't Dustin's trove.

She brushed her hand through the coins to check if there was anything else inside and found nothing. Not a piece of jewellery, not a silver coin; nothing but that sparkling, glittering gold.

"Go call for our boat," Alister said to Pierre. "We need to figure out how to get this onboard without losing it in the water. We'll need everyone's help. It'll be heavy, and if we drop it, I'll probably shoot someone."

Pierre ran towards the edge of the rise so he could whistle and wave his arms. Naeem climbed down to her boat to get half the rowers while the other two stayed inside.

Alister leaned closer to her with a mischievous grin brightening his eye. She couldn't help sweeping her gaze over the eyepatch he was wearing, the one with his family crest.

"If we were alone, lass, I'd take you over this."

He thumbed the edges of it with his free hand, almost a sensual caress. It wasn't hard to tell he wanted to romance the chest like it was a sweet lover.

"Well," she said with teasing mumble. "We do still have to count it."

They often counted loot and coin together, since they were both the captains of their ships.

He gave a warm laugh, wagging his index finger at her. "You're absolutely right, and I hope we have as much fun counting this one as we did last time."

Rosetta had never allowed Alister to bind her hands behind her back so he could spank her and yank her hair while taking her from behind again. She thought once was enough to condemn her soul for eternity.

Still, a flush of desire warmed her chest at his words and

the memories of that day forever imprinted into her memory.

Men came up behind them and they stepped out of the way so they could grab the chest. They tested multiple ways to carry it so it was sturdy before they started making their way down the sharp rocks.

It was so heavy and large, only two people could be in the boat with it and Alister possessively opted to take a position. Derek took the other.

Her boat was overcrowded but manageable as they followed behind back to their ships.

"We should have a celebration," Rosetta commented as they rowed.

"A celebration is a perfect idea!" Pierre yelled loudly so the other boat could hear.

"Oh, aye!" Alister shouted back while rowing the oars himself. "We'll get the good booze out tonight."

"He must be in a good mood if he's willing to share it," Pierre grumbled before turning to her. A wide smile curled his lips. "Since we're in shallows, both ships can party together."

"We'll take watch when we're done," Naeem quickly said, eyeing Rosetta warily. "Since you did it last time."

"Did we? I don't remember." Pierre frowned in thought, placing a hand over his chin. Then, he shrugged like he didn't care. "Suits us. Our crew is a bit more, how do I put this... rowdier than yours?" He slapped his own knee with a chortle. "They'll be happy to hear they can get well and truly pissed. This is probably our biggest pay day ever."

He crawled forward to put his arm around her shoulders, half-laying against others to do it.

"And it's all thanks to Rosetta!" He shouted so loudly, it hurt her ears. "The lass copped a slap so we can cop a fat pay!"

"Rosetta!" one of the other men in the boat chanted, making others do it as well. "Rosetta!"

"Naeeeeem," she whined, covering her face with her

hands. "Please make them stop."

"Rosetta!" Naeem shouted with a laugh, pumping his fist into the air. "Who's the greatest and fairest of them all?"

"I think that would be me," Pierre cut in, placing his hand against his own chest.

"No, you're the dumbest and ugliest of us all."

He lunged for him. "I should push you off this boat!"

"Both of you, stop!" They shook the very full boat and almost made it tip, causing her to grab whatever was next to her in fear. "If you make me fall into this icy water, I have a gun and I'm not afraid to use it."

The last thing Rosetta wanted right now was to be sick from a cold. She had enough problems to deal with.

Eventually, her rowboat settled next to her ship while Alister took the chest to his own. She figured he was planning on them counting it in his cabin.

She climbed up the rope ladder that had been rolled down the side of the hull and crawled onto her ship.

"We found a big chest of gold," she told her crew, who were standing around on the main deck to find out what happened. "You'll all get good wages."

Cheers rung out, arms pumping into the air. Some even threw their hats to the sky in excitement.

Once Alister and his men pulled the boat high enough next to the Howling Death, they were able to grab the chest and pull it onto the deck with a booming thud.

He made a show of it, allowing everyone to come see what profit they had collected. It didn't matter if it was his crew on his deck or hers coming to have a peek.

Rosetta stood next to him to watch.

There was a certain sparkle that seemed to remain in the men's eyes afterwards, like the sun shining on all that glittering gold permanently refracting in them. They were thrilled, and the thrum of energy on both ships almost felt electric. The buzz of it affected all and made everyone livelier.

Months at sea could be tiring and to finally have some reward for it gave them the courage they needed to keep their spirits high.

"Glen," Alister called, getting the bulky, older man's attention. "We're going to host a feast for both ships. Grab the Laughing Siren's cook and every man you need to make something delicious. Don't care what it is, what needs to die, just make sure there's enough and it's ready by nightfall."

His neat and gloriously curled moustache twitched. The large, salt and peppered grey-haired man gave a curt nod before turning to go below. His son, Clint, hurriedly followed behind him.

"Now, lass." He grinned so brightly, it almost seemed blinding. "Let's go count this coin and split it."

They followed behind the men who carried the aged chest into his cabin. Alister pushed his eating table to the side so they could place their bounty in the middle of the room, knocking over the candlestick arbour as they went. They plopped it down with a loud bang and she feared it was so heavy, it would go through the worn timber flooring.

When the men were gone, he opened it once more, as though he couldn't stop himself from wanting to admire it.

"I thought it would be Dustin's trove," he mumbled while he stood staring at it. His tone was darker than she thought it'd be.

She came closer to see he was no longer smiling, as if he'd been putting on a show outside this room. Rubbing his muscled back with one hand, she slipped the other around his stomach to rub his chest as well. It was the best Rosetta could do to be comforting.

She was disappointed for him. "I know it's not what you wanted to find, but it's better than nothing."

He looked at her from the corner of his good eye, perusing

the features of her face. "There's a part of me that doesn't want to find it." He put his arm around her shoulders so she would come up beside him. "I promised Mad Dog I'd find it, and I really do want to, but it also gives me a purpose rather than just sailing across the seas without a real destination."

"Then I'm confused, Alister. Are you upset or not?"

He threw his head back and gave a deep laugh.

"Lass, I don't think I've been happier than I am right now, looking at this chest of gold with you."

His words made her turn her gaze away from him when a terrible pang lanced her through her chest.

He turned and lifted her until her backside was resting on the wooden top. He placed his hands on either side of her on straightened arms, his grin returning once more.

"And it's thanks to you that we have it."

"I have my uses." She waved her hand up and down dismissively, trying to hide that she was a little flustered. He was looking at her all handsome-like with a face of appreciation, and it did things to her insides. "So, when do you start becoming useful?"

He grabbed the outsides of her thighs and pulled her a little forward as he settled his hips between them.

"You're lucky you're sitting on this much gold, or I'd make you pay for that comment."

"You do realise we can do this tonight after we celebrate?"

He shook his head, his grin turning more devilish by the second. The way his teeth were tightly clasped showed just how much tension was beginning to build inside him. It always made her stomach flip with desire so swiftly, she let out a small gasp.

Alister would never know how just a simple look, with hunger and intent obvious in his good eye, could make Rosetta turn to a puddle.

"Nay. Half of it will be on your ship then, and I'm too

excited by the two things currently in front of me to wait."

With a tiny giggle, Rosetta put her arms around his neck and crossed them. She leaned in and placed her lips against his throat, right where his jugular pulsed, just because it made it quicken and him expire.

"Then what the hell is taking so long?" she whispered, nipping at his skin.

"You annoying brat!" He flipped her over so that she was laying over the chest. "You never learn, do you?"

No, never, she thought with a smile.

His actions said he was angry as he ripped her tights down so the waistband collected around her knees, buckling them together. Then he grabbed a large chunk of her hair and pulled so her body arched. He even bit the side of her neck.

She knew she'd said the exact right words to send this man into a lust-filled frenzy she was more than delighted to take.

Alister sat on the ground with a large pile of coins spread out across the floor. They'd emptied the entire chest so they could count it.

The pile was between himself and Rosetta, who had a cute pout of concentration as she counted. Her brows were crinkled, her lips puckered, her nose slightly scrunched.

His sight often veered away from what he should be paying attention to – the coins he was counting – to look at her.

They were about halfway through it, and even though it was a long, boring, mundane task, he was finding great enjoyment in it.

To watch Rosetta's hands constantly filling with rare gold pieces, with that adorable face, as her blue eyes caught the lowering sun from his murky windows – well, that was a sight worth seeing.

Her counted pile was much smaller than his since he didn't have to stop at stacks of ten like her, but he didn't mind he was doing most of the work.

Every time they sat down and counted coins together, which they did often because she couldn't count her own by herself, she got better. Making the stacks was the easy part, calculating them into groups of a hundred, but then calculating those hundreds often got her tangled.

He'd long ago realised she hated doing this – she was embarrassed she'd get it wrong. She was so quick-witted with everything else, so smart and cunning in other ways, that she saw herself as a failure and didn't even want to try. He always made her, though, even when she tried to distract him.

Secretly, he was thankful she wasn't great at it and that her progress was slow-moving.

Alister enjoyed counting coin. He did it often even if he knew how much was in his safe. Pierre had once told him he looked like a money-hungry, greedy pirate.

He didn't care, so long as it brought him joy.

Doing it with Rosetta, teaching her how to do it herself, brought him even more. It allowed him to silently watch her without her opening her dirty mouth to say something that made him want to bend her over something to punish her.

Instead, he was able to admire the beautiful woman in a calm, serene environment. That they were doing this here, in his cabin, in the place he felt most comfortable in, was even better.

"This is taking forever," she groaned after a long while. She changed her position from leaning against her hip to sit on her backside. Bringing her knees to her chest, she rubbed her eyes with her palms. "I hate you so much right now."

He gave a chuckle, pointing to the pile and circling his finger. "We're getting there; only got a quarter to go. It'd go quicker if you figured out how to count to a hundred."

"But that's so many numbers!" She fell back against the timber flooring, letting her arms fall out wide. "It's so easy to get confused."

"Nay," he said with a shake of his head. "It's easy if you break it up."

"I know how to count to a hundred! I just hate it when I suddenly lose focus and forget my number and have to restart!"

"Fine. I have an idea."

She sat up when he pushed over the small pile he had in front of him. He messed up his count on purpose by adding it to the larger one.

"You count out loud for both of us. If you get lost, I'll know where we're up to."

She nibbled the corner of her lips.

"Really?" Her shoulders rolled forward slightly, like she wanted to slump them but refused to. "Won't that slow you down?"

"Aye, but it'll make getting through this pile faster in the long run."

She eyed him carefully as she grabbed a handful of coins while shuffling her legs apart.

When she dropped a coin and he did the same, she said, "One." Another fell between her thighs and one right in front of himself. "Two." Then another. "Three."

She tripped in her count at forty-nine.

"Fifty," he said for her.

With a nod, she continued.

Once that hundred was down, she wrote down the number on a piece of parchment to keep track of the hundreds she put into the pile next to her. Alister just kept a mental note of his total amount, since he didn't need to write it down to do the math.

They started again.

The sun was still shining by the time they finished the entire lot. He made her do the final calculations, under his guidance, of course.

"It took us hours to count this," she grumbled, rubbing her cheek.

"Eight-thousand, nine-hundred and twenty-three pieces of eight." He flicked one of the palm-sized coins into the air with his thumb so he could catch it a moment later. "I think it must have held ten thousand, but the original owners took some with them before they left the chest there."

"What do you think happened to them?"

He shrugged. "Who knows? Died on the sea, murdered, got arrested. What do I care since it's ours now?" He flicked the coin into the air one last time to catch it. "Guess what now, lass?"

She squinted her eyes at his mischievous tone.

"Whatever it is, no. I'm too tired."

"We still have to split it."

Her face seemed to go white with dread. "I'm not counting half of this again!"

Laughter began to rumble from him, even as he shook his head. He pointed to the pile next to her. "How much you got there again?"

"Ah." She started fumbling for her piece of parchment that she'd written everything on. "Three thousand, two hundred, and six."

"How much is the even split?"

Her lips pursed together defiantly.

When he realised he'd thrown her too big of a number to wrap her head around on her own, he gestured for her to put her piece of parchment on the ground between them.

They broke it down together until she knew the amount was half with one gold piece left over – which he claimed.

Then, he helped her figure out how much she needed to take to add to the pile she already had.

Since he had the foresight to know she'd be tired and rather irritable by the end, he'd kept a few of his piles in hundreds by themselves, as well as one in a thousand.

It took him less than ten minutes to give her what she needed for her share from what he'd counted. They dumped her share into the chest to be transported to her ship.

When they were done, he reached across and hooked his arm around her torso to drag her closer until she was laying with her back against his chest.

"You look tired." She usually did after counting.

It did nothing to quell his desire for her, but she didn't usually have dark circles under her eyes. His lips tightened when he realised she didn't just look tired, but completely exhausted.

"I think I need to go for a nap," she laughed, allowing him to hold her as his way of saying she'd done a great job.

He knew it was meant to be a joke, since Rosetta was awake when the sun was, but it hadn't escaped his notice these days that she often went into her cabin by herself for an hour here and there.

He'd once caught her asleep in her bed, as though she hadn't been bothered climbing into her hammock, and had promptly left.

He rubbed the back of his neck.

I have been pushing us all too hard.

Dead Man's Island was the first time they'd stopped for a night for the last nearly three months. He hadn't allowed them to stop, to drop anchor and rest for a day or two along the way. Everyone was exhausted.

Even he was tired.

"We'll be staying here for a few days," he told her, since he'd just made the decision.

She raised her hand and patted the forearm across her chest.

"That's a good idea. Let your men rest." Tilting her head back so she could see him, she gave a small smile. "I'm going to go back to my ship for a few hours, but I think most of my men will want to join yours in the celebration. I will as well."

"Are you trying to say you're going to overcrowd my ship just so you don't have to clean your own?"

She clicked her fingers with a laugh. "Aw shucks, you caught me."

It would annoy him, but he couldn't help thinking, *it'd be nice to see the two crews together on one ship.* To watch them carouse around causing mischief and chaos sounded like an energy he might be able to deal with for a night.

"Alright, lass," he sighed, releasing her so she could get to her feet. "Get your men to fill my boat." He gave her arse a spank. "But remember, I'll be drinking whiskey tonight."

"Then I've changed my mind. I think I'll go celebrate in the cave by myself."

He grabbed her ankle before she could step away from him, careful not to trip her.

"If I can't find you, Rosetta, I might just row to it," he threatened before letting her go.

CHAPTER SIXTEEN

Alister held his fifth bottle of whiskey in his hand while leaning his side against a barrel that'd been brought up to the surface.

It had once been full, but the men had drained it of its contents throughout the evening. Other empty barrels were being used as tables for their games or other activities. Empty crates had also been brought up to be used as chairs and more tables.

"This has been a good night so far," Pierre said as he sat on top of the barrel next to him.

His legs were spread while he used the heels of his boots to prop his feet up on the metal ring that helped keep the timber together.

Alister was leaning his elbow on the top of the barrel next to him to keep himself propped up. He felt himself doing it the more his legs sagged.

They were both in front of Pierre and Derek's cabin door, watching the men celebrate with drunken tomfoolery on the main deck. They were also below and on the Laughing Siren, since the Howling Death got overcrowded at one point.

He was wearing his doublet coat since it was winter and saw most were wearing their own, including Rosetta with her tunic and tights beneath it. It was a rarity to see it buttoned up.

"I worry my ship will sink with the amount of people on

it," Alister joked, but he knew his ship could handle this number.

"They're going to start crawling to their hammocks soon."

The night was still relatively early, but once the feast had started at sundown, men drank like it was going out of fashion. It seemed many of them wanted to consume as much booze as possible, as if they were afraid they'd somehow run out.

It wouldn't; they had plenty in the stocks.

Because he'd been saving the whiskey for a night such as this, there were plenty of barrels available, alongside the many more barrels of cheap rum they had.

As one ran out, it would be taken away and a fresh, full one would be brought to the surface.

A few empty ones remained. They played games on top of them, sat on them, rolled them around the deck. Pierre had claimed this one long ago and Alister had come down from the quarterdeck to be a part of the crowd.

The feast had been epic.

With all the different ways Rosetta had taught their chefs to cook, the food had been delicious. Alister was sure if he went to search for more, there would be none left, everything eaten. It had been enough to feed a small army, and their ships combined was indeed a small army of pirates.

Even though they were soon to hit three months of being on the sea, they weren't eating plain food. Rather, they still had jarred vegetables and fruit, plus dried herbs that would last many more months.

"Most of her men will retire before ours," Pierre added, nodding his head at Rosetta, who still managed to have a plate of food.

Naeem had been guarding it while she flitted around the deck. She spoke with multiple people, being unusually chatty. She often came back to it and Alister shook his head when he saw her do it again.

"I don't think I've ever seen her eat this much."

"Good," Alister snorted, drinking a large chunk of his bottle. "She's putting on weight."

Rosetta had always seemed small to him. She was strong from manning the helm, but that muscle sat beneath a thin layer of fat he barely saw as acceptable.

"Don't women eat when they're sad, though?" Pierre asked, as if Alister would have any clue what went through a woman's head.

"Aye, but they get fat too when they're happy."

A large smile had been fixed permanently on her features this evening, and it often made Alister curl his lips. If he had been worried Rosetta was growing bored, a night of watching her enjoying herself was enough to settle his worries.

She still enjoys sailing with me.

After a day like today, where he'd gotten treasure because of her, taken her over it, then counted it with her, well... he knew he was still infatuated with her.

Cheerful music was being played, and they both watched her drag Glen Darkley to the centre of the main deck and force him to dance. The old chef was unsure of what to do as eyes turned to them, but she took the lead.

The usually expressionless man broke into a large grin, and he started to skip with her. The heavy man became light and spritely on his feet as he brought his arms up high, his elbows in the air.

"I didn't know Glen liked to dance," Pierre laughed. "Look at him go!"

He spun her, even picked her up to twirl her. The horrid squealing giggle she gave made them all cringe.

Alister threw his head back with a deep chuckle before bringing his bottle up and downing the last of it.

As if she was constantly watching him, she broke away from Glen to grab a bottle next to Naeem, who was leaning against his own barrel. Before long, the empty bottle Alister had been holding was swiped from him as she placed a full one in his hand.

She gave him that twinkling finger wave as she backed away, the one he always found flirtatious and got his hackles rising.

He almost shuddered. *Woman knows how to drive me mad.*

It was because of her Alister never had an empty one in his hand. He appreciated it, because he was rather content where he was next to Pierre.

When she returned to dance, she made his brows raise. She'd grabbed Derek by his meaty hands and dragged him to skip this time.

"Come on, Mr Crayley," she said brightly. "I know you can dance, despite that peg leg of yours."

Like poking a bear with a stick, he roared into action.

He grabbed one of her hands while placing the other around her torso, high up on her back. He began to do a close waltz with her, skipping her up and down the deck.

"At least he doesn't have many toes for her to step on," Pierre grumbled.

Alister knew she was able to keep up with Derek with ease. She was allowing the old sea dog to lead and kept up with his movements with practised perfection.

"I'm just surprised he's even doing it."

He was even more surprised when she grabbed Kent. He did a terrible job, and she eventually let the young Clint have a turn.

"The men like her a lot," Pierre commented, elbowing him in the shoulder.

She'd made herself the centre of attention and was bringing them great entertainment. Her laughter and energy seemed to keep the thrill going for the night. There hadn't been a single brawl since she started.

"Aye, I know they do." Alister brought his bottle to his lips, his sight trailing to those who seemed to be waiting in line to take her hand. He'd realised a long time ago that they liked her. "She wouldn't still be here if they didn't."

He wouldn't have allowed a woman to come between him and his men, despite his attraction to her. He was ever thankful it wasn't an issue.

When his statement was met with silence, he turned his head up to look at Pierre. His brow was raised in his direction, as if he had another opinion on the matter.

Alister shrugged, not caring to dig for information if the man wouldn't divulge it willingly.

In their small moment of silence, a short, light wind blew some of his long hair across his neck and billowed one side of his coat.

"I'm going to fix the ship," Alister told him quietly while swirling the remaining liquid in his bottle, looking at him from the corner of his eye.

"What do you mean? Like, restore it?"

"I've got more than enough gold now that I can do what I want and not care."

Alister had never had this much coin on him before.

That chest was going to allow him to be freer with his spending. For the first time, he was going to be able to give the men good wages while also having so much for himself and the ship that it didn't matter what he did with it.

He turned his sight back to the people in front of him before letting it wander over his ship. He moved it over the peeling railing; it hadn't been painted since before he stole it. The sails were patchy because he rarely replaced them.

All Alister did was make sure the hull was in perfect condition, but even then, it was worn-looking.

"I'd like to paint it and replace the timber planks where they're rotting."

"Does that mean you'll be fixing below deck as well?"

He nodded, his lips thinning as he thought about everything that needed doing. It would cost him, and would also be time consuming.

"Aye. I want to make the entire ship look like when we first took it."

Rosetta took better care of the way her ship looked. She made sure it shone, was freshly painted if it withered away in certain spots.

My ship should look as good as hers.

It had little to do with his pride – he thought his frigate was superior simply because it was a warship. It was more that he just wanted their ships to suit each other better.

"You do realise that means you'll have to dock for a few weeks, right?" Pierre laughed while shaking his head. "I doubt you'd do that just to make this ship look good."

Alister looked at him from the corner of his eye once more.

"When she wants to dock again, that's when we'll do it."

Not that Alister was going to tell Rosetta his plan. The longer he could stay at sea, the better he felt. He knew she would want to resupply at some point anyway.

Not yet. They still had another two months of good food before they fell into old habits of smoked meat and dried beans. Then, there were the ships they raided that resupplied their stocks. Still, he knew she would want to give her men a break soon. Alister would use that as a chance to fix his ship.

"What port?"

He shrugged. "Depends on where we are in the world." They had one map left to go to, and Alister still wasn't interested in going south. "I'm hoping to find another head fleet ship to raid for possible maps. I've already told her that."

Rosetta finally released herself from one of the men dancing with her and made her way towards them. She'd barely spoken a word to him tonight, but he often found her eyes finding him.

He let out a sigh of relief when she extended her hand to Pierre.

"No way!" the blond man laughed, leaning his body away from her. "I don't think my toes have healed from the last time we danced."

"I promise, I've improved since then." Her face held innocence behind that smile of mischief.

When Alister saw he was still going to deny her, he slapped the man on the back so he'd fall forwards off the barrel. That gave her the opportunity to unwillingly drag him to the middle of the deck.

"Better you than me, lad!" Alister shouted when he turned his head around to scowl at him.

Pierre was hesitant at first, trying to keep her at arm's length. He must have realised she didn't intend to hurt him for once, because his face grew into a beaming grin. Out of everyone she'd danced with, Pierre held the most skill and he was able to finally show it off.

The man had danced with many women to woo them into letting him up their skirt... for free.

Alister would have been bothered by how closely they were dancing, but he knew Rosetta would never allow him to touch her. Pierre also wouldn't disobey his order. He liked to push the boundaries just to nettle Alister, but he knew it was all under false play.

By the time Alister was three quarters of the way through his newest bottle, he could feel his body swaying a little more. Too many more and he feared he wouldn't be able to stand.

It's been a long time since I've been like this at sea.

Since rum did little to alter his state, it was odd to feel the boat rock under his feet and not feel steady like he usually did. He thought the barrel he was leaning against was the only thing helping to keep him upright.

Just as he considered finding a place to sit, looking around for what was available and what would be comfortable, he felt someone lifting his hand with the bottle in it.

He turned his head forward once more to find Rosetta pulling him. Shaking his head, he pulled his arm back. "Dance with the men, lass."

"But I've never danced with you before."

She grabbed his wrist this time and started to tug heavily.

"Aye, that's because I don't." Despite his protests, she managed to wrangle him to his drunken feet and pull him a few steps. He dug his heels in. "Nay, Rosetta."

Seeing he wasn't going to go much further, she lifted his arm for him and twirled underneath it. His elevated mood soured instantly.

"You don't have to do anything, then," she purred, before twirling the other way.

He grabbed her forearm and pulled her closer to his chest, bending her arm across it to yell directly at her. "I said nay!"

There was a rough break in the music, a partial silence of chatter from the loud, growling sound of his shout.

Alister *didn't* dance. He wouldn't jump around like a foolish monkey on the deck of a ship. He enjoyed watching his men do it, but he refused to participate.

He expected her smile to fall; instead, it deepened into something that had been humorous to almost sweet.

She allowed him to grab her the way he did since he wasn't hurting her. "Didn't you like the chocolate?"

It took him longer than it should have to realise why she was asking him. *I did.* He sighed defeatedly. She was asking him to trust her, and Rosetta rarely asked him for that.

"Fine, lass. Do what you want." If she wanted to dance with him while he stood here doing nothing because he wouldn't participate, then so be it.

With a nod, she took his near-empty bottle from him and

reached it out to Naeem. She received a full one and gave it to him.

Where do they keep getting these from? Why did Alister keep getting them?

Deciding he didn't care, he chugged a small amount while she used his other arm to dance. She twirled underneath it with a giggle. The sound lessened his annoyance.

She spun out and then used her momentum to curl his arm around herself when she spun back in. When her shoulder was against his chest, she reached up and kissed his cheek.

His brows shot up in surprise.

She started moving around him and he felt her hands dip into the side of his doublet coat to slip underneath his tunic, caressing her hand up the side of his torso directly against his skin. It slipped over his lower back, making it straighten in reaction, before her hand fell away.

"Have you been having a good night?" she asked quietly when she came back around to the front of him. She grabbed his hand while placing her other around his neck.

She stepped side-to-side, but she scraped the back of her nails through his hair from his neck to halfway up his scalp before his bun got in the way. His body's reaction to her nails was intense. One of his feet stepped back when he felt a wave of goosebumps prick down the side of his body and make his legs go nearly unbearably weak.

"Aye." He shuddered when she did it again, and he had to right his footing once more. "Had been."

She brought her hand from his neck to run it down his chest, brushing over one of his nipples in the process. She placed her hand on his side and made him spin in a circle with her.

He would have stopped her if she hadn't slipped her hand under his tunic. Most of her actions were covered by his doublet coat, so no one seemed to notice what she was doing.

No one saw the sensual way she was touching him, stroking him.

"How about now?"

She's playing with me. She hadn't just invited him to dance; she had wanted to flirt with him openly, almost secretly, while surrounded by their men on the deck with them. She wanted to fucking tease him, and it was *working*.

She let him go so she could grab his hand and twirl underneath it again before bringing herself closer. The way she looked up at him, how her lips pouted into a teasing smile before she licked at them, caught his attention completely.

"Lass..." he warned.

What he was warning her of, he wasn't quite sure.

I'm too drunk for this. She'd handed him bottle after bottle and now, she was playing with him. He didn't know what he was supposed to do. He knew what he wanted to do, but he didn't often draw attention to them like this in front of the men.

She rarely did, so why was she doing it now?

It didn't matter when they were in port; the men could get their own women. Here, they couldn't; they were stuck with each other.

It was getting late into the night, and he'd already been thinking about grabbing her but hadn't wanted to impose on her obvious fun. He didn't want to misread the signals she was giving him, but that was impossible to do in his current mental state.

Watching her dance. Watching her occasionally grab a piece of food to eat and then sucking on her fingers to rid them of the juice, her sight occasionally falling to him to give a warm smile. All of it was tantalising to him.

What is it that draws me to her? Why couldn't he get this seductive little devil out of his mind?

It often felt like she'd somehow burrowed something

beneath his skin that made him feel tight with tension whenever she looked at him. Spoke to him. Touched him.

The worst part was that none of it needed to be suggestive.

When it was, when she was purposefully toying with him, it got Alister so twisted inside his mind, he could barely stay in control.

"Yes?" she answered oh so sweetly, right before she placed her hand between them and cupped his sac. She rubbed her hand up his hardening shaft, like she knew she'd been giving him an erection.

A groan fell from him before he grabbed her by the nape of her neck and pulled her in.

Fuck. Something inside him fizzled when he crashed his lips against hers, quickly bringing his tongue forward when she accepted the kiss. He licked across her tongue, needing to taste her as a deep expire fell from him.

She's got my sail ropes in knots.

He kissed her hard, holding onto her so she couldn't escape, even though he could feel her lips moving over his just as eagerly. He could taste alcohol from his own mouth, he could taste food from hers, but most importantly, he could taste Rosetta's feminine sweetness.

Her hair was tangled around his splayed fingers, and he refused to let go of her head as he tried to deepen the kiss by pulling her further in.

He hadn't realised his eyes had closed under a heavy frown until they suddenly opened when he heard her giggling. Someone, most likely Pierre or Naeem, whistled at them.

Heat prickled the back of his neck, and he pulled back, his eyes falling over everyone watching them. Most wore grins and didn't seem to mind. They were either all too drunk or too happy with their payday to be bothered this night.

He turned his head back and took a swig of his drink in embarrassment. It turned into him chugging his drink when he felt Rosetta's fingertips pushing the bottle up to make him finish it.

"Screw this," he said when he was done before carelessly trying to throw it into the ocean.

It smashed against the railing instead, making glass shatter into the water. Then he grabbed her, threw her over his shoulder, and carted her towards his sleeping quarters.

Laughter rang out while hands slapped into claps or fists bashed on the railing or barrels.

"Enjoy yourselves; you deserve it after today!" Pierre threw at them.

"Shut the hell up!" he barked back, before chuckling when he heard her laughing as she swung behind his back.

He had to hold onto the railing connected to the stairs, since his legs felt heavier than they did a second go. He was thankful he did when he almost dropped them both.

He shook his head, trying to clear his hazy mind before stumbling his way to his cabin.

He slammed the door closed behind him and walked over to his bed to toss her down onto it before he actually dropped her. She let out a squeak when she bounced.

He gave a confused grin. "Where'd you get that, lass?"

She had somehow managed to grab another bottle, this one full with a cork in it.

"I think Naeem thought we'd need it."

She let it fall against the bed so she could reach up and drag him from his feet to kneel above her. The delighted and warm smile she gave him made his mind ache as she brought him closer.

"I feel like you're trying to get me drunk."

He took her lips in a singular kiss before his mouth started drawing them over her jaw and down the side of her neck. He ran his tongue along it just so he could make her do the little gasp that made his ears tingle.

"I just want you to have a good time tonight," she whispered with a sense of breathlessness as he began to suckle on her skin to bruise it. He was planning on covering her in little red marks from his mouth tonight.

He could feel her hands working on the buttons of her tunic. "You've been working so hard. You deserve a break."

Giving him drinks, dancing with him, speaking such tender words; he realised she just wanted to be sweet with him for once.

He worked on undoing the ties of her tights, but she broke his concentration when she kissed at the side of his neck, pushing his doublet coat off his shoulders.

"Plus, you're so much fun when you're like this."

Alister leaned back on his knees, groaning when he saw she'd already opened her tunic and revealed her perfect breasts to him. He quickly reached for one of her boots so he could remove them, needing to have this woman naked beneath him.

"That's not what you said last time," he told her, his voice husky and strained, even to him.

She makes me so damn horny. His cock felt constricted in his breeches, and he was desperate to plant it inside her.

Maybe she didn't realise it, but Rosetta didn't need to get him drunk to make him take her like that night in Tortaya.

He'd been refraining from doing it again when he'd seen how weak she'd been afterwards, but he'd had many nights since then where he wanted to just take her repeatedly to the point neither of them would be able to walk afterwards.

There was something inside him craved her. What was supposed to sizzle out and die over time, boring him with the same taste and feeling, instead made him hunger for her deeper.

"Then don't be so rough with me," she said when he tossed her second boot behind him to thud against the floor, almost as though she knew that was exactly what he'd been intending.

How else was he supposed to get rid of this feeling?

He often felt, if he just relentlessly fucked her the way he needed to, took out his lust on her, it would stop strangling him, stop controlling him.

Instead, it just broke him in the moment.

What is it about her body that makes me insane? he thought as he leaned down and grabbed a breast as he ran his tongue over her hard, rosy nipple. It was a wide and flat, messy lick.

He let go so he could suck on it freely when she gave him a haunting mew, her fingers coming up to tangle in the loose half of his hair.

Lifting her backside, she helped him strip her tights from her legs. He gripped at her thigh once they were off, pulling on it as he started swirling his tongue.

Sucking hard on her nipple, he pulled his head away until it slipped from between his lips. He moved to the other, wanting to make both red and aching from his *mean* attention.

When she started pulling on his tunic, he lowered his body to help her, placing kisses down her stomach.

He dipped his tongue into the shallow of her scar, liking that her skin wasn't perfect. It made him feel relaxed that she wasn't flawless. Women who had perfect skin made Alister, who was covered in scars, who had killed and taken life, feel unworthy of taking such a fine thing.

But Rosetta was like him, was so dangerous and physically tainted that it made him sink his teeth deep into her side, uncaring if he added to her scars or not.

His destination became undeniable when he started nipping at the skin below her navel. She spread her thighs before he even needed to do it himself. She was welcoming him.

His eyes darted up to her face to see her head was tilted forward to watch him, her cheeks already pink with arousal.

Alister had done this once before while she was sober and able to remember it properly. She'd come quickly upon his tongue. She licked at her lips eagerly when he lowered himself more and a grin spread across his features. *She likes this a lot.*

He was thankful he was able to lay down on his front, since his arms felt a little shaky and weak, but the booze in him did everything to make sure his mouth was savage with her.

Alister wasn't interested in making this slow or teasing. He just wanted to make her feel so damn good, she would fill his mouth with her juices as she came.

Her hands shot down to grip his hair, her back bowing the moment his tongue touched her, like he'd put a hot coal to her body. He flicked over the hard nub of her clit and every time he did, her beautiful thighs twitched around his head.

She moaned when he sucked on it, swirling his tongue, but he was the one who moaned when he finally came down to her entrance to dip inside. There was already a little pool for him, telling him just how much she was enjoying it.

The taste of her made him shove his tongue deeper so he could collect more, eagerly awaiting her spilling inside his mouth.

"Alister..." Her hips twitched, as if she wanted to buck against his mouth, scraping his nose against her clit.

As he ran his tongue from her slit to her sensitive nub, his gaze turned up to watch her body roll all the way from her hips to her shoulders, laying firmly against the bed.

His grin deepened when it happened again while he sucked and lashed at her. *She's about to...*

Before he could even finish his thought, he had to lower his head when she let out a loud cry. He dipped his tongue inside when she came, swirling his tongue so he could lap it up. Her channel rippled around the tip of it.

The way she tasted, her orgasm not mingled with his own, was a treat Alister found himself savouring, something he savoured and drank in an attempt to quench his undeniable thirst for her.

Little, shuddering moans fell from her when she was finished, and he started teasing her clit with his tongue again. He just wanted to make her entire body twitch because of how sensitive she was now.

She started pushing at his head until he was forced to release her. He made his way up her body, leaving wet kisses behind. As he always did, he tongued that scar across her torso, the perfect line to make him speed up the pace. He sucked her already red and swollen nipple just for good measure.

"Take your boots off," she panted, pushing at his chest when he tried to kiss at her neck.

She wanted him naked too.

"I don't think I can wait, Rosetta," he told her, leaning over her more and forcing her to let him place his lips on her.

His cock was paining him terribly, throbbing in his breeches that felt too tight and harsh against the sensitive head.

"Please?" she begged, and Rosetta never begged.

He let out a groan before backing away from the bed.

With rushed movements, Alister bent his knee so he could raise his foot to take off a boot. He had to quickly place his bare foot down before he fell. He took off the other, nearly hopping on one foot.

She was making him more desperate for her by doing this. Alister was growing impatient to fill her, to have her glove him in heat and softness.

When he turned to her to practically dive back into the bed while reaching for the buttons of his pants, he had to pause. Rosetta was on her knees at the edge, already reaching forward to undo them herself.

He studied her face while he felt each button pop before

she pulled his breeches down to reveal his shaft. She turned her face up to him with a bright smile, cupping the underside of him. He felt it pulsate in her palm.

Then she turned her gaze back down, stroking the entire length of his engorged cock. She licked her lips to wet them before they parted. Alister's nose crinkled to stifle his groan; she wanted to suck him.

He palmed the top of her head to run his fingers through her glossy brown hair. He quickly pulled her closer, worried she might change her mind.

She really wanted to treat him tonight. A blowjob from Rosetta was like being sucked by an angel... or a devilish succubus with all her teasing.

The first, deep lick over the tip made him lose all the breath in his chest. She sucked the broad head into her mouth, twirling her tongue all along the flared rim.

His head fell back, letting his neck go loose so he could focus on the difficult task of standing. Even just the wafting heat of her breath had his cock twitching.

When she started sinking her mouth down with her tongue lapping at him, his hand fisted her hair. The other came up to cup the nape of her neck, as though he needed to hold onto her to steady himself.

She wasn't as playful, wasn't as teasing as she usually was when she did this for him, but he didn't need her to be.

Every time she moved her head back and forth, her tongue cupping the underside of him and making the head brush over the ridges on the roof of her mouth, it made his lungs squeeze. He let out a deep groan when she even brought one of her hands up to heft his sac, giving it a light massage. His balls felt heavier than usual, like they ached to release his seed.

She brought her head back to stroke the tip with a wet swirl. Her lips brushed over the sides, all around him, pulling on the skin around his cock when she started moving back and forth again.

With every movement from her, every change, he felt his legs starting to shake. His knees were trying to buckle, both from the booze and the wonderful way her mouth felt.

His head fell forward when he felt a well of precum shudder his entire body.

I want her to keep going. He wanted her to suck him dry and swallow him down, but he had to pull her head back by her hair when her mouth picked up pace.

"I can't," he huffed, stepping to the side so he could kneel on the bed next to her. He'd fucking fall at this rate.

She didn't care that he was stopping her, didn't question him. Instead, she grabbed the sides of his face gently and brought his lips down on hers, turning her head to deepen the kiss instantly. Everything felt heated between them, and Alister's mind and chest ached from her.

He palmed the back of her head, bringing her closer, while the other grabbed her backside to lift one cheek. He thrust his hips against her at the same time, moving her body to stroke him.

He felt her reach a little higher and pull his eyepatch off, revealing his face for her before she threw it against the bed to be lost until morning.

It wasn't the first time she'd done this. She preferred to see his face entirely when they were alone, and it warmed his heart. Something that had been an unspoken insecurity in him was something she'd accepted wholeheartedly. He thought she may even like it.

Just when he was about to push her down, she pushed one of his shoulders to make his body twist and crash against the bed.

It wasn't often Alister felt weakened by her, a creature much smaller than him, but there was something about the way she was tonight that made him submissive to whatever she wanted.

If she wanted him on his back, then he knew what she was going to do was going to mess his mind right up.

He knew he was right when she crawled on top of him to straddle his waist. She slipped her folds over the underside of his cock, moaning into his mouth as she wetted him.

He pulled her doublet coat from her but left her unbuttoned tunic on. He thought it might keep her warmer. The last thing he wanted was her shivering from the cold winter air rather than being lost and mindless while riding him. It was selfish of him, really. He didn't want anything distracting her from his cock.

Then, he pushed his hand between their bodies so he could grab the base of his cock, hoping she'd slip him inside her and put him out of his fucking misery.

The ache bordered on pain, and he knew the only thing that would give him relief was if she swallowed him whole into her heat. The curls over her mound tickled as she ground her hips against him, pushing her needy and swollen clit over the length.

She continued to kiss him, making his tongue swirl with hers in a lazy dance that ate at his resolve. Her breaths were laboured and caught whenever she rubbed her folds over him just right, causing a tiny noise to leave her.

He found himself holding his shaft, unable to stop himself from pushing his hips upwards so she'd stroke it harder.

"Fuck, Rosetta," he said against her lips. "Mount me."

He needed her to. Otherwise, he was going to roll them over and slam so hard inside her, it would probably hurt them both.

She gave a small giggle, showing she knew exactly what she'd been doing.

"You...!"

He was just about to do it, roll them over and take her with feral pumps, when he finally felt the tip of his cock tuck against her entrance. He lost all his unravelling thoughts.

Shit! Rosetta leaned back and mounted all of what her body would allow in one go. His lungs seized in his chest while his hips thrust up so he could try and bury himself deeper. Both his hands came down to her arse with heavy slaps to push her down as heat, tightness, and texture surrounded him. With how wet she was, there had been no resistance in taking him.

Her back arched, her head falling forward as a soft cry broke from her. She dug her nails high on his stomach as she stretched for him, adjusted to his size.

"You always feel so good inside me," she moaned, her brows furrowing so deeply, he would have thought it was from pain if it wasn't for her twirling her hips. She was stirring him inside her, wanting to feel him hit everywhere. "Why?"

He'd often asked himself the same thing. *Can't think.* He couldn't, not when she was trembling over top of him and rubbing his tip against her cervix.

Then she started to really move, and Alister knew he was doomed.

The way Rosetta bucked her hips atop his cock was like a wave that started from her waist and rolled down to her hips. It felt like a grind, the walls of her channel trying to hold onto him while her hips stroked up the front.

How she felt was breath-stealing.

It affected him all the way down to his muscles, his bones, every nerve and cell. It made his shaft throb harder with each stroke of her pussy, made his balls tingle, his groin tighten in blissful agony.

Watching her move was mind-numbing.

His gaze remained fixed, never straying as he watched her.

Her thighs jiggled as they slapped against his hips when she reached deep impact. They were spread wide over his large, muscled body, pulling apart the lips of her folds so he could see her pussy gripping him as the pink skin moved up and down. Her hands trembled on his stomach. Her perky round breasts bounced, jiggling with every movement. Her shoulders curled forward when she twitched, like she was going taut.

It was her face, however, that always stole his sanity.

She would watch him, her blue eyes staying with his face to see his reactions to her riding him like a cock-hungry whore as she moaned.

Her freckles seemed brighter behind the pink arousal that flustered her face, her bottom lip a little redder than the top, as if she'd bitten at it when he wasn't looking.

There was something about her eyes, though. It held a haunting look of need, desire, yearning, like she was melting on the inside. It was present every time, like a hunger she had for him he knew he returned with a savage, determined crinkle to his nose, a fierceness in his gaze.

Sometimes, she could dishevel him when she was on top, could take him to a place where he lost himself. It made his mind useless to do anything but let her take him the way she wanted.

Even now, seeing her tunic slowly slipping down her shoulders ate at him. He knew she'd be feeling a cold bite of air washing over her, but she was too distracted by him inside her to care.

She just wanted him, wanted to ride him. Fuck, she looked like she was loving it.

She bucked wildly, her head tilting back so she could face the ceiling, as though she couldn't hold herself up properly anymore. Her moans grew louder, unhidden, uncaring as she pleasured herself with his cock.

She must have known he was growing impatient, that his hands had started digging into her backside so he could move her himself. He was trying to get her to come down harder on him, trying to lift her hips to get her to go faster.

Rosetta leaned over, placing one of her hands against the pillow behind him while she cupped the side of his cheek. She brushed her thumb over the scar on his face just below his blind eye as she pressed her lips to the side of his neck.

She kissed him with warm breaths as she tried to keep in control of the way her hips moved.

Then, between each teasing draw of her lips, her tongue darting out, she sweetly said, "You can call me Rosie if you want."

Alister groaned deeply. His hands stilled on her as he throbbed so hard, he'd feared he was about to come without warning.

How could her saying that almost shatter him completely? *Bloody hell, she can't say that to me right now.* Alister knew he wasn't far from it.

He released one hand so he could grab the back of her head and force her mouth to his. He kissed her deeply, showing he understood what that meant to her.

I've finally taken her away from that bastard. Alister had gained enough of her trust to steal that nickname from Theodore and claim it as his own.

It was his now, his to take, to say, to tease her with.

He had to break away from the kiss to lay his head back against the bed with how heavy and weighted it felt. His eyes rolled into the back of his skull as he felt his balls starting to draw up.

He could hear her pants of breath were tight as she leaned back, moving up and down on him this time. Then, her head fell as she started letting out loud little cries.

Alister needed to tell her he was about to come so she would hop off him, but everything felt hazy when he opened his lids once more to watch her.

His eyes couldn't help looking to where his agony was

currently escalating out of control, as he watched her spread folds move around his thick girth glistening with her wetness.

"Rosie..." He groaned it, his face twisting into a furrow as he felt himself thickening. He couldn't stop himself from thrusting up into her to meet her movements, knowing it would help ease him. "I'm about to–"

"Oh, Alister!" Her hips became chaotic as she tried to go as fast as she could on top of him, controlling his cock to hit everywhere she desperately needed.

He didn't get to finish his words before he felt her body suddenly grip around his shaft as she drenched him. Her core was quivering so much, it made his jaw drop.

Alister didn't want to break away from her while she was coming and screaming his name with abandon. She was twitching, riding him like a crazed animal, as if she couldn't get enough. Watching her was dangerous, feeling her even more so.

Fuck, feels so good. She was plush, taut, rippling around his cock with spasms, like her pussy wanted to suck him impossibly deeper. *Haa!*

A guttural, growl-like noise rumbled in his chest quietly as she continued to climax over top of him, milking his shaft in heavy squeezes, hungry for him, as he started to come inside her. Inside her heat, her wetness, the plumpness of her inner walls.

His fingertips dug into her arse while the fingers of his other hand did the same to her thigh, grabbing it quickly to help him through this. He felt his legs lightly shake as tension shot through him. His shoulders pressed more firmly into the bed below as he dipped beneath her.

It was almost like his groin wanted to escape what she was doing to him as the intensity of his own orgasm blew through him. Feeling her ride him while he did it was nigh overwhelming.

Alister had lost his mind.

When he was done, he didn't even get the chance to collect his addled brain, to regret what he had just done, to bloody care, because even though her walls had stopped squeezing him, she continued to move.

It lashed his body with heavy aftershocks, his cock so sensitive now, it felt like she was trying to kill him as movement robbed him of breath.

Rosetta didn't know.

He quickly rolled up to sit, grabbing her hips and settling her before she destroyed him completely. Hugging her to him, he buried his sweat covered face against the side of her neck, trying to catch his choking breaths.

"What about you?"

"I already came, Rosie," he said quietly.

Shit, calling her that feels nice. So nice that it didn't make sense.

He wanted to cringe at how she might react, wanted to wince at what he had done, but he was too satisfied to feel an ounce of regret... just like the last time he'd done it back in Tortaya.

"Inside?"

He was going to be in trouble for this. He promised he wouldn't do it again, but experiencing this woman lose herself over top of him was just too much.

"I don't think you should ride me anymore when I'm drunk."

He obviously couldn't control himself and he knew, deep down, if she kept doing it, he'd probably keep losing all sense of reason and fill her again. Even with his mind hazy, his vision blurrier than when he was sober, he knew it was truth.

He didn't understand what it was about the way she felt that got him stupid. *I don't make this mistake with other women.* So why her?

"Hmm," she said thoughtfully. "Once can't be too bad."

He gave a sigh of relief, thankful she wasn't going to berate him for it.

"It wasn't last time," he chuckled lightly.

She gave him a tiny, short laugh in return. They stayed motionless for a small while, holding onto each other's sweat-slicked bodies.

"I like you cock-warming me, lass."

It was like the most intimate cuddle he'd ever received, holding her while nestled inside her warmth and wetness. He could feel her body thrumming around him, and all the sensations were keeping him hard.

When he pushed her hips down on him, he felt his semen squelch inside her, and he crinkled his nose. That wasn't a sensation to which he was accustomed.

"You can be so soft sometimes," she said, shaking her head.

What? He pulled his head back with gritted teeth in anger and gripped her jaw tightly.

"I'm never–"

He blinked, letting her go before he even finished his sentence. He realised she was complimenting him, not calling him weak, like his men would if they were to call him that. She was trying to call him sweet, which right now, he was trying to be.

"Thirsty?" She reached for the bottle of whiskey that had been beside them all along. He was sure his eyepatch was somewhere around them as well.

She removed the cork to hand it to him. He wanted to deny it simply because his body was already swaying, his mind already muddled, his body already heavy.

He was on his ship, not in port. He wasn't used to getting this intoxicated when he had to command his men in the morning. Already, he knew that was going to be a struggle and his vision was already so impaired, it wasn't wise for him to continue.

He didn't get the chance to deny it. When he didn't take it, she tipped it to his lips and started his drink for him. When deliciousness hit his tongue, he took it from her.

She placed her lips against the side of his neck, making his lids feel heavy while she pressed her fingers to the base of the bottle, keeping it upright until he had chugged the entire thing.

Letting it fall off the edge of the bed to roll away, he turned his face to take in the scent of her in a deep inhale.

Smells like her... and gardenia flowers.

"Is it time for more?" she whispered around kisses, grinding her hips against him.

He couldn't help chuckling. She was just as bad as him.

"Oh aye," he said, lifting her and slamming her back against the bed while he was still deep. "Horny bitch."

He didn't wait, didn't want to. He gave a measured thrust, his teeth gnashing when he hit hard and deep.

Why can't I get enough of her?

He brought his hips back and thrust into her again, feeling her bounce beneath him, watching as he stared down at her with straightened arms.

He shook his head, feeling his brows furrow as his mind hammered. As excited as he was, thrilled she was going to take him again and again tonight, there was a part of him that constantly ate at the back of his mind.

It was there, always in the back of his conscious, when he was with her and when he wasn't, when he was busy or had free time.

Alister wanted to know why he couldn't stop with her, why he had a never-ending need for her. No matter how many times he took her, it was never enough, and didn't seem like it would ever be.

Why did her smell make him feel so drugged, it made him

mindless? The way she moaned for him, clung to him when she was beneath him, tore at him when he was in the moment.

Why did looking at her and all the beauty she held standing on a moving ship in the sun make something strange and foreign swirl in his chest?

"N-not so hard," she pleaded, wincing lightly.

Alister wanted to slam into her.

He wanted to break her like it was the answer in discovering what had hooked into him. He knew it was her fault somehow, and every time he fucked her, he wanted to punish her for it. It felt like it was deepening every time, getting worse and worse, and he feared he'd be swallowed by it completely, forever altered.

It was swallowing him whole.

The answer, the reason; it was right there, somewhere in the recesses of his mind that he ignored and refused to acknowledge. He knew it all made sense. It nagged at him like a forgotten word on the tip of his tongue.

He didn't know how to access that part of himself. He wanted to, wanted to take back the control she had stolen because it felt safer.

As he continued to slam his cock home, there was hunger in her features, but also a plea. Alister paused.

Looking down at her face, the way she looked trusting and sweet while somehow holding a wicked glint in her eyes, brought on one question he'd never thought before.

Why the hell do I care so much? Why did he want the answer to his questions? Why let that be the focus of his thoughts when he could just enjoy her, enjoy this?

That's what he decided he was going to do.

He pulled his hips back a little, so he wasn't thrusting so deeply, and hooked one of his hands behind her knee. He spread her, lifting her until she was more at his hip height. It twisted her slightly, but he had no problem holding onto her like this with his strength.

Alister grinned when her mouth fell open and her back arched, turning to her side slightly. He begun to take her faster rather than harder.

Cry after cry fell from her, his shaft grinding right against the sensitive ridge he knew she liked.

A wave of dizziness hit him, and his arm shook so violently, it caved, forcing him to his elbow.

Forced to be closer to her, he buried his face against the side of her neck, groaning against it. He started pistoning his hips, thrusting into her with such quick pumps, it felt like absolute bliss strangling him. The squelching sound of their bodies meeting was erotic.

"Louder." He wanted her louder than ever.

Fuck, he wanted her screaming.

"Too fast!"

Alister wasn't going to give her what she wanted this time. He kept his pace, knowing if he just kept going, she would drench him.

He wanted everyone past his door to hear her. He was determined to make sure they did. He wanted them all to know he was currently inside her, that he was the one taking her, that she was coming around *his* cock.

Usually, he cared how his men felt, would kiss her to quieten her, shove his hand against her mouth. Tonight, though, he just wanted to make them jealous. He wanted to make them envious that Alister was the one who got to take not just any woman, but Rosetta Silver.

He knew Rosetta was gone when she started screaming his name, try to wring his cock in spasms he could barely feel with his speed.

You're mine, lass. For how long, he didn't know. All he knew was that he was bloody content.

CHAPTER SEVENTEEN

Rosetta laid curled into Alister's side.

Watching him sleep, she brushed her fingertips through the black hair on his chest. She was admiring this brutish man in all his masculine glory, finding he looked rather peaceful with his large, hairy chest rising and falling so slowly and steadily.

He'd passed out not long ago.

She'd taken every burst of him. She was a little sore and tender all over, but although he'd been rough with her, she knew he hadn't taken her as deeply as he had in Tortaya.

It might be because she'd made sure he was too intoxicated to truly have his strength. She also knew it would make him fall into a satisfied stupor at some point, which is why she had truly done it.

Everyone has their limits, she thought, taking in his warmth, the feel of him, how she pressed up against him.

Even Alister could get legless, and since she'd been feeding him bottle after bottle, she'd made sure he achieved it. He was so out of it that she was even able to reach up and caress the side of his face without him waking to stop her.

He looks so peaceful like this. It was hard to imagine he was a brutal, cutthroat criminal.

The scar on his face was always a reminder, as were the many other scars on his torso, arms, and even hands, but

Rosetta could no longer think of him as anything hard.

To her, under all that arrogance, he could be sweet, caring, protective, and charming.

She brushed her thumb over the scar, before drawing her hand down so she could palm his muscled chest, moving to his bicep to appreciate it as well. She ran it down his arm until her hand found his fingers and started playing with its golden rings.

She stayed there playing with them, spinning one on his finger repeatedly. He didn't wake, his chest rising and falling with deep breaths of sleep. She played with his family crest in particular.

As much as she was enjoying this silence-filled moment by herself, she hated this bed. It was hard against her soft muscles. She knelt beside him to stare down at his face.

Even with that nasty scar, you're such a handsome man.

A small sad smile curled her lips before she leaned over and pressed her mouth to his, giving him a light kiss.

Then, Rosetta carefully crawled off the bed so she could return to her ship. She dressed in the cold, bitter air, making sure she was presentable before she left the room.

It was silent when she opened the door, the night so late that she was sure the sun wouldn't be far from trying to rise. She was tired and desperately wanted her bed, where she would be comfortable.

There were a few stragglers on deck, those who had fallen asleep on it because they were too inebriated to make it to their beds.

She shooed them by kicking them and flapping her hands. "Off to bed, you lot."

With grumbles and curses swearing she was the devil, they stumbled their way below deck so they could pass out in their hammocks.

There was a long plank between their ships, since they had

made sure they were steady by dropping both anchors on either side. She walked across it, meeting Naeem, who was waiting for her on the other side.

He pulled the plank back into their ship.

"Are you sure about this, Rosetta?"

The look he gave her was one of extreme disapproval. Naeem never looked at her like that. His lips were tight with tension while he looked her straight in the eyes with disappointment... in her.

"No," she laughed nervously.

His look turned into sympathy.

He patted her on the shoulder while letting out a puff of breath of concern. "Fair enough."

"W-Wake the men," she told him, averting her gaze when a heavy swirl of shame twisted her gut.

She turned away when he headed below deck to do as she commanded. Her eyes fell over the Howling Death, trying to give it a smile as she took in its faded sails and rigging.

Rosetta wasn't sure about what she was doing anymore.

All she knew was that she'd foolishly fallen in love with Captain Alister Paine.

CHAPTER EIGHTEEN

Crap! Alister was jolted awake by someone loudly bashing at his cabin door.

Since he'd fallen asleep in the middle of the bed, when he quickly sat up because of the noise, his face was covered by his hammock.

He'd thought he'd find Rosetta next to him. Then he remembered she hated his bed and refused to sleep in it. He often woke with this sensation.

I should have moved us to my hammock. She would have stayed with him then, and he'd come to like her waking in his arms.

He slapped the hammock out of his way as he crawled forward to sit on the edge of his bed, palming his forehead with both his hands.

I haven't felt this hungover in years. Not since the death of his father, to be precise. It hadn't helped that he'd been the holder of the pistol that shot him, even though his father had been the one to ask for the mercy of a quick death.

Alister had drunk himself into a state that night, guzzling booze until he was numb. The splitting headache he had now, alongside a mouth so dry his tongue felt like sandpaper, told him he'd drunk far too much.

"Stop bashing!" he yelled at the door when the person wouldn't cease. He knew it must not be Pierre or Derek, because either one of them would have just waltzed in by now. "I'm getting up!"

It quietened immediately.

Looking around the brightness in his cabin, he knew it must be mid-morning. He'd gotten up later than he should have.

He reached for his breeches to put them on. Despite how much moving made his head throb, he also reached for one boot at a time, lifting his leg into the air to shove his foot inside.

He had duties to perform.

Just as he was about to reach for his tunic, the door burst open, Pierre running inside.

"Bloody hell!" He grabbed the empty bottle next to the bed and threw it at the wall, making him jump nearly out of his boots. Alister hated being woken, and definitely hated it more when he was disturbed right afterwards. "What do you all want?"

He'd told the men yesterday they wouldn't be moving for a day or two to give them a break. They should all be resting, not waking him up so violently. They'd put him in a sour mood. After last night, he should have woken up elated and satisfied.

Rosetta had been like a dream.

She'd given him everything he wanted, as long as he didn't go too hard. She hadn't pleaded for him to stop, hadn't said she was too tired, hadn't started to pass out. She'd taken all of him and returned it with just as much fiery passion.

Pierre's breaths were huffed, as though he'd run to Alister's door.

"It's gone," he said, shaking his head with disbelief.

His brows furrowed. "What's gone?"

"Alister..." Pierre ran his hand over his blond hair, his face torn like he was filled with unimaginable anxiety. It was even pale. "Their ship is gone!"

His eyes widened. "What?"

Despite being partially undressed, he ran straight for the door, pushing him out of the way as he burst into eye-piercing sunlight. He turned his head from side-to-side, searching the horizon, and couldn't see the Laughing Siren.

He stumbled back a step like he'd been punched in the gut. *She's gone...*

Rosetta had finally sailed away from Alister.

Fuck... He placed his hand on top of his head. *Why?*

Why did Rosetta leave? *But last night...* It couldn't have been because she was bored of him.

The woman who had ridden him, moaned beneath him all night, had definitely not been a woman tired of sleeping with him.

His hand fell away when understanding knocked into him. *It had been a goodbye.*

She'd been intending to leave and wanted to give him something as a sweet memory. She'd gotten him drunk on purpose so he wouldn't wake while she left.

As much as her leaving upset him, there was one other problem...

"Our supplies!" he roared, turning to Pierre with so much fury, it spooked even him.

Rosetta had most of their supplies.

"Look down there!" someone shouted, pointing down the side of his ship and into the water.

Alister ran to look over the railing with hands slapping against it. His hair whisked over his shoulders as he looked down.

Next to a rowboat attached by rope to the side of the hull were barrels. Inside the boat were crates, chickens in their cages, and her goat Reginald that unhappily bleated up at them. There were at least ten barrels floating next to it.

She gave us our supplies. She'd done as she promised.

It made him feel worse. She really intended for this to be it, leaving in the middle of the night without saying a word and giving him no reason to chase after her.

How long has she been planning this? Until we got to this location?

He turned back to his cabin, quickly making his way to the safe to check it. When he opened the door, he could see a stack of ten coins at the very front that he hadn't put there.

She knew I'd check to see if she stole from me. He could see she hadn't. Those ten coins were an obvious message. *Cheeky bitch.*

Unable to help himself, he went back outside, as if he needed to double check that her ship really was gone. A vacant horizon greeted him. He'd been hoping it would suddenly appear.

"Why did no one wake me earlier?"

It was mid-morning, for crying out loud! They couldn't have left more than a few hours ago, and he might have seen her on the horizon, would have known which way she'd gone.

"The hatch was locked," someone told him.

Most of his crew was on the main deck, wondering just as much as he at what had happened.

"So was our room," Derek added. "Been trying to get out of it for hours."

"Then how the hell did you all get free?"

Rosetta had locked them all in except for Alister.

Someone from the back raised their hand. "I was asleep in the crow's nest." *She must not have known.*

Alister greeted his eyes with his own and the man turned away at the expression he was wearing.

She fucking left. She'd left him, and Alister didn't like the way it felt, didn't like that her ship wasn't next to his, that he didn't know where she was.

He ran his hand down his face in frustration.

Shit! He covered his blind eye with his hand, heading for his room once more so he could finish dressing. He couldn't believe he'd greeted his crew without a shirt or his eyepatch. He quickly donned them both.

"What do you want to do?" Pierre asked when he emerged, glaring out at the world with a vengeance.

"Nothing," he spat.

Rosetta had left. She was done with him. He wouldn't chase after a woman who didn't want him anymore, despite how much he wanted to.

"But Alister." Pierre reached forward and put his hand on his shoulder to turn him.

He had to clench his hands into tight fists to stop himself from punching or backhanding the man. Rage had settled in, and he refused to take out his anger on his own men.

"What?"

"You like her."

Humour crinkled his eyes as a bellow of a laugh fell from him. "Nay, I don't. I liked taking her hole." He shook his head, his laughter turning dark. "Why would I like a devious, hot-headed, annoying, cunt of a fucking woman?"

She never listened to me. Never did what she was told. She got under his skin so much, he yelled at her all the time.

That lying nature of hers made her dangerous.

He had to constantly be vigilant around her. He never knew what was truth and what was lie, which is why she'd probably gotten him so plastered he couldn't have figured out she was planning to leave.

I should have known. Now that she was gone, the signs were obvious.

She was a whore. Not in her past, he didn't care about that. But she would have freely taken other men in Tortaya despite being with Alister. She would have cheated him out of his fun before he was ready.

He opened his mouth to continue badmouthing her, wanting to vent his anger, but he eventually closed it.

If he truly felt this way, that there were parts of her he should truly and utterly hate, then why did he still want to go after her?

He should hate her, despise her even. So why didn't a single shred of the emotion hit him?

"Shit, lad." His eyes widened further than they ever had. He stumbled back a step, as though he'd been punched in the gut once more. "You're right. I like her."

It had never been about what she could give him, do for him. Alister liked *her*.

The way she looked was stunning. It was those blue eyes that bewitched him, how they changed between lightness and darkness, reminding him of the different depths of the ocean.

Her freckles were wild. They splattered across her face like mud to make her appear dirty in a wicked way that often got him excited. Her nose was small, making her appear cute. Her lips were puffy, soft, so pouted, he'd been addicted to kissing them.

Her body had been a sin: curved but toned from years of hard work. The way the soft parts had squished in his meaty hands had felt sublime. His thumbs had constantly wanted to press into her muscles in small, appreciative massages.

Even just her brown hair that looked like dirt, often messy and knotted, had tantalised him. He'd liked it crawling across his skin.

There had been something about the way she smelled that near felled him every time he was close to her. The perfume that made him feel comforted had just been an addition.

The way she talked was crude. She spoke like a man, and it gave him freedom to never hold his own tongue. He didn't have to watch what he said, how he said it, like he would have with a fancy woman.

There was a deep yell she'd do when calling out commands to her men that had been ugly, but he'd always grinned because it made them listen. She'd demand obedience and she'd get it.

And that laugh... That horrible laugh that made her sound like an animal being strangled to death. It somehow made his stomach tighten in want whenever he heard it.

But it was her personality that ran circles around him that had drawn him in. He never knew which way was up and what was down.

He respected her as a captain, was proud of the brutal pirate she was... because she was just like him.

She was smart, cunning, and had tricked him so many times, it put him to shame. She was so strong, in every aspect, that she didn't need his help with anything. She knew what she needed to do, even if it was to step back and let others do the work for her.

He'd thought it was the sex, her pussy, that he'd wanted the way it scrambled his mind, yet it had never been this good with others.

It was because it was with her, with Rosetta, who was wild, playful, sometimes even defiant because she knew it made him more crazed. She stroked his mind and body to such a feverish degree that he'd often felt burned.

She's like the sea. Untameable. Uncontrollable. Something that looked pretty but was deeper and darker than he would ever be able to see or touch.

Alister had wanted to drown in her, had been trying to do just that. He'd wanted to be swallowed by everything she could give him, not understanding it had been all of her.

He had been lost in those crashing waves constantly throwing his resolve around.

It was the risk, the freedom, the strange adventure he'd

gone on with her, not just with their ships, but the secret battle they'd shared.

She was like the sea, and like the ocean waters, he wanted to dominate her, even though he knew he never could. He wanted to control her, even knowing it was impossible. He could never command her, and like the waves and the wind, he had to steady himself through her force.

He finally understood why he couldn't seem to get enough of her. It's because he never would have.

Something had been growing inside him, something he had thought was physical but had actually been emotion deep down that he didn't understand.

He still didn't understand.

To come to this realisation now... His eyes crinkled deeply in what he thought might be loss.

She left me. Him. She had cast him to the side like he was nothing. But Alister didn't know how to navigate sadness and he instead turned it to anger. *She left me!*

How dare she fucking leave! Without a word, without a reason why.

Without giving him the chance to change her mind.

That woman wants me. He knew it deep down to his bones. If she hadn't given him a sweet goodbye, he might have thought differently. *I will have her back.*

Alister stomped his way to the quarterdeck railing to greet his men. "How would you all feel if I chased after her?"

He wanted to more than anything, a need even greater than finding Dustin's trove, but he wouldn't send his men on a wild goose chase without their permission.

One of them cupped his mouth to make his voice louder. "We'd call you an idiot if you didn't."

A menacing chuckle broke from his chest.

"Aye, then. Let's go find the lass. Bring those supplies onto the ship and weigh the anchors!" As much as he wanted to let his men rest, knowing they were tired and probably just as hungover as him, he wasn't going to let her get far. "Hoist the sails! Let's get this ship moving!"

Moving to stand behind the helm, he narrowed his eyes on the horizon, determined to see her ship.

"Where's our heading?" Pierre asked, coming up beside him as they waited for the crew to unfurl the sails.

"She'll go to somewhere she's familiar."

"Tortaya?"

"Aye, Tortaya." He looked at him from the corner of his eye. "She won't expect that I'll go after her."

"She probably left because she cares for you and got scared."

That could be a real possibility, one he hadn't considered. *Did I realise too late that I care for her?* He wondered if Pierre was right.

He hadn't shown her he might reciprocate her feelings. If he hadn't been so ignorant, so arrogant, so bloody stupid, would Rosetta still be here?

But she didn't tell him, either. She chose to run away like a coward.

Then again, Alister could only imagine how he might have reacted if she'd told him how she felt before he realised what he felt himself. *I would have immediately rejected her.* Then she would have left anyway, probably in shame or embarrassment, and he would have still realised this far too late.

But I would have watched her sail away. He would have realised and been able to go after her before she was truly gone.

The anchors were pulled from the water, the sails unfurled. He needed to steer his ship as it started moving.

It took him longer than it should have to realise... that one of his rings was missing.

CHAPTER NINETEEN

2 months later

Alister stomped his way through the mansion he was currently inside of with unstoppable force. He was like a wild, runaway carriage, unable to be stopped as he barrelled through people carelessly.

Pushing everyone who tried to get in his way, women, men, even a child, he made his way deep inside. He didn't need to ask for directions; he knew the entire layout by heart. He didn't ask for permission, didn't speak to another person as he stormed his way to his destination.

When he finally got to the double doors, he flung them both open and entered.

The woman inside gave him a loud gasp of surprise as she was tying up the back of her dress. The man, still buttoning his tunic but otherwise fully dressed, turned to him suddenly, like he intended to fight.

His face went white at the sight of Alister. He was far bigger and younger than him.

"Has he paid?" he asked, turning his face towards the woman as he made his way to the man.

"Y–yes." She ran forward with reaching hands. "Alister, wait."

"Good."

He grabbed the man by the shoulder of his tunic, dragged

him to the door, and turned him so he was facing forward. He proceeded to kick him in the backside so he would stumble out of the room.

Alister slammed the door behind him so loudly, the thudding bang made the woman flinch.

He turned to his mother. The shock she felt had her frozen.

He was back after so few months at sea, and he was sure she was surprised. He hadn't killed that man as he promised he would, which was probably even more shocking.

"What are you–"

"Where is Rosetta?"

He folded his arms across his chest, keeping his feet planted in a wide stance. His eyes were narrowed in mistrust, in suspicion, as he stared at his frail mother.

Her blonde brows drew together, her head shaking just slightly from side-to-side. "I don't know."

For two months, he had sailed directly to Tortaya, thinking he'd catch up to her, that he'd see her ship if he headed this way.

He never did.

His frigate was faster than her galleon. He knew the truth, but he refused to accept it. He wanted her to have come here, to have given him a clue to find her. She knew his mother, had considered this a place of safety.

"You do. You know where she would have gone."

She'd been here on and off for the past four years! If anyone knew where Rosetta had gone, it was Lillian.

"She left?"

"Aye, two months ago."

Two long, terrible months.

While he'd sailed with tenacity and unbending resolve, something nasty had crawled its way inside him over time. His anger, his sense of betrayal, was accompanied with a pining he didn't think he could handle.

It felt like a venomous, blue-ringed octopus had shuffled its way under his skin with its slimy, slithery limbs and clutched his heart in its tentacles. Squeezing it. Crushing it. Damaging it.

It was painful. It felt disgusting.

If he thought of her, it felt like it moved with a swirl of emotion to strangle his beating heart. Blood rushed through his veins in deep, pounding pumps, like it was going to explode in his chest from the force.

When he remembered she'd left him, it would nip with its beak to pang him.

Alister didn't like it. He didn't want to feel like this.

He refused to show his men the deep, ever-present agony. He was ashamed of it.

With a sigh, the tension in her shoulders lessened. "What did she take?"

"What do you mean?"

Everything. He felt like Rosetta had taken everything from him, which didn't make much sense.

"If you're this determined to find her, she must have stolen something. What did she take?"

"Father's ring," he answered, turning his head to the side to look at the wall.

"That's all?" She gave him a scoffing huff, the noise bringing his focus back to her. "You don't care for his ring much and I can see you're already wearing a replacement."

He wiggled his hand, indeed feeling the ring on his finger. There was always a replica in the top drawer of his desk.

It was the one ring he didn't want to be without, but being on a ship was wet. One slip of a rope, one wet and stormy night, could see any of his rings lost to the bottom of Davy Jones' Locker.

So, just like his father did, Alister always had a replica made and kept safe in the top drawer of his desk, exactly the same. He was sure his father, or perhaps even an earlier relative, had lost the original and had done the same.

"You said you know of her past, that she told you everything. Where would she have gone?"

It wasn't often they had a standoff or argued about something. To see his mother fold her arms and turn her head to the side to dismiss him rather than answer him made his eyes narrow further.

"Leave her alone, Alister." Her arms tightened further, her pale, bony hands turning into little weak fists. "Whatever she's stolen, let her have it. Whatever she's done, let it go."

He couldn't believe it! His own mother was taking Rosetta's side, defending her against her own son.

"I will find her!"

When he did, he was going to wring her neck for leaving him. He was going to kiss those soft lips until they were so bruised and swollen, she would never forget the feel of his own against them.

Lilian threw her arms to the side and quickly raised one to point at him. Her brows were crinkled tightly, her eyes bowed in concern and worry.

"You will leave that girl alone!"

She came forward with fury, continuing to point at him until she reached his chest and poked him with quick jabs. His mother never had any fear of him. She knew, no matter what she did, no matter how many times she slapped him, hurt him, he would never lay a hand on her.

"Rosetta has been through enough torture at the hands of men!" she yelled, tears of sympathy filling her eyes. "She doesn't need another man chasing after her for God knows what reasons just to hurt her! Theodore and the men of this town have done enough to break that woman."

"She's not broken," he sneered. She was too free-spirited, too bubbly, too cheerful, to be broken.

"That's because you're too blind to see the truth!" She took in a shaking breath, trying to bring back her usual calm composure. "I have seen that woman so terrified, she refused to leave a cupboard for days because she was hiding from that cretin. I've seen her so broken that she couldn't leave her own bed to eat. I saw her break down when she got her first ship and crew because she couldn't believe it after everything she'd been through."

She stepped away from him to place her hands on her cheeks, shaking her head with sadness. She stared at the floor, as though she couldn't believe what she'd witnessed.

The more she spoke, however, the more Alister felt his arms loosening. His brows started to crinkle into a knot.

I've never seen these sides of her.

He'd never seen Rosetta cry, even when he'd found her three days after Mr Smith died. Even though he'd been concerned, even disappointed, that she may be grieving for a crew member when it was foolish to get attached, she'd never once cried during those days.

She'd giggled with him, had teased him for letting her lay against him while she got better from her flu.

Not once, in the months he'd been sailing with Rosetta, had he ever needed to comfort her. He'd never needed to bring her in for a caring hug.

"All the things she's told me, I don't think I would have survived it." His mother was strong in will, even if she wasn't strong in body. To hear her say this made his gut tighten. "I thought raising you and your sister while working the streets was hard. I thought losing you was even harder, but what that girl has lost will never come back. What she has been through will never be erased."

She turned her head back up to him, her hands sliding to cover her mouth like she wanted to hide her emotions.

"She lost her family, her friends, her home, everything in

one day. She left a life of unimaginable wealth just to be free."
Once more, her eyes bowed and crinkled in sadness and
sympathy, but they held a beseeching hint in them. "Don't
take that away from her, Alister. Don't make her run again.
Please, I'm begging you. Whatever she's done to anger you,
just let it go. She's already been punished."

Hearing this made that cruel octopus curl its tentacles
tighter, making his chest ache so terribly, a coldness washed
over him.

She's been hiding it. Rosetta had tried not to allow the
depth and darkness of her pain bubble to the surface around
him. He knew it now, and he could remember seeing small
peeks of it.

The day she'd gotten the Laughing Siren, she'd been
embraced by Mr Smith. He'd thought it was in celebration,
but even he'd been surprised by it, since she rarely hugged
anyone, including him.

The last night they'd been at Tortaya, she'd revealed so
much, making him want to reciprocate. He'd told her about
his father, not realising she'd been feeling sorrow before he'd
arrived, had been sharing a small fraction of how she felt about
her past.

She told me she's done things she wasn't proud of. He
thought she'd meant her time with his mother. Now, he was
sure there was more than what he'd been told.

Learning just how deeply her pain ran from his own
mother... well, that was a hard bit to swallow.

He finally unfurled his arms, palming the top of his head
to run his hand over his hair. "I can't."

He didn't want to make her fear for her own life by running
across the sea like she had with Theodore, but Alister wasn't
bent on hurting her like he was.

He wanted her. He wanted to know why she left. Alister
wanted to go after her more than anything.

"Tell me how to find her, ma," he almost pleaded, feeling his hand shaking as he ran his palm across the back of his neck. Alister couldn't handle this woman not knowing he cared for her, not when it could be the reason she wasn't with him.

And, after what he had just learned... well, shit. He wanted to hold her in a warm embrace, see if he could help heal her wounds.

"Alister, please. I've never truly asked you for anything." His face twisted in agony at her plea, and he turned his eyes away from her. "She–"

She suddenly paused.

A long, silence-filled moment thickened between them. He knew she was examining his soul with those green eyes that could always see through him.

"Oh, my dear, sweet boy." She came forward to place her hands on both his cheeks, turning his face gently until he was forced to look at her. "I was telling her to guard her heart when I should have been telling you to guard yours."

Her expression melted into something so remarkably soft that he knew she understood his feelings better than he did.

"You're not after her because she's wronged you. You're after her because you love her."

He wanted to deny it.

He wanted to laugh, as though what she'd said was ridiculous.

He couldn't.

He'd never even contemplated what he'd been feeling was love. How could he, Alister 'One Eye' Paine, the Bloody Storm of the Seas, love anyone?

He was a murderer. He had so much blood on his hands, had killed so many people; how could he feel something so pure?

Hearing his mother tell him what he was feeling, he knew

it was the truth.

I love her. He cringed at hearing his own mind say it for the first time. The tentacles around his heart squeezed tighter.

Lillian lowered her palms from his face so she could tug on his hands, dragging him to the table to sit.

"If you feel this way, why did you let her leave?"

He averted his gaze until she sat in front of him to hold one of his hands on the table.

"She left in the middle of the night," he grumbled. "We anchored near some shallows. They took the watch and made sure no one was above deck to alert me her ship was leaving."

"Then she probably doesn't want you to follow her, dear."

She started rubbing her thumb over the top of his hand in comforting circles. He barely appreciated the familiar warmth.

"Aye, I know that," he admitted, his lips tightening. "But I'm still going to."

"You might be chasing a woman who doesn't want you." Her brows crinkled in worry for him. "You might discover something you may not be able to handle."

He gave a dark, humourless laugh.

"I don't think so." He finally brought his eye to her. "She told me I could call her Rosie, ma."

He knew she would understand what that meant as much as he did. It was one of the reasons he was sure she felt the same way for him.

"Well, that's awfully convincing." She patted his hand before climbing to her feet. "I think we both need a drink."

For his mother to say she wanted a drink of whiskey this early in the day, which she usually reserved for him, told him he'd fried her nerves.

"Nay," he said, shaking his head as he pulled her to sit. "I don't want a drink."

Alister hadn't let a drop of it, except from the grog water, touch his tongue since that night. He wanted to be clear-headed, and he worried that, if he started to drink his sorrows away, he wouldn't stop.

She gave him a strange look , but sat back down.

"If she didn't come here, where would she have gone?"

Lillian shook her head, the yellow waves of her hair bouncing. "I really don't know. The world is a big place, Alister. You could be searching for her forever."

His face clenched into a wince on one side.

The thing was, Rosetta was like him. She may not have a bounty on her head specifically, but there was already a bounty for the captain of the Laughing Siren.

They would soon realise that was her.

If she docked in any port that wasn't a haven for pirates, she and her crew would be arrested.

He just needed to jump from port to port to eventually find her, or at least find people who had seen her ship.

CHAPTER TWENTY

Five months later

Alister stabbed the sharp point of his dagger into the top of the table, twisting it to carve a small hole. How many times he'd done this, he didn't know. At some point, he'd bore his way through the wood if he wasn't careful.

With his other arm folded across the table, he glared out at the bar patrons. The place was loud with chatter, a low flame from the fireplace warming the otherwise cool area. However, that fire, along with many candles, did little to light the inside of the dim, shadowy building.

He was at the rear of a tavern with his back against the wall, a long table sitting in front of him like a desk.

Pierre, Derek, and a handful of his crew sat around him drinking, talking to each other, but no one was allowed to sit in the empty chair front of him.

No one came to talk to him. Not even his own crew spoke many words to him, since they would only receive short replies or wordless grunts. No woman wanted to sit on his lap – not with the murderous look he wore.

His aura was steeped in homicidal tendencies that even his men found it hard to be around. It was as though his rage had manifested into something physical, a bubble around him.

As the months passed, it only worsened.

It had taken him nearly two months to sail directly to

Tortaya in the west and speak with his mother about Rosetta. Since she had no information to offer, he'd docked at every port until he'd reached as far east as it was safe to go.

For five months, he searched, asking the locals if they'd seen her ship when he ported at the many places he'd been. His men asked everyone they could: local fishermen, incoming or departing trading boats. He'd even docked at risky places.

Alister and his men had almost been arrested once, but they'd made quick work of those soldiers and fled before anyone could stop them.

Now there was nowhere else in the northern hemisphere he could go. If he went much further east, Alister would be sailing the Howling Death directly into heavily guarded Queen Mary Anne's waters.

As much as he wanted Rosetta, he knew he couldn't go further than this.

Alister was back at Dunecaster, the last city safe for any pirate or criminal to dock. The island was similar to Tortaya.

So, if he had been everywhere she could have gone in the northern hemisphere, then... *where the fuck is she?*

He knew Rosetta couldn't have sailed off the edge of the Earth. She couldn't have just disappeared. She was alive out there, somewhere.

He refused to believe she'd gotten arrested, had been sunk. She was too smart for that, too good at being a sailor to be so foolish.

Did she go south? Alister slammed the point of his dagger into another part of the table, his lips thinning further.

If she did go south, how was he supposed to follow her?

He knew those waters better than she did, but even he didn't know them well. Sailing unfamiliar seas could find them hopelessly lost.

He didn't know how to navigate those stars as well as he

did the ones currently above him. If he went that way, he could be looking for a lost ship while sailing a lost ship himself. *That's how we starve to death.*

He started twisting his dagger to create another shallow hole, a growling groan of irritation bubbling in his throat.

I don't want to go south. He'd avoided it for most of his life and had only been that way when Mad Dog was captain.

But he wanted to find Rosetta.

Alister was obsessed. She consumed his mind totally, plagued him, haunted his every waking moment.

Seven months of having that woman, memories forever seared into his memory like he'd been permanently branded. They burned him every minute he'd been without her.

He was sad. He was angry. *Fuck, I'm horny.*

He eyed a pretty woman walking across the bar, cringing at her with disdain. He stabbed the table once more, watching himself do it.

He knew his men were just as worried for themselves as they were for him. They'd never seen Alister like this. Dustin's trove had always been his goal, but he wasn't this crazed for it. He had his reasons for searching for it, but he was also fine with never finding it.

His determination to find Rosetta, however, was unwavering.

He knew it was a problem when old man Derek made a comment to Pierre, not realising Alister overheard.

"Cap'in's got that same look in his eye as his pa."

Cole 'Mad Dog' McCarthy had been partially insane.

Watching his own father descend further and further into madness as he spent years searching for fabled treasure had been difficult for Alister to watch. The decline in his mental state, his obsession, his infatuation for something that might not exist, was hollowing for a child to witness.

He'd always feared that would be his own fate.

To hear he might have the same crazed look in his eye now? That hadn't been pleasant to discover. *But Rosetta is real.* She was a living, breathing person. She wasn't some mystery treasure.

It had only taken them four months and two weeks to get to Dunecaster. It had been easier than the three weeks he'd been docked in it.

For three weeks, Alister's feet had touched land.

Every night and day, he sat in this bar, at this seat, with this table in front of him. If it wasn't him, it was one of his men coming to take a shift for him while he slept on his ship.

He didn't sleep long, always returning to his seat.

He ate well, he was rested, but that was because he wanted his energy for when he finally set sail again. He refused to let his body wither away.

I've spent so much gold trying to find her.

His men didn't mind that they were docked for so long. They just chased after the skirts of prostitutes and enjoyed their time here while they could.

Alister, on the other hand, hadn't spent this much time on land since he'd helped his mother to build her fancy little mansion. Before that, since he was eleven.

Every morning, his crew would collect on the pier to find out if they were sailing out that day. When it was a disgruntled no, their eyes would turn away from him, as though they were upset on his behalf.

It was pity, and he hated it.

The number of times he'd lashed out at his men for giving him that look... well, it was enough for them to eventually stop doing it. They just nodded and returned to their holiday away from the sea and hard work.

"How much longer do you want to stay here?" Pierre asked him quietly, leaning closer. He asked him the same question every few days.

"As long as it takes."

Once more, Alister crawled his eyes over the busy tavern filled with drunken morons, flirty women, loud music, and heavy chattering. He was thankful the room was dim.

Someone who has seen her ship will turn up at some point. Another stab of his dagger had his eyes narrowing with impatience.

Stealing a poster of Queen Mary Anne's bounty for the Laughing Siren, which had a picture of the sculpture on the front of it, inspired Alister to make his own posters.

He was offering a reward of five hundred pounds for the lucky bastard who could tell him where it was, or at least what direction it was heading.

It was why he was waiting here. He needed to stay in one place for the bounty to be effective. If someone saw, they needed to be able to hand the information to him – they couldn't do that if he was on the sea.

It would cost him fifty gold pieces.

That wouldn't bother Alister too much, handing out his gold to find her, if it wasn't for every greedy, lying bastard who had taken a seat in front of him. They wanted a quick buck and were willing to cheat him for it.

The third man who had given Alister false hope by sitting in front of him with false information until Alister derailed him enough to reveal he was lying had been violently gutted.

From that moment forward, he'd sat with his own wanted poster of ten thousand pounds on the wall behind him.

It served as a warning.

It was a picture of his scarred face, eyepatch, long hair, and stubble beard. Under the drawing was his name, the full amount for his arrest, then the half amount if it was just his head. The bounty poster was Queen Mary Anne herself, her name signed at the very bottom.

No one else approached him after that.

Good. Piss off. He didn't want to deal with bullshit. He just wanted information, then to leave this sad rock he had no business being on.

So, when a wary and hesitant man shuffled his feet not even two tables down from them, eyeing Alister and the poster behind him, one of his brows raised.

He was an older gentleman, closer to Derek's age than his. He had a receding hairline, fluffy hair on the sides like he needed to cut it but hadn't. It was black but peppered heavily with grey and the occasional white. He had a beard that covered his entire face and glasses that brightened his dark brown eyes.

He was wringing a soft hat in his hands, similar to the brown overalls sitting over his white tunic and whatever pants he had beneath it.

Realising he probably looked menacing stabbing his dagger repeatedly into the table, Alister slipped it into the side of his boot. He leaned back in his chair, folded his arms, and kept his eye on the man while he waited for him to approach.

A candle flickered between them as the minutes ticked by.

Eventually, the man came to stand in front of the table.

"A–Are you Captain Alister Paine?" he asked quietly.

He pointed to the poser above his head to show him it was obviously him. "What do you want?"

He wrung his hat tighter. "I saw on your poster that you're looking for information on a boat with a jolly mermaid on the bow."

"I am." He crinkled his nose into sneer. "What proof do you have that your words won't be lies?"

The man cast his eyes downwards. "None. I don't even know if the boat I've seen is the one you're looking for."

Alister squinted as those of his crew seated around to protect him turned their attention to the nervously trembling man.

Alister kicked the opposite chair to back it away from the table.

His response had at least been honest in doubt.

"Sit."

With jarring movements, the man leaned into the chair until he was seated.

"Better make your story interesting; otherwise, I'll gut you just like the last man who sat in this chair and lied to me."

"Please," he begged. "I'm just a humble fisherman who wants to return to his family. I'll tell you everything I know, but that gold would be enough for me to go home."

Alister leaned his body forward and once more placed his forearm on the table. "I don't give a shit what your problems are. Now, tell me what you know of the ship you saw, and I will decide whether it's enough to warrant the release of my coins."

Seeming to sense Alister's impatience, the man started nervously rambling.

"We were picked up by a trading ship heading to Dunecaster a week ago. My captain and crew... we were out near where the northern waters turn into the southern ones when a giant ship came over the horizon!" Another twist of his hat accompanied a shake of his head with bowed eyes of fear. "It must have seen us because it turned towards us. Then, before we even knew it, it released cannon fire. Our small vessel was destroyed in minutes."

"Did they try to raid you?"

"No. Like I said, I'm a fisherman. We were a fishing boat. There wasn't anything worth stealing on our ship besides fish."

"Did you see a woman on board?"

"I don't remember. I was too busy trying not to get shot! All I remember is it had a mermaid on the front with a jolly wide mouth. It looks exactly like the picture on the posters."

"That's all you have? Many ships have mermaids on the front of them!" Alister bashed his fist on the table, making the man flinch. "Why waste my time with useless information?"

"N–No. That was just the last time I'd seen it, but I saw it before then."

"Where? How long ago?"

"It was docked at Luxor for nearly five months."

A small gasp parted his lips, his fist unclenching as he turned his head to Pierre. "That's where Theodore Briggs is from."

The place Rosetta had run away from was the town of Luxor in the provinces belonging to Queen Mary Anne.

"Why would she return there?" Pierre whispered, a deep frown crinkling his forehead. "She would have been arrested."

Alister leaned forward once more, turning his attention back to the fisherman. "You said it was docked at Luxor for five months, but it sank your ship a week ago?"

The man gave a nod.

"The ship just turned up in port in the middle of the night. When anyone went on board to find a crew or captain, it was completely deserted, like a ghost ship. It looked exactly like the head fleet ship we all thought was lost at sea." His eyes darted to Pierre for a moment before returning to him. "You mentioned Theodore Briggs. He hasn't returned to port for months, but he commanded a ship like that. I saw it then, and seeing it again, months later without its original crew, no one knew what to do."

She went home. She had gone to the one place Alister would never have thought to look, nor could he.

He couldn't go to Luxor. The moment his figurehead was seen from a distance, they'd fire their land cannons at his ship and fish him from the water to arrest him.

As he had mentioned, mermaids on the bows of ships were common. If she had sailed into the port under the cover of night, they could have abandoned the ship before anyone realised what it was.

What he didn't understand was why Rosetta would go there at all. Why would she return? *Why risk being arrested?* What she had done was stupid beyond all reason.

She had docked for five months. That gave Alister the impression she was hiding from something, was running away. *If she wanted to hide from me, she could have gone somewhere safer.* To return the Laughing Siren to its original port? That just didn't seem logical to him.

"When they realised it was the Laughing Siren, they had soldiers guarding it, waiting for the crew to turn up so they could arrest them. I don't know how they managed to set sail again. I was surprised when I saw it coming towards us."

"Do you know of Rosetta?"

The man's brows furrowed. "Rosetta Briggs? Of course, she was Theodore's wife, but she's been missing for four years now."

"You never saw her in the five months the Laughing Siren was docked?"

"No, why would I have? They say she went crazy, boarded a boat, and never returned."

She must have gotten her men to walk the town for her while she hid herself.

Despite the lack of answers, Alister couldn't deny that what this stranger was saying was rather convincing.

"What colour is it painted?" Alister asked, his eyes squinted. "The captain of that ship keeps it in remarkable shape. What colour are the rails?"

Asking him for a strange detail made the man's eyes dart around. "Uh, blue, I think? Light, like the sky."

Alister let out a laugh.

He turned to Pierre, who grinned at the sound. Alister hadn't laughed in months. "Aye, that's her ship alright." He faced the man again. "Before it sank your boat, which way was it heading?"

"South."

That made his laughter and cheer die. "Like south to the islands below Luxor, or south to the southern hemisphere?"

"We were on open water – that's where we get the best sea trout. The ship was heading to the southern hemisphere."

"Shit, Alister, we may never find her again."

He knew that. If she was heading that way, the chances of finding her were slipping further and further from his grasp.

I have a direction now. Plus, he had a time frame that wasn't too long ago. Alister finally had hope he would find her, and it elevated the worst of his hopelessness.

He reached behind Pierre to grab the man next to him.

"You, go to the ship and get me the map on my desk."

He shoved him to get to his feet and do as commanded.

The fisherman darted his gaze towards his crewman, to Pierre, then Alister. "Does this mean I've given you the information you need?"

"Once you show me where you were and where you saw that ship sailing, you will get your coin."

The wide grin of relief that formed on his weathered old face was warming. He really wanted to return to his family.

Alister was too busy figuring out a plan in his head to appreciate his look. He needed to make sure they were prepared, had everything he needed before they set sail.

At first light, they would be leaving this wretched town.

CHAPTER TWENTY-ONE

It was in the dark of night when Rosetta and her men left the mansion they'd desecrated, a place she had once called a home, and had been a place of suffering.

They were following her back to the pier where the Laughing Siren was currently being guarded by Queen Mary Anne's soldiers.

When they first arrived in Luxor, she'd abandoned her ship and headed straight for the vile Briggs mansion. It hadn't taken much to infiltrate it, not with the number of brutal killers she had following her.

Theodore's family thought he was dead and had decided to settle in. They stole his coin and used the power he held for themselves. When they saw her, they were shocked and very much disgruntled about her return. They were obligated to release the mansion to her as his widow.

Their anger quickly turned into fear as she commanded her crew to massacre them all.

Women and men. There were no children, but if there had been, Rosetta would have spared them. Still, she hated this family. They all knew what Theodore had done to her and they had never intervened. For that, they deserved their ends.

For five months, she claimed the land the mansion resided on as a safe place for herself and her men. She wore a dress and answered the gates when anyone came to speak with them, thinking the Briggs family was still alive, playing games to trick them into leaving.

She knew how to act noble, sound noble. No one batted an eye.

She gave the servants, most of whom were slaves, the option to die or join them. All of them had sworn their fealty if it meant they could escape their servitude. The men would join her crew when they set sail, the women released to hopefully start their own lives on this continent. Banksia was a large country.

Until then, they weren't allowed to leave the mansion.

Naeem had a big hand in helping her do all this. A few of them remembered him, since he'd been one of them. The others who first escaped with her were no longer with them.

Her men had lazed around the mansion. Some often went to the town to buy food and water for them, but other than that, there was no reason to leave. It was on the top of a hill surrounded by iron fences, two stories high and nearly the size of a small castle. The grounds allowed them space and luxury while they hid from the outside world.

Not that they did much to upkeep it. The gardens fell to ruin without maintenance. She and her men trashed the place, ripping paintings from walls, smashing vases, leaving rubbish on the floor. She used the portraits of Theodore for knife throwing practice.

No one was ordered to clean, and the filthier the place became, the brighter Rosetta smiled.

What did it matter the state of the Briggs mansion when she intended to abandon it? She didn't care, so long as it wasn't unsanitary whilst they were there.

Once they were done with it, they took everything valuable they could carry, including everything in the treasury. Without Theodore to guard and watch over his own money, his family had been draining it when word of his ship's takeover arrived.

No one yet knew it had been her who killed him.

It had taken her over a month and half to decide where she wanted to go after leaving Alister, eventually making her way to these shores.

Now, a little over five months after docking, she was pleased she was finally able to return to the sea.

Her men were prepared for the small fight they knew would greet them when they walked up the boardwalk of the pier to the Laughing Siren. The rotating soldiers had thinned out after so many months of her ship being abandoned.

It had been silent at first. Men stalked their way up to quietly slit throats from behind until someone shouted an alarm. A bell rang in the distance.

It was too late. With darkness covering them like a blanket of shielding comfort, they killed over half the soldiers present.

With the new additions to her crew, Rosetta now had over ninety men.

Turning her head to the side as she walked behind her men, killing their way through the pier, she peeked at the woman walking beside her. Rosetta now had her first female crew member.

She was a pretty redhead with freckles almost as wild as hers. Her eyes were a light amber, skin as white as freshly fallen snow.

It would take her a long time to adjust to life at sea, but she had offered to stay with Rosetta instead of trying to find her freedom with the other women.

"Nervous, Elizabeth?"

The young woman gave her a curt nod, curly, unruly hair bouncing. Around small, thin lips, she softly said, "I've never been on a boat before, ma'am."

"Please, I've told you not to call me that a thousand times." Rosetta sighed heavily, stemming the urge to roll her eyes. "You'll understand better when we're out at sea. Call me

Rosetta or Captain."

"Y–yes, my apologises," she quickly stuttered.

Rosetta knew she was used to being punished if she didn't speak formally with someone of a higher class. She was no longer of higher class. She was a commoner; she didn't deserve such elegant titles.

"There she is." A smile spread across her tired face when her feet met the gangplank to her ship. "This is the Laughing Siren."

"It's a lot bigger than I thought it would be."

"She's a big boat." Rosetta stepped away from Elizabeth so she could board, giving them some space before she started to shout. "You all know what to do! I want us out of this bay before anyone notices we're gone!"

"Aye, Captain!" they all shouted back.

Men started climbing shrouds, others yanking on anchor chains. Others were carrying barrels they'd procured over the last few days to supply the ship with good food and water.

It wasn't a lot, but she hoped it would last.

"Naeem, I want you at the helm."

With a nod, he made his way to it and stood at the ready.

"Mr Andrews, you and I will count the stocks after I take Elizabeth to her quarters."

She turned to the girl still standing on the boardwalk, like she'd lost the ability to move her feet.

"Come now, don't mess about!" Rosetta shouted, making her shuffle her feet until they hit the main deck. "Follow me."

Rosetta led her up the quarterdeck steps. Unlocking the door to the navigation room, she opened it and led her inside.

She took in a deep breath, breathing in the space she'd missed like an ache. When she heard Elizabeth's light feet patter up behind her, she walked to the left.

There were two sleeping cabins attached to the navigation room. One was for the captain; the other was for the first mate

– both were required to be close to this room.

Rosetta claimed the one on the right long ago. She was giving the second to Elizabeth so that the girl was close and safe. For the first time since she'd acquired this ship, she finally opened Theodore's old sleeping cabin.

"It isn't much, but you shouldn't need to be inside other than to sleep." She showed her the small bed inside with the little table at its foot, the decent sized cabinet mounted inside. "You'll be allowed the use of the navigation room the rest of the time. There is a second desk, but make sure you never touch mine or the safe, got it?"

With a nod, she answered, "Yes, I understand."

"Thank you for coming with me, I appreciate it."

Finally, Elizabeth gave her a warm, sweet smile, her soft personality shining through.

"Of course. I'm thankful to be free of being a maid and you have been so nice to me. I knew the moment you told the men you were going to sail away that I wanted to come."

"You'll come to regret that," she laughed. "The sea is rough."

As soon as she turned away from the woman, any pleasant emotions in her features died. She immediately grabbed Mr Andrews to go below deck to make sure everything was shipshape.

Rosetta didn't feel the need to play pretend for her crew.

They all knew she was torn up inside, that she was in pain. They all knew to leave her in peace and not question her about her sadness, her heartache, the confusing and tormented emotions she constantly bore.

Riddled with guilt, with shame, with regret she would never dare try to rectify. Rosetta didn't feel like she'd taken a proper breath in nearly seven months.

I have made my choices. Now, she must stick with them – not that she thought Alister would have cared that she'd left.

She'd given him his supplies. Other than the ring she'd stolen, which she knew he had a replica for since she'd seen it in his desk plenty of times, there was no reason for him to chase after her.

She'd sailed the other way.

To him, she was done. The prideful and arrogant man wouldn't have taken the rejection well.

She knew they'd both expected it to be him, but when she'd realised what had been growing inside her, she knew she had to leave. She loved Alister, but she wasn't willing to bear the pain of the result if he found out the truth. So, tucking her feelings away, she ran.

Scared and afraid, Rosetta fled.

Without a word of why. Without the opportunity to stop her. Without a chance to find her, just in case.

What point was there in remaining?

She didn't think Alister had the capability to return her feelings. He'd once told her he didn't even have a heart. He even admitted he didn't have the ability to be lonely.

He was a cold-blooded murderer, a man as rough and unforgiving as the storm that had once tried to kill her and sink her ship.

He could be cold, merciless, cruel.

How could someone like that fall in love with her?

Even if he was out there chasing her, she knew it was because of some kind of vendetta that she'd left, not because he cared for her.

He'd showed her he desired her, that he wanted to keep her alive, but he'd never done anything to show her he felt anything tender for her. Not once had she felt free enough to show her inner pain and sadness – she didn't think he'd care.

She always feared he'd reject her if she'd tried seeking comfort in him. To have a crying and weeping woman finally release her inner turmoil? Not many men appreciated witnessing it, nor did they understand it was the final bridge of trust that needed to be crossed to gain all of who they were.

For Rosetta, it was just easier to keep it all buried away. *I'm used to bottling everything up.* Still, despite it all, she felt irrevocably and despairingly alone.

"Looks like the stocks are good enough," Rosetta said, nodding her head in approval.

It was thanks to Alister, though, that she was able to count the barrels of food and estimate how long it would last with over ninety mouths to feed. She could even do the head count herself.

Before long, they were pushing off the Luxor pier and heading out to open ocean, heading as far south as she possibly could.

Quiet and uneventful days passed.

"Sail, ho!" someone called from the crow's nest.

"What kind of ship?" she asked, making her way from the main deck to the helm.

"It's a fishing boat."

Rosetta pulled her spyglass from the box and extended its tapered sections. She looked through it to see the small boat in the distance.

She thought for long moments. *That looks like a Luxor fishing vessel.* They were still rather close to shore, even though they'd been sailing for three days. *Hmmm.*

She turned her head in the direction of the helm while still looking through her magnifying spyglass. "Mr Andrews, turn starboard side. Head for that ship."

"But it's a fishing boat." His dark brows knotted deeply. "It's not worth raiding one of them."

"I know. We can't leave anyone behind to know which way we're heading." When she didn't get a response, nor feel her ship turning, she lowered it to look at him. "Well? I've given you an order."

"But they're innocent men, Rosetta."

"Aren't those we kill on trading ships innocent men? Aren't those on fleet ships innocent men? I don't care what they are. If they recognise this ship from afar, they may tell Queen Mary Anne where we're heading."

She didn't want anyone after her knowing where she was going. Once she was in southern waters, she knew she'd be free. Rosetta was hoping she'd be able to take a proper breath.

"Yes, Captain," he sighed, turning the ship to the right.

Since it was nothing but a fishing boat with spears and nets, they had been no match for the Laughing Siren and her cannons. Just one cycle of cannon fire and she watched that little boat sink as she pressed on into the horizon.

They started their journey south uninterrupted, mostly.

They'd dealt with a few difficult storms as they changed oceans and hemispheres. They also passed a trading boat she'd raided in hope of gaining additional supplies.

It had been a trading boat from the south, one she didn't need to sink on principle. They'd spoken a different language and had darker skin than her. There had been a few men in her crew who were familiar with the language and had been able to relay her commands. They'd easily laid down their weapons and surrendered.

Unfortunately, it had been a ship of wares and only held food enough for the trip they'd been making. She took most of it, leaving them just enough to make it to port.

After a solid month on the seas, though, their supplies were dwindling. Rosetta knew they were going to have to port soon.

"How are we going, Mr Andrews?" she asked as she came up beside him and patted his shoulder lightly.

"We're going well," he laughed. Any transgressions or arguments were generally left in the moment as they tried to hold onto hope and high spirits. "I'm thankful it seems we've passed all the storms. We've had clear skies for almost a week now. It makes manning the helm for long periods easier."

She gave a small laugh, unable to wrestle up a real one. "Now that I know. Naeem is asleep?"

She looked up at the bright noon sun. Their shifts had changed again and Naeem was having a nap in the morning so he could take the afternoon into evening shift.

"Yeah, he's still passed out, but he should wake soon to take over. How about you?" He eyed her up and down, giving a shake of his head with thinned lips. "How are you feeling?"

"Better every day." Rosetta had been dealt a deep injury and had been trying to heal it. "Thank you for taking the wheel in my stead."

"Excellent!" he exclaimed, a bright grin spreading across his face. "We've all been so worried about you, and I'm surely pleased I won't have to work so hard soon. How's the girl?"

Rosetta had really come to enjoy speaking with Mr Andrews. He reminded her of John, just half his age. He was friendly, smart, and held strength in both body and will.

He wasn't as jolly or funny as Naeem, but he did try to be optimistic – which is exactly how John had always tried to be when he wasn't acting like a stern father. Considering he'd taken Thomas under his wing, it was no surprise he'd shaped him into someone Rosetta would need in his absence.

"Elizabeth?" She gave a snort of humour. "She's getting used to the waves, but she's a landlubber."

She mostly stayed in the navigation room except to eat. She wasn't comfortable around the men, no matter how many times Rosetta assured her they were safe.

"What about–"

"Sail, ho! It's a fleet ship!"

Those words ended their conversation and sent relief soaring through her. Just what they needed; a good, solid ship to take down.

"Which way?" she asked as she reached for her spyglass.

Keat yelled back, "Port side! Three clicks away."

That meant it was right on the horizon and far away in the distance.

"Head that way, Mr Andrews. Port side."

She felt the Laughing Siren turn to the left.

"What's a fleet ship doing this way?" she muttered to herself as she raised her lens.

It wasn't rare for the north and south to trade, but Queen Mary Anne mostly traded with the west.

"Maybe she's been opening up her trades," Thomas remarked, answering her muttering. "It would be wise if she opened her borders. The Southeast Trading Company could easily have a trading route through Luxor."

"That's true," she sighed, searching the horizon. "We've been out of the loop while we were with the Howling Death."

Ever since she'd gained her ship, Rosetta stopped paying attention to the shipping routes of the royal fleet. *It's been over a year since I took my ship and looked at the last updated trading alliances and routes.*

"You're right," she yelled to the man above. "It is a fleet ship."

With crisp white sails, she could see the Queen's green flag flapping high in the air attached to the centre mast. She lowered the lens to laugh.

"Looks like we'll be getting our supplies, boys!"

From what she could see, it was a decent sized ship. If it was on a long journey, it should have more than enough stock to fix hers.

She wouldn't need to worry about the life of the men on board since she'd be sending it down to the bottom of the ocean. Rosetta never left those men alive.

She started stomping one of her boots against the ground, making her stomps echo. "Naeem, you lazy sod. Wake up!"

He'd often told her he could hear her stepping around like

she was an elephant. Hopefully, she'd wake him.

When he didn't emerge and she could see the enemy vessel with her naked eye, she went to the main deck and opened the door. She tried to flip him out of his hammock.

"Hey, I said wake up!"

"What do you want?" He started pushing at her face. "I'm tired, since you do jack shit these days."

"You can miss out on all the action, then. We're approaching a fleet ship."

"Well, why didn't you start with that?" he exclaimed, laughing as he rolled out and landed on his feet with ease. He started tugging his boots on, hopping around on one foot. "We always need to be quick with those ships. Otherwise, we sink them before we get what we want."

"Exactly. I'll need you to take the lead with this. You know I can't go over in my state."

"Yeah, yeah, I know." He put his weapons belt on and made sure everything was right. "Alright, let's go."

Rosetta walked back up to the quarterdeck with Naeem in tow. She raised her spyglass once more, looking over the ship better now that it was closer.

The Queen's green flag with the royal coat of arms flapped in the wind. She examined the white crisp sails her ships always displayed, and moved her lens over the red cedar timber that had recently been polished until it shined. Dark, forest green railings were obviously freshly painted.

As always, the fleet ship was in pristine and excellent condition, clean, painted, and restored like it was on its first adventure.

Now, let's guess what your name is.

She'd heard multiple names for her ship besides the Laughing Siren: the Happy Sea-maid, the Jolly Mermaid, the Giggling Water-Nymph.

That last one was Rosetta's favourite, considering she was

the captain.

The moment Rosetta scanned her spyglass over the bow of the ship, it fell from her hands to hit the ground with a distinct shatter. She'd broken the glass inside it.

Without a care for her poor tool, she quickly turned and pushed up on the wheel of the helm, turning it in the other direction.

"Whoa!" Mr Andrews gasped, releasing it to put his hands up in surrender and let her take over. "What are you–"

"That is no fleet ship!" she yelled so loudly, it almost came out as a screech. "Get us out of here!"

A hitch of breath caught in her lungs as a sharp pain shot through her. She had to stop, almost sagging to her knees in agony.

Naeem stepped forward to help her. She managed to stay on her feet, but she couldn't stop the deep pounding of fear accelerating her heart rate. Rosetta was choking on her anxiety.

We need to get away. We need to run.

Following her commands, everyone jumped to action immediately to get them moving as fast as they could in the opposite direction.

If Rosetta was telling them to run from a fight, then they understood she knew they wouldn't win, or she had a good reason.

But it was too late.

"Captain, I'm sorry," Keat yelled down to her from the crow's nest.

He understood as much as she did now what ship it was and to whom it belonged. They both hadn't been able to see its minor details because it had been too far away.

"Prepare the cannons!" She stepped to the railing to shout over it. "You will attack that ship! You will fight when they try to board."

She turned to look over the stern of her ship as the other gave chase.

Why? She didn't need her telescope to know that the skeletal forefinger of the grim reaper pointed at her while its other hand grasped a lantern. It had a harrowing face that looked like it was screaming with a hood over its head.

Why is he here?

Alister lowered his spyglass with a dark and menacing grin, feeling his hair flapping around his neck and shoulders as the wind cut through him and his clothes.

It was windy today, making his sails buckle and concave. The salty air swirling around him made him feel energised for his hunt.

"Looks like we've got her on the run, lads!"

His eye fell on the green flag sitting at the top of his mast bearing the Queen's coat of arms.

He'd known Rosetta would fall for it. He knew she would turn her ship towards his when she saw it in the distance, would help him close that space between them so he could get hold of her faster.

I knew she would try to attack me if she thought I was a fleet ship.

His frigate would always be quicker than her galleon since it was smaller and lighter, but he hadn't wanted to spend half a day chasing her down. She'd turned to him, closing the distance, yet once she'd realised this was no fleet ship at all, she'd wasted no time turning her ship.

Because she was momentarily in place while she turned, Alister was able to close the gap.

Derek had taken over from Pierre to man the helm when

they'd seen the Laughing Siren in the distance. That large and glorious ship... the moment Alister had seen it, the octopus strangling him had started to ease off.

Aye, lass. You can run, but I won't let you get away this time.

He wouldn't have to live with the unanswered questions. If there was a chance Rosetta still wanted him, he was going to make sure he got her. If she didn't, maybe he could move on, but he had an inkling that, if she held even a shred of what he did in her heart, then she would be his again.

Let's find out why you ran away like a coward.

"What are your commands?" Pierre shouted from the main deck, ready to pass on the information.

"Nothing," he answered, turning his head. "Just follow until we're next to her."

"What about the cannons?" He pointed to the hatch leading to below deck. "Shouldn't we start preparing them?"

"Nay." He eyed the stern of the Laughing Siren now that it was in range of his bow cannons. "Just prepare the men."

He winced. He knew he was going to have to let her attack him while he allowed it and didn't return fire. *She won't like it if I hurt her ship.*

Walking over to Derek, he put his hand on the man's shoulder. "When we're next to it, we'll start heading over. Once everyone's across, I need you to get the Howling Death away from it as fast as possible."

"Ye think she's gonna try and sink us?"

"Aye," he sighed. "Could be a possibility."

What he had done to warrant that, he didn't know. If he was the one she was running from, had been hiding from, then he knew she may not react well to seeing him.

He'd already told his men the plan days ago, working out the best course of action. They were all ready, but Alister felt like he wasn't.

He knew what he wanted, but not what he should expect.

He could be walking into a situation that would hurt him. Not physically, but in a way he had never experienced. He barely understood what he felt, why he felt it.

All he knew was he did, and he'd be damned if he let this woman go without trying. At least by the end of this day, he could end this uncomfortable journey.

He narrowed his eyes as Derek started moving the ship to come up beside theirs. *You better want me. I came all this way for you.*

Shouts from both ships called to each other like a war cry.

His men started swinging across. Her ship started firing. Usually, there would be someone below deck to man the cannons, but since he wasn't going to utilise them, he was able to send the brunt of his crew across.

As a swarm, they overtook those on the surface of the Laughing Siren. Half of her men were below deck and he knew his crew would close the hatch so they couldn't assist.

Should have spared the cannons, Rosetta. It may have been a fairer fight if she'd kept hers above the surface as well. He wondered if it was because she thought he'd return fire.

Alister was the last to swing across because he was unable to find her. He expected her to be at the helm.

His ship vaulted to the side, vibrating beneath his feet as the side of his hull was hit by cannonball after cannonball. It was designed for battle and was strong enough to withstand the first round, which would only crunch the timber.

If his ship stayed behind and continued to take damage, those tiny holes of broken timber would become the size of cannonballs.

He stood on the poop deck since it was the highest level and gave him the easiest access to see into her taller ship without having to climb the shrouds.

Shit, where is she? Any longer and Alister would lose his

chance to cross when Derek swung the Howling Death out of firing range.

While he was looking to the back of her ship and scanning back over, he saw her. It looked as though she'd just come from the navigation room, running down the stairs to cross the deck, heading for the hatch.

Alister could see his men had already locked it. He wouldn't let her open it. He needed to beat her.

Pulling taut on the rope in his hand connected to the centre mast, he started running. He ran down both staircases so he could cross the main deck of his ship to pick up speed. Then he ran diagonally towards hers to create an arch in his swing, needing to gain height, as his ship was lower than hers.

Stepping onto the railing, he jumped and kicked both legs forward. Flying through the air, he aimed straight for where he wanted to land with all the skill and precision he'd developed over the years.

Still in the air, he let go of the rope and started to fall. Landing on top of the hatch right before she could get to it, he turned.

As he was bringing himself out of the crouch he'd taken to soften the worst of the impact, he began to tower over her. She quickly had to halt, or she'd crash into him.

Her face whitened in dread as she looked up at him.

"Hello, lass." He took a single step forward to move off the grated hatch. He would've grinned in triumph, if looking at her face didn't make him so damn angry. "Long time, no see."

CHAPTER TWENTY-TWO

Rosetta hurried to transfer everything she needed into Elizabeth's room to hide it.

She felt terrible that the soft-hearted woman was crying.

As soon as she'd heard they were going to be attacked, she'd been steadily shaking, her hands trembling with fright. Then, while Rosetta was trying her hardest to be hasty and quick, the sounds of cannons firing brought the woman to tears.

Despite her fear, her face turning blistering red, she was helping. The sounds of distress she made, the weeping and sniffling, hollowed out her chest, but she was thankful Elizabeth was doing everything she could.

Once everything was moved – no one would think to check a room that had always been empty – she pushed Elizabeth inside.

"You'll be safe in here," she told her while holding onto the doorhandle. "Stay quiet. No matter what you hear, no matter what happens, stay in this room."

"A–Are you going to be okay?" Her hands were covering her mouth, cupping it like she already wanted to be silent. "What do I do if you get hurt or captured?"

"I'll be fine. As long as you stay quiet in here until I get them to leave, everything should be okay. I'll get you once they do."

Rosetta would get them to leave. She had to.

Letting her eyes scan over the woman with an apologetic look, she softly closed the door. Bolting to the door of the navigation room, she threw it open and slammed it shut behind her.

I have to get below deck, have to get away from here.

Without glancing around to know if it was truly safe, seeing Alister's men had already swung across and their number nearly double hers on the surface, she sprinted down the stairs.

She could see the hatch had already been shut, and she didn't care if they reclosed it behind her. Down the length of her ship, men were fighting on either side. Hers were trying to keep those who had crossed over from completely dominating it. It gave her the space to duck and weave around the few who had gotten past.

Her heart was beating so fast, it felt as though it would burst in her chest, her breaths so sharp she feared she'd start to breathe glass from her lungs.

Almost there. She was only a few steps away.

She came scrambling to a halt when Alister landed on top of it.

Shit! No! She would have been safer below deck instead of out in the open like this.

The look on his face appeared cold. "Hello, lass. Long time, no see."

A wash of dread poured over her and she took a step back when he came forward. Rosetta pulled on the handle of her sword to bring it out of its sheath, pointing the tip at him.

He did the same with his cutlass. The large, curved blade seemed overpowering and dangerous compared to her thin, double-edged sword.

How am I supposed to do this? How was she supposed to fight someone who was bigger than her, taller than her... and someone she cared for?

She didn't want to hurt Alister.

She wouldn't hand herself over to him, either. Rosetta wouldn't surrender just yet, not if there was a chance she could still get below deck.

We can talk there.

Rosetta slashed her sword forward, forcing him to step back and deflect it with his own.

"You finally restored that ship of yours."

She didn't know why she thought he wouldn't return her swing with his own. She had to quickly dodge it before she was cut across the shoulder.

"Aye. Thought it was time. I got some pieces of eight because of a certain treacherous woman."

He swung again, not giving her time to think. She deflected it with her sword. The force sent a stab of pain through her abdomen. *My wound still hasn't healed.*

"I can see you finally learned how to dress," she sneered, slashing forward and making him deflect it.

As much as she was riddled with anxiety because he was here, she couldn't help noting Alister looked wonderful in his new outfit. He looked better than when she'd seen him last.

The man was wearing the black eyepatch she'd given him with his blue family crest. She always thought it looked good on him, but it was the white tunic with a deep vee neck and ties that suited him. It wasn't the one she'd picked. This one had a seam of lace that showed it was made of high-quality.

His breeches were black but clean, made like they were a perfect fit. His tunic was surprisingly tucked in; she'd never seen him do that before. She eyed the brown doublet coat around him. It was new, with golden stitching and buttons.

With all of this alongside his neat stubble, clean looking face, and black hair reaching his shoulders tied back neatly, he looked like a man who might have been noble at first glance.

"I had someone show me how to not look poor," he answered, holding the flat edge of his blade up to block her side swing.

He returned it with his own.

Her own attacks were easy for her to do, but every time she blocked one of Alister's heavy blows, a lance of pain hit her. She gritted her teeth and refused to wince.

"Have you figured out how to count your stocks yet?"

"No." She deflected another attack, but his seemed to come faster and faster. "I had a terrible teacher."

His lips curled into a small smile of humour.

"That's not true. I thought I was pretty patient with you pathetically fumbling your way through it." She squinted her eyes into a scowl and stabbed her sword forward, forcing him to jump back quickly or she would have stabbed right through his midsection. "Ever considered it was the student and not the teacher's fault?"

He raised his cutlass over his head and swung downwards. She raised her sword to block it, placing her hand against the flat part underneath to support it.

His blade curved in front of her as she stepped back.

Although it hurt to block, she'd expected his swings to have more force behind them. *He isn't using all his strength.* He couldn't be. This seemed too easy.

She eyed the hatch coming into view; she had been directing them in a circle so she could be within range of it.

"I don't think so."

"How many strikes have rung?"

"Seven," she blurted out, right before she had to deflect his attack again. "Eight."

"Aye, good job. But you're eyeing that hatch now."

She should have known he knew what she was up to.

Rosetta slashed forward in a wide swing so she could get him to back up and give her space.

He didn't dodge it like she thought he would. He swung his cutlass to the side with such a heavy burst of strength, it resonated up her arm when their swords made contact. It speared all the way through her body, making her wince as she tensed.

Her sword swung out of her hand as her grip loosened.

Knowing this was her only chance, she sprinted the two steps towards the hatch and flipped open the lock. She threw open the hatch, but before she could take a single step down it, her shoulder was grabbed, and she was spun around.

A small scream locked in her throat when he grabbed her wrist and curled his body forward. He shouldered her waist until she flipped over it.

"Put me down!"

He continued to hold onto the same wrist, and she used her other hand to palm his back, trying to take away the pressure under her torso.

He used his free hand to let out a loud whistle as he started walking across the deck. His men immediately came up to circle him carrying her like a preorganised signal.

It didn't escape her notice that he'd grabbed her arse firmly when she started kneeing him in the chest.

"Let her go!" she heard Naeem shout behind her.

He must have come to stop Alister. She wished she could help by grabbing her pistol, but he was holding the wrist that could've reached for it.

Unable to see what happened when they halted, she tried to make sure Naeem was still alive when he started walking forward again.

She reached for him.

"Naeem!" She screamed his name in a shrieking cry when she saw someone had their sword to his throat, holding onto him from behind. "Don't you dare kill him!"

She winced every time Alister's foot hit the steps to climb

higher, her body bouncing over his shoulder.

She tried to keep her eye on Naeem, but couldn't see what happened to him when the upper deck blocked her view. She noticed his men clustered around both staircases on either side, as though to block anyone from climbing after them.

Pierre had his eyes narrowed on her in disapproval as he followed up the stairs. He turned to Mr Andrews to point his pistol at him, stopping him from assisting her.

She started bashing on Alister's back when he opened the door to her navigation room. *Nononooo!*

This was the last place she wanted to be, and she worried for Elizabeth currently hiding in her room. She didn't want her to hear what was going to be said, or what this could eventually turn into.

It felt like she was being choked when he didn't put her down to talk. Instead, he started carrying her to her sleeping quarters.

Oh my gosh... He wouldn't, would he?

She didn't think Alister would do something so cruel to her simply because she'd left, but dark emotions could make people callous.

Her heart leapt to her throat when he threw her down against her bed. She pushed her free hand forward, trying to get him away when he kneeled above her.

"No!"

"Let's get this off you." He pulled on the buckle of her weapons belt and ripped it off her, throwing it behind him and out of reach. It cluttered against the wooden floor.

"Wait!" She pushed harder, a mixture of betrayal and fear bowing her eyes so deeply, she could feel the welt of tears wanting to form. "Stop!"

He gripped her flailing arms and pushed them until he had a hold of both her wrists in one of his large hands, pinning them above her head. When he settled into the gap between her thighs, she started kneeing the sides of his legs.

"You and I are going to talk, Rosetta," he said in a calm but stern tone. "Calm down."

Talk? She hadn't realised she'd clenched her eyes shut until she stopped struggling. She slowly peeked them open.

"Then why did you–?"

She thought he was going to strip her!

"Couldn't have you reaching for that pistol of yours." His lips thinned in irritation, his eyes squinting at her. His expression said he knew exactly what she thought he was going to do to her and didn't appreciate it. "I don't trust you won't punch me in the face or kick me in the nuts again if I don't pin you down."

Her lips pouted as she turned her head to the side. "I vaguely remember doing that."

She should have known Alister wouldn't hurt her, but she'd been attacked by men in many ways in the past. It was difficult not to paint them all with the same brush... even if she knew him.

Because he wasn't laying on her, had given her plenty of room to breathe, she could feel her lungs settling. Her anxiety was still present, but it didn't feel as suffocating.

That did little to calm the heavy beating of her pulse as she felt it in her jugular, her stomach, her chest. It pumped so loudly, it seemed almost deafening.

She thought it may have even quickened when she felt him gently brush a curl of her hair from her face with the back of a finger. It was a caring gesture, one she couldn't handle from him.

I can't do this. She couldn't bear to look at him now that a silent truce had been called between them. She couldn't meet his eye after what she had done.

Guilt sailed through her. Regret. Sadness.

She didn't want to look at the first person she'd ever fallen in love with and then abandoned to save herself. Didn't want to feel the depth of it when she took in his features.

I'm such an idiot.

Why did I allow this to happen? She'd known since Tortaya, had recognised what she was feeling and thought she could handle the unrequited emotion as they sailed together.

Alas, it had continued to grow, continued to fester into a painful ache that only seemed to go away when she'd been entangled with him. It didn't matter if it was sexually or sleeping curled up by his side. As long as her limbs had been clutching at him, nothing else mattered.

He was mean, rough, dangerous, but this brute of a man had been gentle with her when she needed him to be, soft and sweet when they were alone.

It was as though his hands thought she was both the most fragile thing in the world when he'd petted her, but also a fierce, wild cat that could take his strength when he grabbed at her. These conflicting touches always threw her off-guard.

His hips had been a never-ending storm, but his mouth had become so affectionate, it made her mindless. She happily let him do whatever he wanted.

She knew he'd started to seek her out because he'd valued her company, like he did any of his most trusted crew. To feel included in that small circle had been heart-warming.

These were things that had little to do with tenderness.

She'd found these warming moments lovely because of how she'd begun to feel, not as a reflection of how he did. They were done for his enjoyment, because of his impulses.

I should have left sooner.

Things might have been easier. He might not be here now if she had.

She didn't even know why he was. She didn't think he would come after her, wouldn't care to chase after her. *I'm just some woman to him.* He would have left her eventually, casting her to the side.

He'd grown possessive of her, and she had found that titillating, but it didn't mean he truly felt anything for her. Men liked to own things, wanted to control things. She was a thing he'd wanted to keep to himself and had figured out the best way to do that and nothing more.

So why chase after her when he be with someone else? *Because I was easy? Available with my own ship?*

He'd once told her he liked the idea of having '*good pussy*' trailing after him on her own damn ship. Was it because he could escape her when he found her annoying or troublesome?

Her bed had been elsewhere.

They'd shared each other's when they wanted to, but he didn't have to face her when he didn't. Sometimes, he didn't.

I hate this. She didn't want him here, pinning her to the bed, didn't want him so close, he could steal everything away from her.

He smelt of salt, of sea, of him, of the warm, woodsy musk that belonged to Alister. It was one she'd found so wonderful, she would lay with him for a little longer in the mornings just to take him in when he was asleep.

Her brows crinkled as guilt lashed her even harder. *I don't want to lie to him.*

For someone who wanted to talk, he said nothing.

I want this over with.

"What are you doing here?" she finally asked quietly, refusing to move her gaze from the long, gridded windows on one side of her narrow sleeping chamber.

"I should be asking you the same thing."

"You told me I could sail away whenever I wanted, so I did."

She felt his fingers dig and curl into the hollow concave at the base of her throat. He started rubbing against her jaw lightly.

"You took my father's ring," he commented, continuing to brush his fingers over her skin while the chain to which it was attached swayed across her throat.

Is that why he's here? Something hurtful swirled in her torso.

"I saw you had another in your desk. If you want it so badly, take it and leave. You can have it back."

She wouldn't have taken it if she'd known it was the reason he'd come after her. He dropped it.

"Nay, you can keep it." He lifted his hand, drawing her attention for a moment "Already replaced it."

She could see he was wearing the replica on his ring finger already. "Then what do you want?"

"Damn." He grabbed her jaw and forced her head forward to face him. "You're prettier than I remember."

Looking up at him, his eye like the sun from the light shining through her window as it darted over the features of her face, she felt like he'd gouged into her chest.

Her brows drew together so tightly, a crinkle formed in the middle, her lips tightening into an agonised pout. Then her eyes widened when his hand shot through her hair to hold her still as he lowered his head and crashed his lips against hers.

The feeling in her chest gouged deeper, but despite it, Rosetta felt a tremor of desire and longing flip low in her belly. Her entire body tensed beneath him, and her hands clenched into small fists.

The low and heavy groan he gave when he tilted his head and moved his lips to kiss her deeper made her ache in so many ways, she didn't know how to handle the conflicting emotions.

I missed him. She missed that roughish sound. She missed the feeling of his lips against hers, the way he smelled. His voice. His face. His touch. How his stubble tickled her face.

She'd hated herself for missing this man, and it only

worsened every second he was in front of her. She knew it was going to hurt more now that she'd gotten another taste of him when she sent him away.

Like a poor, pathetic, hungry woman, Rosetta couldn't stop herself from kissing him back. Just once she allowed herself to take from him before she finally turned her head to the side to violently break the kiss.

All she wanted to do was cry, but she refused to show she cared.

CHAPTER TWENTY-THREE

Looking down at Rosetta while he let his mind quietly soak in all her beauty, Alister couldn't stop himself from kissing her.

He should've been focused on speaking with her, but a deep-seated craving had gripped him. He thought if he hadn't gotten to feel her lips like this again, he would've died.

As he drew his lips over hers, only one thought came to mind. *So damn soft.*

They felt silkier than he remembered, like parts of him had forgotten just how amazing aspects of her were, just so he could be enthralled when he finally saw her again.

When she'd kissed him back, he thought he was going to get lost in her until she ripped herself away. He hid just how heavy his breaths suddenly became just from that quick contact, how much it affected his body.

He stared down at her.

She didn't smell of gardenias and he figured she'd run out of that perfume a while ago, but she smelled of herself. It made his lids want to go heavy.

She was avoiding his gaze again, and he didn't like it.

"Why'd you leave?" he asked with a dangerous bite.

With her arms above her head, she still managed to shrug. "Got bored."

He let out a bitter laugh. "Nay, I don't believe that one. Try again, *Rosie.*"

He watched her wince.

She'd made a mistake in telling him he could call her that. She'd given him permission to wield such a heavy word and in doing so, she'd given him hope she wanted him just as much as he wanted her.

Her goodbye hadn't been empty, but filled with emotion. Alister didn't think he had been alone in his feelings; at least, he didn't want to believe he was.

He wanted her to admit to it.

He wanted her to admit she left because she was afraid, just so he could tell her he'd chased her all this way because he understood. He wanted her to tell him she loved him so that he could be free to tell her the same.

Because... Alister was deeply petrified of showing his vulnerability, just to find out he was wrong. If he told her what had driven him to find her and she laughed at him, scorned him, it would destroy his stone heart.

He wanted to know she felt the same so he knew he wasn't alone in this. If he was, then he had been the biggest fool.

He would have no one else to blame but himself.

She may feel something, but if it wasn't as deep as what he'd come to discover inside himself, then he had been a moron for coming here.

He wasn't sure.

In Tortaya, the way she had so easily accepted him with other women, would have accepted other men, had sent a woman to his lap? Looking back on that had been difficult. She hadn't seemed to care, and it meant she may never have.

She had come to start sleeping in his hammock, but that had been because she was cold since it'd been winter. She knew he wouldn't have accepted it if she'd slept with anyone else for warmth, even if it was Naeem.

He hadn't known it then, but he'd allowed her to occupy

his space because he'd liked her being in it.

She didn't say anything for a long time, thinking to herself while he'd been lost in his own thoughts.

"You got me drunk, locked down my ship, stole my ring, and left in the middle of the night without a fucking word, Rosetta. I came here to find out why."

The more he spoke, listing what she had done, the more his nose crinkled and his blood pumped in rage. *She left me!* Made him chase after her for seven months!

She drank in his anger and wielded it for herself, like she needed it for courage. Her head turned to give him a direct glare of narrowed eyes.

"Why should I have stayed? The sex may have been good Alister, but why should I have stuck around for a stupid, arrogant man who yelled at me whenever I didn't do what he told me?" His head reared back in surprise, and hers came forward in determination. "You always treated me less because I was a woman! Why would I have stuck around for that?"

Shit. That was hurtful.

He grabbed her beneath her jaw, wrapping his hands around her neck to hold her still. He bent his head over her with a snarled expression.

"I may be arrogant, but I stopped seeing you as something less than me a long time ago." His gaze flickered between her eyes, making sure he held her stare completely. "I have respected you as a captain since that storm that separated us. I treated you like my equal and I showed you that!"

How dare she try to twist something good he knew he'd done into something nasty.

"You kept punishing me for stepping off my ship!"

"Because it was fun! Taking you on a ship we'd destroyed together or raided..." Well, it had started to become the highlight of them doing so.

When there was something they could attack on the horizon, Alister knew he'd bend her over something on it and take her with brutal thrusts. If the ship had been sinking, it put a time limit on what they were doing, making him even more excited.

When her face didn't change in surprise or confusion, his lips thinned in annoyance.

"You knew it, too." The rest of her words may have been truthful, but the ending had been a lie, and he almost hadn't noticed.

It was obvious she was going to keep lying to him.

He knew she wasn't aware of the battle inside him, how her reactions were making those tentacles squeeze around his heart, crushing it.

It hurt so badly, it made his lungs feel dry, like he couldn't breathe. Alister was starving of oxygen.

What did I do wrong? Even if he hadn't realised what he had been feeling, he knew he'd done things that often confused him.

Wanting to count coin with her. Having her lay on his chest because she'd been unwell. Taking her to bed alone in port, and then caring for her afterwards. Letting her always get her way and scratching at his head afterwards, unsure of why he was letting her.

Alister had shared with her the story of his father. *I even told her who my mother was.* If she had been anyone else, he would have backed out of that room and left them with unanswered questions, but he'd trusted her.

He trusted her more than any of his crew.

"Why do you even care that I left?" She started squirming beneath him, as though she wanted nothing more than to be free. "It's been seven months. Go back to the port girls and prostitutes you've been taking and leave me the hell alone!"

A dark chuckle fell from his lips as he raised his hand and

pointed his forefinger at her, shaking it up and down.

"I knew you'd bring this up." He continued to chuckle –
despite the fact it lost its humour with each roll. "That if I did,
you'd use it against me."

"What's that supposed to mean?" she sneered.

"I haven't fucked another woman since I met you!" he
roared so loudly, she winced.

Her eyelids fluttered in surprise, her bottom lip falling
slightly. "Y–you're lying," she stuttered, her gaze darting
around, as though she couldn't handle the intensity of his
stare.

"Nay." He felt her hands suddenly tighten with his fingers
as he held her down. "Only lass I've been with is you since
you abandoned me in Dunecaster."

Even back then, he'd been too focused on getting his ship
back. There had also been something about watching her sail
away, the back of his own ship heading further and further into
the distance. It had stopped him from taking a woman then,
simply because he'd been so turned on by her doing that that
he'd wanted to take it out on her, punish her.

Realisation settled into his entire being. He let out a huff
of laughter as he shook his head. *I've bloody liked her from
the beginning.*

He'd liked Rosetta from the moment she'd stolen his ship,
simply because she'd had the audacity to do it.

"Well, I have," she said quietly, turning her head to the side
and looking at the wall with shame.

Just like that, Alister felt like he'd been gutted with a knife.
Still, he leaned a little closer and cupped her cheek pressed to
the bed gently by slipping it between them. He let his thumb
brush over it once.

"Aye, I thought you might," he said softly, making her
visibly cringe. Even her legs tensed beside him.

He'd known it was a possibility, one he'd prepared himself

for. He despised it, but she had chosen to sail away.

In her mind, why would she have kept to herself?

He'd needed to accept it before he came to her because he hadn't reacted well when he'd originally had this realisation. He'd almost shot someone in rage. Yet, he'd had it and still came here for her.

I want her. The more she continued to talk, saying things as if she wanted to extinguish the fiery yearning he had for her, the more he wanted to know if she still wanted him at all.

He should have released her by now. What she had told him was damning enough for him to walk away and know it was hopeless, but he didn't want to.

She'd kissed him back before. He thought maybe, he just needed to spark her back to him after so long.

With desperation and determination clinging to him, Alister wrapped his hand around the nape of her neck and once more crashed his lips to hers.

Her reaction had been instant.

Rosetta's lips moved beneath his like she couldn't help herself. A flutter of hope swirled in his gut. He refused to let her break away when she tried, holding her still as he deepened the press of his mouth.

By the third time their lips moved over each other's, she gave him the little mew she used to give him when he knew she was enjoying it. When her eyes closed and she gave him another, Alister's body felt heavy after a wild shudder rolled through him.

He pulled back, seeing a subtle flush of arousal had already pinkened her cheeks and the bridge of her nose. It even reddened her chest as she huffed with shallow pants.

His grin grew and lifted his cheeks as it spread, becoming wider when she peeked her eyes open with that softness she'd occasionally gifted to him.

There was no denying it. Despite the reason she'd run from

him, Rosetta still wanted him. She'd given him what he needed. *I'm not backing down.* If this was the way he needed to do it, then so be it.

Alister took her mouth again, making her eyes shut once more. He ran his hands higher. With one, he gripped both of hers to hold them tenderly, and with the other, he ran it through her hair to grip her.

Tilting his head, he waited for her lips to part and then he slipped his tongue forward to lick her. She gave a moan, her tongue hesitantly brushing against his.

He'd half-expected her to bite it.

The longer he kissed her, the more relaxed he felt her becoming. He slipped his knees back and lowered his body until he was laying between the nook of her legs.

A groan strangled its way from his lungs and up his throat when he gave a heavy thrust with his hips, his hardened shaft stroking against her.

Alister had been hard the moment he'd pinned this deceitful, beautiful woman against this bed. With just that one simple movement against her, he knew he'd lose his ever-loving mind if he got the chance to slam his cock inside her again.

A loud gasp broke from her, pausing her kisses and making her eyes snap open wide. He didn't care. He just wrangled her lips back into the kiss with force, taking complete control.

She didn't stop him, was no longer trying to break away.

The passion he had for this woman burst inside him tenfold. It heated his skin, quickened his mouth, tightened the grip he had on her.

He thrust against her again, knowing he must be hitting somewhere pleasurable when her breath hitched. For good measure, to make sure, he did it again, just to hear her breath hitch once more.

"*Fuck*," he groaned, finally breaking from her lips so he

could start a path down her jaw. He licked at the skin over her pulse before he nipped at it. "I want inside you so badly."

The last time he'd told her those words, she'd melted for him. The night in Tortaya when he'd been gentle with her had been one he hadn't been able to forget. It had been filled with emotion after sharing parts of himself, after finding out she accepted his horrid face the way it was.

"I–I can't," she whispered around sweet little pants.

It wasn't a no. He grinned against her skin when he stroked his tongue across her neck and felt her shiver in reaction.

Oh aye, she wants me alright. He knew it when he slipped his hips over hers, and this time, he felt her ankles brush up against his thighs like she wanted to wrap them around him.

She only did it when she didn't want him to get away.

"Let me have you, lass."

He released her hair and brought his hand down. He hefted her breast, thumbing her nipple through her tunic. A sharp gasp snapped from her, like his touch had scalded her.

"I met someone else," she blurted out so fast, he'd barely understood it.

But he had, and he pulled back to glare down at her.

He let go of her perky little breast he'd much rather play with than hear a lie like this.

"Nay," he refused, such a dark bite to it that he watched her head press harder against the sheets. "Then where is he?"

Where was he to stop Alister, who knew he wasn't far from getting Rosetta to a place where she wanted him pumping inside her as much as he did? Why hadn't he come to protect her? To take her out of his arms?

"H–He's not here." She wouldn't meet his gaze as she turned it to the side to look at the bed beneath her.

He noticed her eyelids flicker, similar to the tale his mother had told him. His mother hadn't been useful in finding her, but she had given him some information to help him.

"But he's sweet, and wonderful, with hands that aren't covered in blood." Seeming to grab more courage with each word, she turned her head forward and met his eye with unwavering doubt. "Someone who isn't covered in scars. He's everything to me you could never be."

He thought his heart might have stopped beating.

"You love him." It wasn't a question but a statement.

"Yes."

Alister's nose crinkled so tightly, it bunched the skin around his cheeks and made his eyepatch dig in.

He reached down, grabbed his dagger from his boot, and sunk the blade of it into the mattress right next to her head.

"Then I'll fucking kill him."

Someone had stolen what he wanted, all because she'd run away and hadn't given him a chance!

It should have been me! If she hadn't run away, he may have been the one to gain her love for himself! He wanted it, wanted it just as badly as he wanted her body to swallow his.

A sense of betrayal cut him so deep, he had to snuff out the impulse to turn his dagger on her.

She knew she'd made a mistake when he saw her face drain of its rich colour completely.

"He has to be on board, Rosetta, because I know you're not stupid enough to return to Luxor."

Her eyes went stark. "How did you know I was in Luxor?"

"You sank that fishing boat, but you didn't kill everyone." He lowered his head with a sneer. "A man turned up in Dunecaster. You led me right to you."

He watched her chest start to heave in quick bursts, anxiety riddling her expression. It was obvious she had been hoping he didn't know where she'd docked, because it would have made her story more believable.

"Aye. Let's go find him, shall we?"

Alister would gut him, push his corpse in front of her, and

then walk out that door.

If she had replaced him so easily and given her heart away after everything Alister had done to find her, he wanted nothing more than his love to turn into unbridled hate.

He started to back up onto his knees once more.

"I told you, he's not here!"

He pointed the tip of the blade at her. "He's either not here or he's not real."

One of those statements was a lie, because it couldn't be both. If she loved this so-called man, then she wouldn't have left him in a port she couldn't return to again, or head towards a hemisphere where it would be impossible to find her once she was far south enough to dock.

"I–I..." she stuttered, her eyes falling everywhere but to his face. Her bottom lip trembled so wildly, it was making it hard for her to talk.

She was trembling so much, he could feel it in his hand as it shook her arms.

"I said it because I just wanted you to leave," she admitted, her body falling limp. A tearless sob fell from her as her eyes defeatedly fell to the side. "I didn't ask for you to come here, to do this to me!"

Everything inside him felt like it was spinning out of control, a cyclone of emotions all at once. That octopus slithered in his chest and clutched at his mangled heart. His gut felt twisted. It felt like his insides were wriggling and writhing beneath his skin in such an intense way, it almost felt disgusting.

Was there someone else, or wasn't there? Did she want him, or didn't she? Did she hate him because he was covered in scars, had a history of blood, and was arrogant, or did she possibly care for him?

He felt like he hadn't gotten a single answer he'd come here for. *And I'm hurting her.*

His mother had begged him not to hurt this woman. He'd come here with no intention of it, but he could see that him being here was eating at her.

I don't want to hurt her.

Alister knew what he needed to do. If he wanted the truth, then he had to stop being a coward.

She'd told me I held the sun and the moon in my face. If she hated his scars, she wouldn't have called what most found repulsive something so mystical.

He dropped the dagger and cupped the side of her head, an apologetic expression filling his face. He cringed at his own behaviour. *Shit. I frightened her.* He was as bad as every bastard she'd ever met.

"I–" he started before he winced.

He didn't want to lay his heart on the line. He'd never been a hesitant man, never afraid, and yet, he couldn't even speak three bloody words to this woman!

Three words that could solve everything, or nothing.

"Rosetta, I'm–"

A strange sound caught his attention.

He paused, his eyes widening as he stared at her. *We're not alone.* There was someone else in the navigation section of her ship.

Neither spoke as a silence fell upon them.

He knew it was true when he heard it again, a soft sound he couldn't distinguish. Rosetta tensed beneath him.

There really is someone else.

Alister grabbed his dagger and yanked her off the bed. Pulling on one of her arms, he dragged her from the room.

He'd decided he wouldn't kill him, wouldn't do that to her because he was angry and selfish. She'd been through enough. He finally wanted to give someone who actually deserved it mercy.

However, he wasn't going to confront a man who could

possibly be holding a weapon without having one himself. He'd dropped his cutlass when he'd knocked her sword from her hand. It was easier to block a sword with a dagger than with a pistol.

He flung open the second bedchamber he knew was there, ready to grab a man and fling them both into the middle of the navigation room so he could look at them. *What kind of coward hides while their woman is captured?*

He wanted to see him for himself. He wanted to know what kind of man had stolen Rosetta. He wanted to sear the image of them together in his mind, so that if he tried to let his pain and loss bother him, he would remember she was beneath someone else.

What he hadn't expected to find was a woman.

"Take one more step... and I'll blow your brains out," Rosetta threatened.

The moment he'd opened the door, she'd ripped her wrist from his hand that had loosened its grip in confusion. Then, she'd grabbed his pistol from its holder and put it to the back of his head.

She cocked it to show him she was serious.

What the hell is going on?

CHAPTER TWENTY-FOUR

Alister stared at the woman in front of him. Her hair was a fiery red, curled, with rich brown eyes widened in shock and fear.

Then, his bewildered gaze greeted someone else.

"Elizabeth, leave," Rosetta demanded. "Go to my room and stay there."

Alister didn't dare grab her as the stranger ran past him. He was too busy staring at the other person in the room.

A baby? His head reared back with confusion. *Why the hell would Rosetta have a baby on her bloody ship?*

It was bundled up in a soft-looking grey blanket, all tucked in and warm, resting in a small, child-sized hammock.

Deep blue eyes looked back at him, observing him with little hands in the air as it squirmed and kicked. With a tuft of fluffy black hair on top of its head, Alister knew it didn't belong to the woman who had just ran from the room.

The strange sound he'd heard was this child struggling to be free of its blanket. It wasn't hard to know who those blue eyes belonged to, not when he'd been staring at them not even a moment ago.

His own widened. "You knew you were pregnant. That's why you left."

"Yes."

His stomach tightened, while everything else inside him seemed to release. Alister had his answer.

A sense of ease pulsed through his system and the dagger fell from his limp hand. It clanked against the floor, but the sound seemed distant in comparison to the thoughts that raced through his mind, the emotions that ensnared him.

He went to take step forward, but she shoved that pistol harder against him. "I told you. If you move, I'll shoot you."

Alister put his hands up in surrender.

"It's my child, Rosetta!" He wouldn't allow her to keep him from his own child!

Shit. I'm a father. It was freshly born, couldn't be more than a month old.

"I don't know who he belongs to," she callously rebuffed.

"Aye! You fucking do."

It may have blue eyes like her, but its hair was as black as his.

"I don't know who his father is." He heard the sneer in her voice, knew her eyes must be squinted into a glare that he thought he could feel the cold stab of in the back of his head. "I had plenty of fun in Tortaya."

Such words cut him terribly. "With me, lass!"

She could lie as much as she wanted, but Alister knew. He knew looking at this child that it had to belong to him. She'd referenced a boy twice now. *I have a son.*

What she'd said to him earlier suddenly made perfect sense. This was the man she loved. A child, her child, *their* child. Of course, Alister could never compete with him.

He also didn't have to.

"You will let me meet my son!"

"N–no. He's mine." He heard a tremble in her voice before she cleared her throat. "If you want to live, you will forget you ever saw him."

"Nay! Never."

How could he? What she was asking of him was ridiculous. How was he supposed to just sail away and forget that she'd had his child? That he was on the seas and Alister had no idea where he was? That he couldn't return to him to make sure he was well?

She'd left him in the middle of the night to steal his child away with no intention of telling him he had one! *How fucking dare she!*

"He's mine!" she yelled, and he thought he might have even heard her stamp her foot. "Y–You can't have him."

The gun pressed to the back of his head started to shake. Her hand was trembling and Alister recognised if he didn't get it away from her, she might actually shoot him.

"I won't let you take him away."

He turned his head slowly so he could look back to her with a spiteful squint to his eyes. "You have no right to–"

His words were cut short by the sound of a sharp sob, before he even took in the sight of her.

Alister quickly ducked his head to the side and back, bringing the pistol next to his face so it was pointed at the wall. He swiftly reached for it, grabbing it from her before she even had the chance to pull the trigger.

When he turned to her, she flinched so deeply, it made his stomach twist in gut-wrenching agony. She thought he was going to hit her; just like Theodore, just like every other man she'd known.

Holding the pistol, he hooked his free hand around the back of her head and yanked her towards him. He pressed her face against his chest, slipping his arms around her shoulders to keep her to him.

"No!"

She bashed the bottom of her fists against him, hitting him randomly across his shoulders with weak, little punches.

A shuddering, trembling, heart-rendering cry fell from her as she started to weep against him. It was slow to build, but grew stronger with each passing second that he refused to let her go – no matter how much she struggled to get away.

For the first time since he'd met her, Alister was seeing Rosetta's pain.

What he'd seen when he'd turned around was a blotchy, ugly, swollen red face of tears. Her forehead had been so scrunched with fear and anxiety that it nearly felled him the moment he saw it.

Seeing those drops falling freely from her eyes, moving down the crease of her nose on one side and onto the other cheek, had felt like a slap across the face. Alister coming here was the catalyst, and he didn't like that he was.

When she realised bashing on him wasn't working, she gave up on trying to get away. She curled her fingers into his tunic to grip it tightly, burying her face against him.

"Y–You can't have him. You can't take him away from me. P–Please..." It was plea.

Rosetta was begging him, and he held her tighter because of it. *She left because she was afraid I'd take him like my father did me.* Rosetta was afraid of ending up like his mother.

Why wouldn't she be? If it had been done to his mother, in Rosetta's eyes, why wouldn't he have followed in his father's footsteps?

She's already had one child taken from her. One that had never even taken a breath, one he now could see she had desperately wanted.

He didn't understand it, but with how much pain she was in now, Alister knew she had wanted that bastard's child. He'd originally thought she might have been relieved in some way to not have birthed it, but she wouldn't be this frantic and hysterical if she didn't.

He uncocked the hammer to his pistol and gently dropped it to the floor so he could free his hand and pat the back of her hair. He slowly, to not spook her, brought her in for a comforting hug, surrounding her in his arms.

This poor woman.

"I'm not going to take our son from you, Rosetta." A louder cry sounded from her at his words, almost like a shriek, and he felt her clutch his tunic tighter. "He's yours."

Her entire body began to tremble, her feet slipping beneath her like they couldn't take the weight of what she was feeling.

"I'm sorry!" She took in a shaking breath before it came out as a squeaking, yet quiet, heave. "I'm so sorry. I didn't know what else to do."

"You should have told me."

She started to weep harder as she shook her head. "I c-couldn't."

He was thankful he was already holding her as her legs gave way. He lifted her, supporting her small frame on her useless legs as everything inside seemed to give.

"I-I didn't know what you'd do. I didn't know if you would try to make me get rid of him."

Fuck... What kind of person does she see me as? Was it just because of how the men had treated her in the past? He wanted to believe Rosetta didn't truly see him as that kind of monster; otherwise, why would she have stayed with him so long?

Alister turned his head to the ceiling, trying to draw strength from it. He was trying to kill his anger, trying to snuff it.

His mother had been right, and he'd been blind this entire time. *She's broken.* A scared, broken woman who had done everything she could to protect herself. Confused.

Alister couldn't blame her for this, not when it wasn't rational, just as him chasing her halfway around the world hadn't been rational.

"I–I knew it was wrong," she started. "To just leave in the middle of the night without telling you. But I didn't know how you would react, and I was so *scared*."

"How long did you know?" How long had she kept this

secret from him before leaving?

"A–A month."

He'd not once noticed.

She'd been napping through the day. Eating more. Had spent less time at the helm. He'd even thought she was putting on weight.

"And you chose that night because it was easier to trick us so you could leave quietly, and you had the coin to last you."

She gave another sob, this time nodding her head.

Everything made sense.

If I didn't go after her, I would never have known.

"I want to meet him, Rosetta."

She finally turned her head up to him, and he winced at the state of her, the obvious pain and guilt in her eyes.

"You will let me hold him," he demanded with a deadly tone as he looked down at her through his bottom lashes.

The way her brows furrowed said she didn't want to let him, as if she worried he might bolt with him the moment he had him in his arms. She eventually, finally, nodded.

When she started to settle, Alister slowly put her back on her feet until she was steady. He backed up from her, eyeing her carefully as he moved towards the hammock. He may have been a little worried she'd dive for the pistol.

With her hands clasped in front of her near her chest, she watched him as he turned to look down at his son.

He hesitantly reached up and removed his eyepatch, wanting him to look up at all of his father for the first time.

Gently and as carefully as possible, so as not to hurt or crush him in his meaty hands, Alister scooped the boy up. He slid him around in his arms until his head was tucked near his elbow.

He only needed one arm to hold him, cushioning him completely across his forearm.

Rosetta gave him a few minutes to soak in his first

moments with him alone. He didn't seem to mind Alister's ghastly appearance as he cooed at him, happy to be free of the hammock and blanket before giving a joyful squeal he didn't appreciate.

A small smile curled his lips.

Perhaps it should bother him this had happened when it was never his intention, something he didn't want. Alister had never wanted a child, but if he was going to put a babe in anyone, he was thankful it was Rosetta. *She gave me a son...*

"He's beautiful, isn't he?" she asked quietly, with a voice raspy from crying.

She eventually came up to them so she could brush the tip of her index finger against his chubby cheek.

"Aye, he's just fine."

Alister thought he looked like an over-cooked potato, but he wouldn't dare tell her that. He'd never found babies cute. He'd mostly found them abhorrent.

He snapped his head to her.

"And he's mine?" She nodded. "Without a doubt?"

She looked up to him to meet his gaze. "Yes."

Knew it. His shoulders sagged in relief. He just wanted her to admit it.

Then a thought crossed his mind, something from what she'd said earlier. Since he had one arm free, he reached forward and gripped her jaw to lift her to his eyes as he leaned down.

"Did you fuck other men while carrying my son, Rosetta?"

He couldn't think of anything worse!

Knowing she'd been carrying his child while having another man's cock thrusting inside her... something dark frayed the edges of his vision.

"No. I wouldn't do that." Her brows drew together in an almost sympathetic frown. "I haven't been with anyone else since I met you. I lied."

His sight flickered between her eyes as she steadily held his. He believed her.

He slipped his hand forward and palmed the back of her head, pulling her towards him. Alister crashed his mouth on hers, bringing her in for a deep kiss that tasted of salt from her drying tears.

Relief, ease, and contentment rolled through him like a gentle wave, washing away all the pain and loss he'd felt, bit by bit.

He broke from her when the boy made another squeal, a little quieter than before. Alister looked back down at him.

"Would you have told him about me?"

She once more started brushing her fingertip against his cheek, occasionally moving it up to push the black hair on top of his head to the side.

"Yes. That's why I took your ring."

Alister's brows drew together, looking between them. "You were going to give it to him?"

"I'm going to tell him all the tales I've learned about you." She turned her head to give him a small, yet sad, smile. "About how his father is the great Captain Alister 'One-Eye' Paine, the Bloody Storm of the Seas, the most wanted pirate of the Seven Seas of Old Gaia." She turned her head down once more with a snort of laughter. "I doubt he'll believe me."

The boy grabbed a small chunk of Alister's long hair that came past his chest and yanked on it with a surprisingly strong pull. He didn't care, not when his frown deepened as he listened to her. *She wasn't going to hide who I was from him.*

"When he's old enough, I know that he will probably want to find you."

It took him a long time to realise she was talking in future tense rather than a reflection of what she'd been intending. She was speaking like she was still intending for it to be the same, even though he knew of his existence, was here now.

"I knew if he wore your ring, you'd believe he was your son. I knew you would be upset that you were only just finding out, if you were even still alive, but you would take him under your wing." Then she smiled once more. "That's if I wasn't with him on the Laughing Siren."

There was a long pause as he took in this moment.

Holding his son in his arms for the first time. Watching the way she was looking at him with complete and utter adoration.

A warmth filled his chest.

"Marry me," he demanded, looking over her beautiful face.

"P–Pardon?" she stuttered, suddenly lifting her face to him with a frown.

"Aye, you heard me." He wasn't going to repeat himself; he'd had a hard enough time blurting it out the first time.

"Alister... no. It's okay."

Her eyes darted over his features, a confusing mix of worry and anxiety crossing over him while he did his best to hide the hurt at her rejection.

She turned to the boy to fix the blanket around him to distract herself.

"I was prepared to do this on my own. I'm not going to ask you to stay with me just because of him. You don't have to take responsibility. I can pay for him, care for him on my own."

Rosetta hadn't left him because she didn't want him. She'd left because he'd made a mistake that night in Tortaya and she'd fled in fear.

This was his fault.

He lifted his hand and pointed his index and middle finger at her. Squinted eyes filled with suspicion, he shook them up and down.

"You love me, don't you?"

Behind that pinkness from her earlier crying, he saw the rest of her pale.

I knew it! He shook his head in disbelief, at her obvious unease about him figuring this out.

"You're smarter than this, lass. I didn't chase you for seven months for no reason." He bounced the boy lightly when he started to squirm, worried he was going to cry. He brought his eyes back to her. "I realised once you left that I was in love with you. I was always going to ask; the boy has nothing to do with it."

"I don't understand. I didn't think you would ever..." She trailed off, her gaze falling to the side like she really couldn't comprehend this.

"Aye, me neither." Alister didn't think he'd had a heart until he met her.

There was a shyness in her eyes he'd never seen before when she looked back to him, perhaps a pinkness to her cheeks that had nothing to do with the tears she'd cried.

"I'm asking you to sail with me forever, Rosie. As my wife."

It was because Rosetta could sail with him, wouldn't be some woman he'd be leaving on the land, that he'd ever considered this. If he was going to have a wife, it would need to be someone who would be with him always.

He was a man who liked to fuck, but he would be faithful to the woman he chose. He wouldn't have wanted to go without sex for an extended period, possibly years, because she wasn't with him.

But it wasn't just because she had her own boat. He wanted her because of who she was. Rosetta was like the sea. Both were untameable, both wild, both full of depth and beauty, both just as annoying.

"I–If you're sure," she said softly, nibbling on the corners of her lips.

"Was that an aye?"

"Aye, lad, it was a bloody yes."

He gave a deep chuckle. "Atta girl." Then he shouldered her lightly to get her attention. "My ship missed yours."

It was his own way of saying he'd missed her, because he didn't think he could say something so... lame.

She let out a small laugh, shaking her head as though she understood. Then in a quiet murmur, she said, "I love you too, by the way, you great, big idiot."

A grin curled his lips before he turned his head down as he continued to bounce his son. "What's his name?"

"Um, Alister..."

There was a long pause.

Bloody hell. What horrible name did she give him if she had to pause before she told him?

"Aye?" he answered to get her to continue.

"No," she laughed awkwardly. "That's his name. It's Alister."

His face twisted in repulsion. "I'm not going to have you moan our son's name when I'm taking you."

"Well, I didn't think I was going to again!" she grumbled under her breath in annoyance. "Fine, we'll change it. It's not like he knows what it is anyway."

She reached forward to try to take him.

He quickly moved his arms out of reach. "Nay, you've had your turn to hold him."

An entire month of it!

"Give him back, Alister."

"I said nay, lass! You'll wait your bloody turn."

She puffed her cheeks and folded her arms across her chest. At least she'd conceded.

Then her arms loosened as she said, "We should probably stop the men from killing each other now."

"Aye, but my men have been ordered not to kill yours." He wagged his finger at her. "I knew you wouldn't have been happy with me if they did, or if I blew a single hole in your ship."

Her lips thinned as she muttered, "I didn't give them the same command."

Well, they bloody better not be dead! He'd kill them all over again if they decided to die here and now.

Alister stormed to the door of the navigation room.

"Wait, let me get Elizabeth." Rosetta ran to the door of her sleeping cabin and opened it slightly. "Everything's okay now. You're fine to come out."

The redhead peeked through the gap, saw Alister was still there, and immediately backed into the room again to hide.

As Rosetta came up to him, he put his eyepatch back on in preparation of going outside.

"Who's the woman?"

"She's been helping me take care of him." Her eyes fell on his son. "I couldn't do it on my own and I'm still healing from giving birth."

Speaking of which...

"Are you okay?" he asked with true concern, sweeping his gaze down her body.

He gripped her hip, as if he could somehow check her state. Their son wasn't small, and even Alister could tell he was a big babe.

"My ma almost died giving birth to me, said I was the biggest baby she'd ever seen."

"It was tough, but I'm fine," she laughed. "Lost my sea legs, though."

"Nay," he said with a tone of disbelief. "Your sea legs are almost as good as mine."

"It's why I had to port in Luxor. It was the only place I could think of to house all my men but was safe to hide."

"From me," he stated with narrow eyes, his lips thinning into a scowl.

Not wanting to answer him, she turned the door handle to

step outside.

No one was fighting but swords were raised at each other as they shouted back and forth. His men were acting as a blockade so hers couldn't come up the stairs and interrupt them. Alister had organised it that way; he hadn't wanted to be disturbed until he got his answers, and hopefully, her.

"Oi, you bunch of scurvy dogs," he called loudly, but not in a way that would upset the boy. "Who wants to meet my son?"

A pause and a blanket of silence settled over the deck while they digested his words. Gazes flickered between each other in surprise and shock.

Then a loud, excited cheer sounded, making his son shriek and cry from the sudden noise. Alister quickly handed him to Rosetta, as if his hands had suddenly caught fire.

One thing was certain: Alister was unsure if he was excited to tell his mother or not. *She'll rip my ear off for this.*

CHAPTER TWENTY-FIVE

Alister grinned down at Rosetta as she stared up at him, the sun washing over them, warming their skin. They were standing face to face, barely a metre apart as the ship swayed beneath their feet.

Like it always did, the light made the blue of her eyes look like shallow waters and they sparkled with a warm depth he thought might be deeper than the ocean itself.

It had been a month since he'd found Rosetta, gotten all his answers, discovered he had a son, and they'd once more set sail together.

She liked his ship a lot more now since he'd restored it. He'd even gotten his mattress replaced because he couldn't stand her refusing to lay in his bed. They had yet to.

She didn't like to part from Adrian, his son, for too long. He'd liked the name because of its relation to the Adriatic Sea. Rosetta had rolled her eyes at him for it.

They'd returned to the northern hemisphere, making their way to Tortaya after going to Dunecaster for supplies. He'd discovered Rosetta had been nearly out of food and water because she'd been fleeing him. She hadn't had the freedom in Luxor to stock her ship properly.

They were heading west because he wanted to show his mother what he'd accidently done, get abused for it, and then wait for her to cry in joy. He knew his mother well enough to know she would, knew she would enjoy meeting her grandson – only because he was intending to marry Rosetta and not abandon her like his father had done to his mother.

Before they'd left the southern waters, they'd quickly stopped off at the location on the map they'd acquired. It hadn't been too many days from where he'd caught up to her, a volcanic island right in the middle of nowhere.

One side had been covered in lava, constantly spewing down the mountainside because of a large crack in the volcano. The other side was covered in grass and sand, peaceful by comparison.

Anchoring their boats on the calm side, as though there wasn't a violent, raging river of fire and melting death right next to it, they'd rowed to the sandy bank.

After climbing a ledge of unsteady rock with just his men, since Rosetta didn't want to leave Adrian, they'd searched for the entrance to a small cave against the volcanic mountain.

As soon as they'd entered it, sweat dotted their brows as warm air swirled around them. It wasn't too unbearable, but it definitely wasn't a cool cave like most.

After only a short walk in the narrow passage, it had opened up to a large space.

Shovels dropped from hands. Gasps rang out.

Alister had almost fallen to his knees.

They'd found it. They'd found Dustin's trove.

Hidden and nestled away in the southern seas, on an island nobody would think to check, in the middle of nowhere so far from other land that no ship would pass it on purpose, was a cavern filled with an abundance of treasure.

Loot spread from grey cave wall to grey cave wall. Golden vases, candlesticks, and even coins littered the ground, as if they'd run out of chests to fill. There were silver plates, cutlery, and every kind of valuable item there could ever be. There were even chests of high-quality clothing and garments.

Everything had been tossed carelessly into piles.

There were five chests of varying sizes, mostly medium, spanning the cavern. Mixed inside were bronze, silver, and golden coins, as well as sparkling gems and jewellery.

"It's real," Pierre gasped, turning his head in every direction.

"Mad Dog was right," one of his lower ranking men remarked.

"He was still insane," Alister commented.

He may have been right, but his father had truly been a madman. Still, Alister reached down and grabbed a coin from the ground, feeling its warmth under his fingertips.

To hide all this booty on an island that could destroy it... Alister clenched the coin in his fist. *I can't believe I found it.*

He'd finally done what he'd promised, and there was one thing he could take to prove it. Dustin 'The Raider's' infamous pirate flag, a winged skeleton symbolising death, was draped over one of the chests.

"What do you want to do, Alister?" Pierre asked, finally bringing him out of his trance of breathless, wordless shock.

"Take the largest chest." He pointed to the one in the middle. "That'll be enough to pay everyone's wages and make them happy."

He walked towards the flag, wanting to touch it with his fingertips, to hold it. Hell, he even wanted to brush it against his cheek in admiration.

"What about everything else?"

"We leave it," he said, turning his head back to his men right as he reached the flag. "We're the only ones who know where it is. With this flag, we can tell the world we were the ones to discover it."

"The finders of Dustin's trove," Pierre laughed, placing his hands on his hips and throwing his head back. "Our names will go down in history as the greatest treasure hunting pirates ever."

"Aye," Alister grinned, ripping the black flag from its resting place. It stirred up dust and soot. "Perhaps they'll stop calling me 'One Eye'."

He really hated that name.

They left most of the treasure behind, taking just one chest and the flag. They could return to it anytime they wanted.

It had been one of the most joyous days of his life. He'd finally completed his goal, finally done what he'd set out to do.

He'd been searching for it with his father since he'd been eleven, and then five years by himself. For nineteen years, since he'd recently turned thirty, it was all Alister thought about.

He thought he may have been a little disappointed he no longer had direction. There was nothing making him point in a certain direction with determined glee, nothing keeping him on the sea.

In a way, he'd almost felt like he'd lost his purpose.

That was, until Rosetta reminded him he could still hunt other maps. She told him, if he wanted to, he could add to Dustin's trove and claim it completely as his own by building on it.

It wasn't because she'd told him this that brought him relief, though.

Alister realised she still had goals, was still going to follow him, and he could focus all his obsession on her instead. He could follow other maps, travel the world freely, and do it all while having this pretty woman by his side.

He was still going to be a cutthroat pirate, but he could plough her in every ocean while loving her. She gave his life purpose, alongside the son he would raise and shape to be like him...

To be like her.

Strong like him, smart like her, and as fearsome as them both.

That's why, the day he'd found Dustin's trove, the happiness he'd felt was overshadowed by the one he was experiencing now.

He was surprisingly nervous about the eyes of nearly a hundred and fifty men staring at them on the quarterdeck of the Laughing Siren.

He tried not to look at them and focused purely on Rosetta, who had a strange flush to her cheeks that he rarely ever saw.

Her gaze darted to the side to avoid his, before flicking back as though she knew she had to look. He was without his eyepatch; he'd done that purposefully.

He wanted her to look at him completely, at what was good, what was ugly, and know only this scarred face would be above her every night.

He'd slit the throat of anyone else who tried to touch her.

He'd never noticed how she could be a little awkward and shy. Perhaps it was because this was a strange day for both of them. He knew neither of them had ever expected to be doing this with anyone, not least each other.

He was in his best clothes, which just so happened to be what he usually wore.

She was in her dark green dress. Why? He didn't know. He thought he might have preferred her in her usual getup but was just content that she was here.

There was a stranger on her ship, a man neither one of them knew, speaking to them. Or rather, at them.

His voice was shaking with fear.

With two guns pointed at his head, one held by Pierre, the other Naeem, he should be afraid.

He was the captain of the small fleet ship they'd sunk just a few days ago and had imprisoned until they found some shallows in which to drop anchor.

"D–Do you, Rosetta Silver, take Alister Paine to be your lawfully wedded husband?" he asked her.

Both Alister and Rosetta could have done this, since any captain of any ship could technically marry two people. It was legal and binding, as long as it was recorded in their ledgers.

Neither had wanted to state the binding words, though. It felt like it would've cheapened their marriage if they had. They just wanted to agree to the vows like any normal person.

So, when there was a fleet ship on the horizon, they'd both agreed to imprison its captain and force him to do it. They'd gotten his name, gotten him to sign their ledgers, ones they would later sign themselves.

Alister wanted to do this on the seas rather than on land; Rosetta hadn't cared. He just wanted to do it sooner rather than later. He knew she was a runner – that often got his hackles rising.

"Yes," she answered without hesitation.

"A–And do you, A–Alister Paine," the man started, his voice growing shakier by the second. His fear worsened when Alister turned his eye to him with a foul glare for ruining this. He swallowed deep, and continued steadier, "Take Rosetta Silver to be your lawfully wedded wife?"

"Aye." He immediately winced. "Fuck, shit. I mean *yes*."

He'd bloody practiced this!

"Then I pronounce you legally married. You may now kiss your wife."

Alister shot his hand out and wrapped it around the nape of her neck, pulling her towards him. Then, he dipped her slightly by twisting her body and covered her lips with his.

She returned the singular but lingering kiss, her fingertips gently placed against the sides of his jaw.

Their crews applauded and cheered, throwing their hats into the air in congratulations. A few even discharged their pistols.

"Please meet Mr and Mrs Paine," the officiant said with his arms raised to the crowd, finalising his duty.

"Rosetta Silver," Rosetta muttered when their lips parted.

"Paine," Alister rebuffed, squinting his eyes at her.

"Silver."

"Paine, lass!" She *would* be taking his last name!

She started to giggle quietly, throwing him off guard. She was teasing him, and he almost threw his head back in laughter.

What did I just agree to?

"Come here, you annoying woman." He scooped her up, hefting her into his arms so he could cradle her.

"Wait, Alister!" she yelled when he started walking her towards the navigation room door. "We're supposed to participate in festivities."

"Don't give a shit," he answered, managing to open the door with the hand under her legs by fumbling the handle. "I'm going to fuck my wife."

His own words made him grin, partially because of what he was now able to call her. She was permanently tied to him.

Well, unless...

"You're not going to shoot me like your last husband, are you?" he asked with a chuckle, using the back of his boot to shut the door.

Right before it closed and the area went silent, both Alister and Rosetta heard a gun fire. Neither one jumped at the sound, nor cared when they heard the fleet captain's body hit the deck with a thud.

Her lips puckered into a brattish pout. "As long as you don't do anything to make me."

"So, a good spanking is on the table or nay?" He leaned his head forward to kiss her again as he moved them towards her sleeping quarters.

She laughed beneath his lips as he placed her on her feet at the foot of the bed.

Pulling at the ties on the back of her dress, he loosened it enough so he could push it down her body, letting it pool around her feet.

His kisses halted when he circled her waist and hips with his hands, shocked nothing was slung around them.

"No weapons?"

She kept that precious pistol of hers on her nearly twenty-four hours a day. He'd even seen her sleep with it like a teddy bear. To not find her wearing it came as a surprise.

"I didn't want to wear them today."

He didn't understand why she averted her gaze, or why she grew slightly flustered, blushing as she looked to the floor.

"But I'm wearing mine."

Was, at least. She'd just unbuckled his own weapons belt and let it fall to crumple around his feet.

"One of us needed to," she said, unbuttoning his breeches so she could untuck his shirt. "I chose for it to be you."

As much as he should have been sensually roaming his eyes down her curving, wickedly naked body – besides her boots – he found himself focusing on her face as she spoke.

She may not have said it outright, but she just told him she trusted him to protect her had something gone awry.

With a groan crinkling his nose, he grabbed her right in the crease where those glorious round cheeks of her arse met the tops of her thighs. He lifted her, forcing her to wrap her legs around his hips.

Kneeling on the bed, he ate at her lips, kissing her with feverish, heated draws she tried to escape like she was being burned. His mouth followed hers, unwilling to let her go as he reached back and removed each of her boots.

His eyes suddenly widened when he faced her, and she reached her hand up to stroke his cheek.

He halted for a moment. *Shit, I almost forgot. Lucky I still have my pants on.*

He reached into the coin purse tied to his open breeches and fumbled around inside it. When he took what he wanted from it, he grabbed her left hand and shoved a plain golden band onto her ring finger.

"What's this?" She brought her hand forward to inspect it.

"If you ever take that off, Rosetta, I'll throw you into the ocean as punishment."

He'd fish her from it again, but he wanted the world to know she belonged to him without needing to shadow her.

She better not lose it. He'd found it in the chest they'd taken from Dustin's trove.

She gave him a soft look, one filled with an emotion he was learning to understand within himself. She reached forward to grab the sides of his face and pulled him down for a searing kiss.

He laughed against her lips. *I half-expected her to throw it back at me!* Instead, she pulled his tunic off, dragging it up his back.

He only broke the kiss to let her pull it from him, then he was right back at her. *Need inside her.* Alister was desperate for it.

She managed to turn her head to the side so she could breathe while he was distracted pulling his cock from the gap in his unbuttoned breeches.

"Your boots and pants."

Her breaths shuddered when he slipped the head of his cock up her folds and ground against the hard nub of her clit. He was sucking at the place on her neck that always had her arching for more.

"Nay," he said in huffs. "Don't think I can wait that long."

"Be gentle with me."

"Fuck, Rosie," he groaned, slipping his tongue against her skin before roughly kissing her. He let his shaft go so he could grind the length of it against her. "I don't think I can do that either."

Alister had eight months of celibacy and sexual frustration built up inside of him. She had still been healing, had asked him if he would be patient, to wait until he married her to give her time.

Despite how much that pained him, he had told her he would.

It was why he had rushed to find someone. The moment he saw a ship on the horizon, he didn't care who it was, what it was. He was adamant about ripping the captain from it and shoving him into the cell of his ship.

The longer it took him, the longer he had to go without her. "Please."

Without taking his lips from her neck, liking the way her breath hitched and how her skin warmed, he slid his hand down her body.

He flicked her nipple along the way with each of his fingers, not lingering but giving the overly sensitive, hardened bud a tease. As much as he wanted to pet Rosetta, if he didn't get his cock in her soon, he was going to burst.

Slipping two fingers around her clit, he caressed her entrance and shoved both inside, all the way to his rings.

Her body tensed and her back arched as she gave a gasp, her little nails digging into his sides.

Shit, she's tight. He'd thought she would be looser – all things considered.

He started moving his fingers back and forth. *Crap.* Alister had almost slammed himself into her core without preparing her first.

Need to calm down. She'd asked him to be gentle, but he felt like an uncontrollable cannonball grenade about to go off. His shaft was hard, throbbing unbearably.

He could even feel a coolness against the tip, where the air had cooled the dollop of precum that already formed just from seeing her naked. If Alister didn't calm down, he was going to hurt her in his carelessness.

When he felt she was accustomed to his two fingers, he dipped in a third, feeling her tense once more.

"Ohh," she moaned, lifting her head to bury it against his shoulder. She gave him another groan when he spread them.

I don't think I've ever prepared her like this. Once she took him, if he got between her legs before she started to shrink too far, Alister could just thrust inside like the impatient, horny bastard he was.

The first time he'd taken her, things between them had been rushed. Same with the second. This was the first big break they'd had since she'd obtained the Laughing Siren.

When she started bucking against his hand, showing him she wasn't far from her climax, Alister pulled his fingers from her wonderfully damp channel. He wouldn't let her have what she wanted until he could feel it around his cock.

He pulled back on a straight arm and grabbed her thigh to drag her closer. He looked down to watch himself grab the base of his cock and tuck the head against her entrance. Just the light kiss of their bodies made him shudder.

He pushed in slowly, drawing out the moment. A groan dropped from his lips as his broad head popped inside and he felt the tight squeeze of her pussy, the intense heat.

His shaft pulsed again, the slowness like torture, and he pushed in a little more hastily. Drawing his hips back when he was halfway to collect her wetness, he speared forward.

"Oh!" Her head tilted back, her chest lifting as her back bowed when he was seated deep and stretching her completely around the girth of his cock.

Alister's own head fell forward to look down at her folds spread around him. He could feel her core quivering in reaction, and it only intensified as he ground himself deeper.

This ain't gonna last long. Already, his cock felt taut with tension, her body sublime around his. A huff of breath flew from his lungs in relief at the feel of her.

He pulled back to give her a measured thrust, placing both hands against the mattress to steady himself. When he gave another, a breathless groan shuddered from him as his eyes closed in bliss, feeling them starting to roll back.

Feels as good as I remember. Feeling her grip him made it perfect; she was always so wet, it felt like she was drenching him every time. *Fuck, I love this pussy.* He loved her, everything about her, everything about this.

His hips started to pick up speed, started to thrust harder, and his eyes finally rolled back.

"Yes!" she gasped beneath him, her hands slipping around him so she could dig her nails into his back. "M–More."

He figured they didn't need to be as gentle as they originally thought they did. His breaths grew short when he hit harder, felt like he was reaching deeper. They clogged his chest, strangled him.

Alister was drowning just the way he liked it – in her. Her sounds as she started to release moan after moan. Her smells. The way her nails scored into his skin, like she wanted to add to the scars she'd permanently left on his back.

"Alister..." There it was, his name.

She always cried it when she felt good, when she was lost. She was calling to him, letting him know there was nothing on her mind but him.

She yanked him down to her, and he barely had the chance to catch himself on his elbows so as not to crush her. She wanted to hold him closer, moving her arms so she could cross them over his shoulders.

He leaned on one, using it to prop him up as his thrusts came faster, need lashing through him. His hips were starting to go wild, needing to take everything she could give him.

His self-control was slipping a bit more every time he thrust into this beautiful woman, this devious, playful, sinful little creature, a nymph in disguise.

She was going to plague him for the rest of his life. She was going to tease him relentlessly, and he knew he would want to be with her every chance he could.

I claimed this. Claimed her. She was his to take.

"I missed this," she moaned, burying her head against him as their bodies started to sweat and slip. "I missed you so much." She wrapped her legs around his waist and locked her ankles so he couldn't escape without a fight. "Waited so long to have you inside me."

She couldn't do this to him right now.

He was trying his damned hardest to be careful, to not go too hard, to not injure this precious thing, but if she kept talking to him like this, she was going to break his resolve.

"Quiet, Rosie," he barked softly, barely able to wrangle up any strength to his voice.

"But you feel so good..." she cried, her head falling back. "So big. I feel so full. I've always loved it."

His control snapped.

He shoved his hand down their bodies and grabbed the back of her knee. He gave it a firm yank to unlock her feet and pushed it to her chest, spreading her as far as he could.

He gave himself the room and freedom to start pumping his hips quicker, faster, slamming his aching cock harder. He burrowed as deep as he could until he knew he was hitting the end of her, destroying them both.

"Oh, Alister!" she screamed before she lost the ability to formulate the words, just releasing cry after cry.

She fluttered around his cock as he delivered frantic thrusts, and she squirmed beneath him as she wrung him, spasming, clenching.

Heaven. It felt like plump, pillowing bliss as he speared

through it.

It pushed his electrified body over the edge.

He hissed in a breath when he felt his shaft swelling. Delicious agony started to spread, a deep ache that pierced the hard rod jutting up from between his hips.

Just as her body started to go lax around his, giving him some reprieve to think, to concentrate on his own body hardening with his own release, his head started to fall back. He pulled her leg further to the side to keep them unlocked and open for him, his fingertips digging in so hard, he knew he must be bruising her.

"Haa!" His body started to shake as it built, as his gut tightened. "Oh, f–"

He couldn't even finish his sentence.

He just groaned so loudly, he worried the outside world would hear him as he started to release heavy, wet bursts of his seed. Rope after rope, it climbed his wildly pulsating and throbbing cock.

His vision went hazy as he stared at the wall near-blindly. He was unable to pull himself from his taut and tensed position as he released eight months' worth of frustration, eight months' worth of need, desire, lust, and yearning. It felt like his heart and lungs had stopped working.

He pumped his hips with shuddering twitches that wracked his entire body. When he finally finished, his cock and sac felt so sensitive, he feared if he pulled from her, it would kill him. Alister needed her to soothe him with her warmth.

As much as he wanted to hold her, he knelt back onto his knees so he could catch his choking breaths. He held her waist with both his hands.

Alister stared down at her, watching her pant as she peeked up at him. She looked dazed, lax. He soaked her in for a long while, feeling her core pound around him as she collected herself.

Her soft look didn't last long.

"You came inside?"

"Oh, aye." He'd spread her legs, held them open, pushed deep, and purposely started filling her. "You're my wife now, Rosetta. I can do what I want with you, and I can come in you as much as I like."

She would spend the rest of her life warming his come for him. The thought made him shudder.

He ran his hands down her sides so he could grip her hips, pushing her onto him when he started to go soft, giving her the inches she couldn't take when he was hard.

Usually, his erection would stay for a second round, but he'd come so intensely, his body was demanding a reprieve in between. He would make sure it wasn't long.

"Not if you don't want to get me pregnant again!"

Alister placed his hand against her belly as he caressed the skin of it with his calloused fingertips.

"Not going to be upset if I put another babe in you, to be honest," he answered with a shrug.

Her brows drew together tightly. "You want another?"

"Not particularly, but if it happens, it happens."

Coming inside this woman felt remarkable. He wanted to do it, had for a long time before she'd left. He should have known then that if he'd been willing to risk it, despite no woman ever making him want to do so, then he must have been growing to care for her.

Now when he pulled out, it would be just to cover her in him for his own enjoyment.

Her lips pursed together, her gaze fluttering away before coming back.

"I'm actually surprised it happened the first time," she admitted in a small voice. "I thought I couldn't have children after what happened."

A small frown crossed his features. *Is that why she hadn't seemed upset that first time?*

"Well, I'm glad you can." Adrian may have been an accident, but he was glad his son was born. "So, how about it?"

"How about what?" She squinted her eyes at his gleeful tone and the cheeky grin slapped across his face.

It may also be because she could feel his shaft growing hard inside her.

"Let's fuck until we make another." He leaned down and grabbed her jaw, knowing she secretly enjoyed it when he did. She rarely pulled away. "And then let's fuck some more."

She gave him a naughty smile that told him she liked the idea of that. "Take your boots off first."

Nay, he thought to himself.

That required him pulling away from her completely. Although he pulled his cock from her just to watch his own seed literally *drip* from her channel, making him shudder once more in deep-seated want and harden completely, he wasn't willing to part from her for long.

Alister thrust back in all the way with a cheerful grin, feeling their mingled wetness. *She's all mine.*

Rosetta gave a small, mumbling groan as she rolled over with an exploring hand, searching for warmth and a welcoming cuddle.

When she found nothing but sheets, she let her heavy lids flutter open to find the space next to her was empty.

Where'd he go? She knew she'd fallen asleep laying against Alister's chest, partially on top of him.

She'd curled one leg between his while her arm crossed over his stomach, clutching him tightly. As she'd nuzzled her face against his dark chest hair, a smile of contentment had turned the corners of her lips up when she felt his fingertips lightly tickling up and down her spine.

He'd told her he was going to stay with her all night, and she knew he had when she remembered waking a few times with his arm and body heavily draped over her.

The way he held her while he was asleep, as though he was worried she'd escape unless he was holding onto her, was sweet. It wasn't because she'd fled from him; no, he'd been doing it for a long time.

So, to not find him in the bed next to her, when she always woke up before him, was strange.

She turned to see how high the sun was and instantly covered her eyes. *Someone shoot the sun!*

She'd known it must be high, considering how bright her cabin was. She just hadn't expected it to be *so* high – it was mid-morning and stabbing her directly in the eyeballs!

Another groan fell from her. *We were going all night.*

Even though he hadn't had a sip of booze until they both decided to join the festivities celebrating their crude and short wedding, by both their requests, he'd taken her in the same way he did when he was drunk. He hadn't been.

She only ever woke this late in the day when he kept her up all night. Actually, she vaguely remembered him waking her when the sun had already been up with his cock hard inside her.

She covered her lips with her hands. *I don't think we've ever done it in the morning.*

Since she was always up before him, and doing it in a hammock seemed near impossible, she'd never experienced that particular activity.

She let out a small snort of laughter.

It's probably why he doesn't like that I'm awake before him. Alister probably wanted to start his day with sex.

With a shake of her head, she pulled her aching body from the mattress to sit on the side of the bed. Naked but knowing it was unlikely anyone would walk in, Rosetta covered her face in her hands.

She still couldn't believe she'd married that brute!

Although she agreed to it when he asked, and they'd been planning it since they'd imprisoned the captain who'd unified them, it was different now that she'd done it.

She was happy she had. He was self-important, high-handed, and so hubristic that Rosetta feared she'd roll her eyes so hard she'd go blind one day, but she loved, truly loved, this overbearing man.

Now that he'd started holding her in more comforting embraces, she'd never thought she would find a meaty man's muscled body so soothing as it trapped and squeezed her.

Instead of dominating her with abuse like others had, trying to discipline and control her, Alister's strength surrounded her like a blanket. He gripped her hard sometimes, tossed her around, threw her over his shoulder, but she found it so arousing when he did.

He overpowered her with touches she liked.

With a sigh, she turned her mind towards other things. *I need to feed Adrian.* She'd fed him right before she'd gone to sleep.

Elizabeth had given Rosetta a break by taking care of him for the night so she could be with Alister. The easily frightened girl was adjusting to the Howling Death and its crew, but Rosetta could tell she was still uneasy.

They were a lot meaner looking than her own crew, with missing parts, who often responded with grunts rather than words. They weren't the easiest to warm up to.

Rosetta was sure Pierre would make her feel right at home once he successfully got under her skirt. She had a feeling he would at some point. She'd seen the way his mischievous little face eyed the pretty, naïve redhead.

Since Naeem had also noticed Pierre's interest, he was doing the best he could to make the man jealous since he was already close with Elizabeth. It often made Rosetta smile.

Still, the girl was such a help with their son in the meantime.

Searching the cabinet mounted inside the wall, she found her usual clothing of tights and tunic. She'd worn her dress the previous day because she'd thought it would be easier to get out of. She knew Alister wouldn't want to wait and would grow impatient. If she was being truthful, she had been impatient, too.

After putting on her boots and then her weapons belt, Rosetta left her sleeping quarters to check on Adrian.

She had two, small, child-sized hammocks: one in her room, where he usually slept except for last night, and one in the navigation room so Elizabeth could watch over him throughout the day.

He napped often. He was a sleepy child, considering her ship rocked gently from side-to-side all the time and put him to sleep.

When he was awake, he observed the world with big blue eyes filled with awe and wonder.

She loved it when he looked at her with a cheerful squeal, as if he was happy to see her. He always reached up and grabbed her hair to tug on it. He was already strong and that relieved her. He wasn't weak and frail, wasn't a sick newborn like she knew some were.

Rosetta knew he would grow to be big and tough, just like his father.

With that thought making her smile, she walked over to his hammock to feed him, only to find it empty.

Where is he? She rustled through the empty hammock before running back to her cabin to check that one as well. It was also empty.

Rosetta sprinted to Elizabeth's door and threw it open, making the woman sit upright so quickly, her eyes hadn't even opened yet. She looked tired, and Rosetta knew she must have been up most of the night.

"Where is Adrian?"

Her confused and dazed face turned into a deep frown. Her brown eyes drew to Rosetta, as if she didn't understand.

"He should be in his hammock. I haven't heard him cry for a while, so I thought he was asleep."

"Well, he's not!" she yelled, heading straight for the door of the navigation room.

Alister took him. He must have him.

It made her stomach tighten in tension. She bolted outside, hoping to see him holding Adrian on the deck of her ship. She couldn't.

Naeem must have seen her from the corner of his eye because he turned his head to her suddenly. He winced at the face he saw.

She didn't like that look one bit!

"Where are they?"

"I told him you'd be upset when you found out." He pointed to the Howling Death sailing next to her ship.

Rosetta sprinted for the railing and held onto it as she searched it. She didn't need to scan her eyes far.

"You'd better not have swung over there!" she screamed.

Alister was manning the helm with one hand while his other arm held Adrian.

He threw his head back, as though he'd let out a bellowing laugh. Then he pointed to a plank leaning against the railing of his ship. He'd walked across it! Sure, probably holding onto a rope for extra security, but he'd taken her child off her fucking ship!

I'll kill him for this! What he'd done was dangerous!

But that wasn't why she was upset.

Rosetta had nearly had a damn heart attack when she saw Adrian wasn't where she thought he'd be. She was protective and possessive of him, cherished him more than she did anything else.

She pulled her pistol from its holder, waving it in the air as a threat. Alister covered Adrian with his arm, making her realise what she was doing.

Putting it back in its holster, she went down to the main deck of her ship to find a rope to swing across.

However, when she turned back around with one in her hand, she noticed the Howling Death was slowly moving further away. Alister was creating a gap so she couldn't cross and yell at him.

Once more, she could see he was laughing.

She walked to the railing of her ship and folded her arms across her chest. Her eyes were narrowed so far into a squinted glare, she could barely see.

She knew he'd want to give him back when he started screaming for her breast. He'd hate it. The way Adrian cried when he was hungry was ear-piercingly horrid.

She knew she'd have him back very soon, but she still couldn't help thinking, *I want a bloody divorce already!*

EPILOGUE

23 years later

Adrian Paine drifted his gaze over the weathered grey sails that flapped and hollowed in the wind. The backdrop of the blue, near cloudless, sky behind them showed bright weather.

Beautiful clear skies, tranquil rolling waves, and the perfect wind to fill the sails. His father had warned him that a day like this could see him getting fucked over.

Apparently, devious wenches like to fly across the ocean on perfect days and steal everything from gullible men if they weren't careful. Of course, he also knew his father had found something precious on a bright sunny day just like this, something he coveted deeply.

From his spot on the ship, Adrian watched a man sprint across the runner of a sail post before using a rope to twirl his way back down to the main deck.

He checked the directional compass hanging around his neck and turned the wheel of the ship to the left a little, righting their direction.

For twenty-three years, Adrian had lived his life on ocean waters. He barely knew the land. He barely understood it.

The idea of a class system, of a government, was foreign to him. He didn't understand how it worked, how there were high, middle, and lower classes. Not when all he had ever felt was freedom.

He'd been swallowed by riches every time they brought this ship back to the Paine Trove, which had once belonged to some dead pirate called 'The Raider'. It was nothing but a legacy now, since they had stolen it for themselves and added to it.

They also spent it freely.

So, seeing poor commoners when he did touch foot on land was strange. Adrian could spend his share of wages on whatever he wanted, had so much of it that he never needed to worry or care.

Apparently, he was too much like his father had been when he was his age. Adrian spent his money on booze, gambled it away, and took multiple prostitutes.

He didn't like the land, either.

His legs felt shaken. It was too sturdy, too hard beneath his feet. He often walked around like he was drunk, even when he hadn't had a drop of alcohol.

He was an ocean dweller and would never be anything else. He much preferred to have the waves beneath him, whether violent or calm.

He liked having the wheel of the helm in his strong grasp, enjoyed controlling the vessel he currently manned. It made him feel powerful, like he had somehow tamed an untameable element. *Da told me he felt the same way.*

He also commanded men like a king. He told them what to do, where to go, how to do their jobs.

He'd been on the sea all his life; he had more experience than over half the people here. Perhaps not hands-on, but his young eyes had watched every aspect of a ship moving and he knew it better than anyone.

Although he had been carefully watched by his mother, someone extremely protective of his life, he'd started working when he was young.

Adrian had started climbing the shrouds when he was

seven, had pulled on ropes when he was eleven, and manned the helm when he was sixteen. He killed his first man at eighteen.

He'd seen much of the world, had much spilt blood on his hands. He was a pirate who already had a small bounty on his head, just like both his parents did.

A smile curled his lips, his blue eyes trailing over the crew working on the deck below him.

He'd never forget the day he first stepped off the ship onto dry land after he'd murdered someone. His father had headed straight to a port after he did, telling them they had to celebrate.

It was all under a guise.

His father was a strange person who told him he was a man now that he'd taken a life and should be treated as one. Behind his mother's back, because he didn't think she'd approve, he'd bought Adrian his first woman.

He'd been more frightened of her, of losing his virginity, than he had been of gutting a man.

His lips curled into a brighter smile as he laughed at himself.

That was definitely no longer the case now that he was twenty-three and had bedded many, but it often made him chuckle, especially when his gaze turned back to look at the vessel following his own.

At the helm of that ship, he could see a boy who looked fairly like himself.

His hair was black like his, his eyes blue like his. Actually, if it wasn't for the fact that they were five years apart, they almost looked like twins.

He doesn't know what's coming. Adrian had decided not to ruin the surprise.

Maddox Paine was his name, and he was his younger brother.

The sound of a footstep followed by the thud of a wooden peg leg sounded behind him.

"You've got that stupid look on your face," his father said as he emerged from the cabin behind to him. "Can only imagine what trouble you're up to."

"Just remembering when you made us dock right after I took my first life."

"Are you now?" Alister chuckled as he put his arm around his shoulders and leaned most of his weight on him. "Why are you thinking so heavily on the past?"

He turned his head to the side to look at him, his smile turning mischievous. "Well, I'm sure you'll be treating Maddox to the same, considering he just killed his first man in that last raid."

Alister had directed them to shore, despite having more than enough supplies to last them months.

"Aye, lad, you're bloody right about that!" He threw his head back with a great, bellowing laugh, patting him so hard on the back, he almost stumbled into the wheel. "Don't tell your mother; she'll slap me around a bunch if you do. She doesn't know I did that for you back then."

His father patted his head and ruffled his short hair until it was unkempt.

"You couldn't even talk to a woman!" He made a scoffing noise. "Couldn't have my own son being such a pansy."

He let out a pout. "I wasn't a pansy."

"Despite my haggard appearance now, I used to plough my way through shore wenches before I met your mother. I expect my boys to do the same."

Perhaps because Adrian had never really known more than the Howling Death he currently manned, and the Laughing Siren on which he had spent most of his life, he was turning into someone just like his father. He was his role model, and like father like son, Adrian mimicked him in almost every aspect.

"Ma tells me I'm going to be just like you."

"Aye, and while you and Maddox have her eyes, you both look just like me too."

It was hard to tell now, considering his father's state.

Adrian turned his head once more to look him over.

Although he wore an eyepatch with their family crest imprinted into it, just like the ring Adrian wore on his forefinger, Adrian knew what lay beneath it. The cloudy, milky blue eye blindly stared while the other was light brown and often appeared to glow in the light.

It had been like that all his life, but the scar running over it was accompanied by another, newer one, he almost considered worse.

On the same side, like that side of his face was cursed, was a gash that ran from the corner of his mouth, all the way to his cheek bone, and even nicked the tip of his ear. It was deep and nasty, and it meant part of his face was permanently twisted due to the tendons and muscles being cut.

Adrian had been there when his mother sewed his father's face back together after being slashed with a sword. He'd been protecting Maddox's life four years ago, and instead of worrying for himself, he'd protected his son.

Pirate hunters had set their sights on them.

It was a tough battle. There had been more than one ship to fight, two ships matched against two ships. They'd been hunting his parents and knew to bring more than one hunting vessel armed to the teeth with cannons.

Watching his parents fighting, side-by-side, back-to-back, defending each other, had always been awe-inspiring to Adrian. They were so in sync with each other that one knew when to duck so the other could shoot someone above their head. If they were fighting together like this, one of them rarely got hurt, and Alister was always there to shield Rosetta with his own body if he needed to.

He hated it when any harm came to her.

Even though he was supposed to be hiding, because Rosetta hadn't deemed him old enough yet to participate in fighting, fourteen-year-old Maddox had taken it upon himself to take up a sword, like some stupid hero who wasn't skilled or experienced.

With no one knowing to back him up, he'd gotten cornered. Alister had jumped in and saved his life, copping a strike across the face, instead of a blade slashing for Maddox.

Now, that side of his face was not only blind but also twisted into a mangled scar. His long, stubbled beard, now peppered with grey, only helped to hide it a little bit.

The other side of him was nearly perfect, not a scratch on it. Adrian knew to judge what he would look like when he was older by that side rather than the other.

The rest of his father's body was covered in scars, but he was as strong as an ox, and Adrian had yet to beat him in an arm wrestle. He often challenged him to one.

Adrian's gaze fell to his father's feet. Despite his peg leg, Alister refused to stand back when there was a battle to be fought. He was at the front of every attack.

He was still the captain after all, and Adrian knew he would never gain the title until he died.

But how he had obtained his peg leg was not as grand of a story as his face. *Ma often picks on him for it.*

He'd lost his foot to footrot by not changing his boots enough. Apparently, she'd warned him it would happen, but he didn't often listen to her. An 'I told you so' had fallen from her lips the moment they realised why parts of his toes were turning black.

Adrian still thought he was brave, and a little insane too, because of it. After the rot had spread from his toes to the rest of his foot, Alister demanded that someone, in his words, 'cut the fucking thing off.'

So, from just below his calf muscle, Pierre, who was still his first mate, had hacked it away with a cleaver. His mother had helped to heal the wound as best she could afterwards.

She hadn't been right for a long time after.

Neither of them had been.

Rosetta had manned the helm of the Howling Death for the months Alister had been unable to walk. She spent every other hour of the day looking after him and helping to rehabilitate him until he could walk on a peg.

Once he was able to, despite his pain, he was an irritable asshole until he'd grown accustomed to it. His mother took it in stride, no matter his temperamental attitude, and eventually, they were back to their usual selves.

"Speaking of your mother, where is that woman?" He watched Alister turn his head to look for her, showing him the back of his head. His hair was still thick and was half-plaited rather than in a half-bun, meaning Rosetta had gotten to it recently. "She was out of bed before me."

"Doesn't she always do that?" Adrian laughed. The early morning sun had only just finished rising.

"Aye, but I always wish she wouldn't."

"I don't know where she is. Last I saw her, she came out to speak with me before going to Maddox."

She'd woken up to check on her children.

Today, she'd greeted Adrian before lightly tapping him on the cheek from saying 'aye' and 'nay' and speaking similarly to his own da! She didn't want them speaking like they were morons, even though she'd wedded one who did.

She often confused him. Adrian didn't understand his own mother and had never met a woman like her.

I consider her more insane than Da. Still, he loved her dearly, and she loved him just as much back, perhaps even more.

He hoped he found someone just like her for himself.

"Then where is Scarlett?" Alister asked. "She's probably with her."

Adrian shook his head. "Nay, Scarlett is in the crow's nest on the Laughing Siren having a tantrum because I wouldn't let her man the helm."

Scarlett was his younger sister. She looked nothing like him.

Her hair was mud brown, her eyes brown, and she had freckles peppering her pale skin. She looked more like their mother, which meant she was a pretty little thing. She also acted like her, which meant she bickered with everyone.

"Aye, good. She's too young."

"No, she's not," a feminine voice said from the quarterdeck steps as his mother came up them.

"Nay!" Alister argued. "She's not old enough to man the helm by herself."

With a squinted glare, her lips thinning in irritation, she stood before them with her hands on her hips. Her attire had barely changed as Adrian grew older, but she'd recently bought herself a navy-blue, doublet coat and wore it most of the time. She was always cold, even in summer.

She gestured her hand towards Adrian. "If he and Maddox were allowed to man the helm at sixteen, then Scarlett can at sixteen."

Alister stepped forward to point his index and middle fingers at her. "She's not strong enough!"

"That's because you never let her do anything!" She grabbed his fingers and held them in a small fist to direct them away from her face. "Just because she's your daughter doesn't mean you have to be so protective of her. The only reason I don't let her man the helm on her own is because Adrian doesn't have his own ship and Maddox is still learning."

Soon, Adrian would be allowed to commandeer a ship of

his own and become a captain. He was just waiting for the right one.

I want a warship, just like Da. He wanted a smaller one, a faster one, one that could hold almost the same number of cannons.

He wanted it so he could protect his brother and sister, and his parents when they were too old and useless.

A small grin formed across his face.

He could picture it: he and Maddox manning a frigate each while they sailed on either side of Scarlett on the Laughing Siren. An unstoppable force. A family that killed and raided side-by-side.

He was excited to become a captain under his father's fleet. With the guidance of his parents, he knew he could do great things. He was just like his father, but Adrian was cunning and intelligent like his mother. Not even his siblings could measure up to him.

"I let her climb the shrouds and work the sails!" Alister yelled back at Rosetta. "I've seen her, and I know she can't do it yet."

She rolled her eyes. "Yes, she can. I've been with her on my shift and let her. She's good at it, just like me."

"She can't touch the Howling Death until she's got experience."

"And she won't get experience unless she gets to steer the Laughing Siren, but Maddox is currently at the helm."

They were all learning the same way. They would start with the Laughing Siren, since it was bigger and able to cut through the waves rather than being knocked around like the Howling Death. It was easier to control, even though it required more manpower.

Adrian's grin grew. Hearing his parents' squabble like they usually did brought him entertainment. He also knew a secret, one his mother didn't know, and one his father didn't think he was aware of.

While they were all sleeping, with Naeem at the helm of the Laughing Siren, Pierre steering the Howling Death, Adrian often came to stare out at the stars, hidden away somewhere on one of the two ships.

Alister would sneak onto the Laughing Siren once he thought everyone in their family was asleep and wake Scarlett from her sleeping quarters in the navigation room.

Then, he would shove Pierre out of the way, stand behind her, and let her man the helm of the Howling Death. He'd guide her while standing behind her, his hands holding two of the wheel handles while she did the same with a different two.

He'd tell her how to map the stars, instruct her when to turn the wheel into an on-coming wave.

He'd done this with all of them.

He didn't often show it, but his father was proud of all of them and their capabilities. He was rough, often threw them into the deep when it came to learning, but he was hands-on.

He wanted to make sure they were all ready if they wanted to sail by themselves. He refused to have his children die before him and often told them he didn't plan to die anytime soon.

Alister came to put his arm around Adrian's shoulders once more. "Well, when he gets his own ship, she can man the helm of yours and Maddox can come here."

"Fine." Rosetta folded her arms across her chest and turned her head to the side. "But I'll still be letting her learn with me. None of this, *'she can't man the helm because she's a girl'* bullshit."

"She's too much like you for me to have those kinds of thoughts," he sighed back, removing his arm from Adrian. He moved closer to her. "Where you been, anyway? Woke up in a cold bed by myself."

Her arms tightened further.

"Was checking the stocks of both ships. I don't know why we're going to port when we have more than enough to last."

Adrian and his father shared a wary look between them.

"It just doesn't sound like you."

Shit, she's catching on. He tried not to let his face fill with humour. *She's too smart for us.*

Adrian could see the wheels turning in his father's head. He was trying to figure out how to distract her.

Alister reached forward and turned her head to face him again by pinching her cheeks with both hands. He yanked on them with harsh pulls. "When did you start turning into a wrinkly bitch?"

"Right when you stopped being a complete man."

She kicked Alister in the peg leg, making it slip back. He stumbled forward, having to grab a handle of the helm to stop from falling flat on his face. Adrian helped him by having a good strong hold on the wheel to hold him up as he righted himself.

"I'll show you a man!" he bit, grabbing her around the nape of the neck and forcibly pulling her to him. "Come here, you annoying little devil."

He kissed her while grabbing her arse and pushing her hips against his. As she usually did when he did this, she responded by crossing her arms over the back of his neck and kissing him back just as deeply.

It was Adrian's turn to roll his eyes as he watched his parents stumble. Alister was leading them back into the cabin on the Howling Death that they shared.

Before long, he knew he would hear things he would much rather not.

When the door slammed behind him, he threw his head back with a laugh. This wasn't an odd occurrence, nor strange behaviour between his parents.

His mother didn't care that his father's appearance had

turned monster-like. She loved him just as he loved her; and neither cared who knew it – even their children.

It was normal to them, to their entire family. Sex was not a foreign ideal and it wasn't shunned.

But I still need to hurry and get my own ship. Then, he could perhaps find a woman to be the same with. Someone beautiful, reckless, but perhaps a little bit easier to deal with. He gave a singular snort of laughter through his nose. *Now wouldn't that just be ideal?*

The End

CPSIA information can be obtained
at www.ICGtesting.com
Printed in the USA
LVHW042137280623
751101LV00031B/119